DISLOYAL OPPOSITION
BOOK ELEVEN OF THE LUNAR FREE STATE®

John E. Siers

Theogony Books
Coinjock, NC

Copyright © 2025 by John E. Siers.

All rights reserved. No part of this publication may be reproduced, distributed or transmitted in any form or by any means, including photocopying, recording, or other electronic or mechanical methods, without the prior written permission of the publisher, except in the case of brief quotations embodied in critical reviews and certain other noncommercial uses permitted by copyright law. For permission requests, write to the publisher, addressed "Attention: Permissions Coordinator," at the address below.

Chris Kennedy/Theogony Books
1097 Waterlily Rd.
Coinjock, NC 27923
https://chriskennedypublishing.com/

Publisher's Note: This is a work of fiction. Names, characters, places, and incidents are a product of the author's imagination. Locales and public names are sometimes used for atmospheric purposes. Any resemblance to actual people, living or dead, or to businesses, companies, events, institutions, or locales is completely coincidental.

Cover Design by Shezaad Sudar.

Ordering Information:
Quantity sales. Special discounts are available on quantity purchases by corporations, associations, and others. For details, contact the "Special Sales Department" at the address above.

Disloyal Opposition/John E. Siers -- 1st ed.
ISBN: 979-8893191547

*To the Lunar Free State
In Whose Service We Stand.*

Prologue

15 March 2123

Privateer *Aquila*, Sacagawea System, Near the Hyper Limit

"We're being hailed." Castro gave a little snort. "Do they really expect we will answer?"

"Which one is hailing?" Andrew Zimmer turned to his tactical officer. His expression reflected mild curiosity with no trace of concern.

"The destroyer. They claim not to be Moonie, however. Their ID shows HMS *Torrent*—British, if we are to believe them. They're threatening to fire on us if we don't respond."

"Hmmm… maybe they are who they say. There are rumors that the Brits and Americans are expanding their interstellar commercial efforts." Zimmer stroked his trim beard as he considered the matter.

"Makes no difference." He shrugged. "Our sponsors say anything other than a CNE-flagged ship is fair game. Better if they are not Moonies; Moonie destroyers can be nasty."

Not nasty enough to deal with the three of us, he thought. *The Sillies know how to build a commerce raider.*

For the past two years, he'd been prowling the Akara frontier with *Aquila* and *Lobo*, a pair of Sillascaritan-built fast frigates, but the Lizards had gotten better at anti-piracy operations, and he'd decided to take a break. They'd holed up for a while at a Silly port in the Golden

Braid, where they'd been contacted by a shady character from Earth with a proposition.

It seemed there were certain people back in the Sol System who would fund the purchase of a third ship for his little squadron if he would concentrate his efforts on certain Moonie-controlled shipping lanes. Not Odin or Coleridge—the Moonies were a bit too vigilant there. They had, however, become complacent about their other, long-established protectorates at Rothstein and Sacagawea.

The sponsors hadn't asked for much else—a small cut of the proceeds, to be collected by their agent in the Golden Braid, where Zimmer would need to come to dispose of whatever he collected. They were more concerned about making life difficult for the Moonies; Zimmer could keep most of the profits from the enterprise.

He'd hesitated. He really wanted that third ship, but in the end, he was a businessman. One reason pirates didn't flock to the systems in question was that profits were low. There was little in the way of commercial shipping between Sol and Rothstein or Sacagawea, and almost nothing in the way of high-value cargo. To make such an enterprise pay, a pirate would need to take his victims intact, force them to surrender with little damage to their ships. The ships themselves would represent the primary spoils of the operation.

Zimmer considered himself to be a skilled professional in the piracy game, not some crude brigand who would batter a prize into helpless submission, murder its crew, and loot the derelict hull. The thought of capturing ships intact and forcing their own crews to take them to the prize port intrigued him. He'd accepted the proposition and taken the "earnest money" they had provided to purchase his third ship, which he'd named *Tigre*. While his squadron was being fitted out and provisioned, he'd gone back to Earth to gather intel on shipping for the target systems.

He'd selected Sacagawea as his primary area of operations, and now he was closing the range on his first target, a pair of freighters escorted by a single destroyer. The smaller of the two was typical of commercial traffic calling on Tatanna. The larger ship—his scans indicated it was nearly six hundred meters in length—was an unexpected bonus. He wondered what it might be carrying. He assumed it would be some high-volume bulk product of little value to him. No matter. A hull that size would be worth plenty.

The targets had arrived on the direct line from Sol and had been challenged by the Moonie system picket shortly after they'd dropped out of hyper. Zimmer had watched it happen; with typical Moonie efficiency, the picket force—a heavy cruiser and two destroyers—had dropped in from hyper behind the newcomers, had satisfied themselves as to the convoy's identity, and had hypered out again. It was fortunate, Zimmer thought, that they hadn't decided to stick around. If they had, he would have had to let the target go. Moonie destroyers were bad enough; he had no desire to tangle with a heavy cruiser.

He would need to take out the target's escort. To that end, he studied the tactical display. The destroyer was keeping tight formation with the large freighter, a somewhat timid posture. An aggressive escort commander would have ordered the merchies to run away and would have gone out to meet the incoming threat. In this case, it wouldn't have made any difference; his squadron could deal with a single destroyer without breaking stride. He would, however, have to caution Burgess and Petroni not to hit the freighter by mistake. That was the big prize this time, and they needed to take it intact.

He noted with amusement that the smaller freighter was trying to run, angling sharply away from the other two and pouring on the delta-*v*. Again, it wouldn't make any difference. His ships were built for speed, faster than most destroyers. The merchie was showing impressive acceleration for a commercial vessel, but he would still be able to run it down once he had secured the larger prize.

* * *

ICV *Majorca*, Inbound for Tatanna

They've got to be targeting me. Lilly Maria Buxton felt a cold chill of despair in her heart. *Four times, four separate trips, and I've got pirates on my ass again. The Confeds must know I've double-crossed them, and they're out to get me.*

This bunch, however, looked like pirates, not CNE warships pretending to be "privateers." *Maybe the Confeds have decided not to waste time chasing me themselves. They've put a bounty on my head.*

She couldn't be sure, but based on information shared among merchant skippers, the incoming ships appeared to be Sillascaritan design. They were fast and well armed; they would be able to run her down with ease.

Assuming they get past the Brits. A spark of hope pushed back the darkness inside her. *They're coming on without fear, but maybe they're making the same mistake the Confeds made the last time. Because of her size, they think* Prince *is another freighter…*

* * *

Privateer *Aquila*

"Cap, we've got a problem." Zimmer looked up sharply at the note of concern in Castro's voice.

"What?" He turned his attention to the tactical display.

"That big freighter just brought up a bunch of what look like targeting systems. It also cut its drive and is turning broadside to us. The destroyer's matching the maneuver.

"The big one's hailing us and…" Castro's voice trailed off for a moment. He stared at his comm display, and his eyes went wide.

"Christ! That's no freighter! It's a fucking *warship!* Hailing ID says HMS *Prince of Wales*, and they've opened fire!"

Zimmer watched in horror as the ship they had taken for a freighter spawned sixteen missiles. The destroyer added six of its own to the salvo.

"Shoot!" he ordered. "Shoot back at them."

"Range is too long," Castro protested. "That's a cruiser. We'll never get past their defenses."

Cruiser my ass! Zimmer thought. *It's a battlecruiser! The bloody Brits have got themselves a battlecruiser!* As he watched, the two ships rolled over and sent another 22 missiles his way.

"Shoot anyway," he told Castro. "Keep their defenses busy!" He stabbed an icon on his comm display.

"Burgess! Petroni! Bug out!" he ordered. "Three-way split. Go for the hyper limit. We'll link up later. You're on your own.

"Helm, up ninety and redline the drive." He tried to keep his voice level as he issued the order. It was the best option for escape; his ships had too much incoming vector to reverse course and would simply slide deeper into the enemy's missile envelope. A sharp right angle course change would get them out of that envelope with the least amount of engagement time.

Castro had gotten off two missiles from *Aquila's* chase tubes, but the maneuver had scrambled his targeting solutions, and he was unlikely to get another chance to shoot; he'd be too busy dealing with the incoming Brit missiles.

Still too close. Zimmer ran a quick calculation and gave the helmsman another order, adjusting the ship's vector slightly away from the British warships. *It'll mean more time in their missile envelope,* he thought, *but it'll keep us out of energy range.* His ships mounted adequate missile armament for their size, but their small-bore lasers were intended for precise targeting at short range. He had no desire to get into a beam engagement with real warships. He didn't know what kind of armament the Brits had, but one hit from a battlecruiser-sized graser would likely take *Aquila* out of the battle.

He turned to the tactical display again and drew a sharp breath. *Shit! Burgess screwed up!*

Petroni had copied Zimmer's maneuver, a sharp 90-degree turn away from their original course. *Lobo* was angling away from *Aquila* in an effort to go wide around the Brits. Burgess, however, had first tried to reverse course, fighting against all the incoming vector they'd built up.

The Brits had noticed; all 44 missiles from their first salvo were going for *Tigre*.

Burgess had apparently recognized his error, altered course, and was trying to claw his way out of the engagement. It was too late; even if he survived the missile barrage, he could no longer avoid coming within energy range of the warships.

That means Petroni and I will get clear. Zimmer shook his head. The warships hadn't fired again. His evasion tactic had forced them to adjust their targeting, and apparently, they'd decided to let *Aquila* and *Lobo* go. Technically, the two ships were still in missile range, but the chance of a hit had been greatly reduced. Since he was disengaging, the Brits had elected to hold their fire.

He watched as the first missiles reached attack range and began to detonate, spawning powerful x-ray lasers. To his surprise, *Tigre* absorbed more than a dozen hits before one found her fusion plant and she vanished in a ball of nuclear fire.

He forced himself to relax. *Lobo* and *Aquila* were nearly out of missile range, and the warships were not pursuing them. Instead, they had returned to their original course and were moving to rejoin the third ship. *I guess that one really was a freighter,* he thought. *A non-combatant, in any case.*

Who would have thought it—two warships escorting a single freighter. Where did the British get such heavy hardware? I guess I should have gone to Rothstein instead. For sure, it'll be a cold day in hell when I try Sacagawea again.

* * * * *

Chapter One

15 March 2123

New York, New York, USA, Planet Earth

"What is the problem?" Pierre DuMorne scowled across the broad expanse of his desk. "You've done us a service. You've been suitably compensated. Are the investments not working out?"

"The investments have done well, as you promised they would." Roger Stuart shifted uncomfortably in the expensive leather armchair in front of the desk. "My only concern is that they not come to the attention of the wrong people."

"The wrong people at TerraCorp?" DuMorne waved a hand in dismissal. "They'll never know. We set up a blind account in your name. Your involvement will never be known."

"I am also concerned about that 'service' I've done for you." Stuart's eyes narrowed. "I had to call in some favors on Copper Hills. If it came to light that we helped you with that…"

"You did nothing more than introduce us to your Lizard contacts and advise us as to proper protocol. Nothing will come of it, unless your Copper Hills people choose to make it an issue."

Stuart chose not to press the matter; DuMorne was right. He had more to fear from his own TerraCorp people than from the CNE agents he had been dealing with. Fortunately, there was only one person on Copper Hills who knew anything about it.

Kline won't talk, he thought. *I've got too much dirt on him, and he knows it.*

All the same, his nervous discomfort wouldn't go away. He turned away from DuMorne and took in the impressive panorama beyond the broad windows of the corner office—the Manhattan skyline, seen from the eightieth floor of the skyscraper that served as the headquarters of Freres Le Fleur.

I'm just uncomfortable being on Earth. It's not like I'm actually in the Confederated Nations. I've got perfectly good reasons to be in New York. Everybody does business on Wall Street.

That had been his justification for the first trip three months ago, and no one at TerraCorp had questioned it. His staff had gotten used to him taking an extra day or two on each trip, supposedly to see the sights and enjoy the nightlife in the Big Apple.

In DuMorne's office, he was as close to the CNE as he could get without actually being in Europe. Freres Le Fleur was a financial giant, one of the movers and shakers of the Confederated Nations, and every bit as powerful as its American Wall Street counterparts.

Fortunately, this was his last trip for a while. He'd concluded his business with Freres and could put it behind him. *Time to get out of the spider's lair and catch a flight back to LunaPort,* he thought. *I need to get off this planet.*

"Fine." He got to his feet and nodded to DuMorne. "I got what I wanted; you got yours. *Quid pro quo.* I think we're done."

"We are done for now." DuMorne smiled but did not get up. "I hope we can do business again… soon."

* * *

Office of the Chief Executive, TerraNova City, Luna

"You're telling me the Confeds are going to be mining gold on Ragnarok." Robert O'Hara scowled at the woman sitting in front of his desk. "Worse, you say we've got to let them do it."

"The Akara are the gatekeepers." Vice Admiral Martina Easley threw up her hands in a gesture of helplessness. "They granted the lease—in exchange for a share of the gold, I'm sure."

"Technically, it's not the Confeds. They've simply granted a commercial lease to a private corporation, which happens to be headquartered in one of the Confederated Nations—Germany, to be exact. They don't see any difference between that and the heavy mining equipment they buy from Sweden. Visit any Akara mine on Ragnarok and you'll see Volvo's name on nearly every excavator and rock truck. For that matter, visit one of our own mines, and you'll see the same. We may have issues with the CNE, but TerraCorp has no problem doing business with its member nations.

"The difference," O'Hara growled, continuing, "is that the mining equipment gets delivered by our own freighters or haulers from independent nations. We've banned all CNE traffic from the system—with the concurrence of the Lizards, I might point out."

"Well... that's why they brought it to our attention. Apparently, they want us to modify that policy. We can still ban military traffic, but they say we will have to allow CNE commercial traffic in support of the German mining effort."

"Wonderful." O'Hara rolled his eyes. "Just wonderful."

"It's not a big deal." Easley shrugged. As the head of Luna's Diplomatic Corps, she had been jousting with the Confederated Nations for years. "Okay, they've pulled off a diplomatic coup, but they haven't damaged our relations with the Akara, nor are they interfering with our own mining operations. As I understand it, there's plenty of gold on Ragnarok to go around."

"It's not that simple." O'Hara shook his head. "The Confeds have used commercial ships twice to insert agents and provide supplies to the rebels who are trying to overthrow the Wan government. That's one of the reasons we've banned all of their shipping. That heavy mining equipment you mentioned—including the equipment for our own mines—arrives on ships registered to independent nations, because we don't let Confed freighters into the system, and they refuse to use our TerraCorp ships.

"Now, we're not only going to have to let their ships into the system, we have to let them land people and equipment on the planet. Will the Lizards allow us to conduct inspections of incoming ships? We've been doing that for the independent shippers, but technically we don't have the right, since it isn't our system. The Lizards haven't objected because the shippers haven't complained, but I'm damned sure the Confeds will."

"Ouch!" Easley grimaced. "You're right, I hadn't considered that aspect of it. Our diplomatic efforts with the Wans haven't produced much, mostly because they're a slippery bunch who haven't been straightforward with us. All the same, we certainly don't need a renewed offensive by the rebels; we've already decided we don't want to get involved in that little war they won't admit they're having.

"I guess maybe I'd better raise that issue with the Akara, but I think they'll side with the Confeds this time. As far as they're concerned, the bastards have as much right to be there as we do. The Lizards don't care about the Wans and the rebels; the way they see it, that's our problem. Most of all, they want to avoid getting in the middle of the conflict between us and the Confeds."

Easley sat back and made a note on her pad. Both of them were quiet for a moment, then O'Hara spoke again.

"There's another problem. I had a discussion last week with Lisa Woods, mostly regarding our own gold mining operation." He turned to the screen on his desk and brought up a report.

"A hundred years ago, mines on Earth were producing about ninety-five million troy ounces of gold per year—about three thousand metric tons in total. Over the last century, that number has dropped dramatically. Mining methods are better, but a lot of areas have been mined out, and new sources are hard to find. Last year, all of Earth's mines—and those in the asteroid belt—produced only about a thousand tons of gold.

"Ragnarok, by comparison, is incredibly rich in gold. The Lizards have been mining there for over ten years, and they've still barely scratched the surface—despite which our people estimate that they took more than five hundred tons last year. We have been much more modest in our efforts, but we still took over sixty tons in the last twelve months.

"Some in TerraCorp want to drastically expand our efforts, but the board has decided not to do that for one simple reason: we don't want to crash the gold market on Earth. For whatever reason, our founders decided that the Lunar Free State should have its currency based on the gold standard. That allows us to bury that incoming gold in our currency reserves and use it to fund the colony on Xanadu, rather than dumping it on the gold market. Still, we've increased the Sol System's gold supply by about 6 percent, and the markets have noticed.

"Since we are on the gold standard, any drop in the price of gold immediately decreases the value of the Gold Lunar. That impacts our economy across the board, since we still import so much of our daily needs from Earth. For a simple example, we grow a lot of our produce under the domes, but we still import meats from down there. The price of beef on Luna has gone up as the price of gold has dropped on Earth. In addition, we employ Earth-based contractors in our shipyards at TransLuna. Our contract with Hyundai-Sumimoto requires that they be paid in Japanese Yen, which means they get more expensive as the exchange rate changes.

"We also have the unaligned nations—the Consortium—on the scene. So far, their mining efforts have been modest, but we estimate they are taking almost as much as we are. At present, more than 10 percent of the gold hitting Earth's market is coming from Ragnarok.

"Consider what will happen if the Confeds start mining there. They have no reason to restrict their efforts; their currency isn't gold based. CNE credits have no hard basis at all—they print money as needed on the nebulous theory that the GNP of all CNE nations taken together will cover them. They get away with it because they set the exchange rates for all the nations within their group. They have to keep it within limits, or the non-CNE nations will take their business elsewhere, but so far, they've gotten away with it.

"In short, a decline in the price of gold will hurt us a lot more than it hurts them. For some of them, that alone would be a reason to push their mines to the limit."

"I see your point." Easley nodded. "And we don't know what that limit is. It will pretty much depend on the terms of the lease the Lizards gave them. I think we need to make some discreet inquiries with the Akara about that, to get a heads-up on what to expect."

"Right." O'Hara returned the nod. "We need to get with our own financial wizards to determine the impact. Depending on how the numbers work out, they might want to reconsider their decision to restrict our mining efforts. Gold might be worth less, but we'll get more of it. Unfortunately, that's not pure profit because it would also increase the cost of our mining operations."

"Ugh!" Easley shuddered. "Diplomacy would be a lot simpler if we didn't have to worry about economic factors. I hate these financial things—too messy, too complicated."

"I hate them, too." O'Hara chuckled. "Life was a lot simpler when I was in command of a fleet of warships and didn't have to worry about how to pay for them.

"Now, however, I have to worry about that stuff every day." His expression sobered. "The Xanadu colony effort is getting *very* expensive. It's eating every bit of the Ragnarok gold production profits.

"We have to keep growing the colony, and once again, it's because we're trying to match what the Confeds are doing. It's getting to the point where the cost of it is impacting other areas of the economy. Fleet's already cut shipbuilding and maintenance to the bone; next thing you know, we'll be decommissioning some ships to cut expenses. This Ragnarok issue will only make it worse."

Again, they lapsed into silence for a moment. This time, Easley spoke first.

"I still wonder how the Confeds pulled this off. They've never been close to the Akara, never showed much interest in developing a relationship. Their embassy on Copper Hills looks like nothing more than a token effort compared to ours.

"A deal like this requires a great deal of familiarity with Lizard customs and business practices, as well as careful navigation through the tangled web of Akara bureaucracy. The Confeds have never demonstrated any ability in that area. It almost makes me think they got some help with this, and there's only one place that help could have come from."

"Our people?" O'Hara looked up sharply. "Where… and who?"

"Don't know." She shrugged. "Our Copper Hills Trade Mission people certainly have the expertise, but I don't know them—they work for TerraCorp, not Diplomatic Corps. Beyond that, there may be people on Luna, again in TerraCorp, who know how to arrange something like that.

"Like I said, it's speculation on my part. I don't know for certain that they got help; I just don't think they could have pulled it off on their own."

* * *

Kosetsu Resort, Sapporo, Japan

"So… what exactly are you saying, Andre?" Mohammed Al Sharif scowled at the Frenchman. "Is this going to be a problem for us?"

"Not so much a problem as a situation worth watching." Andre DuMorne shrugged. "If you are heavily invested in gold, you might consider either shifting to other commodities, or simply holding your gold and waiting out the temporary depression in price."

"I *am* heavily invested in it," Al Sharif growled, "as you certainly know. You handled the investments."

"True." DuMorne waved off the comment. "It is still only 10 percent of your total portfolio. In your case, I would recommend simply holding it. We know the market will fall for some time, with the noteworthy increase in the gold supply. It will fall faster when the CNE mines get going.

"The demand for gold is relatively constant due to its increasing use in technology applications. What used to be a bauble for the rich is now a critical component in certain electronic devices, particularly in military applications. The fact that the Lunar Free State's currency is based on it tends to further stabilize the demand.

"As a result, any disruption in supply produces an immediate spike in price. Should it become necessary for you to liquidate, Mohammed, a temporary disruption in supply can be easily arranged. It is the long term effect on the LFS economy that serves our purpose. The Moonies are forced to divert more of their own production into their reserves in order to keep the price up. If Gerhardt's mining operations get into full production, that will not help them."

"Economic warfare!" Al Sharif snorted. "Like trying to kill your enemies with slow poison. I prefer more direct methods. Fortunately, while you and Gerhardt are enriching yourselves, you have also given me an opportunity to conduct a campaign more to my own liking."

In an age of unlimited electronic communication, the Invisible Hand—the five most powerful men on Earth—still preferred to meet face-to-face to discuss the fate of nations. They were wealthy beyond measure, possessed infinite patience, and laid plans that would take decades to mature.

They met as equals, always requiring a round table at their chosen meeting place. They spoke English, so that none should have an advantage, since it was not the native language for any of them. For each meeting, they chose a chairman by drawn straws; this time it was Al Sharif's turn.

"Ragnarok?" Gerhardt Richter chuckled. "We leave that in your hands, Mohammed. The situation there is a perfect fit for the Jihad."

"The rebels are still infidels—" Al Sharif shrugged "—but their revolutionary zeal lends itself well to subtle conversion. Our first efforts will simply be to support them in their war against the oppressive Wan government. By opening the planet to commercial exploitation, you and Andre have given us the opportunity to put people on the ground. If some of those people happen to be true believers as well as competent fighters, it will serve my purpose as well as yours."

"It's perfect for all of us," DuMorne replied with a huge grin. "Gerhardt's mines will feed his own bottom line and enrich my investors. They will also fund your revolution, Mohammed, for which Butos will supply weapons and mercenaries. Huang's shipyards will build several ships in support of the operation. Best of all, it required nothing more than careful navigation around the Moonies through the bureaucracy of the Lizards. Once they gave us the mining lease, the Moonies were powerless to stop us."

"They still won't allow CNE warships to enter the system." Gerhardt Richter directed a scowl toward the Frenchman. "That leaves them in control of the situation."

"I disagree." Butos Kimba joined the conversation. "The Moonies control the space around the planet, but their diplomatic efforts with the Wans have made little progress. The action in this system is down on the planet, because of the gold mines. The type of guerrilla operations Mohammed's people do so well render support from space ineffective. Consider the lesson of history: the Americans controlled the air over Viet Nam, but in the end, victory went to the Viet Cong."

"Much of it had to do with the fact that the US was supporting a corrupt government in Saigon, but that is another similarity between

DISLOYAL OPPOSITION | 23

that conflict and the one we are supporting on Ragnarok. The Wans are another corrupt dictatorship, another apple waiting to be plucked."

Across the table from Kimba, Huang Chang Li wore his usual guarded expression, giving nothing away, but inwardly he felt a mild flash of humor at Kimba's comments about corrupt dictatorships. The African warlord's domain included a dozen such dictatorships on two continents. Kimba had been such a dictator himself, until he decided to let others do his dirty work while he raked in the profit from their efforts.

I'm surprised he isn't on the other side of this one, providing support to the Wans instead of to Mohammed's fighters, Huang thought. *I suppose it doesn't matter; he makes a profit either way, and the Hand has decided that Mohammed should handle this one. Their combined participation in the Ragnarok operation should make DuMorne and Richter happy.*

The French financier and the German industrialist had often grumbled that Al Sharif and Kimba took no interest in the interstellar conflict between the CNE and the Moonies, and they were instead focused on manipulation of the wars and revolutions among the Third World nations of Earth. For once, the warlord and the jihadist were engaged and cooperating on an operation in another star system.

Still, in Huang's view, the Ragnarok rebellion was no more than a minor part of the overall issue. He straightened up in his chair and raised a hand, drawing an immediate nod from Al Sharif.

"If we might return to the economic issue for a moment, I can report that the Moonies are already feeling the pinch. It may not be due to the fall in gold prices, however. More likely, the cost of building the Xanadu colony is weighing heavily on them. I have been advised that there will be cutbacks in my shipyard contracts for naval maintenance at TransLuna station. They have already cut new ship construction almost to zero, but they are also reworking maintenance schedules.

"That might be a financial concern for me, were it not for the fact that the Americans and Brits have dramatically increased both new construction and ship maintenance at Mid-Pacific and L5. My people at Hyundai-Sumimoto tell me the increased revenue from those operations will more than offset the decrease at TransLuna."

"Hah!" Richter exclaimed. "Your profits from the Americans and Brits are serving you well; however, the CNE is not happy about Hyundai-Sumimoto's move from Circum Terra to L5. I might wish you had discussed this with us before you decided to make that move."

Among the Hand's members, Richter was most heavily connected with the Confederated Nations of Earth, home to most of his industrial operations. DuMorne's financial interests were also heavily invested in the CNE, and the two of them exercised more control over the bloated bureaucracy than did the elected officials of the CNE's nominal governing body.

"The decision was out of my hands." Huang shrugged. "Hyundai-Sumimoto is a Korean and Japanese conglomerate. The governments of those nations exerted heavy pressure and offered significant incentives in favor of the move."

"Interesting…" DuMorne stroked his chin. "Japan and Korea exert influence on behalf of the United States and the British Commonwealth. It would appear that this new 'Consortium' is more than a commercial venture, more like a political alliance.

"And you, Chang, stand to profit from that alliance, since your contractors supply shipyard services to the Americans and Brits, as well as the Moonies."

"I should point out that I do the same for the Confeds at Omicron." Huang raised an eyebrow in DuMorne's direction. "Gerhardt's electronics firms also supply all of the players involved."

"True, true." Richter waved off Huang's comment. "I should not have been critical, Chang. After dealing with the CNE bureaucracy for so long, I should realize that it is not always possible to make governments do what we want them to do.

"I am more concerned with the growing strength of the new alliance. We have long assumed that if we set the CNE and the Moonies at each other's throats, they will destroy each other, leaving a power vacuum we can exploit. Now, however, it appears that the Consortium may be the ones who will benefit from the conflict. We absolutely must begin to take them into account."

"I have been thinking about that," DuMorne replied. "My people tell me there are two people who are driving the effort—Elizabeth of England and Redwing of the US. The others are significant players, particularly Japan and Korea, which are economic powerhouses, but the British queen and the American president are the leaders who are driving it forward."

"Hmmm…" Kimba produced a feral grin. "Is it possible we need to be thinking about cutting the head—or heads—off the serpent?"

"Good Lord, no!" Richter glared at Kimba. "Not yet, and not unless there is no alternative. The Americans and Brits may not be up to Moonie or CNE standards in space, but on Earth, they have significant military strength—enough to trample the CNE's Peacekeeper forces into the ground, and they are more sensitive to such things than the Moonies are.

"Remember the 9/11 attacks of the early 21st? The Americans lit up the entire Middle East over an attack that killed only a few civilians.

With them, it always depends on who is in charge at the time, but my impression is that Redwing is not to be trifled with—and if you take him out, his vice president may be worse. As for Elizabeth, the Brits love their monarchy in general, and her in particular. Mess with her, and the CNE might well see a new Normandy invasion happening."

"You assume they would blame any assassinations on the CNE." Al Sharif shrugged. "What if my holy warriors did the job? We are a shadow organization, not located in any specific nation."

"Your holy warriors—or their predecessors—were responsible for the 9/11 attacks on the US," DuMorne replied. "While they were hunting down the ones actually involved, the Americans took out their wrath on a few other Islamic nations. I don't think a conflict like that will serve our interests at present. I am inclined to agree with Gerhardt. We must keep an eye on the Consortium, but I don't think we have yet reached a point where direct action is necessary.

"In the meantime, let us concentrate our efforts on wrecking the Moonie economy."

* * * * *

Chapter Two

15 March 2123
LFS Colony, Eurasia, Planet Xanadu

"Still a lot of empty shelves." Kim Jin Yi shook her head in disgust as she surveyed the interior of the Xanadu colony's general store. In the past year, the store had more than doubled in size—not surprising, since the population had grown to over five thousand colonists. Unfortunately, most of the goods the store carried still had to be imported from the Sol System, and supply consistently failed to meet demand. The store was doing a booming business, but that only meant that each new shipment sold out within days after arrival. Meanwhile, colonists learned to improvise, adapt, and do without.

"Plenty of field rats." Darius Jefferson grinned at her. "Nobody's going to starve."

"Hmmph!" Jin snorted as she tapped a fist against his arm. "Unlike a certain ex-Marine I could mention, some of us don't consider 'field rats' to be proper fare for daily consumption. The colony's producing more of its own food now. They need to cut back on the prepackaged rations and import more clothing, tools, and hardware."

"I'm happy Morell's dairy is producing fresh baby formula." She turned to bestow a motherly smile on baby Jasmine, sleeping peacefully in the carrier slung across her husband's chest.

"Just in time, too." Darius glanced down with a look of fatherly pride. "Our daughter… first baby born on Xanadu. Who would have thought?"

"Well… technically, she wasn't born on Xanadu." Jin grinned up at him. "She was born in orbit."

The Marine assault carrier *Omaha Beach* had been permanently assigned to Xanadu since the earliest days of the colony, not only to serve as a base for a division of Lunar Marines, but also to provide hospital and medical facilities for the colonists. Now the colony had grown, and medical professionals had been recruited. A small hospital on the ground was under construction; however, it was not expected to be in full service for a few more months.

Xanadu's heavy gravity—25 percent higher than Earth standard—presented some health risk to women colonists in the later stages of pregnancy and during childbirth. Jin had taken a leave of absence from her job as director of the Oceania Protectorate to spend the last month of her pregnancy and the first weeks after Jasmine's birth aboard the carrier. As the medics had predicted, the girl had been born with a very strong bone structure due to exposure to the heavier gravity during the first months of development; she would grow up better adapted to life on Xanadu than her parents.

"She may have been the first born among our colonists," Jin insisted, "but we don't know what's been happening at the Confed site in Eastasia. They're twice our size. They might have had several kids born earlier than Jasmine."

"Bah!" Darius grunted. "You always break my happy little bubble with facts and logic. You sound like a research scientist."

"I *am* a research scientist," she told him with a chuckle. "It says so on my business card. I've also got to be back to work in two days, and this time I'm taking Jasmine with me."

"Are you sure? I mean, you've got a lot of work to do with the protectorate and all."

"Mostly office work, indoors, under one gravity." She shook her head. "You've got the farm to run. Natty Rutledge has to go back to school, so you won't have a nanny who can come in to watch her while you're working."

"That's true." He nodded. "Spring term starts in a week."

When the local school system had been established, the colonists had chosen to adopt the Lunar model, in which classes were held from the Vernal Equinox to the Winter Solstice, recessing in the spring rather than the summer. When Jin had gone back to work after Jasmine's birth, they had hired the teenage daughter of a neighboring farmer to come in and tend to the infant while Darius worked the fields.

"Besides," Jin continued, "I promised Storm Shadow and Vine Weaver I would bring her up to the village. They can't wait to see what a human 'kitten' looks like."

* * *

LFS *Valkyrie*, in Xanadu Orbit

"Well, it's official." Rear Admiral Lorna Greenwood turned away from the screen to face the two people seated in front of her desk. "Luna will not be assigning a permanent colonial governor."

"Uh… excuse me, Admiral, but that's not the way I read the order." Commander Jessica Guerrero tried and failed to suppress a smile. "They *have* assigned a permanent governor. They've removed the 'acting' designation in front of your name. Sorry, ma'am, but you're it."

Lorna gave her a look that should have turned her chief of staff to stone, but Guerrero's smile didn't waver. Worse, it appeared to be contagious—Commodore Peter Yoric, *Valkyrie's* captain, was grinning as well.

"Go ahead, smile about it," she growled. "Be advised, however, that this means I'll be dumping more of my fleet responsibilities on the two of you."

"Understood, ma'am." Guerrero was still smiling. "It occurs to me, however, that if they're going to ask you to do two jobs, you ought to have two staffs. Maybe you should ask the Colonial Commission to send you—send the 'governor,' that is—a couple of administrative assistants."

"Hmmm… you're right; I should do that." Lorna sat back with a thoughtful look on her face. "But then I'd need to ask them to expand the size of the colony admin office down on the planet. Most of the 'colonial governor' notices I've gotten from Luna lately are complaints about how much the colony is costing."

"They're starting to get some returns." Yoric shrugged. "The colony produced a bumper crop of cotton last year, and almost all of that got shipped back to Luna for sale on Earth."

"True, but cotton's a low-margin product for TerraCorp." Lorna shook her head. "They have to pay the colonists a fair market price for it and cover the cost of shipping it back to Sol. It wouldn't be worth doing if the demand for cotton on Earth wasn't so high. The same is true for corn, our second largest export. Earth is chronically short of food, mostly because of over-regulation of agriculture and mismanagement in distribution. If they ever got their act together down there, the price would drop to the point where it wouldn't make sense to import it from Xanadu.

"Those exports are good for the existing colonists, making them pretty much self-sufficient where the necessities of life are concerned. What's costing Luna so much is the continued expansion of the colony. New colonists arriving on planet have to be supplied with a start-up package of supplies and equipment, a basic hab module, and a light vehicle. They also have to be subsidized for the first two years to give them a chance to get going. I've seen the numbers from the Colonial Commission; the cost to add a single colonist to Xanadu is staggering.

"That doesn't even consider the cost of ever-expanding essential services for the colony in general: emergency services, the new hospital, maintenance and operation of the landing field, not to mention the cost of maintaining a full battle group and a division of Marines in orbit. I get the impression that some people back at Lunar Command are questioning whether we should have started the colony project to begin with."

"Hmmph!" Yoric snorted. "Too late to back out. The Confeds are building twice as fast as we are, and now the Consortium nations are getting into the act."

"Hah!" Guerrero rolled her eyes. "We're building a colony. The Confeds are building a concentration camp, or that's what it looks like from orbit. They stopped letting us overfly it with drones because they didn't want us to see how bad it was getting."

"I might be generous and call the Confed operation a penal colony," Lorna said. "However, I am inclined to think that maybe the Consortium nations have the right idea. They started out building a commercially viable operation. They've got four copper mines, close enough together for mutual support and operational efficiency, with the minimum number of people needed to keep them running. They were self-supporting as soon as they started producing copper. Now they're building a refining and smelting operation—costs money, sure, but at the same time, it reduces the cost of shipment back to Earth, since they are only sending the refined product.

"Is it a colony? No, technically it's not, but they do have people living there permanently, the beginnings of a sizable town with support services established. Initially, the mine workers were unaccompanied, but they're starting to bring families in. The difference is that the governments of the Consortium nations aren't pouring a lot of money into the development of it. If anything, they're sitting back and collecting taxes from the operators."

"They do have a military presence in orbit," Guerrero pointed out.

"Hmmph!" Yoric snorted again. "A cruiser and two destroyers—with ships rotating in and out every couple of months as seven different nations share the load. Currently, we have an American cruiser and two Australian destroyers. They aren't putting a serious dent in any one nation's military budget."

"Benefits of a capitalist society." Lorna shrugged. "Let private enterprise do the heavy lifting while the government sits back and skims the proceeds. Face it, people, Luna's model is very much socialist by comparison."

"It had to be, in the beginning," Guerrero insisted. "Our government—Lunar Command—had to bear the cost of the infrastructure needed to live on the Moon in the first place. It's not like the original citizens could go out and set up a farm in the middle of Mare Imbrium. TerraCorp was built after the fact, as a way of funding the whole effort."

DISLOYAL OPPOSITION | 33

"That's true," Lorna agreed. "My point is that we didn't have to do it that way here. In a way, we're doing it the same way as the Confeds, with their super-socialist nanny state, in which the government pays for everything. The only difference is, our citizens have more freedom, more rights guaranteed under our constitution, and—unlike Luna—our colonists are not as dependent on the government for their daily necessities.

"That also means that the Confeds—who have a larger economic base than we have in the first place—can build faster than we can. They can also populate it with colonists who are less than enthusiastic about leaving Earth, whereas we are limited to willing volunteers. Luna can preach about their lofty goals for the Xanadu colony until hell freezes over, but unless they send me more colonists, and more support for them, we are never going to meet those goals."

She sat back and lapsed into silence. Guerrero and Yoric said nothing. Finally, Lorna sat up and gave them a wry grin.

"Sorry, people, didn't mean to vent. I'm a Navy officer. I feel like this whole colonial governor thing is a poor fit for me."

"Part of our job description, Admiral." Yoric returned the grin. "We're supposed to stand by in case the CO wants to blow off steam."

"Right." Lorna chuckled. "But maybe if I blow off more of that steam in Luna's direction, they'll get tired of it and send a real colonial governor out here."

* * *

CNE Colony Site, Eastasia, Planet Xanadu

Leonard Moravec winced as one of his bodyguards buttstroked the man who had tried to accost him. In theory, the man was one of his colonists, who had a right to bring his grievances to the governor general; however, there was a proper process for that, one that did not involve running toward Moravec with the supervisor of the man's work detail in pursuit.

Yes, there's a process, Moravec thought, *but this one wouldn't have had access to it.* The man had been wearing the orange and black–striped vest that marked him as a "pressed" colonist, a political dissident or convicted felon from somewhere on Earth, who hadn't immigrated to Xanadu voluntarily.

Moravec had stopped briefly and gotten out of his LAV to view the construction of a new barracks that would be used to house more of the incoming rabble. Not surprisingly, it was being built adjacent to the Peacekeeper compound that was home to the new battalion of troops that had been sent to serve as the colony's security and police force.

Muttering apologies, the supervisor dragged the man to his feet and gave him a shove back in the direction of the construction site. The pressed colonist was bleeding from the mouth and nose; he would need dental work, assuming the colony's sole dentist had time to see him.

Moravec turned to look at the other barracks across the muddy excuse for a road that ran the length of the developed area. The two-story building was surrounded by a high mesh fence topped with barbed wire, accessible only through a gate guarded by a full squad of Peacekeepers. *You would think some precious commodities were being stored there.* Moravec shook his head. The barracks was home to about a hundred women who had been likewise shipped involuntarily, mostly a nasty lot drawn from women's prisons in CNE nations.

In truth, they *were* a precious commodity. Men outnumbered women among the colonists by approximately three to one. A few of the pressed women in the barracks had been designated as "trustees" and worked at various administrative jobs during the day. Others had gained the favor of various functionaries and colony officials and served their patrons in a more intimate fashion. Those that did well might be allowed to move out of the barracks and become full-time mistresses.

Moravec had not chosen to take a mistress, though his chief of security, Amari Nwosu, had suggested it might be an appropriate mark of his lofty status. At one point, Nwosu had brought five of the women—ones he had personally selected for their beauty—to Moravec's office and offered him a choice. He had been tempted but had refused the offer, knowing that any such companion would become a pipeline of information by which Nwosu would keep tabs on his nominal boss. Moravec might be the governor, but Nwosu's first allegiance was to CNE Central Intelligence Services back on Earth.

Still, Moravec was a man and subject to typical male needs and desires. He satisfied those needs through encounters with a mousy little trustee, a relatively unattractive, simple-minded girl in her late teens who had been assigned to cleaning duty in the governor's office. She came three days a week, arriving at nominal closing time. One night he'd been working late and had struck up a conversation with her. One thing had led to another, and now he stayed late on most of her assigned nights for an intimate encounter on the sofa in his private office. She was cheerfully willing to accommodate him, and he was considering abandoning all pretense and taking her on as his full-time companion.

As for the other women in the barracks, most had put their names on the list for the monthly auction, to be sold to some "freeman" colonist who could come up with the money and haul his prize off to an outlying farm. Those who did not get bought would remain in the barracks. Their first duty was to service the male—and a few female—Peacekeepers. To that end, they were "invited" to attend social gatherings in the Peacekeeper barracks. Those who refused the invitation (or were deemed not worthy) were sent to the male colonist barracks. Not all of the women survived these encounters. According to the records kept by Moravec's assistants, three of them had been buried in the past two months, cause of death unspecified.

Still, that's a lower death rate than we're having among the men. Moravec paused to scrape most of the mud off his boots before climbing back into the LAV.

"Back to the office, Georgi," he told his driver. He decided to avoid the landing field on his inspection tour this morning. Another group of people would be arriving, CIS special operators, the people he was officially not supposed to know about. They would be headed for their own camp ten kilometers out in the jungle. Where they would go after that was not his concern.

* * *

Community Meeting Hall, LFS Colony, Eurasia, Planet Xanadu

"As you were, people… take your seats."

It had been more than two years since the militia company had been formed, but Darius still hadn't gotten used to the idea that people should come to attention when he entered the room. That he was wearing shiny new gold oak leaves on his collar only added to his sense of the surreal. *Not bad for a guy who was a buck private in Fleet Marines ten years ago.*

His was a reserve commission, rammed through Lunar Command with a heavy hand by Admiral Greenwood in her capacity as the colonial governor. Darius had retired from active duty with the LFS Marines as a staff sergeant, a disability retirement due to wounds received that left him with a slight limp. The colonists had drafted him to lead the newly formed militia, and Greenwood had confirmed the appointment.

He was not surprised that she'd supported him; a decade earlier, he'd served his first tour after Basic Training aboard LFS *Lynx*, which was Lieutenant Commander Lorna Greenwood's first command. He'd spent the better part of a month covering her six down on the planet after *Lynx* was shot down over Tatanna during the Bug War.

Darius made his way to the podium with only minor assistance from the cane that was his constant companion. The rest of the group settled into chairs, with two exceptions. Yellow Eyes and Ridge Runner, the two native Kitties, settled down on their haunches, curling their long tails around their feet.

The cats normally moved on all fours but could stand and walk fully erect if the need arose. They had insisted on following human military customs; when they stood at attention, they immediately became the tallest people in the room. Ridge Runner stood a full two meters in that position, but Yellow Eyes topped him by a couple of centimeters. They had also learned how to salute, which caused some consternation among newly arrived officers on the Marine base at the colony airfield. The cats were officially assigned to the Marines but also attended militia meetings.

"We'll be doing monthly equipment inspection today, followed by a trip to the firing range for small arms evaluation, but first, I have a few announcements."

"First of all, be advised that our request for a fourth LAV has been put on temporary hold. Don't ask me what 'temporary' means. Luna has, however, approved a replacement core power unit for our first LAV, so we'll be able to put that one back in service as soon as the unit arrives. Again, however, don't ask when that will be.

"Meanwhile, we have received a shipment of ammo for our LARs and rounds for the 75mm mortars. We have enough to increase our range time and hopefully turn all of you into expert marksmen. Today's results will tell me which of you will need that extra time."

He paused for a moment to let the chuckles die down. A few of his troops had shown little aptitude in the use of small arms. The militia company was an all-volunteer unit, though, so he had to work with what he had. *We're lucky to have enough to call ourselves a company, albeit a short one.* His 65 volunteers were organized into two platoons; a regular Marine company would have three.

"Next item is an intel report, passed along to us from *Omaha Beach*. Orbital surveillance shows the Confeds have built a military facility of substantial size about ten klicks from their primary colony site. Our analysts are not speculating about Confed intentions at this point, but they note that it appears to be capable of supporting a battalion-sized force—maybe larger, because it looks like they are still expanding it.

"They also note that—based on equipment in sight—it is intended to support regular military forces, perhaps special ops types, as opposed to the 'security force' they have serving defensive and police missions within the colony itself. That's *another* battalion-sized installation located within the colony perimeter.

"That brings me to the next item, and this is strictly scuttlebutt, people, so don't go spreading it around. Word is that once we get the hospital in full operation down here, *Omaha Beach* is going home.

"That doesn't mean they are leaving us on our own." He held up a hand to stop the rumble of comment from the group. "They don't think they need to have an entire Marine division tied up here. Word is they're going to cut back to a single battalion, supported by an assault transport rather than a carrier. They're also going to leave a full air-support squadron behind, but it will be based at the port down here instead of up in orbit.

"Again, this is scuttlebutt and should be treated as such. You can talk about it among yourselves, because we need to figure out what it's going to mean for us, but don't spread it around outside the company. In particular, do not discuss it with any civilians, not even your family. Our own mission hasn't changed, and we're not going anywhere, so let's not get carried away."

He paused to scan the group, giving each of them a serious, no-bullshit look to make his point.

What he had told them was more than scuttlebutt. He had gotten the word from Lieutenant Colonel Moira Bouchard, CO of the Marine division's 2nd Battalion, currently stationed at the colony port facility. In all likelihood, Bouchard's battalion would be the one left behind when the carrier departed. She had told Darius to pass the word discretely, so the colonists wouldn't get a shock three months hence when the redeployment occurred. Despite his directive, his people *would* discuss it with their families. *Hell, they're volunteers, weekend warriors, not LFS Marines. They'll talk, and word will get out.*

He shrugged and looked at his pad for the next item on the agenda.

"One more thing, people. To encourage you to put forth your best efforts on the range today, Lieutenant Peabody is offering free drink coupons for the Last Chance Saloon for the top three shooting scores."

That brought a round of cheers from the group. For the militia, Sarah Peabody was the CO of 2nd Platoon; in everyday life, she was the owner and sole proprietor of the colony's only saloon. A Navy veteran, she had started off as the company's first sergeant. As the unit grew in size, she had reluctantly accepted a commission and now wore the "brown bar" of a second lieutenant.

"Uh… Major, sir…" In the front row, Lucius Gerard raised a hand.

"Yes, Corporal?" Darius nodded to him.

"Are you gonna declare Yellow Eyes and Ridge Runner out of the running for the free drinks?"

Darius chuckled as he mentally passed Gerard's comment to the telepathic cats. They had learned to interpret human English, but Darius and Peabody were the only members of the group that could speak and receive Kitty mind speech.

He got a mental chuckle in return from the feline warriors. The two cats had not only learned to handle, shoot, and maintain the Light Assault Rifles with which the militia was equipped; they were also the best shots in the entire company, thanks to steady hands and extremely sharp eyesight.

"Okay… since they don't drink alcohol, and rarely visit the saloon, they've agreed not to compete." Darius smiled at the rumble of amusement from the group. "In addition, Lieutenant Peabody and I will also be ineligible to win. I can't make it any easier than that. Are there any other questions?"

He paused for a moment. There were no more questions.

"Equipment inspection in five minutes. Move with a purpose, people. Grab your gear and meet me in the gym."

* * * * *

Chapter Three

19 March 2123

LFS *Sorceress*, in Tatanna Orbit

"Are we having fun yet, Emily?" Rear Admiral Rebecca Ling asked with a chuckle.

"I don't know that I would call it fun, Admiral." Commodore Emily Bernard raised an eyebrow in Ling's direction. "It has been… how should I say it… interesting."

Bernard had arrived on station three months earlier to take command of *Sorceress*, Ling's flagship, replacing retiring Commodore Roger Corbett. Prior to that, she'd commanded the heavy cruiser *Norseman* during the Bug War.

"It's all my fault." Ling shook her head sadly. "When you got here, I made such a point of telling you how quiet and uneventful things had been recently. Now we've got pirates operating in the outer reaches of the system, a smuggler who turns herself in to us and claims she's actually working for Naval Intelligence back on Luna, and Bug scout ships screwing around out at the hyper limit."

"Not to mention a British battlecruiser parked next to us in orbit." It was Bernard's turn to chuckle. "Where did *that* come from?"

"We knew they had one." Ling shrugged. "That was in the intel briefing we got from Luna six months ago. What we didn't expect was to see it at Tatanna, bringing a diplomatic mission to meet with King

Arne. What's more, according to the message I got when they arrived, that mission isn't only representing the Brits.

"It looks like they're finally willing to admit that this seven-nation 'Consortium' really is an alliance, not just a joint commercial venture. Maybe we'll find out more at dinner tonight. It's going to be an interesting night."

As the senior LFS officer in the system, Ling had been invited to a formal dinner aboard the battlecruiser in question, HMS *Prince of Wales*. The invitation had included senior officers, at her discretion, with an RSVP so the Brits would know how many to expect. Ling had chosen Bernard and Commander Thomas Birdsall, her chief of staff.

"Thank you for including me," Bernard said with a smile. "You know I really want to get a look at that ship. It may not be quite up to *Sorceress'* standards, but it's impressive all the same."

"Yes, it is," Ling replied, "and Naval Intelligence is telling us *Prince of Wales* was already involved in an action between Odin and Sol—thoroughly trashed a group of Confed-sponsored pirates, with a little assistance from our people.

"And, to the point, tonight's dinner may be a social event, but it's also an opportunity to gather intel. They didn't invite anyone from our embassy on the planet, so I plan to spend as much time as I can with the Consortium ambassador. As for you, young lady, you might want to do the same with that young British admiral, Sir John Bryant.

"When he finds out you're the captain of *Sorceress*, I'm sure he'll be more than happy to tell you all about his shiny new ship. Besides, you're a lot younger than I am, and much better looking—and what man could possibly resist that lovely French accent?"

Bernard had immigrated to Luna from France as a teenager, bringing with her an impressive academic record that had earned her admission to Lunar Fleet Academy. Now, two decades later, with an equally impressive service record, she had been given command of one of Luna's most powerful warships, but her voice still carried the melodious tones of *une jeune française*.

"So... you want me to play the *agent provocateuse?*" There was a twinkle in Bernard's eye. "You want me to charm this British admiral into telling us all their secrets?"

"Well, I don't think we need to go quite that far—" Ling grinned at her "—but just between us girls, men are always less discrete about such things when they are trying to impress a pretty woman."

* * *

Peacemaker Cantina, Blue Star Station, in Tatanna Orbit

"Interesting choice of a meeting place, Captain." Lieutenant Colonel Marjorie Lyman leaned back in her seat and surveyed the interior of the bar. The station ran on Luna time, and it was 1600 hours. The lunch crowd was gone, and there were few patrons. Most of them were in uniform, but Lyman was not, nor was her companion. The two of them faced each other in a booth in a corner farthest from the bar.

"I had no reason to go down to the planet." Lilly Maria Buxton shrugged. "If I had, someone might have noticed—especially if I had visited your office. I'm sure the CNE has operatives down there."

"I'm sure they do." Lyman chuckled. "We have people watching them, too."

"Likewise, someone might have noticed if you visited my ship. Your customs inspection was already done. You had already seized the contraband and taken it off. You had cleared me to depart.

"I was told this place was mostly frequented by LFS people, though an occasional merchant spacer might use it. CNE people don't come up from the surface, and the decor is intended to discourage CNE spacers from patronizing the place."

"Yeah, you could say that." Lyman chuckled again. The bar was run by Nils "Gunny" Pederson, a retired LFS Marine who had chosen to decorate the place with Navy and Marine memorabilia and other appointments with a Lunar theme. The flag of the Lunar Free State was on full display over the main bar.

"So what's your point, Captain?" Lyman leaned forward and gave Buxton a serious look. "Why are we here?"

"As I told your customs inspection officer, I am in a rather delicate position. The CNE believes I am a reliable delivery contractor for… shall we say, *sensitive* cargoes."

"Smuggler." Lyman rolled her eyes.

"Please… I hate that term." Buxton gritted her teeth. "Everything I do is within the law. If it were not, your people would have arrested me long ago. Let's just say, I am discreet. As long as the paperwork is in order, I ask no questions."

"Right, but in this case, you led our customs inspector directly to the contraband shipment—a pallet loaded with buckets of nails, which would have been fine, if one bucket's nails hadn't been pure copper. Do you know how valuable that would have been on this planet?"

"No." Buxton shrugged. "I'm told that copper is a precious metal here, but I didn't know what was in the shipment. As I told your inspector, I only knew there had to be something there because my CIS contact gave me special delivery instructions. If I didn't have an LFS warship watching me come in, I was to deliver that entire pallet at coordinates to the northeast of the capital city using a drop pod and remove all trace of its existence from my shipping records.

"I asked them what to do if I was shadowed and couldn't make the drop. They told me to simply make normal delivery at the port. I assume they hoped it would get by your customs people down on the planet."

"It might have," Lyman admitted, "though that's one thing we tend to look for. So what you're telling us is that you are a double agent, and history says that such people are notoriously untrustworthy. Why should we trust you?"

"Your Naval Intelligence people have chosen to do so. I showed you the chip I got from them—my credentials, so to speak. If you doubt their authenticity, you can verify them with Commander Drew at NavInt on Luna."

"Right—on Luna, which is nearly half a light-century away," Lyman said with a snort. "I could verify it by hyperprobe in a little over a month."

"But—" she held up a hand to stop Buxton's protest "—let's say I accept your credentials. I repeat, why are we having this meeting? What can I do for you?"

"You can exercise a little discretion in dealing with me," Buxton replied. "I would like to keep serving this particular run. Despite the petty pirates who showed up this time, I have reason to believe it is safer than certain other star systems. To do that for profit, however, I've got to have those sensitive cargoes from the CNE. I have reason to expect they are going to keep sending shipments like this, stuff you have declared contraband for whatever reason.

"They give me the paperwork to cover my ass, because they know there is a chance I will be intercepted and the cargo discovered. If so, they write it off and move on to the next one. So far, they have not faulted me for any such interceptions, but they are going to get suspicious if I keep coming back to them with reports of delivery failure.

"What I am asking is simple: when I tell you I have one of these cargoes, you simply ignore it. Let me land it on the planet and discover it during your customs inspection. That way, I can go back and report that I completed my part of the delivery successfully. I don't need to know whether you seized it down on the planet. All I need is the standard delivery receipt that says I dropped it at the port. Not my fault that Moonie customs are so good.

"Ideally, if I tell you I have one of these remote drop shipments—like this one was supposed to be—your patrol ships could be a bit lax in following me and could let me make the drop. That might be to your benefit if I give you the coordinates to which I'm supposed to drop the load. You could send your Marines, customs inspectors, or whoever out to see who picks it up. You would then know who on this planet is receiving the shipments.

"Meanwhile, I can go back and report to CIS that the clandestine drop went without a hitch. If you do your part as I suggested, they'll never know what happened to their shipment, and you will have captured the intended recipients."

Buxton sat back, lifted her glass, and took a sip of her drink. The Cantina offered a variety of distilled spirits and beer imported from the Sol System, but Tatanna produced some very good local wines. Buxton favored them and had already ordered several cases to stock *Majorca's* liquor locker.

Lyman also sat back and gave the merchant captain a thoughtful look. After a moment, she nodded.

"That makes sense, but there's one other thing we have to consider. I can't call up Colonel Purdue's Marines and send them off chasing a contraband drop outside the city. We do customs inspection and screening at the request and with the permission of the king. Despite what the Confeds may have told you, the Lunar Free State does not rule Tatanna.

"We will have to figure out a way for you to send us a coded message while you are still inbound from the hyper limit. We'll have the choice of intercepting you and escorting you to orbit—which we do for all incoming commercial ships these days, since the Confeds started dumping all this stuff on us—or letting you slip by. That will depend on whether we can get the king's permission to mount a mission to intercept the drop.

"The earlier we get word from you, the more likely we can do that. I don't know whether we will be able to get a message back to you, but you can always assume that if you don't have one of our destroyers on your tail, you are cleared to drop. If we put an escort on you, you can proceed to orbit.

"Let me talk to Colonel Purdue and the king's people and get back to you on that. Are you planning to depart anytime soon?"

"No, actually, I am thinking of giving my crew leave to go down and play tourist." Buxton smiled. "I might go down myself for a day. Tatanna's an interesting planet, a look at what Earth must have been like in the Renaissance period. If I do go down, however, I'll stay clear of both your offices and the CNE Trade Mission—have to maintain my image of innocent neutrality, you know."

Lyman had just lifted her own drink to her lips; she spluttered as she tried to suppress a laugh.

"Innocent neutrality… right." She put the drink down and looked at Buxton with a grin. "You're a rogue, a smuggler, and a double agent, Captain, but you do have a certain style. I'll talk to the people down on the planet and get back to you within a couple of days. Try to stay out of trouble in the meantime."

* * *

LFS *Sorceress*, in Tatanna Orbit

"Captain, wake up, please. I have a priority message."

Emily Bernard blinked and sat up in bed. The lighting in her cabin had come up at the sound of the voice, putting an end to what had been a deep, restful sleep.

"Yes, Sonja." She rubbed her eyes and glanced at the time display on the wall: 0407 hours. "I'm awake. What is it?"

"We have word from Blue Star Control of a major translation event, indications of a multi-ship arrival at the hyper limit on the bearing designated 'Bug Alley.' Per protocols, the picket force has been notified and is preparing to jump to identify and intercept the incoming ships."

Bernard slid out of bed. She was still getting used to the luxury of a full-sized bed and separate sleeping cabin that a battlecruiser's captain enjoyed. She'd spent much of her career with no more than the standard Navy bunk space typical of officer and crew quarters on smaller LFS warships.

She was also still trying to get used to the idea that her new command was actually alive, thanks to an integrated artificial intelligence. Sonja was Bernard's constant companion, hers to command at any hour. The AI's voice seemed to come from mid-air, and Bernard had already gotten into the habit—common to all of the battlecruiser's officers and crew—of looking up at the overhead when responding to Sonja's calm contralto tone.

"I'm on my way to the bridge." Bernard pulled the uniform tunic over her head and reached for her pants. "Are there any more details from the event?"

"Unfortunately, the arrival point is far around the ecliptic from Tatanna's present position. The best Blue Star could give us is the system operator's rough estimate of twenty or more ships, with five or more of them being of capital mass.

"Admiral Ling has asked me to advise you that she is also awake and will be on her way to the flag bridge shortly. She has also asked that the entire group be brought to Condition Blue."

"Right. Pass the word to the other captains and bring us to Blue. Who has the watch?"

"Ensign Perkins is on the bridge, Captain."

Bernard chuckled. Perkins was a tall, gangly young man on his first deployment after getting his commission. He was the most junior officer aboard *Sorceress* and would not have been officer of the watch for anything other than an anchor watch in orbit. The upgrade to Condition Blue meant he would soon be relieved—she would relieve him herself if she reached the bridge before another senior officer arrived—but for the moment, he was in charge of one of Luna's mightiest warships.

"I'm on my way." Bernard finished sealing her boots and stood up. "Advise me if anything changes."

* * *

The system picket had done its job. The cruiser *Iroquois*, with destroyers *Mantis* and *Orca*, had been guarding the approach from Sol outside the hyper limit. They had jumped into hyper, gone nearly halfway around the system, and dropped back into n-space behind the intruders. Twenty minutes after Bernard reached the bridge, *Sorceress* received the FTL flash from *Iroquois*.

"Two Bug carriers, five cruisers, and a dozen of their destroyers." Bernard raised an eyebrow toward Ling's image on her screen. "The carriers are the real concern. The others are only there as escorts. Do you agree, Admiral?"

"Yes, I do," Ling said with a sigh. "Their small craft did more damage to us during the war than their heavy warships. I lost a destroyer to them in Tatanna orbit."

"We took damage from them, as well, trying to clear the orbitals." Bernard nodded in agreement. "I had *Norseman* at the time, and this force is almost as large as what they had defending the planet. They also had small craft launched from the planet in that battle."

"Right," Ling replied, "but we also had two full battle groups. Doesn't matter, we've got to deal with it. Bring the group to readiness for departure. I want to break orbit within the hour.

"I'm also going to call up CruRon 2. Wilcox can stay and hold the orbitals with *Navajo* and *Gryphon*, but I'll want his other two cruisers with us. Plan your formation accordingly. We've advised the civilians in orbit and down on the planet, and…" Ling glanced at another display off camera. "It looks like the British are calling me. I'll get back to you."

* * *

"I appreciate the offer, Sir John—" Rebecca Ling regarded the image on her screen with chagrin "—but this really isn't your fight. We're the ones who took this system from the Bugs in the first place, and we're the ones who promised King Arne we would defend his realm against them."

"Oh, I quite understand." Sir John Bryant was in uniform but appeared to be still in his quarters aboard *Prince of Wales*. He would have gotten word of the incursion as part of the courtesy notice Blue Star passed to all ships in orbit.

"We, however, are in process of establishing diplomatic relations with the king. I've suggested to our ambassador that we ought to do this simply to show that we are also willing to come to the defense of his realm. I'm also rather certain that her Britannic majesty would endorse the action."

"Well…" Ling hesitated. "Would you be willing to place your force under my command for the duration? I think it's important to have a single point of control, and…"

"Of course." Bryant waved his hand in dismissal. "I believe you might be senior to me, and you certainly know more about these bloody Bugs than I do."

"Yes, I guess I do." Ling gave him a grim smile. "I had a destroyer squadron during the war. All right, let's get under way. We can discuss strategy and tactics en route. I'll have my comm people talk to yours to set up channels and callsigns."

"Right." Bryant nodded. "I'm bringing *Torrent* with me. Use her as you see fit. Bryant, out."

"Sonja…" Ling looked up as the British admiral's face disappeared from her screen. "Advise Captain Bernard that the Brits will be joining us. I'll get with her to discuss tactics once we're under way."

***

ICV *Majorca*, in Tatanna Orbit

I must be living in those "interesting times" the old curse talks about. Lilly Maria Buxton felt a lump in her throat as she watched the entire force of LFS warships back slowly away from the anchorage and form up in battle order. A moment later, her eyes widened as the British warships joined them. *Prince of Wales* had been moored less than a kilometer from *Majorca*; she could clearly see the Union Jack displayed on the battlecruiser's forward hull.

They're going out to kick somebody's ass.

The thought brought momentary relief, which faded a moment later as another thought took its place. *They wouldn't be going out with everything they have unless something really bad is coming in.* The alert from Blue Star Station had simply said "hostile forces" were inbound, with a projected ETA of 72 hours. It had gone on to advise that all departures from Tatanna orbit were temporarily on hold to allow for a military deployment. Once that deployment was complete, commercial traffic could resume.

In other words, I'm free to get my pretty ass out of the system before the "hostile forces" arrive.

Unfortunately, three of her five crewmembers were down on the planet, enjoying a well-earned shore leave. Thanks to bans on imported technology on Tatanna, she had no way of contacting them once they left the port facility. According to the Tourists' Guide to Tatanna (supplied by the Moonies upon arrival), they could be staying at any of a dozen inns in King's City that were labeled as friendly to off-worlders.

Majorca's crew were all female, but none of them were shy schoolgirls. The idea of exploring the nightlife in a medieval city appealed to them—had appealed to Buxton, as well, but she'd opted to stay aboard ship and mind the store. The trip to Blue Star Station to meet with Lyman had been her only off-ship time on this trip.

And damn it! I still haven't heard back from Lyman. She wanted to have those communication issues settled before she departed, so her next Confed "smuggling" contract would go smoothly; she would make her delivery as the Confeds requested, and the Moonies would still seize their contraband goods. Those runs were worth good money to her, in addition to the satisfaction she got from screwing the CNE bastards.

She took a deep breath. Her girls were due back aboard tonight. Hopefully, she would also hear from Lyman today. If not, she could afford to wait another full day before making a run for the hyper limit. By then, maybe the Moonies would have kicked ass on those "hostile forces," and she wouldn't have to run after all.

* * * * *

Chapter Four

24 March 2123
LFS *Sorceress*, Outer Reaches of the Sacagawea System

Emily Bernard studied the tactical display. 2nd Fleet's 3rd Battle Group was currently decelerating to match vectors with the incoming Bugs; they would not reach standard missile range for another hour.

Her formation was short a cruiser and two destroyers—the picket force, which was slowly closing on the Bugs from behind—but was augmented by *Aborigine* and *Dragon* from CruRon 2. In addition, she had *Prince of Wales* and *Torrent*; the British battlecruiser was holding station on *Sorceress* five kilometers off her starboard side. Ling had slotted the Brit destroyer into her forward screen. Based on what they knew of Bug technology, the LFS had a superior force. Lunar warships were better than anything the Bugs had in offense, defense, speed, and maneuverability.

They may have improved, she thought, *but we have improved, too.* There had been no serious engagements with insectoid Ay'uskanar since the Bug War, nearly twelve years ago. Lunar missiles now had longer range and better targeting systems.

The real threat was from the Bug carriers. During the war, Bernard had seen a single carrier launch a hundred small craft in less than ten minutes. The carriers might also have improved; for that matter, the small craft they carried might be better, as well.

Bernard realized she was sailing into the unknown, but one thing was certain; the best way to deal with the Bug carriers was to hit them before they could get their attack craft launched.

"Pass the word to the cruisers," she ordered. "Prepare for Wolfpack launch."

The Wolfpack long-range missile delivery system had been developed in the earliest decades of the Lunar Free State's history and had been used successfully against the Mekota, the Otuka, and the Bugs. More recently, in a battle in this star system, the Confeds had seen it for the first time. They had not enjoyed the experience, which had contributed to the near-total destruction of a Confed battle group.

The current version of the system consisted of a long-range delivery vehicle that carried four of the latest generation of Viper missiles. The vehicle was fired from far beyond normal missile range. Using guidance provided by the host ship, it would accelerate at its maximum initially, then go ballistic. It would not power up again until it got within Viper range of its targets.

At that point, the Vipers themselves would lock on and launch, while the delivery vehicle powered up an ECM package to confuse the enemy's defenses. In addition, the delivery vehicle carried a warhead and would attempt to engage a target, though its slower speed made it more vulnerable to missile defenses.

The Wolfpack system was a large and bulky package that could not be fired from any warship's internal missile tubes. Instead, Wolfpacks were carried in belts around the largest warships. Battlecruisers carried two belts of twelve, heavy cruisers a single belt of eight. That put 48 Wolfpacks at Bernard's disposal, a total of 192 Vipers plus the delivery vehicles—240 fusion-fired laser warheads.

The system was best used in a closing engagement against a large formation of enemy ships, which was exactly the situation they were facing. The group was decelerating, turned away from the enemy. They would launch the Wolfpacks to the rear; their own gravity wake would help to hide the launch from the enemy.

"All Wolfpack ships report ready, Captain," Sonja advised. In battle, the AI's primary function was to coordinate defensive efforts for the entire group. The tactical officers of each ship would be free to concentrate on offense. Sonja's advice meant those officers were waiting for a command from the flagship.

"Admiral, we are in Wolfpack range." Bernard turned her attention to Ling's image on her screen. "Request permission to engage."

"Weapons free, Emily. You are cleared to engage." Ling nodded. "Give 'em hell."

Bernard keyed her group command channel. As Ling's flag captain, her job was to pass the admiral's orders to the group and coordinate their efforts.

"All ships, weapons free, defenses free, we are cleared to engage. Wolfpack launch on my mark." She paused for a moment. "Three, two, one, mark!"

At the command, the Wolfpacks launched and headed downrange. It would take them nearly forty minutes to reach attack range for their Viper payloads. *The battle has begun,* Bernard thought, *though the Bugs don't know it yet. Hopefully, when they find out, it will be a most unpleasant surprise.*

* * *

HMS *Prince of Wales*

"I presume you're recording all of this, Teddy."

"I am indeed, Admiral." Captain Theodore Wilshire grinned at Sir John Bryant's image on his screen. "I believe the Moonies have given us a look at that secret weapon system they've been using to thoroughly trash the Confeds recently."

"Yes, it appears they have." Bryant returned the grin. Wilshire was at his command station on *Prince's* bridge, while Bryant occupied his own station on the flag bridge. Having placed his force at Admiral Ling's disposal, Sir John considered himself mostly an observer at this point.

"I imagine the Admiralty will be most interested in the tactical data we bring back from this one." Bryant chuckled. "There! Look! Those packages have gone ballistic. They're off the plot, and I'm willing to bet the Bugs never saw the launch. I can't wait to see what happens when they get downrange."

* * *

LFS tactical doctrine said the best way to use Wolfpacks was to fire them so that they would arrive just as the battle group reached standard missile range and could add a full double broadside that would overwhelm the enemy's defenses. Rebecca Ling had decided not to do that; she had chosen to fire them earlier with the entire salvo targeted for the two Bug carriers, hopefully to hit them before they launched their fighter craft.

The Wolfpack system had its range limits. Though the delivery vehicles made most of the trip with their drives shut down, they still required course corrections along the way, each of which used drive power that would limit the system's maneuverability at the critical end point of their run. Bernard's orders had sent them on their way at what was considered to be the maximum range for the system. They would arrive nearly twenty minutes before the battle group reached standard missile range.

Unfortunately, they didn't get there early enough. The Bug carriers began launching their attack craft a few minutes before the Wolfpacks arrived. They continued to launch even after the Vipers went hot and bored in on the carriers. The Bug missile defenses took out a significant number of the incoming missiles, but most of them reached attack range and detonated, spearing the carriers with dozens of powerful x-ray lasers. One carrier simply disintegrated; the other vanished in a star-bright flare of thermonuclear fire, having taken a direct hit to one of its fusion plants.

Before being destroyed, however, they had launched more than a hundred of their small craft, which immediately formed up and came at the Lunar and British force at speeds no regular warship could match.

* * *

Bridge, LFS *Sorceress*

"Recommend we concentrate missile fire on the Bug cruisers, Admiral." Bernard checked the seals on her shipsuit; *Sorceress* was about to come under fire. "The attack craft are too small and fast. The Bug War taught us they will be better engaged with beam weapons."

"Right." On the screen at Bernard's command chair, Ling nodded. "Hell, if they get close enough, we can hit them with point defense and countermissiles. Sonja, take note."

"Noted, Admiral," the AI replied on the command channel. Point defense and countermissiles were part of the integrated group defense that Sonja handled. They would not normally be used against attacking ships, but the Bug fighters were not like other attackers.

"Mister Stockwell, give priority to Bogies Three through Seven for missiles, if you please." Bernard checked her tactical display. "Ignore the fighters until they get within beam range."

"Aye, ma'am…" Lieutenant Commander Jason Stockwell, the ship's Navigation and Tactical officer, acknowledged. "Missile fire targeting Bogies Three, Four, Five, Six, and Seven. Hold fire on fighters until within beam range."

And hope the Bugs haven't got any more surprises, Bernard thought. She had already noted that the small craft appeared to be faster than those the LFS had encountered in the Bug War. *Well, it has been twelve years. We should have expected that.*

She was more concerned about incoming missiles. During the war, Bug fighters had carried four missiles each, but they were smaller and faster than those carried by regular Bug warships. They were relatively short ranged, requiring the fighters to come within beam weapon range of an LFS warship in order to attack. She fervently hoped that was still the case; otherwise, they would have to go after the fighters with missiles after all.

"Missile range in thirty seconds," Stockwell reported. A moment later, his voice took on a more urgent note. "Enemy missile launch… approximately a hundred and seventy incoming, two minutes to our defense envelope."

"Acknowledged." Bernard drew a deep breath. So far, the enemy had not shown anything unexpected, but their tactics were sound and logical, as usual. The fighters would arrive in time to add their own missiles to the incoming barrage from the Bug cruisers and destroyers.

"Sonja, the defense net is yours."

The chronometer she had set counted down to zero. She waited five more seconds before keying the group command channel.

"All ships, commence missile fire."

* * *

Flag Bridge, LFS *Sorceress*

Rebecca Ling nodded in grim satisfaction as two of the Bug cruisers staggered and fell out of formation. *Their missile defenses have gotten better,* she thought, *but not by that much.* Unfortunately, their missiles have gotten better, too.

The Bug cruisers and destroyers had sent a lot of missiles downrange in their first wave. Their missiles were longer ranged but slightly slower than LFS Vipers; that was no surprise. What was different was their cycle time. The second wave of missiles was on its way less than a minute after the first, and the Bugs got a third wave off before the first LFS missiles reached attack range. While that still wasn't as fast Ling's ships could cycle their launchers, it was a great improvement over what the Bugs had been able to do during the war.

Again, the Bug missiles hadn't shown much in the way of evasive maneuvers, but their targeting systems were too dumb to fool with ECM. They carried no warhead, only a massive penetrator in their noses that relied on the kinetic energy of direct collision to wreak damage on their target.

As expected, the Bug fighter craft had launched their own first salvo at exactly the right moment to add another hundred plus missiles to the incoming first salvo. To do so, however, they'd come into range of the primary graser batteries of Ling's heaviest warships, which had opened fire on the small, fast-moving targets.

From that point on, Ling had been forced to leave the battle in the hands of her captains and their tactical officers—and Sonja, who directed the group's defenses with the cool AI precision that made LFS battlecruisers such a formidable force in a firefight such as this.

Despite the AI's best efforts, Ling's ships took damage. There were simply too many threats to handle with the available defensive resources. The Bugs were logical and understood basic tactics; they concentrated their fire on the biggest threat—LFS *Sorceress*. The battlecruiser's armor was intended to resist energy beam weapons and the x-ray lasers spawned by missile warheads. It was less effective against the kinetic penetrators the Bugs used, and *Sorceress* had already taken damage. Ling ignored the incoming damage control reports and concentrated on the tactical situation.

Knowing the Bug attack craft would be coming for *Sorceress*, she had arranged her destroyers in what had become known as the "*Lynx* defense"—named for the single-ship defense of the carrier *Iwo Jima* by the destroyer *Lynx* during the Bug War. Effectively, the formation put the destroyers directly in front of, but slightly below the path of the incoming fighter craft, where they could engage the incoming enemy while staying out of the line of fire of the battlecruiser's own formidable weapons.

That tactic had never been intended for use against such a large swarm of fighters, however. Many of the incoming Bugs had been taken out; many of their missiles had been swatted down before reaching their target. Now, however, the survivors were inside the destroyer screen, in the zone where neither *Sorceress* nor her escorts could

DISLOYAL OPPOSITION | 63

effectively engage them without fear of hitting each other. It was time to change tactics. Ling touched the icon for the group command channel.

"Flag to all ships…"

Before she could issue the order, the flag bridge exploded around her.

* * *

"Flag bridge is omega, Captain. You have group command." Sonja's calm, clear voice sent a chill through Emily Bernard.

Putain de merde! In moments of extreme stress, Bernard's brain had a tendency to fall back on her native French. *Suis-je prêt pour ça?*

Group command… those two simple words had placed a dozen destroyers and cruisers under her command, not to mention the two British warships. *Am I ready for this?*

Bernard had come up along what Fleet called the "tactical track"— had served as the tactical officer aboard a series of increasingly larger warships as she rose in rank, before finally being made executive officer, and later captain of the heavy cruiser *Norseman*. She had distinguished herself in battle, and proven her competence to command, but until this moment, she had never commanded a multi-ship formation.

Get yourself together, girl. Forget Sorceress; *your people have her well in hand. Focus on the big picture. First, pass the word.* She keyed the group command channel.

"All ships, this is *Sorceress* Prime." To her surprise, her voice came out calm and level. "Admiral Ling is down. I am assuming group command. I have the flag. Acknowledge."

On her display, the icons for all twelve ships blinked green with the standard acknowledgment symbol—message received. There were no comments or protests. She was Ling's flag captain, the most senior officer in the group after the admiral.

She studied the display. The Bug fighters were inside the screen. The destroyers were no longer able to defend *Sorceress*, and in fact were hindering the battlecruiser's own defenses as her tactical officer tried to avoid any "friendly fire" incidents. She had to do something about that.

"Flag to all destroyers, break formation. Proceed independently to target the Bug cruisers and destroyers. Form up on *Copperhead*—Captain Lucas, you have squadron command."

Martin Lucas of *Copperhead* was the most senior among the destroyer captains. Bernard regretted that she hadn't gotten to know all the group's captains yet, but Lucas seemed to be a solid type.

"Acknowledged." The response came back immediately. "*Copperhead* Prime has destroyer squadron command. Destroyer squadron, switch to TAC-3."

Sorceress shuddered as another pair of missiles got through her defenses. More red messages appeared on Bernard's damage control display—Missile 4 omega, Point Defense 6 omega…

"Captain, we have lost 45 percent of portside defenses and 28 percent of missile and beam weaponry on that side." Sonja's calm voice reminded her that she still had to attend to her own ship.

"Mr. Stockwell, if you have portside missiles ready, fire them now," she ordered. "Rollover in ten seconds. Helm, roll right one-eight-zero degrees on my mark. Sonja, adjust defense accordingly… four, three, two, one, mark!"

Despite battle damage, the ship's ability to maneuver had not been compromised. To Bernard's relief, her orders were carried out with textbook precision. Stockwell fired another seven missiles downrange before *Sorceress* rolled over, presenting her relatively undamaged starboard side to the attacking enemy. Sonja continued to track the incoming fighters and took out two more of them with bottom turret grasers as the rollover proceeded.

"*Dragon, Wraith*—" Bernard hit the group command channel icon again "—cover *Prince of Wales*, top and bottom. Sonja, integrate defenses accordingly."

She had noted a shift in targeting in the latest salvo of missiles from the surviving enemy cruisers and destroyers. Apparently, the Bugs had decided that *Prince* was a priority target, and *Sorceress* was best left to their fighters to deal with. Bernard's order sent the two light cruisers to beef up the British defenses.

It was a good call on Ling's part to let the Brits join us, she decided. *They've certainly thrown their share of missiles, and they've fitted in well, despite never having been in action with us before today.*

She nodded in grim satisfaction as the group's latest salvo wiped out another Bug cruiser in the brilliant flare of a failed fusion plant. Meanwhile, Lucas' destroyers had flanked the Bug formation and taken out two enemy destroyers in the process. The Bugs would keep fighting until the last one was destroyed. They would not surrender, nor would they retreat. A crippled ship that could no longer fight would self-destruct. It was the Bug way of doing war.

Sorceress shuddered as yet another Bug penetrator got past her defenses, but a glance at her display showed Bernard that the damage was not critical, and few of the enemy fighters were still in action. Two more of them vanished as she watched, victims of the battlecruiser's main graser batteries. The small craft had run out of missiles; those that remained were in kamikaze mode and would try to ram *Sorceress* if they could. Their chances of getting past Sonja's defenses were poor to zero. For all intents, the battle was won.

Maintenant c'est tout… she thought. *We have done it!*

Bridge environmental system is working, so why am I sweating like this? She resisted the urge to wipe her brow. *Remember this moment, girl, the next time you start wishing for those admiral's stars.*

* * *

LFS *Sorceress*, in Tatanna Orbit

"Bit of a bloody dust up, there." On Emily Bernard's screen, Sir John Bryant shook his head. "Can't imagine what you people went through during the war. I'm glad our first encounter with the bloody Bugs was in company with someone who knew how to deal with them."

"And I'm happy we had *Prince* and *Torrent* to reinforce us." Bernard smiled. "The Bugs have been quiet for years. We never expected them to open hostilities again. I'm sorry that your introduction to Tatanna has been so hostile. It's a very nice planet with good people, which is why we thought it was worth taking away from the Bugs to begin with."

"Glad to be of assistance. I spoke with our diplomatic people a few minutes ago, and they are absolutely delighted. They tell me your ambassador has already advised King Arne of our participation, and he has invited them to the palace for a meeting. He's concerned about the Bugs and wants to move forward with an alliance."

"I'm sure he will." Bernard nodded. "Arne came to the throne when his father was assassinated in the middle of the Bug War. He knows what life under the Bugs was like and has no desire to see them back again.

"But I have to ask, Sir John… did your ships take much damage in the engagement? My people say that *Prince* took at least two hits. They aren't sure about *Torrent*, but both of you were in the thick of it."

"Not as much as you were." Bryant waved the notion aside. "From our viewpoint, it looks like they threw everything at *Sorceress*—practically ignored everyone else in the battle. They knew where the real threat was.

"Yes, *Prince* took two hits, lost a drive node and a missile battery. Two crew casualties there, neither one fatal. They never touched *Torrent*. I'd say we got off rather lightly. How about you?"

"*Sorceress* has seen better days," Bernard admitted. "We have thirty dead, and twenty other casualties, including Admiral Ling. She survived the hit on the flag bridge, but two of her staff did not. Unfortunately, her injuries are severe enough that we are going to send her back to Luna in cold sleep, along with four others of the injured.

"We have several other ships that took hits. The destroyer *Mantis* took enough damage that she had to be towed in. *Iroquois* made it back under her own power, but she's far from combat effective. Three other ships took minor damage. Altogether, we've got forty-seven KIA and close to a hundred wounded.

"In a full-on confrontation with the Bugs, I would say we also got off lightly. I assume you noticed that none of the Bugs survived. When they go all out like that, surrender and retreat are not options for them. We learned that the hard way during the war.

"Admiral Ling's injury makes Commodore Wilcox of our cruiser squadron the senior LFS officer in system. He has advised me to offer you the use of Blue Star Station for any repairs or other support you may need. It's the least we can do in return for the support you provided."

*****

Chapter Five

17 April 2123
Chief Executive's Office, TerraNova City, Luna

"Well? You forwarded the report to me, Mac." Robert O'Hara frowned as he took a cigar from the humidor on his desk. "What do you recommend we do about it?"

"Info only, Admiral." Admiral Charles "Mac" McGruder shrugged. "At this point, I'm still trying to figure out the implications. I've got my own staff and all the battle group flag officers in port working on it, not to mention NavInt and the Diplomatic Corps.

"About all we know at this point is that the Bugs came back with a serious military force. All attempts to contact them and determine their intentions failed—as is the usual case with the Bugs—so Rebecca Ling opened the whole can of Whoop Ass and dumped it on them."

"And took serious damage in return," O'Hara growled, "with Ling herself being one of the casualties. Where does that leave us as far as defense of the Sacagawea System is concerned?"

"Not sure yet." McGruder leaned back with a thoughtful look on his face. "Based on Bernard's preliminary report, we still have a significant force out there. *Sorceress* took the most damage, but she's still combat effective. *Iroquois* also took damage, but with CruRon 2 in place, we are heavy on cruisers. My inclination is to not send reinforcements, but I've passed the word to make *Chesapeake Bay* ready for deployment. It sounds like some damage may be beyond local repair ability. We have one destroyer that isn't hyper-capable."

"What about Ling? The report says they're shipping her back here."

"Right. They took five casualties judged serious enough to put them in cold sleep and ship them back. Ling was one of them. They have others they'll be sending back, but five was the maximum they could put on the embassy's fast courier boat. Damned Bugs got lucky with a hit on *Sorceress* that penetrated all the way to the flag bridge.

"The hyperprobe also had medical reports on the casualties. I turned those over to the medics and convinced them to give me a prognosis on Ling. Those guys invoke patient privacy at the drop of a hat, but I signed off on a 'needs of the service' request. They are talking about severe spinal damage. Assuming they can put her back together again, she'll need six months to recover and learn how to walk again. They say she may never have full mobility.

"That leaves us with Wilcox as the SO at Sacagawea. He's senior to Bernard by a couple of years. Curiously enough, he wasn't involved in the engagement at all. Ling ordered him to remain in orbit with *Navajo* for planetary defense in case any of the Bugs got through… which they didn't. Under the circumstances, Bernard did an outstanding job. Wilcox says he's not moving his flag to *Sorceress*; he'll stay with *Navajo* and leave Bernard in place.

"It's kind of an awkward command arrangement. Technically, she's still the flag captain of the battle group, but he's in charge of the whole show. Neither of them has time-in-grade for promotion, but we really need a two-star out there. We can't wait for Ling to recover—if she ever does."

"So, what do you recommend? Hopefully, we are going to send somebody out there, not send another battle group." O'Hara rolled his eyes. "I'm struggling with the Navy budget already. The last thing we need is another war, but the Bugs have no respect for our problems."

"No, we don't need to send another group. Unless the Bugs show us a lot more than they have, we should be okay. We've got some repairs to do, but that'll bring us back up to strength. What we don't want to do is reduce forces at Sacagawea. That last notice you sent me on the subject has me concerned."

"I know, and you and I still have to talk about it. There are going to be cutbacks, no doubt about that. I need you to tell me where those cutbacks will do the least damage to our mission. That's for a later day. Who are you thinking of bumping to Sacagawea?"

"We've got a few one-stars with necessary experience and time-in-grade, but again, I have to look at which one can be pulled with the least amount of damage. Since we're talking about a possible war zone, we'll want someone with command experience, preferably in combat. I'm thinking of Peter Yoric."

"Yoric? From *Valkyrie?*" O'Hara blinked. "You're going to steal Greenwood's flag captain?"

"Yeah, well, that's part of the reason I picked him. Greenwood has a good backup available with *Valkyrie's* exec. It'll mean bumping Winfield to commodore, but I've looked at his record, and I think he's ready."

"Okay, but Yoric's all the way out at Coleridge. Even if we send an e-boat to pick him up, it'll take the better part of two months to get him to Sacagawea. Can we wait that long?"

"I don't see a problem with that." McGruder dismissed the issue with a wave. "We're tightening up the command team. I'm confident Wilcox and Bernard can handle anything that happens in the meantime. If our past experience with the Bugs is any guide, it'll take them a lot longer than that to move again.

"Hell, they've been quiet for over ten years. I think they were testing us. They got their insect asses handed to them, and they may not be back for another decade."

"Fine." O'Hara sat back and took a couple of puffs on the cigar. "I'll sign off on the promotions. Get it in process. The Bugs may not be back for another ten years, but I want us back to strength out there in no more than three months. Let's talk about the Brits. What possessed Ling to take them along on her engagement with the Bugs?"

"I guess we can ask her when she wakes up." McGruder chuckled. "Actually, it turned out rather well, I'd say. Sure as hell ought to improve our relations with them."

"Really?" O'Hara raised a skeptical eyebrow. "What happens if her majesty isn't so happy about them getting involved in our war with the Bugs? I think you, me, and Martina need to have a talk about that. There are diplomatic implications we may not have considered."

"Hey, I'm not a diplomat." McGruder shrugged. "From a military standpoint, we got our first close-up look at their battlecruiser in action. Bernard included the full tactical dump from the engagement, and I have to say, I'm impressed."

"Has it occurred to you that they got an even better look at our ships in action? Until now, we haven't shown them anything bigger than destroyers, when the Cat Pack rescued them from those so-called 'pirates' on the Odin run. This time they saw what a fully integrated battle group can do in an all-up attack.

"But... water under the bridge." O'Hara dismissed the issue with a wave. "We've got other things to talk about, but I wanted to get your first take on the Sacagawea situation. I've got Martina coming in this afternoon. If you're available, let's talk about the diplomatic situation."

"Admiral..." McGruder shook his head with a chuckle. "Has it ever occurred to you that the CEO never needs to ask if somebody is 'available' when he wants to have a meeting? Being 'available' is part of my job description."

* * *

Le Paradis Sur Terre Resort, St. Moritz, Switzerland

"What is the source of this information?" Huang Chang Li gave Gerhardt Richter a questioning look.

"Diplomatic flash message from Sacagawea," Richter replied. "The CNE is wary of putting a warship in Tatanna orbit in light of past experiences, but they maintain an embassy support ship there with hyperprobe capability. They've also got an e-boat making regular runs between Luna and Tatanna, but apparently somebody decided this was urgent enough to expend a probe."

"I would be inclined to agree with whoever made that decision." Andre DuMorne chuckled. "This offers so many intriguing possibilities. Are the Bugs about to start another war with the Moonies?"

"CNE Intelligence thinks not." Richter shook his head. "They think it was only a probe to test Moonie defenses, and the rapid Moonie response will have convinced them not to do it again."

"Hah!" The bark of laughter came from Butos Kimba. "Just as their response convinced the CNE not to mess with them at Sacagawea a couple of years ago. The Confed Navy is still recovering from that one, and the even bigger thrashings they got at Odin and Coleridge."

"The CNE is content to sit back and build up its strength," Richter insisted. "The Moonies have a firm grip on Sacagawea and will not be easily dislodged. I am more concerned over the involvement of the British in this one. We are starting to see increasing evidence that this new 'Consortium' of the unaligned nations is a strong military and diplomatic alliance, not a commercial venture.

"We have American and British Commonwealth warships at Odin and Coleridge already—admittedly in support of commercial efforts in those systems—but now we have the Brits showing up at Sacagawea, where they've had no previous dealings. The report also says they brought a diplomatic mission there to establish relations with Tatanna's monarchy. What's more, they were able to land that mission successfully, which means they must have agreed to the Moonie technology and trade restrictions, since the planet is still a Moonie protectorate.

"These are matters of concern to us. I believe we must give them serious consideration."

"Indeed we must." Andre DuMorne stroked his chin, a thoughtful look on his face. "Our basic plan has always been to pit the Moonies against the CNE, so that ultimately they will beat each other to a pulp, leaving us to mold what remains into a single entity which we will control, a government for all of the Sol System with extensions out to the stars. We could build an interstellar empire of sorts, bringing the humans of New Eden, Tatanna, Ragnarok, and the new colonies of Xanadu into the fold.

"However, we must now consider that there is another entity to account for. If both the CNE and the Moonies are made too weak, these people may move into the power vacuum and establish themselves as dominant. They are already building a colony of their own on Xanadu and have mining operations on Ragnarok. If Gerhardt's report is correct, they are moving to establish themselves on Tatanna."

"I think we must put our grand designs for a stellar empire aside for the moment." Mohammed Al Sharif scowled at the group. "You have often accused Butos and me of having no interest in the stars, but I am telling you that we must attend to matters closer to home.

"I agree that the Consortium is a threat to our plans, but the seven nations within it are all on Earth. *This* is where we must deal with them. Andre, you have financial interests in the US and Canada; you are in the best position to extend our influence into the governments of those nations. Chang, you have heavy industrial interests in Japan and Korea. You are also most familiar with the culture of those nations. Again, you have the best chance of gaining government influence there.

"I believe this is a direction in which we must move. Do all of you agree?"

There was silence around the table for a moment, then Huang nodded. By drawn lot, he was the chairman of today's meeting.

"I agree. We have neglected the Consortium nations for too long, which may be why they were able to form their alliance in the first place. Andre, do you agree with Mohammed's assessment? It would seem that you are in the best position to extend our influence in North America, as well as to the British Commonwealth."

"I agree." There was a note of resignation in the French financier's voice. "But consider that I am also the one conducting our current project to subvert the Moonies from within. Do not expect rapid progress with the Americans, Canadians, and Brits. This will be a long-term effort."

"That's why I suggested we concentrate our efforts in the Sol System." Mohammed chuckled. "If we control what happens here, the stars will follow. I'm not saying we should abandon our efforts out there. It costs us nothing to let the CNE and the Moonies confront each other on Xanadu, and my revolution project on Ragnarok also requires little attention on our part. I'm saying that our priorities should be given to the efforts closer to home."

Again there was silence around the table. Huang, whose expression rarely betrayed his thoughts, favored them with a rarely displayed smile.

"Do you realize what we have done today, gentlemen?" he asked the group. "We have extended our reach to virtually every part of the Earth—and the Moon, for that matter.

"Gerhardt has always controlled the CNE; Mohammed has always had the Islamic nations as his domain; Butos controls Africa and South America. You have motivated me to extend my influence in the Far East, with an eye toward managing the nations there more directly. With Andre's acceptance of the plan, we will add North America and the British Commonwealth to our sphere of influence.

"As for the Moonies, Andre can continue his efforts at subversion through his TerraCorp contacts. I will also suggest that Gerhardt and I should examine our military contracts with the Moonies to see what we might contribute to their eventual downfall."

* * *

30 April 2123
Lunar Command Executive Conference Room,
TerraNova City, Luna

"What the hell is this, Admiral?" McGruder's tone of voice reflected the angry frustration his words expressed. "You're telling me we've got to mothball almost half the fleet."

"That's a bit of an exaggeration, Mac." O'Hara frowned. "Nothing is being 'mothballed.' We are taking three battle groups off the ready line, but the ships will still be powered up, tended by reduced crews, and will be our ready reserve. The plan calls for them to be brought back online within ten days if needed."

"That 'plan' was developed by dockyard people," McGruder growled. "They know how to repair and maintain ships. They're not qualified to judge whether a ship is ready for action, and they're not the ones who have to take that ship into battle. Why the hell did you not involve me or any of my command staff in the planning phase of this?"

O'Hara shifted uncomfortably in his chair. He was the chief executive. He didn't have to answer the question, but he knew McGruder was right. He hadn't wanted to argue about the necessity of the force reductions, so he hadn't included his fleet commander in the planning of it.

"For one thing," McGruder continued, glancing at Vice Admiral Marjorie Whitman, CO of the fleet anchorage and dockyard facilities, "I'm sure they can restore the ships to readiness, but what about the crews? You are talking about putting thousands of Navy people on half-pay, 'ready reserve' status.

"Never mind the fact that it will put a lot of them in a financial bind—especially since they won't be living aboard a ship and getting three meals a day. I'm also concerned about that 'ten days to get online' issue. If the shit hits the fan, and we need those battle groups, rounding up the crews for them and getting them back to fighting trim will be impossible to do in a month, let alone ten days."

O'Hara looked at the others around the table. In addition to McGruder and Whitman, the meeting included Martina Easley and Lieutenant General Mark Mercer, commandant of the Lunar Marine Corps.

"Point taken, Mac." O'Hara sat back in his chair with a sigh. "That's why we're having this meeting. This is a preliminary plan, and we need to refine it and fix any problems before it goes into effect; however, it *will* go into effect. The reductions in force are necessary. We simply cannot afford to maintain the fleet at current levels. The alternative would be to decommission two battle groups entirely and discharge their crews—no half pay, no possibility of recall, and no ready reserve. It's that bad, people."

He scanned their faces again. Easley's eyes widened, but Whitman nodded. *She's seen it coming,* he thought. *She's already seen the cuts, no new shipyard construction, maintenance schedules being stretched, repairs delayed. Her people are already feeling the cutbacks. We haven't shifted anyone to reserve status yet, but it's coming.*

McGruder still looked unhappy, but his anger appeared to have cooled a bit. Mercer showed no reaction at all; he simply looked at O'Hara with an intense but neutral expression.

"Mark? Any comment?"

"You haven't said anything about the Marines yet, sir." Mercer showed the faintest hint of a grim smile. "I think I know what's coming, though. I was a little surprised when you told me to bring 1st Division home from Xanadu, but I figured that we're pretty much settled there. We're still in a pissing contest with the Confeds, but it's not going to be open combat, because we've already proved we can kick their asses in orbit. Bouchard's battalion should be able to handle anything that happens dirtside.

"I'm wondering what's going to happen when Sakura gets back, and we've got two assault carriers and two divisions parked at the anchorage. I'm pretty sure I'm not gonna like whatever it is, but if things are really that tight, I guess we're gonna have to suck it up."

"Yes, you will." O'Hara nodded. "You and I will have a separate chat about that, but my thought is that you will keep 2nd Division intact and online with *Iwo Jima*. 1st Division—minus the battalion they left at Xanadu—will go to ready reserve, with *Omaha Beach* taken off the ready line like Mac's battle groups.

"With that in mind, study the plan, point out flaws, suggest improvements, and let's make it work. Any questions?"

"One question." McGruder looked up from his pad. "According to this, we're going to pull 4th Group—your son, with *Isis*—off Ragnarok and leave only a cruiser squadron in place. With all that's going on there, especially with the Confeds now mining gold on the planet, is that the smartest move right now?"

"I had concerns about that myself," O'Hara admitted. "I was going to leave John out there and bring Rebecca Ling home from Tatanna instead, but the Bugs pissed all over that plan.

"In order to keep the fleet running, we can only leave two full battle groups deployed. That will leave six groups at Luna, of which three are going to be pulled off the line. Of the remaining three, one is going to be stripped to provide cruisers and destroyers so that we can give minimum coverage to two systems that won't have full groups. That leaves us with two full groups online to defend Luna and stand by to respond if we need a force in a hurry somewhere.

"This is where I had to bring Martina into the picture. We knew we had to cover Sacagawea, because the Bugs are testing us there again. Of the other three systems, which one was most in need of protection? The Odin System belongs to the Lizards. We are there for two reasons only—to mine gold and to look out for the interests of the native humans on Ragnarok. We've also banned Confed warships from the system, though we have to allow their commercial ships in to support their mining interests.

"On that basis, we concluded it was a low-threat system, and we could pull back. The next one was easy—New Eden has always been a low threat for us. We reacted by sending a full battle group out there when that rogue Confed group, or whatever it was, attacked back in '13, but that was ten years ago, and we've never had a whisper of trouble since. The Confeds don't seem to have an interest in it, so reducing our forces there made sense.

"That left Xanadu, which is damned important to us because we seem to be engaged in a colonization race with the CNE. Incidentally, that's where all of Luna's money is going, which is why we need to make these cutbacks to begin with. Leaving a full group there is a matter of protecting our investment.

"Martina, do you have anything to add?" He looked at Easley.

"Not really," she replied. "From the standpoint of interstellar diplomacy, it makes sense. Everybody's focused on Xanadu, and the last thing we want to do is look weak there."

"And yet we're pulling *Omaha Beach* and 1st Division off station." Mercer raised an eyebrow.

"We can justify that." Easley dismissed the objection with a wave. "We're telling people the carrier was primarily there to provide a medical facility for the colony. Now they have their own hospital down there and won't need the support. As for ground forces, we're still leaving one battalion of Marines to augment the colony's own militia."

"Hmmph!" Mercer gave a snort. "Militia! A single company commanded by a reserve major. No—" he held up a hand to stop O'Hara's comment "—I signed off on it. More importantly, Sakura signed off on it, and I'll take the word of the on-scene commander over the bean counters and the diplomats—no offense, Martina—any day."

"None taken." Easley smiled. "I try not to question Marines in such matters, either."

"All right, people." O'Hara sat back in his chair. "Let's get to work on the details. I want a written list of objections and suggestions from each of you in three days. We'll meet again to discuss it after that."

* * * * *

Chapter Six

5 May 2123

Lunar Commercial Shipping HQ, TransLuna Station

"Hmmph. Escorts, no escorts… make up your mind." Marcus Carter waved at the report on his screen. "Fleet needs to get its head of out its ass. Ever since O'Hara took over from Ling, there's been no direction from above."

"What have they done now?" Roger Stuart suppressed a chuckle. "Typical military bullshit, I presume."

"No complaints about the military," Carter grumbled. "People on the line follow orders. It's the brass on top that keep screwing up. 'As of the date of this notice,' they say, 'it will no longer be necessary to form escorted convoys for transit between Sol and Odin. Commercial vessels are advised to proceed at captain's discretion.'

"Escorts and convoys were never needed. The only thing pirates wanted was the gold coming from Ragnarok to Luna. Once we started shipping the gold by express courier—too fast for pirates to catch—the problem stopped."

Stuart resisted the urge to roll his eyes. *The problem stopped because the stupid pirates ran into a British battlecruiser supported by our own destroyers,* he thought. *No more pirates, no more problem.* Carter was a useful tool; no sense pissing him off by pointing out flaws in his thinking.

"So, what can I do for you today, Marcus? We owe you a favor for getting the docking restrictions lifted at TransLuna. I don't like having to ship stuff on CNE freighters, but Lunar Commercial doesn't have the capacity, particularly on the Alpha Akara route."

"Those restrictions are also a throwback," Carter growled. "The terror attack in '15 took Ling out, and O'Hara ordered them in as a knee-jerk security measure. They were never necessary in the first place. Hell, the damned terrorists used a British freighter for the job. Why blame the CNE?"

Again, Stuart resisted the urge to grimace. The restrictions that prohibited CNE-flagged commercial ships from docking at Trans-Luna had nothing to do with the terror attack eight years ago. They had been implemented in reaction to a series of direct military confrontations with CNE warships in distant star systems. Carter was a wellspring of misinformation today. Stuart simply smiled and waited for him to end his rant.

"Hell, they pay docking fees like everybody else. Lunar Command keeps telling us we need the money. If it was up to me, we'd have lifted those restrictions years ago. Fleet has a wild hair up their asses where the Confeds are concerned. You TerraCorp people are much more reasonable. You do business with them all the time."

"Why not, if there's profit to be made?" Stuart shrugged. "Like you say, Command keeps telling us we need the money, so they can piss it away on the Xanadu colony project. That thing's a black hole where profits are concerned."

"Right." Carter nodded in agreement. "And that's my problem, too. You're having to ship stuff by CNE-flagged freighters while our own ships are tied up supporting the Xanadu colony. I keep telling them we need more ships, but they say the shipyard has a moratorium on new construction. I was hoping you people at TerraCorp could help me convince them to loosen up the purse strings and put another couple of medium-hull freighters online for me."

"That's going to be tough." Stuart shook his head. "We're being asked to tighten belts while at the same time they're asking us to increase profits to feed the colony project. One of the reasons we wanted to use CNE freighters for shipping is that they were offering sweetheart deals, shipping bulk cargoes cheaper than we can do it on our own ships."

"I have no control over that," Carter growled. "My job is simply to provide the ships and keep them running. They make it hard enough to do that with cutbacks in shipbuilding and maintenance. Shipping rates are set by the bean counters. The rates we give TerraCorp are already lower than we give to foreign shippers, and they tell me that's the lowest we can charge based on cost of operations. How can the CNE people ship for less?"

"Maybe their overhead cost is lower." Stuart shrugged, dismissing the question. "They've got a bigger fleet, so maybe they've got some economies of scale that let them do it cheaper."

I really don't want Carter to get any more ships, he thought. If that happened, he might have to cut back on the contracts he was giving to his CNE friends—contracts that cemented what he expected to be a personally profitable relationship. In reality, he was not getting a lower rate for shipment from them; now that TransLuna was open to them, he and Pierre DuMorne would be splitting a kickback from the CNE shipping lines. It occurred to him that he might need to cut Carter in on the kickbacks in the future.

"Look, we know what the real issue is," he said. "The Xanadu colony is tying up your ships and eating my profits. If you want more ships, perhaps you need to focus on that. The colony is Lunar Command's pet project. If they started having problems with shipments to and from Xanadu, maybe they would take notice."

"Problems?" Carter frowned and raised an eyebrow.

"Shipping delays, damaged shipments, ships out of service. Just enough to make them take notice; nothing that can be blamed on you—you've been telling them all along you need more ships. Hey… people get overworked, ships get worn out, shit happens. You can point to all of the requests you've made and say, 'I told you so.'"

"Hmmm… you may be right." Carter stroked his chin with a thoughtful look on his face. "Last week I got a notice from the yards about extending maintenance intervals due to lack of yard capacity. Like you said… shit happens."

"Right." Stuart smiled. "And if enough of it happens, somebody has to take notice."

* * *

LFS *Valkyrie*, in Xanadu Orbit

"Wow! This is… unexpected, to say the least." Peter Yoric stared at his pad. "I don't know what to say."

"Congratulations, Peter." Lorna Greenwood smiled across her desk. "I should be upset that they're stealing my flag captain, but I've got another set of orders bumping Jake Winfield to commodore to take your place. He's served us well and deserves to move up."

"That he has," Yoric agreed. "If you don't mind, I'd like to be there when you break the news to him."

"I knew you would. I'm going to call him in as soon as we get you squared away, but first, I've got something for you."

She reached into a desk drawer and produced a set of rear admiral stars. "This is a spare set of mine. I wanted to get word to you right away and didn't have time to check with supply to see if they had any. You can pin them on; according to this, the promotion was effective two weeks ago."

"Thank you, ma'am." He took the two-star emblem and pinned it on, replacing the single commodore's star on his collar. "I'd rather have a set of yours than a new pair from supply. It's been a pleasure to serve with you."

"And you can drop the 'ma'am,' Peter," she told him. "As of now, we are equal in rank. Call me Lorna."

"Thanks." He grinned at her. "I think you've got a couple of years of seniority on me, though. Besides, my flag is about a hundred light years from here. Wow! *Sorceress*... but what happened to Admiral Ling?"

"That's covered in a flash report that was also included in the dump from the courier. Apparently, they had a fight with the Bugs." Lorna frowned. She'd had her own baptism of fire with the Bugs in the Sacagawea System, even before the war. "Report says we won, and our forces are still combat effective, but apparently Rebecca Ling was a casualty and had to be shipped back to Luna. The report's classified, but I'll drop a copy on you. Under the circumstances, I think you have a need to know. I'm sure they'll have more details when you get back to Luna."

"Right... back to Luna." He winced. "They aren't giving me much time for goodbyes. These orders say I've got to report to NavInt for briefing in three weeks."

"Relax." She chuckled. "You've got a few days. The courier boat has been ordered to hold for you. That'll get you back to Luna in eighteen days. For the record, I've already told Jessica to set up a formal dinner for tomorrow night—hail and farewell for you, congratulations for Jake."

"I guess I'll need a day or so." Yoric shrugged. "I need to spend some time with him for the transfer of command. Hell, he already knows everything he needs to know about the ship and the job; he's been my exec for a long time."

"Here…" He placed his commodore's star on the desk in front of her. "When he gets here, you can give him this one, just like you gave me yours."

* * *

7 May 2123
LFS *Sorceress* in Tatanna Orbit

"It seems that our new flag officer is on the way." Roy Wilcox looked pleased to share the news. "They've bumped Peter Yoric to rear admiral and are sending him out."

"Yoric?" Emily Bernard's brow wrinkled. She tilted her head toward Wilcox's image on her screen. "I don't know him. Do you?"

"Not personally, but I've heard of him. Came up in cruisers, like I did, and had CruRon 1 for a year or two. They gave him *Valkyrie* when Greenwood got her flag, and he's been with her ever since. They've seen some action and come through the fire with flying colors.

"He's got a couple of years' seniority on me. I've got no problems serving with him. Truth is, I'll be happy to go back to running my cruiser squadron again. I don't envy you, having an admiral looking over your shoulder all the time."

"An admiral and an AI." Bernard smiled. "Admirals are off duty sometimes; AIs never sleep. No offense, Sonja, but I'm still getting used to the idea that I am never alone." She cast a glance up at the overhead.

"None taken, Captain." The AI's voice held a hint of humor.

"So when is Admiral Yoric supposed to arrive?"

"Not until early July, if all goes per schedule," Wilcox advised. "*Valkyrie's* at Xanadu, so they had to send a courier boat to get him. We are advised to expect him by 10 July, but with the travel distances involved, that looks tight to me. I assume he's going to want *Sorceress* for his flagship. How are your repairs coming?"

"The ship will be ready." Bernard nodded in satisfaction. "We are combat effective, though not 100 percent. We had to requisition some spares from Luna, but we got the requests off as soon as the battle was over. Given that we are holding the fort in Sacagawea, I expect they'll expedite those to us. I'm more concerned about replacements for our casualties. I have not heard back on that yet.

"As for the admiral, the flag bridge has been repaired, and his quarters have been cleaned out. All of Admiral Ling's personal gear has been shipped back to Luna. Do you have any word on her?"

"Yes." Wilcox nodded. "I got a general information report that I'll forward to you. She came through surgery okay and is in recovery. The doctors say she suffered severe spinal damage, but they were able to repair most of it. She'll be able to walk again, but she'll need months of therapy and may never get full mobility. Report doesn't say, but I'm guessing she'll end up with a disability retirement."

Bernard shook her head. "I am sorry to hear that. She was an outstanding officer. From a purely selfish standpoint, I had hoped to learn much by serving under her."

* * *

LCS *Sea of Serenity*, TransLuna Station

"Sorry, Skipper." Mike Rowland shook his head. "Dockyard says it'll be another week before they can slot us in. I can't do anything. They have to pull the unit to get at the internals, so they'll probably replace the whole thing."

"Damn! I still want to know how the fuck this happened." Jack Dawson turned an angry scowl on his chief engineer. It wasn't Rowland's fault, but he had to vent his frustration on somebody.

"I'm telling you, Skip, that unit was fully functional when the inspector showed up. I checked everything yesterday when we found out he was coming. He goes down there, screws around with it, and the next thing I know, I have red lights all over my board."

"Okay, I believe you, but I'm asking again; how could it have happened?"

"I keep coming up with a nasty word." Rowland heaved a sigh. "Sabotage."

"By a port safety inspector? Are you serious?"

"It's a sealed compartment, Skipper. Nobody had access from the time I tested the system until he showed up. He goes down there, we power the system up in test mode, and suddenly we've got a fried delta wave coupler controller. I mean, that thing is toast, doesn't even respond to diagnostics.

"Wouldn't be hard to do. Take the cover off the power feed terminals, short the hot side to the control port—the one he had to plug into to run his test. Wouldn't have taken a whole lot of current to wipe out the internal electronics. No arcing, no smoke, no fire—a quick zap, and you turn a secondary hyper generator into a collection of scrap metal. Everything looks fine on the outside, but it's dead."

"Is there any way he could have done it by accident?"

"Nope. Like I said, he would have to take the cover off the power terminals to make the connection. He would also need an adapter to plug into the port, but hey, a dummy plug of some kind would do that. If he was planning to do it in the first place, he could have had one in his pocket.

"His test unit couldn't have produced enough current to do that kind of damage, and he had no business removing that cover. I checked it afterwards. Cover might have been opened, but I couldn't be sure."

"And nobody was watching him when it happened?"

"There's only room for one person down there." Rowland shrugged. "Those guys are supposed to know what they're doing. We've never had a problem before."

"First, we get a notice to hold departure for unspecified reasons. Next, we get notice of inspection." Dawson's shoulders sagged as he slouched down in his bridge command chair. "Then this guy shows up and wrecks a piece of equipment without which we can't go anywhere. Hey, I believe you, Mike. I can't understand why this is happening. Did we piss somebody off?"

"Don't know." Rowland shook his head. "Maybe somebody doesn't want us to make the run to Xanadu."

* * *

25 May 2123

Farmers' Cooperative, LFS Colony, Planet Xanadu

"Do these people not understand? Corn has to be harvested when it's ready. Markets back on Earth are waiting for it. We can store it here, but nobody gets paid until it gets shipped back to Sol. The bulk hauler was supposed to make orbit next week. Now they say it's 'delayed indefinitely.' What the hell does that mean?"

"I feel your pain, Charlie." Darius Jefferson shook his head. "At least you can sell some of your harvest on Xanadu. Until we build a textile plant, all of my cotton goes back there. Same thing for that jade you people are always breaking my chops about. Back on Earth, it's a valuable gemstone; here, it's a rock that'll tear up your gear if you don't dig it out of the ground."

"There's more to it than that." Eddie Bronson joined the conversation. "That same hauler should have been bringing stuff we ordered months ago. I'm still waiting for a shipment of poly panels to finish my barn. TerraCorp makes money in both directions, so why the hell can't they keep the ships moving?"

"They've done pretty well until now." Darius shrugged. "It's only in the past month we've started having problems. Hopefully, it's a temporary glitch. In any case, there isn't much we can do about it."

"We could complain to Governor Greenwood," Bronson insisted. "She's supposed to be the one responsible for our welfare."

"Sorry, Eddie, but it doesn't work that way." Darius shook his head. "She got tagged to be governor because she's the senior Navy officer in this system. You need a battlecruiser to go kick butt on the Confeds up in orbit? She's got you covered. You need Marines to clean some Confed rats out of the jungle? No problem.

"You need somebody back on Luna to get their heads out of their asses? Sorry, Fleet carries no weight with TerraCorp. She can't snap her fingers and make them shit a freighter for us.

"All the same," he added. "I'm going to lodge a complaint with Todd Taylor. It'll take a month to get to the Colonial Commission back on Luna, but maybe they have more influence than the Navy has.

Besides, I'm sure he'll send a copy to Admiral Greenwood, so we should have both of them on our side."

* * *

ICV *Majorca*, Outbound from Luna for Xanadu

I *certainly never expected to be making this run.* Lilly Maria Buxton studied the hyper transit data for a passage from Sol to Coleridge. *It would seem that playing both sides like this can be profitable.*

She had gotten the codes from Lyman before departing Tatanna. In addition, to her surprise, she'd gotten a cargo contract from the Moonies. For the Confeds, a run to Tatanna was pretty much a one-way trip. They shipped stuff to the planet but shipped nothing back. For that reason, they paid her a "deadhead" fee, expecting she would be coming back empty.

The Moonies did ship stuff back, mostly local arts and crafts, but that type of cargo was relatively high value for its size and mass, which meant it also commanded a premium shipping rate to cover insurance. The Moonies usually shipped it via their own freighters, but somebody—Lyman, perhaps—had advised the exporter to contact her. She had gone back to Sol with a couple of containers in her number one hold—far from a full load, but a tidy addition to the Confed deadhead bonus.

As a result, she'd ended up unloading at TransLuna Station instead of the Confed port at Circum Terra. She had expected to make the short hop to Earth orbit to look for another cargo from her Confed sponsors, but again, she'd gotten a surprise. She had barely docked at TransLuna when she'd gotten a call from Jolene Drew, her contact at Moonie Naval Intelligence.

Drew had asked if she could possibly take on a cargo for Xanadu, a full load for a mid-sized freighter like *Majorca*. They had offered her a premium rate and a promise of a full load returning from Coleridge to Sol. She'd wondered why the offer was coming from NavInt rather than TerraCorp, but Drew had assured her that there was no smuggling involved. She'd offered a rather vague explanation that hinted at some sort of administrative issue between Lunar Command and TerraCorp.

Buxton had chosen not to ask questions; now she was outbound from Sol, several days into hyper. She had relaxed after the first day; anyone hunting her would have had to give chase from the hyper limit to have any hope of catching her. She was still convinced the Confeds were out to get her, which was another reason not to go to Circum Terra to ask them for another contract. With luck, they hadn't known she'd gotten back from Sacagawea.

Being a double agent was fun, she decided. It was also profitable. It did, however, come with certain hazards to one's health.

* * * * *

Chapter Seven

31 May 2123
LFS *Isis*, in Ragnarok Orbit

"We're being recalled?" Eurasia Brown looked up from her pad and blinked, her face an expression of disbelief. "With no relief from Luna?"

"That's what it says." Rear Admiral John O'Hara nodded. "We're directed to leave three cruisers and one destroyer as a 'system security force'—whatever the hell that means. There's a separate set of orders for the SO of that force, but I haven't had time to read them."

"Let me get this straight." Brown's eyes narrowed. "We're mining gold here, in competition with the Lizards, the Consortium, and the Confeds. We've got diplomatic negotiations in progress with the Wan government down on the planet. We've seen pirate activity on the run from here to Sol.

"We're also responsible for enforcing the ban on Confed warships in the system. With that in mind, Lunar Command has decided to *reduce* our presence here to something less than a cruiser squadron. With all due respect, sir, does that make any sense to you?"

"No, it doesn't," he admitted. "I'm not privy to what's going on back on Luna, though, so I'm not going to start second guessing them. I've been getting hints about budget problems and fleet cutbacks for a while, but this is *not* something I expected.

"They've specifically directed us to leave the two heavy cruisers behind. That will make Tremaine the SO of the force, and *Apache* the flagship. They've left it to us to pick the light cruiser and destroyer. What do you think?"

"Hmmph!" Brown snorted. "Depends. Do you want to leave the best we've got here, or keep them for ourselves? Hell, for that matter, they're all good; I don't want to leave any of them behind. Do we have any idea what our mission will be after we get back to Luna?"

"Not a clue." He shook his head. "Return to Luna; that's all the orders said."

"In fairness to Tremaine, I guess we should leave him the best. For the cruisers, it's a tossup, but *Kraken* is almost due for a major overhaul back at Luna. On that basis, I'd give him *Chimera*. By the same logic, I'd give him *Redhawk* for the destroyer slot. She's the newest, commissioned only a year ago."

"She's also got the greenest skipper." O'Hara frowned. "She's Talbot's first command."

"Yes, but I have no issues with her performance. No combat experience, but she's done well in all the exercises."

"Okay, I'll go with your judgment on it. We've got more work to do getting the rest of the group ready for the trip back to Luna. I'm calling a meeting of my staff for tomorrow morning; by then I'll have had the chance to study these orders in detail. I find it strange that we're pulling back at the same time the Consortium nations are building up."

Two American warships—the heavy cruiser USS *Atlanta* and the destroyer *Farragut*—had arrived in system two days ago; *Atlanta's* captain had advised both O'Hara and the Akara Heart of System Operations that they would be in the system for an indefinite period. He had asked O'Hara for a meeting to discuss "coordinated efforts for system security." *I guess he'll need to have that meeting with Tremaine.*

"I still can't believe it." He sat back in his chair and shook his head. "Your first reaction was right on target; Ragnarok is a hot spot. You would think if they were going to pull back a battle group, they'd have done it from a quieter system, like Rothstein. Hell, nothing's been happening at New Eden for the last ten years or so."

* * *

LFS *Medusa*, in New Eden Orbit

"We're going home—" Vice Admiral Walter Simms smiled at the small group seated at the conference room table "—or most of us are. We'll be leaving five ships behind to serve as a system security force, but the rest of us will be headed back to Luna as soon as we can get organized for departure."

There was silence around the table for a moment. Commodore Redford Stallings, *Medusa's* captain, was the first to speak.

"Let me get this straight, Admiral. We're not being relieved by another group? Are we talking about a reduction in force for the system?"

"Yes, Red, that's exactly what we're talking about. Orders arrived by hyperprobe this morning. Apparently, Lunar Command has decided to dial things back to the force level we had ten years ago. Can't say I blame them; nothing much has happened here since then."

"You said five ships, Admiral." Commander Jeffrey Donaldson tapped his pad, bringing up the group TO on the conference room screen. "Which ones?"

"Cutting right to the chase, Jeff?" Simms raised an eyebrow. "Orders say we leave both heavy cruisers. They want us to also leave one light cruiser and two destroyers, but they leave that to our discretion."

Donaldson made additional entries on his pad. On the screen, the display highlighted the cruisers *Huron* and *Acadian*. Simms smiled. *Trust Jeff to keep me organized.* The ability to focus on important issues was one of the things he liked best about his chief of staff. They would need to settle this before they could plan for departure.

Five captains and their crews were going to be disappointed. They'd been at New Eden for nearly two years and had been expecting Fleet to send another battle group to relieve them. Now some of them would be going home, but for others, the deployment had been extended indefinitely.

* * *

LFS *Valkyrie*, in Xanadu Orbit

"What's the problem, Admiral?" Jessica Guerrero gave Lorna a quizzical look.

"Not a problem, just a bit of a surprise. We're losing the Cat Pack. DesRon 12 is being recalled to Luna. "Orders arrived this morning with *Thermopylae*. The good news, I suppose, is that we won't have to provide an escort for *Omaha Beach* when she heads back to Luna."

"Maybe they've got a pirate problem somewhere." Guerrero grinned. Destroyer Squadron 12 had been temporarily redeployed to Ragnarok last year to deal with pirates on the Odin to Sol run.

"I don't know," Lorna admitted. "The orders only say they're to report back to Luna. Harry Oldham's people ought to be happy about that. They've been here as long as we have."

"Is *Thermopylae* here to support the reduced Marine force? I assume that's the case, but haven't seen anything official about the new order of battle down there." Guerrero rolled her eyes. "The Marines operate in their own world; if we're lucky, they let us Navy types know before they conduct a major combat operation on the planet."

"It's not quite that bad." Lorna chuckled. "They usually keep me well advised, but that may be due to my long-time relationship with Nova Sakura. She was my first-year roommate at Fleet Academy."

"Really?" Guerrero blinked. Brigadier General Nova Sakura commanded 1st Marine Division aboard the assault carrier. "I didn't know that. I guess you're going to lose that connection when *Omaha Beach* goes home."

"Not really. Nova's leaving Bouchard's 2nd Battalion behind. I go back a long way with her, too."

"Oh, that's right…" Guerrero nodded. "The priestess was CO of Valkyrie Company when she was a major."

Lieutenant Colonel Moira Bouchard was an ordained priestess of the Goddess on planet Tatanna, a distinction that earned her a chaplain's badge in the LFSMC. She was also a holder of the Lunar Medal of Honor, earned in combat on Tatanna during the Bug War. The standard joke among the Marines was that she could kick ass or save souls, depending on mission requirements.

"Oh, we go back further than that," Lorna said. "I got caught in a dirtside action with her on Tatanna that ended with both of us getting the LMH. After that, she served as my Marine CO aboard *Werewolf* at Rothstein. Our paths have crossed so many times, I often think maybe the Goddess has sent her to save *my* soul."

* * *

12 June 2123

Jefferson / Kim Farmstead, LFS Colony, Eurasia, Planet Xanadu

"So we're officially on our own." Jin shivered. "That's a little scary."

"Well, we're not *totally* on our own." Darius chuckled. "They did leave a battalion of Marines and a bunch of air assets behind. They've also got *Thermopylae* up in orbit for overhead observation and support."

"I'm not talking about combat Marines." Jin shook her head. "I'm more concerned about *Omaha Beach* and the medical facilities in orbit. Our little hospital just opened last week with two doctors who haven't had time to get adapted to Xanadu's gravity.

"Sally Schroeder just told me she's pregnant. She won't have the advantage I had of being able to spend the last month in orbit under one gee. She'll have to tough it out down here through delivery and recovery. They're supposed to add a one-gee ICU section to the hospital, but the way things are going with the supply chain from Earth, I wonder whether it will be ready in six months when Sally needs it."

"Yeah, well, I've been wondering about that, too." Darius frowned. "Why didn't they build the whole hospital for one gee to begin with?"

"Supply chain, again." Jin shrugged. "I'm told they couldn't get grav plates made up and sent out to fit the hospital floor plan. They didn't want to delay the construction of the main hospital, so they only ordered plates for the ICU wing.

"It's not like the hab modules." She waved a hand to take in their surroundings, the modular farmhouse they'd been living in since they had settled on Xanadu. "That design was standardized at the beginning of the colony project, and they've been in production at TransLuna ever since. Even so, last I heard, there were a hundred families waiting to come out here when the modules are delivered for them.

"They've got a long wait, since we're only seeing about four modules per month. The rest of the equipment—power systems, tractors, stuff like that—is no problem because it's being imported from Earth."

"Wow! You're full of news tonight, love." Darius looked at his wife in surprise. "Where do you hear all this stuff? I haven't seen any of it on the colony news feed."

"The protectorate gets information copies of all the stuff that the Colonial Commission sends to Todd Taylor. You need to convince him to share those reports with the Council."

"Hmmm... yeah. You're right. If we really are going to serve as the governing body for the colony, we ought to be on the distribution list. Not Todd's fault, though; he doesn't want to listen to complaints from us about things that aren't under his control. I won't ask him to broadcast the information, but the Council needs to know what's going on.

"On the good news front, though, a freighter finally arrived with those building materials Eddie Bronson's been waiting for and a bunch of other stuff. I haven't checked with the store yet, but they might have that sewing machine you ordered.

"More importantly, it'll be headed back to Luna in a few days, loaded with stuff from the colony's farms, including our cotton. I've got a call in to the export office to see if they've got room for a couple of those jade boulders we dug up in the southwest corner.

"Funny thing, though; it's not the TerraCorp bulk hauler we were expecting. It's a medium-sized freighter out of Earth. Supply chain issues must be pretty bad if TerraCorp is having to hire independent shippers to get stuff out here."

* * *

Last Chance Saloon, LFS Colony, Eurasia, Planet Xanadu

"First time on Xanadu?" Sarah Peabody placed a drink in front of the merchant spacer.

"Yes." Lilly Maria Buxton smiled. "No offense, but the gravity here sucks. How do you people stand it?" She glanced around the bar to make sure no one was close enough to eavesdrop, then dropped her voice to a stage whisper. "It's fine in here, but outdoors, my boobs feel like bowling balls."

"You're a little heavier than I am in that department." Peabody chuckled. "I've been here for a couple of years—was one of the first group of colonists. You get used to it, mostly by developing more muscle, like pectorals to better support your boobs.

"I'm curious, though…" She examined the logo on Buxton's tunic. "ICV *Majorca*. You're not a TerraCorp ship. What registry? Confed? Consortium?"

"None of the above," Buxton replied. "Ibiza, my native country. I'm independent. Delivered a shipment from Tatanna at TransLuna, then got lucky and landed the contract for this one. Not only my first time on planet, it's my first time in this system. I'm surprised to see how much traffic there is."

"Welcome to the party." Peabody grinned. "We've got the LFS colony here—over five thousand population—and the Confeds have one three times our size on the big continent. We've also got that new Consortium building mining operations about a thousand klicks west."

"Ah… competition." Buxton grinned. "Good for business, especially for me. I'm not a Moonie, a Confed, or a member of this 'Consortium.' I can haul freight for anybody. If I can land the contracts, maybe I'll make this a regular run."

"Good! I wish you luck with it." Peabody returned the grin. "Hey, if you come down often enough, your boobs won't be drooping anymore."

* * *

Tempete de Neige Resort, Swiss Alps

"It would appear that your efforts to cripple the Moonies are having the desired effect." Huang Chang Li nodded to Andre DuMorne. "My people at Trans-Luna tell me they are expecting the arrival of two battle groups that are being withdrawn from other star systems. In addition, one of their largest docking slips is preparing to receive an assault carrier—*Omaha Beach*, I presume. The Moonies only have two carriers, and *Iwo Jima* is already there. No preparations are being made for departures, so it appears no replacements are being sent out."

"It will be interesting to see which groups they are pulling back," DuMorne mused. "That will tell us much about where their priorities lie."

"I can already tell you they are still guarding their colony project—and their precious Kitty Protectorate," Gerhardt Richter said. "Confed Intelligence received a hyperprobe this morning from Xanadu. The carrier *Omaha Beach* has indeed departed, along with five destroyers, but the battlecruiser *Valkyrie* remains on station with her full battle group. The destroyers were an independent squadron attached to the group.

"The report also noted that one of their assault transports, identified as LFS *Thermopylae*, arrived on station a week earlier. This type of ship typically supports a battalion of LFS Marines, as opposed to a carrier like *Omaha Beach*, which can support an entire division. That suggests that they have not completely withdrawn their Marine forces from the system, though they may have reduced them."

"No matter." DuMorne waved a hand in dismissal. "The point is that they are feeling the economic pressure and are reducing their forces accordingly. At present, I do not think we should confront them with military force at Xanadu. I would suggest, Gerhardt, that you convince your CNE people to restrain themselves in that regard."

"I may not be able to do that." Richter scowled at the French financier. "CIS has already landed another of their Peacekeeper special operations units on the planet. I don't know what mission they have already given to that unit, but I suspect they are not going to simply conduct training exercises. CIS has reverted to their old ways of secrecy; my contacts do not have full details of everything they are doing."

"What does it matter?" Butos Kimba joined the conversation. "If they strike at the Moonie colony, the Moonies may be forced to send more Marines, which will only serve to further stress their economy. Either way, it will serve our purpose."

"Perhaps," DuMorne replied, "but such things tend to get out of hand. If we press the Moonies too hard, they may respond with naval force rather than Marines. It will *not* serve our purpose if they level the CNE colony with kinetic strikes."

"They will not do that." Mohammed Al Sharif shook his head. "The Moonies have an old-school concept of honor. They will not hit civilian targets in response to military action against them—nor should they need to. A battalion of their Marines is worth a division of CNE Peacekeepers."

"I am more interested to know from which systems they are pulling back. New Eden is an obvious choice; absolutely nothing is happening there, though we might want to consider a little creative mayhem in that system if they reduce forces there. That leaves Ragnarok and Tatanna. Have any of you seen anything to indicate a withdrawal from either one?"

"The CNE has no military assets at either one." Richter shrugged. "They have commercial interests at both, however, and my people should have reliable connections. I will look into it."

"They can't abandon Ragnarok," DuMorne insisted. "They have gold mining interests there, in competition with the CNE and the Consortium."

"Nor can they abandon Tatanna, with the Bugs challenging them again," Richter replied. "And yet, according to Chang's report, they are about to pull back at one or the other. I'm sure Mohammed would prefer it to be Ragnarok."

"Indeed I would," Al Sharif agreed. "It would certainly bode well for the little war we are orchestrating there."

"It would also further disrupt the Moonie economy," DuMorne agreed, "assuming you could convince your rebels to only target the Moonie gold mines, not the CNE or Consortium ones; however, that is another reason why I think they will not pull back from Ragnarok."

"There is no point in speculating." Kimba shrugged. Per the usual drawn lot, he had been selected as chairman for the current meeting. "We will know soon enough. Andre, I believe you wanted to give us a report on your efforts to subvert the Moonies from within."

"Yes." DuMorne smiled. "I can report that those efforts are going well. My brother Pierre has developed a conduit into the Lunar Directorate itself. Moonies are supposed to be 'incorruptible,' but we have thoroughly disproved that myth. We have a TerraCorp executive, who is also a member of the Directorate, who is… how do I say it, 'in our pocket' for certain. We know enough about him to ruin him on Luna, perhaps even cause the Moonies to charge him with crimes.

"He, in turn, has involved several others—including some of their people on Copper Hills, who helped secure Gerhardt's gold mining lease on Ragnarok. More recently, he has influence over an executive of their commercial fleet and is using it to hamper their efforts to supply the Xanadu colony.

"In the Directorate, he advocates restraint in development of the colony, while at the same time in TerraCorp, he profits from their efforts to expand it. I believe he is working in concert with several other TerraCorp executives, several of whom may also be members of their precious Directorate.

"From our standpoint, he is a valuable asset, and I must credit my brother for finding him. We will continue to seek additional corruptible contacts among the Moonies; it is never good to rely on only one, as we discovered years ago with Admiral Hutchins. For now, however, this one is serving us well."

"If I may comment…" Richter raised a hand. Kimba nodded to him.

"I now understand a curious report that my people recently received from CIS, a passing note regarding Moonie commercial traffic." Richter nodded to DuMorne. "It appears that your Moonie contact's efforts to disrupt their commercial fleet are already producing some effect.

"According to the report, the Moonies are hiring independent shippers to make up for their own shortcomings in the supply chain for Xanadu. Curiously enough, one of those they hired is a ship's owner and captain that CIS has used in the past to conduct smuggling efforts to Ragnarok and Tatanna. CIS plans to contact her when next her ship returns to the Sol System, to see if maybe she might perform other services for them. If nothing else, she could prove to be a good source of intelligence.

"In addition, the Moonies are allowing CNE-flagged commercial ships to dock at TransLuna. While they are not likely to be giving any significant cargoes to those ships, the Moonies continue to buy products from CNE nations. Those cargoes no longer need to be transshipped at Circum Terra to Moonie transports for the final leg to Luna."

Smiles punctuated the momentary silence around the table. Al Sharif chuckled.

"It would appear, gentlemen, that my earlier concerns about the slow pace of economic warfare were unjustified. At this rate, the Moonies may be brought to their knees within the year. I still believe, however, that a little military action will hasten the process."

"I am inclined to agree." Richter nodded. "Mohammed, you have your rebellion going on Ragnarok, and I am certain the CNE is planning something on Xanadu. We want to challenge the Moonies in as many places as possible, so perhaps it is time for the CNE to push back against their efforts to retain military control in the Sacagawea System."

"The last time you did that, it cost the CNE a lot of warships," Huang pointed out.

"True." Richter chuckled. "What I have in mind this time would be a diplomatic confrontation, not a space battle. The CNE could simply send a couple of warships to test their resolve. Worst case, the Moonies turn them back. Best case, the CNE gets a foot in the door."

* * * * *

Chapter Eight

15 July 2123

Castle Boroson, King's City, Planet Tatanna

Why do I feel like I've gone through a time portal into the Middle Ages? Emily Bernard smiled at King Arne T'Boroson, absolute monarch of Tatanna's realms. The king was quite young, handsome, and rather charming. He was also married, but that wasn't an issue; polygamy, particularly among the nobility of the planet, was common practice.

Romance, however, was not on the menu for tonight's dinner. Bernard had come down to the planet primarily to introduce her new boss, Rear Admiral Peter Yoric, to the king and his advisors. The event had been arranged by Harold Wilkerson, the LFS ambassador to Tatanna. Wilkerson had only requested a royal audience, but Arne had insisted on making it a dinner to welcome the new LFS senior officer in system—a private dinner, a sign of the close relationship between the Crown and the Lunar Free State.

It wasn't a first for her. Arne had thrown a similar dinner party a few months ago when Rebecca Ling had brought her down to introduce her new flag captain to the king; this time she was performing the same function for Yoric.

"I was most distressed to hear that Lady Rebecca had been injured." Arne spoke English with barely a hint of an accent. "Have you had word of her condition? I know it takes a long time for news to travel between your world and ours, but I have been concerned about her. She was in charge of your forces here for many years and was always a friend of the Crown."

"Yes, we have, Majesty." Bernard smiled. "A courier arrived this morning. She is still receiving treatment, but the doctors say she will be fully recovered in a few months. Fleet has already offered her a new command, but not in space. They want her to take over as commandant of the Lunar Fleet Academy, the school where we train officers for our Navy and Marine Corps."

"You have a special school for that?" The question came from Sir Regas D'Narr, the king's high sheriff. "Your forces must be numerous, to require such a thing."

"We graduate a class of a few hundred officers per year, Sir Regas," Peter Yoric replied. Bernard had been amused to find that her admiral was more subdued in the presence of royalty than she was. Aboard *Sorceress*, he was a confident, outgoing leader, all that she expected from a flag officer of the LFS.

He's also a rather handsome devil, she thought. *Especially in this setting, in his bravo dress uniform.*

She suppressed the thought. He was her immediate superior; she wasn't supposed to find him attractive. Unfortunately, her libido had little regard for military regulations and had been sending her stray thoughts like that ever since he'd come aboard a week earlier.

Unfortunately (or fortunately, depending on one's point of view) he seemed to have no such attraction to her. He'd been nothing but completely professional toward her, with the easy familiarity one might expect from an officer toward his next-in-command.

"Hmmm… a few hundred." Sir Regas wore a thoughtful look. "That's enough officers for many thousands of regular soldiers. I doubt we would need more than ten new officers per year in the Crown's Guard."

"Still…" He turned to the king. "The idea of a special school to teach our guard officers the art of leadership has merit, Your Majesty. It is worth thinking about."

"Indeed it is," Arne said with a chuckle. "Our off-world friends refuse to share their marvelous technology with us, but sometimes they let slip an idea for something we can do with the tools we have at hand."

A sharp *chirp* in her earbud got Bernard's attention. Her small data pad was hidden in a special pocket in the tunic of her bravo uniform. The people who had designed the garment had decided that an officer or noncom might need communications during formal dress-up events.

Fortunately, she did not need to retrieve the device to respond. She touched the tiny button on her earbud to take the call.

"*Information only, Captain, no action required.*" The voice was that of Commander Robert Rochford, her executive officer. "*Blue Star picked up an incoming hyper signature on the direct line from Sol. The picket jumped to intercept, and we just got the FTL flash. We have two Confed warships—one CA, one DD—inbound.* Vampire *challenged them, got no response. Garvey chose not to engage, pending orders.*"

She raised an eyebrow. Sacagawea had not seen a Confed warship for years, not since the abortive attempt to take the system that had cost the CNE an entire battle group. Confed merchant ships still arrived at regular intervals in support of the CNE trade mission on

Tatanna, but the LFS had issued a warning back home that any warships that entered the system would be considered hostile.

"I've taken the precaution of bringing the group to Condition Blue, but I'm waiting for the light speed follow-up message before taking further action. That should arrive in another two hours. Based on the numbers in the FTL flash, the Confeds are a minimum of thirty-seven hours from planetary orbit. The picket will continue to shadow, but we have plenty of time for a group intercept. Unless I hear otherwise from you and the admiral, we will continue to stand by."

Bernard decided there was no need to spoil the dinner party. She reached up and tapped the earbud button twice, sending a simple acknowledgment that the message was received. Across the table from her, Yoric noticed the gesture and raised an eyebrow. She gave him a small shake of the head. *Not an issue.* She hoped he would agree with her assessment later, when she had a chance to tell him about it.

To her surprise, King Arne had also noticed. He turned to her with a smile.

"A message from your ship, Lady Emily?" Seeing the look on her face, he continued with a chuckle, "I have been around your people long enough to know about these marvelous devices you possess, magical tablets that can show images from far away, and convey messages over great distances—and those tiny things that can whisper voices in your ear."

"Yes, Your Majesty." Bernard returned the smile. "A captain must always keep in touch with her ship, but it was of no concern. A small matter, not important enough to take me away from this wonderful table you have set for us.

"France—the country of my birth back on Earth—prides itself in serving up the finest food in the world. Your royal chefs have shown me, however, that Tatanna is its rival in the culinary world."

Noting smiles of approval from both Yoric and Wilkerson, she patted herself on the back for her diplomatic skills. Arne was beaming; she congratulated herself at having neatly diverted him from any further questions about the message.

He's already upset about the return of the Bugs; no sense telling him we might have another issue with the Confeds.

* * *

King's City Spaceport, Planet Tatanna

"Good call on all counts, Emily." Yoric settled into his seat and fastened the restraining harness. "No point in airing our dirty laundry with the Confeds in front of the king, and no need to interrupt a diplomatic dinner. Nothing's going to happen until we get the detailed report from the picket. The Confeds are a long way from the planet; we've got plenty of time to plan a measured response."

"That was my thought, Admiral. We've had another flash from the picket, but it was nothing but a status report. The Confeds are ignoring all hails and are proceeding in system. They aren't showing any signs of haste, just cruising as if they were on a routine mission. *Cobra* will shadow them and maintain contact. The rest of the picket has returned to station."

"Sounds like everyone's got their heads on straight up there." Yoric nodded in satisfaction. "This might be a feint to draw our picket off station. If so, it didn't work."

"From what I've seen so far, you've got a good team." He favored her with an engaging grin that brought butterflies to her stomach. "I think we'll work really well together."

Yes, Admiral, we will, she thought, *if I can keep my hormones under control.*

She said nothing more, just smiled and nodded as the craft lifted off, carrying them back to *Sorceress.*

* * *

CNS *Achilles,* Inbound for Tatanna, Sacagawea System

"Reverse course and leave this system, or we will open fire." The Moonie admiral's face on the screen wore a neutral expression. His voice was calm but firm. "What part of that do you not understand?"

Captain Manuel Cortez gritted his teeth. This was not the response CIS had predicted. The Moonies were supposed to make a lot of noise, threaten severe diplomatic consequences, then give in and allow him to proceed to Tatanna. His was to be the foot in the door that would allow the CNE to station a permanent squadron in the system. He stabbed the icon on his screen to open the channel.

"My orders are to proceed to Tatanna orbit in support of our embassy and trade mission there. You have no right to stop me." He gave the Moonie an angry scowl. "If you fire upon us, we will reply in kind, and you will have created an interstellar incident. Your superiors back on Luna will not be happy with you."

He hoped the sweat on his brow wasn't obvious. His threat to return fire was an empty one. *Achilles* was accompanied by a single destroyer, CNS *Chevalier.* In front of him, spread across his track, were a Moonie battlecruiser, two heavy cruisers, and a half-dozen lighter units. Any exchange of fire was likely to result in a very short engagement, with victory going to the Moonies.

"Your people back on Earth have been advised." The subtext on the screen told Cortez the speaker was LFS Rear Admiral Peter Yoric.

"We allow your embassy and trade mission to operate on Tatanna, supported by commercial traffic, on the sole condition that no CNE warships enter this system. You are in violation of that requirement and will be dealt with accordingly. You have thirty seconds to stand down and reverse course."

Cortez swallowed hard. He had cut his drive when he first detected the Moonie force in front of him. He was coasting in on the ballistic remnant of his original course, but the range was closing. He was already within missile range of the Moonies, and they were painting him with targeting scans. More importantly, he had gone to battle stations on first approach, and his ships were targeting the Moonies. Both sides were poised to open fire.

He glanced at the weapons console, where his tactical officer wore a look of pure hatred. Habib Okele was an Islamist who considered Moonies to be the ultimate infidels. His hands were poised over his controls as he glared at his tactical plot. The panel in front of him showed rows of red lights, indicating missiles armed and ready for launch.

Okele was otherwise a competent officer, more so than most in the middle ranks of CNE's navy. Today, however, Cortez would have preferred to have someone else at the weapons station.

"Weapons to standby, cease targeting," he ordered. "Helm, flip vertical to reverse course, go to one-seven-zero gees. Comm, pass the word to *Chevalier* to—"

"No!" Okele's voice was a snarl. "Die, infidels." His fingers danced over his console, and two missiles streaked away from the cruiser's forward chase tubes. "Helm, come left nine-zero degrees."

Cortez recoiled in horror. "Helm, belay that order. Okele! Stand down! Safe your weapons! You are relieved!"

* * *

CNS *Chevalier*

"Sir! *Achilles* has opened fire on the Moonies!" *Chevalier's* tactical officer turned to stare at his captain in consternation.

"I see it. We are engaged. You may open fire."

* * *

LFS *Sorceress*

"Defenses free, weapons free." Emily Bernard felt mild surprise at how calm her voice sounded. "Pass the word to all ships, engage at will."

She turned to Peter Yoric's image on her screen for confirmation. Yoric nodded. "Stupid bastards… give them hell, Emily."

The LFS formation had turned its broadsides to the approaching enemy. Bernard felt the familiar vibration as *Sorceress* hurled eighteen missiles at the enemy ships. A moment later, her consorts added 48 additional missiles to the barrage.

Overkill, she decided, *by an order of magnitude.* The Confeds hadn't bothered to turn broadside and had fired only their chase tubes. Only four CNE missiles were incoming.

"All ships, hold fire," she ordered. "Let's check results before we waste any more missiles. Sonja, mind the defenses."

"Yes, Captain." The AI's voice was calm and cool, as always. "Countermissiles going out, point defense standing by."

* * *

CNS *Achilles*

"Engineering, report!" Cortez choked on the acrid smoke that filled the bridge. The intercom appeared to be working, but he was getting no answer from main engineering. "Any section, report, anyone who can hear me." He waited through long moments of silence. *There may still be survivors,* he told himself, *but they don't have communications.*

The smoke told him that the bridge had not been breached. That was a good thing; his shipsuit cowl and faceplate had been ripped off in the struggle to get Okele away from the weapons console. In the end, the helmsman had grabbed a rescue tool from the overhead rack and bashed in the tactical officer's head. Okele's body still lay in a corner of the bridge.

Unfortunately, the struggle had involved not only Cortez but the entire bridge crew. As a result, *Achilles* had not defended herself nor taken evasive action against the Moonie missiles, and had been hit by dozens of powerful x-ray lasers as the unchallenged warheads detonated. Remarkably, the bridge had not been hit; the smoke came from the engineering console, which had been fried by power spikes originating elsewhere in the ship.

Neither of the ship's fusion reactors had gone critical. Either none of the Moonie lasers had penetrated their containment, or—more likely—fail-safes had worked and vented the plasma-filled cores to space. *Achilles* was no more than a tumbling wreck, with few systems still functioning under emergency power.

At that, she was better off than *Chevalier*. The tactical displays on the bridge were no longer functioning, but the last view before they failed had shown Cortez an expanding cloud of star-hot plasma where the destroyer had been.

Cortez looked around the bridge, dimly illuminated by red emergency lighting. His helmsman, two systems technicians, and comm officer stared back at him.

"Kristina, do we have any communications?" Cortez noted a few still-illuminated indicators on the comm panel.

"The emergency rescue beacons triggered and are operating, sir." Kristina Ivanova's face was streaked with tears. The young lieutenant had never been in combat before today. "We have one ship-to-ship channel that appears to be working, but there's no one out there to talk to."

Except the Moonies, he thought. *I can only hope they respond to our beacon. Otherwise, we're all dead.* Even if his surviving crew members could get to lifepods, they were in the empty outer reaches of the star system. Life support would fail long before they got anywhere near the planet that had been their destination.

* * *

LFS *Sorceress*

"The hulk is already on a general course for the planet," Bernard advised. "Without power, it will not arrive for months, and Tatanna will have moved on in its orbit. My people are recommending we take the survivors off and put a beacon on it."

"I agree. Towing with a warship is always a tricky proposition." Yoric nodded. "We have *Chesapeake Bay* in system with tugs available; we might as well take advantage.

"As for taking the survivors off, remind the Marines to be careful," he cautioned. "Survivors on a derelict don't usually resist being rescued, but with the CNE, you never know. There are a lot of anti-Moonie fanatics in their Navy ranks."

"True," she agreed. "I wouldn't expect survivors to resist rescue, but I wouldn't have expected them to open fire against such overwhelming odds. That must have been one of the shortest engagements in history."

"I believe it was." He chuckled. "Good call on holding the second salvo, by the way. There was no way they were going to survive the first one."

"I thought so, too," she said. "I wanted to concentrate on defense. I would have felt very foolish if we wiped them out, and one of those four missiles they fired got through to us. I still don't know why they fought so stupidly. They fired only their chase tubes, never turned broadside, and kept coming straight at us. We had crossed their 'T'—they had to know what was going to happen.

"The cruiser never defended itself. The destroyer made an effort but couldn't mount an effective defense against that many incoming. What were they thinking?"

"Hmmph!" he snorted. "Maybe if we can find a senior officer among the survivors, we can ask them."

* * *

HMS *Prince of Wales*

"Thought you'd like to know, Admiral. The Moonies have returned to orbit."

"Have they, now?" Sir John Bryant raised an eyebrow. "Any sign of battle damage? Anything unusual?"

"No, nothing obvious." Wilshire shrugged. "Looked very much like business as usual. I suppose it could have been a training exercise.

Almost certainly not a Bug incursion. They headed out on the line for Sol, almost exactly the opposite direction from Bug Alley. Besides, we fought with them against the Bugs last time. I'm sure they would have given us a call if they had more incoming."

"Not sure about that." Bryant wore a thoughtful look. "Admiral Ling would have. Not so sure about this new fellow, Yoric. He strikes me as being a little less flexible about things like that.

"That's only an impression, mind you. He's just arrived, and he's new to the system. Now we won't have time to get to know him. Are you ready for departure tomorrow?"

"Yes, sir, I am. Tatanna's a pleasant port, but we've been here longer than expected. Frankly, I'm ready to go home. Can't tell you how happy I was when *Dauntless* and *Defender* arrived. Diplomatic duty is fine, but we are her majesty's only battlecruiser. We should be showing our colors in the home system."

* * *

LFS *Sorceress*

"Just FYI, Ambassador; the Brits have departed." Yoric nodded to Wilkerson's image on his screen. "Or two of their ships have; *Prince of Wales* and *Torrent* broke orbit an hour ago and are headed for the hyper limit. The two destroyers that arrived last week are still here, as is the diplomatic courier boat that arrived with them."

"We expected that." Wilkerson shrugged. "They wasted no time getting their embassy set up, and they've done their homework. They acquired land next to the spaceport, hired a local contractor to build it for them, and petitioned Arne for the Tatannan version of diplomatic immunity. They certainly did a better job with it than the Confeds did."

"Right, and they've made an agreement with Luna that allows them to lease space on Blue Star Station, all of which suggests that they intend to have a permanent military presence in orbit."

"Oh, it's more than that, Admiral." Wilkerson shook his head. "I've looked at the copy of the agreement Luna sent us. Yes, they're leasing space, but that space will be accessible to any of the seven Consortium nations. The Brits are taking the lead on this one, but next thing we know, we might be sharing orbit with an American cruiser."

*****

Chapter Nine

15 July 2123
CNE Peacekeeper Camp, Eastasia, Planet Xanadu

"*Einkommen... setz dich...*" Lieutenant Colonel Heinrich Doernberg waved his two subordinates into his office. As with all CNE military units, English was the official language. Doernberg's special operations battalion included troops from seven different nations, but he and his two company commanders were German. Among the three of them, occasional linguistic lapses were common.

"*Ja, Oberstleutnant.*" Major Diedrich Loeffler took one of the chairs in front of Doernberg's desk; Major Helga Vollmer took the other.

"CIS has given us two missions, both in Eurasia, and both involving a certain amount of deception." Doernberg nodded toward the map displayed on the large wall screen. He tapped a few keys, and a small red circle appeared on the map. "Diedrich, you will take the one against these 'Consortium' people. Your target will be their copper mine and the adjacent community on the west coast. This is the largest of their four mining sites, the closest to a permanent settlement they have built.

"Yours will be the more conventional mission. You will engage and destroy targets of opportunity, evade their security forces, and disappear into the jungle. You will do this repeatedly, but with moderate restraint. You are not to destroy them completely or wipe out their population. They currently have around two thousand people on or near the site.

"They have a platoon-sized security force, and those you may engage at will; however, your primary objective will be to disengage, leaving nothing behind that will tie your people to the CNE. Instead, we will provide you with an assortment of artifacts of Moonie origin that you will leave to be discovered. The objective of this will be to convince these people that the Moonies are conducting these operations against them."

"Does CIS actually think they will believe such a thing?" Loeffler's eyes widened, and his jaw dropped in disbelief.

"Who knows what CIS is thinking?" Doernberg's lip curled in a hint of a smile. "I doubt the Consortium will believe any such thing, but perhaps it will put small questions in their minds. My only concern is that you strike repeatedly and disengage safely without leaving anything that would connect you with the CNE. Is that clear?"

"*Ja,* we can do that." Loeffler nodded.

"As for you, Helga, yours will be a much more subtle task, requiring a great deal of stealth." Doernberg turned his attention to Vollmer. "I have not yet accepted this one. If you tell me it cannot be done, I will tell CIS to go screw themselves. I won't risk my people on an impossible mission for little or no return.

"Your task will be to infiltrate the Moonie colony. They have over five thousand people, with more arriving at regular intervals. At this point, not everyone knows everyone else. They are recruiting people from all over Earth, various ethnic types from different cultures. Their security consists of a battalion of Lunar Marines whose primary focus is to defend against attacks from outside the colony. You will not be doing that. You will need to get past them to enter the colony, but once you are in place, the Marines should not be of concern to you."

"You are asking us to enter the colony posing as Moonies?" Vollmer gave a skeptical snort. "To walk around the colony like we belong there?"

"Not like Moonies, like *colonists*," Doernberg insisted. "This will be a small unit operation, not even a full platoon, more like a single squad. You will choose your best people, with consideration to their ability to operate undercover and their skill in field operations. Stripped of uniforms and combat gear—which is how they will be operating for this mission—they should be able to pass as ordinary people, fresh out from Earth and starting a new life on a new world."

"And how long are we expected to maintain this charade? Do you actually expect us to live among them?"

"Of course not." He waved the suggestion aside. "All you need to do is get close enough to the colony center to do a little creative sabotage. Take out their power plant, hit their water purification plant, blow up a few buildings, kill a few people, and fade into the jungle. One coordinated strike, and your mission is done. As simple as that."

"With a battalion of Lunar Marines hunting us." Vollmer rolled her eyes. "I'm sure CIS has no concerns about that, as long as we do a sufficient amount of damage to the Moonies."

"They may not be concerned, but I am." Doernberg growled. "As I said, if this mission does not appear to be something you can accomplish without losing your team, I will tell CIS where to stick it."

"The intention is that you will get in, install time-delayed charges, and get out before they go off. You should plan your exit strategy to be beyond the colony perimeter when that happens. Experience has shown that your people should move through the jungle alone or in pairs, not in groups. The Moonies are very good at spotting things in the jungle that aren't supposed to be there. Don't make it easy for them.

"Here is the most detailed information we have on the Consortium settlement and the Moonie colony." He touched an icon on his pad and waved at the screen, where the view split to reveal a pair of detailed maps. "I will transmit the data to your pads. Study it. I want a mission plan from each of you tomorrow afternoon.

"In your case, Helga, I will also want a go or no go decision. For you, Diedrich, I will assume your mission is a go unless you discover some show-stopping factor we have not considered."

The two officers pulled out their pads and prepared to receive the files.

"If you have questions in the meantime, come and talk to me." Doernberg tapped his own pad to send the data. "Otherwise, be here tomorrow at 1400, and we'll get to work planning these missions."

* * *

Marine Battalion HQ, Colony Landing Field, Eurasia

<<*To… orbit, Priestess?*>> Three Moons tilted her head to the side, a questioning gesture in Kitty body language. <<*You mean up to the heavens, the realm of the moons and stars?*>>

<<*Not so far as that.*>> Lieutenant Colonel Moira Bouchard smiled, careful not to show her teeth. She had learned their body language as she had learned how to mind-speak with the cats. Only one human in a hundred could communicate with them at all; in less than a year, Bouchard had become one of the best Kitty-speakers on the planet, her only rival for the top position being Kim Jin Li.

<<We will go high, above the ocean of air, but we will be much closer to the world than any of the moons; the stars are so far, I cannot describe the distance in terms you will understand.>>

<<We do not understand now.>> Yellow Eyes purred. <<We learn quickly, Priestess. I will be most pleased to make this journey, but I am curious. What is the purpose of the meeting?>>

<<Blue Eyes wishes her people to meet you, that they might better understand why we have taken the course we have with your people.>> Bouchard projected the avatar for Admiral Greenwood. <<Our objective is not to interfere with you, but to protect you from others who would interfere. It is an important part of our mission, and Blue Eyes is our chief.

<<I want you to go because you are the senior warrior who is working with us. I want Three Moons because she has become my personal aide. I consider her to be a member of my command team.>>

<<Understanding these tribal relationships has been the hardest part for me,>> Three Moons admitted. <<You are chief of warriors but not of the artisans and shamans of the colony. Also, Dark Giant is chief of a small group of warriors that is not under your authority. He is also one of the council of chiefs for the artisans and shamans. Blue Eyes is chief of everything on this planet but must answer to another chief on a distant world. At times, it is confusing.>>

<<Sometimes it is confusing for us as well.>> Bouchard allowed a bit of amusement to color her mind-voice response. <<Blue Eyes has two roles. She is chief of the warriors of my group aboard her ships in the sky. She is also chief of the colony—the artisans and shamans, and Dark Giant's small group of warriors. Sometimes one group wants one thing, and the other group wants something else. She must decide which is more important.>>

<<And that is why I will always be a warrior.>> Three Moons purred. <<I do not want to be a chief or a shaman. I am one of your warriors, Priestess. If you say I must fly higher than the sky, then I am ready.>>

* * *

LFS *Valkyrie*, in Xanadu Orbit

"This meeting has a certain historic significance," Lorna told the assembled group. "Most conferences involving nonhuman participants—the Akara or the Otuka, for example—are conducted by telecommunication. We don't invite them to our ships very often, nor do they invite us to theirs.

"This is a rare exception." She nodded to the two cats to her right. Chairs had been removed to give them the positions of honor at the table. "This is also the first time any of their kind have been off the surface of their world."

The meeting was being held in *Valkyrie's* flag conference room. To her left, newly promoted Commodore Jake Winfield faced Yellow Eyes across the table. Jessica Guerrero sat to Winfield's left, facing Three Moons. Moira Bouchard sat to the right of the cats, with the only civilian present, Kim Jin Li, seated to her right. The other members of Lorna's staff were seated to Guerrero's left in descending order of rank.

"Doctor Kim is here to see to it that our guests don't suffer any cultural trauma." Lorna regarded Jin with a smirk. "Personally, I think she is being a bit overprotective. We have done our best to make them comfortable."

A purr from Yellow Eyes told her the Kitty warrior was following her remarks. The Kitties had taken a long time to learn to understand human speech, but Yellow Eyes had been in contact with humans since the earliest days. Kitty vocal apparatus wasn't suited to speech, but their hearing was exceptionally keen.

"We originally thought Xanadu had no intelligent life. Doctor Kim's discovery of the Kitties came as a complete surprise, and it came after the decision to develop a colony had already been made back home. I'm told there was serious discussion back on Luna as to whether we should continue with the colony project, but the arrival of the Confeds convinced Lunar Command to proceed. We had to regroup and establish the protectorate, but that was based on some invalid assumptions.

"We assumed that our furry friends were a primitive society whose culture needed to be protected from contamination by more advanced humans. We failed to understand that their simple lifestyle was a matter of choice; that their failure to develop an advanced technology stemmed mostly from a lack of need. From their standpoint, they were already living in the Garden of Eden and had no need to constantly strive to improve their lot.

"In fairness, Doctor Kim originally suggested that might be the case, but people back home did not accept her theory until other studies—notably by Doctor Levin—confirmed what she had been saying all along. It turns out that the critical factor that no one accounted for was telepathy.

"Yes, it's true, they communicate telepathically. You've all seen the reports, but the reality of it is something else. I know that for a fact, because I've had this guy—" she turned and nodded to Yellow Eyes "—talking to me in my head."

"No, Web, they can't read your thoughts." Lorna chuckled. Timothy Webster, her flag lieutenant, had been regarding the cats with an uncomfortable expression. "They can hear you thinking—at a great distance, I might point out—but it's just noise to them. At best, they can get a sense of your emotional state.

"Those of us who can communicate with them have to learn to project our thoughts in a certain way to be understood. It's easier for us to understand them than for them to understand us, but that's because projecting comes naturally to them. For the record, as far as we have been able to determine, only one person in a hundred can hear or speak to them telepathically. This meeting is unusual, because there are three of us who can—Doctor Kim, Colonel Bouchard, and me.

"At that, I have not had much contact with them and can't do it well yet. Doctor Kim assures me, however, that with practice, I will improve. To that end, she is proposing to have Yellow Eyes spend more time with me, up here in orbit. You people—" she nodded to her staff "—will need to prep *Valkyrie's* crew for that, so that nobody freaks out over a chance encounter. Val, you'll need to make sure that everyone gets the word."

"Yes, Admiral." The AI's voice seemed to come from mid-air.

<<*Hear voice, feel no presence.*>> Yellow Eyes tilted his head toward Lorna in a questioning gesture.

<<*Not human person…*>> Lorna tried to convey the idea that the ship itself was speaking. Her limited mental vocabulary failed her, and she looked to Kim and Bouchard for help.

<<*Difficult to explain.*>> Jin ducked the issue. <<*We will talk about it later.*>>

"I told him it's complicated, Admiral." Kim chuckled. "I told him we'll discuss it later, but I'm not sure I can explain artificial intelligence to them."

For reasons not yet understood, humans who could talk to the cats couldn't converse telepathically with other humans. Jin had heard the query from Yellow Eyes, but not Lorna's reply, nor had Lorna heard what she had said to the cat.

"Right." Lorna returned the chuckle. "We can try later. In any event, we're doing this because we believe the Kitties can offer us a great deal, especially in military situations. We've already seen it in combat operations on this planet.

"We thought we would need to protect them against attacks by certain bad actors, notably the Confeds. We still have concerns in that regard, because they have no defense against attacks from air or space. What we have discovered, however, is that they need no such protection against conventionally armed forces on the ground.

"I've studied reports from the actions where they were involved, and I can tell you that a regular ground force moving on foot would have no chance against a sizable force of Kitty warriors in the jungles or rainforests on this planet. Would you say that's a fair assessment, Moira?"

"Yes, ma'am." Bouchard nodded. "With nothing more than their natural weapons—their fangs and claws—they've taken out regular Peacekeepers and mercenary special operators. In the field, Yellow Eyes and his warriors are invisible, move silently, and can hear you thinking from a kilometer away, no matter how much cover you have. In addition to telepathy—which lets them communicate silently with each other—Kitty eyesight and hearing are off the charts by human standards. They also have a sense of smell that bloodhounds back on Earth would envy. If they haven't already heard you thinking a kilometer away, they can smell you if the wind is right.

"While you're slogging along through the heavy gravity of this planet, they can leap at you from ten meters away and take you out with a single swipe of a paw. Body armor doesn't help when they hit you hard enough to crush your ribcage or rip your head right off your shoulders. Our people have to train hard to become warriors. These guys are born that way.

"If that's not enough, they are highly intelligent. Yellow Eyes learned how to field strip, maintain, and shoot an LAR by watching my Marines do it. I've seen the targets he's turned in on the range; if he were one of my troops, I'd be recommending him for sniper school.

"Most of the time, however, he doesn't need a rifle, nor will one be of much use to a human in his territory, where visibility is limited to about five meters by natural cover. By the time you see him, it'll be too late to deploy a weapon."

With that, Bouchard sat back and nodded to Lorna.

"Thank you, Colonel." Lorna returned the nod and scanned the faces around the table. "That brings us to the point of this discussion. We are embarking on a… call it a military research project.

"So far, we have two competent 'Kitty communicators' in Colonel Bouchard's battalion, and three more Marines who show some promise. In addition, Major Jefferson of the Colonial Militia has the ability, as does his company first sergeant, though at a lesser level. The cats will be working with both the Marine battalion and the militia company for this project.

"Colonel Bouchard is still developing ideas on how best to use their special abilities in a combat situation. Right off the top, however, she has suggested that they are well suited to reconnaissance and scouting missions. I'm not a Marine, people, but it seems to me that any ground operation would benefit from having a Kitty on the team.

"Yellow Eyes is going to be spending time with me, primarily to help me develop my own communication ability—mostly for my alternate job as colonial governor. In addition, I would like you, Jessica, and the rest of the staff to consider any possible way in which the Navy might benefit from having Kitties aboard ship. At the moment,

I can't think of anything, but I will entertain any suggestions you might have."

* * *

Wardroom, LFS *Valkyrie*

<<So... this is a 'cat' from your world?>>

Dusty, the ship's wardroom cat, regarded the Kitty warrior warily from the end of the bar but did not flee. Yellow Eyes gave the smaller feline a slow blink, accompanied by a low purr. To Lorna's surprise, Dusty responded in kind.

<<The family resemblance is quite remarkable.>> Lorna detected amusement in the Kitty's mind voice. <<I also sense a kinship in spirit. He is a warrior in his own mind.>>

<<Kim says you are very close in...>> Lorna paused as her mental vocabulary failed. She had no idea how to say "biology." <<...in flesh and blood.>>

<<Do not worry, Blue Eyes.>> The Kitty warrior nodded. <<There are many things Kim cannot explain to us, but we have learned to trust her. As time passes, we will come to understand you, your people, and your works. That is one of the reasons I am here, to learn about such things.

<<I had not realized there would be so much to learn, however.>> He waved a furry hand to take in the wardroom, but his comment carried an image that extended the gesture to include the entire ship. Lorna was learning to pick up those subtle colorations in Kitty mind speech. She had not yet learned to project them, however.

I must sound like a kitten learning to talk, she thought to herself, *but it's important for me to learn this. We can't move forward on this planet without taking the Cats into account.*

<<*Tomorrow,*>> she told him, <<*I will take you on a tour of the ship. I will try to explain everything, but you will need to help me. In that way, I will also learn.*>>

<<*Blue Eyes*—>> Lorna felt the hesitancy in the cat's mind voice <<—*this is not my place. It is a wonderful experience. It opens my eyes to things I never knew existed, but it is not a place for my people, not yet.*>>

<<*I understand.*>> Lorna nodded. <<*Among humans, only a select few can live and work in this environment, and we have been traveling among the stars for a very long time. I sense that your people are not yet ready to do that.*>>

<<*No, we are not. We are becoming comfortable with your people in our own world. We work well with Priestess and her warriors, because we understand their purpose. They are protecting the people of your tribe—your 'colony'—as our warriors protect ours. We can be useful to you in that mission, because we have warrior skills that you do not have.*>>

<<*Thanks to you, we are learning that our own world is larger than we imagined.*>> His mind voice carried a mental chuckle. <<*For now, that gives us much to explore. It will be a long time before we are ready to go out to the stars.*>>

* * * * *

Chapter Ten

15 July 2123

LFS *Isis*, Lunar Fleet Anchorage

"I haven't seen anything like this since... well, hell, before the Bug War." John O'Hara waved at the large wall screen on the bulkhead, currently set to an external camera view of the anchorage.

Isis was moored at the far end of the top tier of the docking array. On the screen, five other battlecruisers occupied the rest of the tier. The view didn't show them, but he knew the tiers below were full to capacity with heavy and light cruisers.

"Top rack's full." Eurasia Brown nodded. "If another battle group comes home, they'll have to dock at TransLuna."

"Some of the lighter units are doing that already." O'Hara snorted. "They pulled the Cat Pack from Xanadu, and they're talking about bringing CruRon 2 back from Tatanna."

"So we're home." Brown shrugged. "We've been here for a couple of weeks. Do we have any orders?"

"Not yet. I've been bugging Admiral Simms about it on a daily basis. He says he has no orders. He got the same recall notice at New Eden that we got at Ragnarok: leave some cruisers and destroyers, come home. No further orders, no explanation. Truth is, he's been sort of hinting that maybe I ought to ask my dad what's going on, off the record."

"Seriously?" Brown blinked. "Kind of a big jump over the chain of command, isn't it?"

"Yeah… and I told him that. He says Admiral McGruder doesn't have any word, either. He's suggesting I drop some heavy hints on my old man that somebody needs to pass the word down the chain. We've got six battle groups sitting here. Only one of them—currently Jacobs with *Nike*—has a mission, and that's strictly system defense."

"So… what are you going to do?"

"I'll talk to my father." O'Hara sighed. "I'm going to suggest that Lunar Command needs to get its collective head out of its ass and pass the word down the chain of command. I can do that much without violating any regs about jumping the chain. He doesn't have to tell me anything, he just has to tell McGruder. Hopefully, Mac will pass it down the line to Simms, and the rest of us will get the word."

* * *

Chief Executive's Residence, TerraNova City, Luna

"It's good to have you home again, John." Candy Parks smiled at her son across the table. "It's hard to believe you were out there for two years."

"Yes, Mom, time passes quickly when you're having fun," John O'Hara replied with smirk. "For us, though, it was a mostly tedious and boring tour."

"Well, you did have the pirates to deal with," Robert O'Hara joined the conversation.

"*I* didn't have the pirates," the younger O'Hara insisted. "They were in hyper, on the Odin to Sol run, beyond my jurisdiction. I was lucky somebody thought to send the Cat Pack out to deal with them. For that matter, we were even luckier they picked the wrong convoy to attack. The Brits took a big bite out of them, and Harry Oldham cleaned up the rest."

"Yeah," the elder O'Hara replied with a chuckle. "That was a real clusterf—" He stopped abruptly and glanced at his wife, who shook her head and rolled her eyes.

"Sometimes you Navy types are as bad as the Marines. Go ahead and finish it. It's not like I haven't heard it before."

"—uck." Her husband grinned at her. "Anyway, it was a comedy of errors on the part of the pirates."

There was silence around the table for a moment, then John gave his father a serious look. "Dad… what's going on?"

"What's going on about *what?*" The elder O'Hara's voice held a defensive note.

"The Navy." John shrugged. "Three quarters of the fleet is sitting at the anchorage, idle, waiting for orders. I've only been here for a couple of weeks, but I'm hearing that this has been going on for months. 1st Fleet's 2nd and 4th Groups have been taken offline.

"Crews have been reduced to minimum anchor watch levels. Officers and enlisted have been transferred to half-pay reserve. Systems have been shut down or taken offline. If we needed those ships for action, it would take weeks to get their crews rounded up and everything restored."

"Can you think of any possible scenario where we would need more than four battle groups online?" Robert O'Hara scowled at his son. "For that matter, here in the home system, we don't need more than two."

"Does that mean you're planning to take another two offline? Is mine going to be one of them?"

"I think you're getting into things that are above your pay grade." The scowl deepened.

"I think it's time for me to leave the table." Parks got to her feet.

"No… you two stay." She waved them back into their chairs. "I'm used to this, discussions about things I don't have a need to know. Matters of state security and all that."

Father and son stared after her as she left the dining room, then turned back to each other.

"Okay, maybe it's above my pay grade—" John returned the scowl "—but how far up the ladder would I have to be? I've talked to Simms, and he tells me he hasn't got a clue. I'm pretty sure he's talked to his boss, and if McGruder doesn't have the answers, something is seriously wrong at Lunar Command."

"Mac knows what's going on," Rob O'Hara admitted. "He's been told not to spread the word to the lower ranks."

"Why the hell not?" John's jaw dropped. "You've got a couple thousand Navy people who have been kicked off active service and had their pay reduced to half, and nobody's told them why.

"A lot of Marines have been dropped, as well. We've got two assault carriers sitting in orbit without a mission."

"Not for long." Rob shook his head. "2nd Division's being deactivated, transferred to reserve status. *Iwo Jima's* going to be taken offline, like *Athena* and *Cassandra*.

"Mark Mercer got the orders this morning. He'll be moving over to 1st Division. Sakura's being sent down here to take command of the Marine Corps Training Center—which will *not* be training any new recruits for the foreseeable future. All recruiting efforts have been shut down. MCTC will remain in service, but only for advanced training and proficiency maintenance for active-duty Marines."

John O'Hara's jaw dropped. He stared at his father in silence. The elder O'Hara sat back in his chair with a sigh.

"You're right, son. We owe these people an explanation. I'm not going to give it to you tonight, lest you be accused of violating the chain of command." A hint of a smile crossed his lips and was gone. "I'll give Mac a heads-up in the morning, and we'll set up a briefing for all Navy flag and Marine general officers. You'll get word of it through regular channels."

* * *

Docking Bay 12, TransLuna Station

"Perfect." Roger Stuart nodded in satisfaction. "Looks all proper and secure."

"It should be." Marcus Carter frowned at the scene in the docking bay below. "I left that part of it to the Marines. They elected to use the rapid response team rather than regular TerraNova Security. Bunch of brainless goons, but they put on a good show. That's all we need to keep Lunar Command happy."

The two men watched from the gallery as the security team covered the entrance to the bay while cargo handlers transferred the sealed containers from the interstellar express courier *Javelin* to the Marine light assault lander.

"They'll land the shipment at MCTC and escort it to the treasury on Level Seventeen." Carter shrugged. "It'll get weighed in, and they'll start minting lunars. All the paperwork will match; everyone will be happy. *Javelin's* crew will close up the ship and go off duty.

"Nobody will notice the service tech who shows up later to do a little work on the ship's environmental system. He'll have a proper work order, and he'll bring a large tool bag with him. After that… well… a certain package will find its way to your friends in New York."

"*Our* friends in New York." Stuart gave Carter a sharp glance. "You'll see results, too."

"Whatever." Carter shrugged. "I'm not complaining."

"I have to say, you've set this up very well." Stuart turned away from the observation window. "It's been running smoothly so far, but I wanted to see the process for myself."

"Hmmph!" Carter snorted. "What you've seen is what everybody sees, a normal transfer of gold from the Ragnarok mines to the treasury. What you did *not* see is what's going on beneath the covers. Nobody sees that except the people involved."

"I've been meaning to ask you." Stuart lifted an eyebrow. "How many people is that, exactly?"

"Only one of *Javelin's* crew, the engineer. That's why it was so important to convince the Navy to use express couriers instead of escorted freighters for the gold transfers. *Javelin* only has a three-person crew, and the flight deck people rarely go aft to the engineering spaces. I've got the same arrangement with the other courier—*Arrow*—but the two engineers have no contact with each other. Each thinks he's the only one doing it.

"After that, we've got two people—the tech who retrieves our package, and your TerraCorp guy who takes it from the tech for shipment to Earth.

"The important thing is, each person in the chain only knows his part of it. Your guy at the mine is the only one who knows what's in the package, and he only delivers it to the engineer on the ship. The others may suspect what's in it, but it's a sealed package, and they know better than to open it. It's a five-kilo package, they pass it on, ask no questions, and get paid. Our friends on Earth take care of you and me. I presume they also get a cut, but there's plenty to go around."

"Right." Stuart chuckled. "Five kilos works out to 160 troy. At current market, that's around $300,000 USD, the bulk of which goes to you and me. Our New York friends only get 5 percent, which leaves plenty to pay off the little guys along the line."

"Hopefully, none of those little guys are directly connected to us." Carter scowled at Stuart. "The two in the middle are well down the chain from me, but you set up the guy at the mine, and the shipment guy works for you directly."

"The mine guy is the site superintendent," Stuart advised. "That gives him an excuse to accompany the shipment up to orbit. He was hired from Earth for his mining expertise, with a few things on his record that we were willing to overlook. I was able to exploit that when we set up this operation. As for the one who handles the final shipment, yes… he's one of my own subordinates. He follows orders, doesn't ask questions."

"Best we can do, I suppose." Carter sighed. "Nothing more to see. I'm heading back to my office."

"Me, too." Stuart turned away from the viewport. "If I hurry, I can get the 1500 shuttle back to Luna."

* * *

New York, New York, USA, Planet Earth

"You have done a masterful job on this project." Andre DuMorne beamed at his younger brother. "I am truly impressed."

The brothers were seated in comfortable armchairs, enjoying glasses of wine from Pierre's well-stocked sideboard. It was Pierre's office, but the younger DuMorne had come out from behind his desk upon Andre's arrival in deference to the elder's status as the company's chief executive. Andre's own office was in Paris; he had arrived in New York by private jet this morning.

"It was nothing," Pierre insisted. "Once we found the first corruptible Moonie, it was like opening the gates. Now we find them everywhere we look. On the gold project alone, we have six names—two of them of some significance—all of which are tied to us by investment accounts we control.

"Stuart is the most useful. He is not merely one of the top executives of TerraCorp; he is an elected member of the Lunar Directorate. Through him, we have made contact with other directors. Next in importance is Carter, the managing director of their commercial fleet. Apparently, he's had an axe to grind with the LFS Navy for some time.

"As for the others, one never knows." Pierre shrugged. "Perhaps someday we will find use for a Moonie mining engineer or a shipyard technician. Stranger things have happened. In addition, it is rare that one of our Moonie subversion projects produces a profit, but the commissions we receive for investment of the gold are a nice additional benefit.

"You will be amused to learn that the gold itself is being minted into counterfeit lunars by a company in the Bronx that normally makes commemorative coins and medallions. The US government looks with disfavor on the sale of bullion whose origin is not documented."

"Genius, brother." Andre chuckled. "But you told me you had other news. What else have you got for me?"

"Hmmm…" Pierre favored his brother with a conspiratorial grin. "How do you suppose Richter would react if you offered him access to data on the Moonies' FTL communications gear?"

"What?" Andre blinked. "I'm sure Gerhardt would pay dearly for such information, but where did you get it? Subversion is one thing, but have you developed sources for military espionage?"

"Remember that little bit of fluff you turned over to me some years ago, the lovely Christine?"

"Yes, I remember. Lovely, indeed, but I would hardly call her *fluff*. The woman has a good brain and a talent for espionage, but her information is usually related to Moonie fleet deployments or TerraCorp business strategies, not Moonie technology. Huang has better assets in place for that than we do."

"True, but you will recall that she once gave you information she obtained from a naval officer she encountered by chance—information that ultimately led the CNE to engage the Moonies at Ragnarok. She dropped the relationship with that officer when he was no longer useful to us.

"Recently, however, she encountered him again, and he seemed to be somewhat distressed over his current situation. Such things offer an opening for a clever female agent to obtain information by pretending sympathy, so she decided to take a chance that he might prove useful again.

"As it turns out, his story confirms that our other efforts to disrupt the Moonie economy are succeeding. He was an engineering officer who was taken off space duty and assigned to the LFS Navy yards at TransLuna. The Moonies are cutting back on shipbuilding and maintenance, and he has been taken off active duty entirely.

"Apparently, the Moonies borrowed a custom from the British Navy of the Napoleonic era. When they take their officers and ratings off active duty, but want to keep them in reserve, they put them on half pay. That is what happened to this one, and he is not happy about it. He could seek civilian employment, but he considers that to be beneath his dignity.

"He is talking about wanting to leave the LFS altogether, to come to Earth, and maybe join the American, British, or even the Confed Navy—at a much higher rank, because of his extensive knowledge and experience. It seems he has a greatly inflated opinion of his own worth.

"Our dear, lovely Christine has told him that she might know somebody who could make that happen for him. She is telling him she can get him connected with the American Navy—she is an American, after all, though she works for us. She suggested that he needed to supply some kind of technical material—something unique to the Moonies and not available from other sources—to prove his credentials to the people she would be talking to.

"She didn't really expect he would do it, but a few days later, the stupid, naïve bastard produced an electronic file, which she sent to me. I am not a technical expert, brother, but it certainly looks like detailed technical information on their warship FTL comm systems."

"Unbelievable." Andre shook his head. "We have already debunked the myth that Moonies are incorruptible; now it appears that not all of them are as intelligent as they claim to be. Perhaps we should let this fellow emigrate to the CNE. He would fit right in with the morons who are running the show over there.

"As for this technology, I think your first instinct was correct. If Gerhardt's electronics firms were to suddenly develop an FTL comm system that was as good as that of the Moonies, the CNE would be delighted and would pay him a lot of money to equip all of their warships with it."

* * *

**Conference Room, Chief Executive's Office,
TerraNova City, Luna**

"Are all of you ready?"

Rob O'Hara looked around the table at his council of advisors—key people in the upper levels of the Lunar Free State, including Admiral Abraham Moskowitz, Luna's judge advocate general. The JAG represented the judicial arm of the LFS government, effectively Luna's Supreme Court.

Of the others in the room, Admiral Vandana Prashad, commandant of the Corps of Engineers, was the senior officer, followed by Vice Admiral Martina Easley, head of the Diplomatic Corps. The one civilian present, Lisa Woods, was an executive director of TerraCorp, and also a member of the Lunar Directorate. The lowest ranking person in the room was Commander Randolf Burgess, O'Hara's chief of staff.

Getting nods of assent all around, O'Hara drew a deep breath.

"All right, Mike," he addressed the comment to the other, unseen participant, "make the connection."

Screens along the wall of the conference room came to life, each filled with rows of windows. Captions showed the names and ranks of the participants—virtually every Navy flag officer currently in port and two Marine general officers. Eight additional windows showed the avatars of the AIs currently in port—the six battlecruiser "ladies"—as well as Mike of Lunar Command, and Louis of TransLuna station. Seven more windows showed civilians, executive directors of TerraCorp.

Officially, the Directorate was not part of this meeting, though a number of the attendees were also elected members. Absent, however, were representatives of the Lunar Research Institute, the scientific and educational community. The LRI would need a separate meeting, as would the Directorate when its members were in session.

He drew another deep breath.

"Ladies and gentlemen, this is the first time in the history of the Lunar Free State we have attempted a meeting on this scale. For the moment, I will take no questions.

"What I am going to present to you are simple facts, not subject to dispute or argument. What I need from you are suggestions on how to deal with these facts and mitigate their impact on the Lunar Free State. I do not expect solutions today. What I want you to do is think about what you hear and pass your questions and suggestions up your chain of command.

"You have seen drastic cuts in your areas of operation. Unfortunately, these cuts are absolutely necessary. We are presently facing a crisis the like of which our nation has not seen since the earliest days of the Lunar Free State. The crisis is financial. We've extended ourselves beyond the ability of our small nation to sustain the effort.

"We have operations that require military presence in four other star systems. We are currently engaged in a competition with the Confeds to build a colony on Xanadu. We have thousands of colonists in place already, and hundreds more waiting for transport. The colony also provides a support system for the Kitty Protectorate, to which we are committed by a constitutional mandate.

"This is a critical project, one that we must continue to prevent the Confeds from taking over the entire planet and the protectorate. At the same time, it represents a drain on our resources, and it becomes more expensive as the financial crisis deepens at home. Like Luna, the colony is dependent on products only Earth can supply.

"Until now, TerraCorp has supplied us with the means to keep moving forward. Our basic sources of income at home—asteroid mining, smelting, low-gravity manufacturing—continue to produce. Tourism continues to grow as a profitable industry. Our commercial fleet continues to profit from trade among the stars.

"Unfortunately, we haven't done as well with our investments in Earth's financial markets. A recent downturn in those markets, combined with the declining value of the Gold Lunar, has put us in a position where our expenses exceed income by a significant amount. We had a reserve in the Lunar Treasury, built up over many decades of financial success. That reserve has all but disappeared.

"From the earliest days, our founders insisted that the Lunar Free State would never operate at a deficit. They felt so strongly about it that a balanced budget is mandated by our constitution. Were it not for that mandate, I could borrow billions of lunars tomorrow, but that would mean that someone on Earth would own a piece of our nation, and through financial leverage, could dictate our national policies. We've seen this happen on Earth many times in the past.

"The only solution is to make drastic cuts in spending. We can't cut much from the Corps of Engineers, since most of their budget goes for maintenance of our national infrastructure. Without that, air and water don't get recycled, and the lights go out in TerraNova City. We have, however, put all expansion and remodeling projects on hold.

"We also can't cut very much from TerraCorp, because money spent there produces the income we need to pay for everything else. We can, however, stop any increase in expenses. There will be no pay raises or bonuses for TerraCorp people, and shareholders will not be getting a dividend this year.

"That leaves the Navy and Marines. Again, we can't cut much from the Marine Special Services Division, because they provide services essential to the wellbeing of the nation—police and first responders for TerraNova city and TransLuna station. We do not, however, need two full divisions of combat Marines online.

"To that end, 2nd Division is being decommissioned. One battalion has been moved to 1st Division to fill in the gap left by the battalion detached at Xanadu, but the rest of 2nd will be released from active duty and put on half-pay ready reserve status. *Iwo Jima* will be taken offline. Except for a small maintenance team, her officers and crew will also be transferred to ready reserves."

He paused for a moment to survey the faces on the screen. None were smiling, but none looked ready to protest.

"Regarding the Navy—" O'Hara focused his gaze on McGruder, who wore a grim but neutral expression "—I'm sure all of you noticed that there are six battle groups in port. The anchorage is crowded to the point where we are forced to expand its facilities. That expansion, however, is the only new fleet construction in progress.

"1st Fleet's 2nd and 4th Battle Groups—*Athena* and *Cassandra*, and their supporting units—have been taken offline. Orders are being cut to do the same with 1st's 3rd Group and 2nd Fleet's 4th Group—*Nike* and *Isis*, and their supporting units." O'Hara's gaze flicked involuntarily toward his son's image on one of the screens. John's face showed no reaction; he'd been expecting this.

"As with the others, the officers and crews involved will be placed on ready reserve status, with the ships taken offline and serviced only by skeleton maintenance crews. Details will be contained in the orders, but in conjunction with this reduction in force, the system defense mission will be taken over by Admiral Simms, with *Medusa* and 2nd Fleet's 1st Battle Group.

"We've already made corresponding reductions in shipyard maintenance and construction activities. At the moment, no new ships are being built, and maintenance schedules have been adjusted.

"There are more details; those will be shared with you as orders are issued. For now, we have covered the main points. We believe these actions will bring the Lunar Free State's budget back into constitutional compliance; the goal is to have the nation back on its feet by the beginning of next year.

"Until then, however, you people are going to have to suck it up."

* * * * *

Chapter Eleven

3 August 2123

LFS *Valkyrie*, in Xanadu Orbit

"Damn, it's getting crowded up here." Jake Winfield studied the tactical display. "Next thing you know, we'll have the Akara showing up."

"It's only six ships, but they're parked a lot closer to us than the Confeds are." Lorna Greenwood shrugged. "They took up station over the Consortium mining operation. According to the message, three of them will be going back home tomorrow."

The newcomers had dropped out of hyperspace and been challenged by the LFS system picket. They had identified themselves as the American heavy cruiser USS *Ticonderoga* and two Korean destroyers, RKS *Jeongjo* and RKS *Sejong*.

Ticonderoga's captain had sent messages to both Lorna and the Confed SO in system, advising that they had been sent to relieve the current force—USS *Chicago* and a pair of Australian destroyers—in support of Consortium interests on the planet.

"The Consortium." Winfield shook his head. "Seven nations operating as one. They're like the anti-Confeds."

"There's a big difference," Lorna insisted. "The nations of the CNE give up a big part of their own sovereignty. They bow to the CNE Council in Amsterdam and turn over their military assets to the Confed Navy and the Peacekeepers. These people may be closely allied, but they are all independent nations, even the British Commonwealth members. The Brits don't tell Canada, Australia, or New Zealand how to run their own countries, like the Confeds do with theirs.

"That puts us—and the Confeds—at a disadvantage. We have to treat them as individual nations, though we see them acting together. We haven't figured out how to deal directly with the Consortium, because there's no unified authority that speaks for all of them. They've got a tight alliance, but they won't admit to it."

"Politics, diplomacy… I hate that stuff." Winfield rolled his eyes. "That's why I made a career in the Navy. Hoped I would avoid all that."

"Hate to disappoint you," she replied with a sigh, "but once you get a star on your shoulder, it comes with the territory. I felt the same way you do, but now I'm knee-deep in it."

"I can see that." He chuckled. "One minute you're the admiral, next minute you have to be the governor."

* * *

Confed Strike Team Alpha, Eurasia, Planet Xanadu

"We will hit them after midnight." Diedrich Loeffler scanned the faces of his two lieutenants and their platoon sergeants. "Simple destruction is not the objective. We know they only have a platoon-strength security force. If they are forced to respond to two separate incidents, you will outnumber the responders and will have the additional advantage of ambush.

"That is why we must coordinate the strikes. We have maintained comm silence, but we have probably been overcautious. We are not dealing with the Moonies. These people do not have a dozen warships in orbit and a battalion of Marines to drop on our heads. Use comms as necessary to ensure simultaneous execution.

"Your people have been trained in comm discipline. Make sure they adhere to it, but don't let it hamper your operations. Hit your targets, deal with the response, and get out. Don't forget to leave the little presents that CIS has gone to such trouble to provide for us.

"Are there any questions?" He scanned their faces once again. None of them spoke.

"Very well… the order is given. Move out."

* * *

Confed Strike Team Beta, Eurasia, Planet Xanadu

"This is as close as we can get as a group." Helga Vollmer peeled the wrapper off the ration bar and took a bite. This would be the last meal she would share with her team. "We are less than five kilometers from the edge of the colony. The Moonie drone patrols follow along the perimeter, and their software is good enough to alert them to a group this size, even if the operators are asleep at the controls.

"Fortunately, they have gotten complacent. Orbital surveillance shows they run those patrols on a regular schedule at sunrise and sunset each day. Plan your approach to reach the perimeter at midmorning. That will give you time to stow your gear and assume your 'Moonie colonist' disguises."

She looked around the circle; all of them continued to eat, but their attention was focused on her. They were a hand-picked team, nine of her best troops. She had chosen to lead the mission herself, leaving her lieutenants in charge of the company back in Eastasia. They'd flown to the CNE's research station in Eurasia aboard one of the regular shuttle flights. From there, a stealth flight had dropped them within a hundred kilometers of the Moonie colony. A three-day trek through the intervening jungle had brought them to their present position.

Including herself, four of the team were female. She'd selected them on the theory that a male-female couple would draw less suspicion from the Moonies than a pair of males. She would have made it an even split but had not been able to find a fifth woman sufficiently qualified for a mission of this type. She'd given her all-male team the most accessible target—the Moonie grain storage facility located in the middle of the farmlands to the south of the colony's center.

She'd selected the least experienced troop as her own partner, a young man named Halverson with just three years of service who was a creative genius when it came to explosives. She'd also chosen the least accessible target, the water treatment plant adjacent to the landing field. They would need to pass through the center of the colony to reach it.

"Try to exit by the same route you came in, so you can retrieve your gear on the way out. From what we have seen of this jungle, you will need it; you will be on your own until you reach the extraction point. We will not regroup until then."

She checked the chrono display on her pad: 0400 hours, local time. In two more hours, the Moonie drone patrol would do its morning sweep along the colony perimeter.

"You all know your targets. Some of you have farther to go than others, so move out at your discretion. Good luck. I expect to see all of you at extraction."

One can always hope, she thought, *but we are about to stir up a hornet's nest. Most likely there will be a few faces missing at our next meeting. Maybe mine will be one of them.*

* * *

Consortium Mining Town at Crooked Creek, Planet Xanadu

"What the fuck?" Leo Halsey sat up in his chair. He was alone in the central security office; no one had heard the expletive. He checked the time hack on the screen in front of him. *Crap! Ten after midnight. What's going on?*

A second explosion rattled the windows. Halsey was a military veteran, had been a US Marine before joining Firecat Security; he knew the difference between an industrial blast and incoming fire. *We're under attack!*

He had already punched the General Alert icon on the screen when another thought hit him; who would be attacking a little town in the middle of nowhere on a planet almost sixty light-years from Earth? There was no intelligent life native to the planet except the Kitties, and they were primitives; high explosives weren't likely to be in their arsenal. That left the Moonies and the Confeds. To his knowledge, neither had any beef with the Consortium.

He was still pondering the question when a window popped up on the screen with the name of his boss, Jeffrey Barnes, the Crooked Creek security director. *Audio only… probably got him out of bed.* As he reached out to accept the call, a third explosion rocked the building.

"What's up, Halsey?" Barnes wasted no time on formalities. "Who's blowing the shit out of what?"

"Don't know, sir. Haven't got any reports… stand by." Another window had opened, showing the face of Jennifer Rockwell, the rookie trooper who had drawn the midnight shift at the mine gate.

Rockwell's eyes were wide, and her lips were moving rapidly; she was talking without waiting for him to take the call. The image bounced—she was running with her pad held in front of her. Halsey tapped the window, opening the connection.

"… assembly area. I've got incoming!" Rockwell's frantic tone matched the expression on her face. "Source unknown. I'm trying to reach…"

Her image disappeared. The window flashed Call Disconnected. Seconds later, the sound of another explosion arrived.

"Call everybody in," Barnes ordered. "Open up the armory, tell them to gear up as soon as they arrive, but nobody goes anywhere until I say so. I'll be there in ten minutes." Without waiting for a reply, he switched off, leaving Halsey staring at an empty screen.

Names began to appear in a text box as troopers acknowledged the alert. *Shit!* Halsey ground his teeth. *They're on the way in, but by the time they gear up, we're gonna lose the damned war. We're a security guard force, a bunch of rent-a-cops, like a small-town sheriff's department. Most of us are combat veterans, but this is* not *what we signed up for.*

To Halsey's horror, another sound split the night—the sound of automatic weapons fire, and it seemed to be coming from the opposite direction from the explosions.

* * *

"We've got hostiles with automatic weapons in the northeast quadrant of the housing area." Halsey strapped on his body armor while he reported. "They're on foot, shooting at anyone they encounter. Looks like they're headed for the power plant.

"The mortar attack hit the mine right at shift change. Swing shift was coming up and going home, midnight shift in the assembly area waiting to go down. I think we're gonna have a lot of civilian casualties when it's over."

"Might not be anything left," Barnes growled. "Armed force of unknown strength, attacking an undefended village. If they'd rolled in with any kind of mechanized support, they'd already own the town." The security director strapped on his own gear. On arrival, he'd taken Halsey off the communications console, replacing him with a less experienced trooper. He'd divided the rest into two teams as they reported in.

"I'm going to take my group to secure the power plant." He nodded to Halsey. "You take the other over to the mine entrance. I'll keep my team on channel one, you keep yours on two. We'll use three as the command channel so we can talk to each other. Got it?"

"Got it." Halsey ran a quick check on his comm unit. "Chief, those guys were laying mortar fire on the mine assembly area. That means they've got tubes in the jungle to the north." He pointed to an area on the large wall map. "Do you want me to go looking for them out there?"

"At night? With this crew?" Barnes gave a snort of disgust. "Hell, no. You might have done a few jungle ops in a previous life back on Earth, but we're not trained for it. On this planet, the jungle is not somewhere you want to be after dark, even without a bunch of armed terrorists out there. Secure the mine assembly area, and deal with any hostiles within the village perimeter."

* * *

"Incoming!" Halsey dived behind the trash bin, hoping his team had heard his shouted warning. They'd been strung out across the assembly area, moving cautiously in the direction of the mine entrance, when he'd heard the whine of incoming mortar rounds.

He'd taken point, supposedly the most exposed and dangerous position; as it turned out, that had brought him closest to the trash bin, the only cover in the area. An instant later, the first mortar round exploded less than twenty meters away. He'd covered his head, but the sound of the explosion battered his ears, mingled with the clanging of fragments hitting the steel sides of the bin.

Three more explosions followed at about five second intervals, each a little farther from his position. *Single mortar tube,* he decided, *and they had their targeting dialed in. Means they haven't moved it since they hit the compound the first time. Bastards were waiting for us to arrive.*

He'd seen the dead scattered across the open assembly area when they arrived. One of them had been Rockwell, her broken body crumpled against the perimeter fence where she had fallen. The rest—a dozen in number—had been miners. The survivors, if any, had apparently fled the scene before Halsey's team arrived, taking any wounded with them.

Halsey checked the comm pad on his wrist. The display was still active but showed three of his five-person team offline. He touched the transmit tab.

"Bravo Team, report," he ordered. No answer.

The mortar fire had stopped. He got to his knees and peered cautiously around the corner of the bin. *Oh, shit! They're* all *down.* The five troopers who had been following him lay in a ragged row across the area, none of them moving. Two of them might still be wearing functional comm pads but were in no shape to use them.

There were no craters or other impact marks on the ground. *Proximity frags,* Halsey thought. *Anti-personnel.* He'd been lucky; the steel container had provided exactly the right sort of cover.

He was still contemplating his fortunate survival when the sound of heavy automatic gunfire rolled across the open area. From the sound of it, the action was taking place near the village center, a kilometer away. To Halsey's trained ear, it did *not* sound like fire from the Ruger A24 carbines the security troopers carried.

They were waiting for Barnes, too! The realization came as a shock. *Who the fuck are these people?*

* * *

Schmidt Farmstead, LFS Colony, Eurasia, Planet Xanadu

"I'm Erica Vollmer. This is my nephew, Hans." Vollmer gave the Moonie farmer a hopeful smile. "We are your new neighbors, to the south. We went out to look at the place, but the truck broke down—some sort of electrical problem, so we have no comms. Can you help us?"

"I can do that." Eric Schmidt returned the smile. "Are you newbies, just arrived in system?"

"Yes. Only three days ago. Most of our gear is still back in town. We came out to look first, before we moved in, but..."

She resisted the urge to pull out her concealed pistol and force her way into the hab module. She hoped that Halverson was following her lead and not doing anything to arouse suspicions. This was a test to see if they could really pass for colonists—a safe test, since, this far out in the farmlands, they could always take appropriate action without attracting attention if the charade failed.

"Hmmm… well, I could call somebody to come out and fix your truck," Schmidt suggested, "but if all your gear is in town, maybe it would be best if I give you a ride back there. I need to go into town anyway."

"Oh, thank you." Vollmer shot a glance at Halverson, pleased to note that he had nothing but a boyish grin on his face. "That would be wonderful."

She had come up with the "neighbors to the south" story after they had passed a newly built, unoccupied module at the end of the road, not far from where they had emerged from the jungle after stowing their field gear and changing into their civilian clothes.

"Come inside, relax for a minute while I get my gear together." Schmidt waved them toward the entrance. "One gravity will feel good. Do you need water or to use the bathroom?"

"No, we are good." Vollmer accepted the invitation and followed Schmidt through the door. Halverson followed, and they found themselves in a small but comfortable living room. The drop in gravity came as a relief; Vollmer hadn't realized how much the morning's hike had taken out of her. She'd done the heavy-grav conditioning on the way to Xanadu and had been on the planet for the better part of six months, but the gravity still took its toll on her. They'd been on the move for hours without a break. With a sigh, she settled into an armchair.

Schmidt disappeared into a back room. Vollmer leaned forward to speak with Halverson, who had settled into another chair next to hers. She kept her voice low, little more than a whisper.

"I would like to get to the objective without killing anyone," she told him. "We're not here to slaughter Moonies, we're here to damage their colony infrastructure. Focus on the mission."

* * *

Grain Storage Facility, LFS Colony

"Jesus!" Luis Morales stared at his partner. "You didn't have to shoot her!"

"Yeah, I did." Ron Randall slipped the pistol back into its holster and pulled his shirt down to cover it.

"She could have sent a message."

"How? The comm unit's on the table by the wall. She couldn't reach it without getting up."

Morales walked around the desk for a better look at the victim, a woman in her twenties who had tumbled backwards out of her chair when the bullet struck her between the eyes. "Awww... Christ, man! She's pregnant—must be about six months gone."

"She *was* pregnant." Randall shrugged. "Now she's just dead."

The two of them had reached the grain storage facility—a pair of towering silos that rose above the surrounding farmlands—by midday. The ten-kilometer trek should have been easy, being on level ground and mostly over a gravel road, but Xanadu's heavy gravity and the hot, humid climate had exhausted them.

They had gone straight to the little office next to the silos and found immediate relief in the climate-controlled environment. The young woman had greeted them with a smile. Randall had drawn his pistol and shot her.

"Search the body," he ordered. "She must have keys for that truck outside. I'd rather not walk all the way back to the jungle after we set the charges."

* * *

Battalion HQ, Colony Landing Field

<<*Someone has died.*>> Three Moons glanced sharply at Moira Bouchard.

The cat had come into Bouchard's office to discuss the training of other "Kitty speakers" among the Marines of 2nd Battalion.

<<*Who? When? Where?*>> Bouchard's response was the generalized Kitty query for more details.

<<*Human. Sudden death. Too fast to be sure who or where. That direction.*>> The cat pointed in a southerly direction with her tail. It was a gesture that Bouchard normally found amusing, but not today; the mental message was too distressing.

She paused for a moment; this was not something for her Marines to handle. The colony had first responders for domestic emergencies. She turned to the interface on her desk and touched an icon. A moment later, the local dispatcher's face appeared on her screen.

"Emergency Response… How may I help you?" The young woman's voice was calm and level.

"This is Colonel Bouchard at Marine HQ. One of our Kitties is reporting that someone has died. I don't have a location, only that it's somewhere south of my location at the landing field."

"Uh… say again?" The woman gave her a look of confusion.

"Ah… how do I explain this?" Bouchard gritted her teeth. "The Kitties can sense strong emotions, shock, pain… things like that. They can sense it from far away. Three Moons says somebody died, but it happened suddenly, and she got only a general idea of direction. In the past, she's been able to sense strong emotions several kilometers away. I'm sorry, but that's all the information I have."

"You said south of the field, right? There's nothing much down there but farms; it could be any one of a dozen." She shrugged. "Without anything more to go on…"

"I'm sorry, that's all I've got." Bouchard ground her teeth in frustration. "For the record, though, I trust the Kitties without question on things like this."

"I'll pass the word," the dispatcher replied. "That's all I can do."

"Fine. Thank you." Bouchard cut off the call and punched another icon. A moment later, the face of Colony Administrator Todd Taylor appeared on the screen.

"Colonel, what can I do for you?" Taylor smiled as he took the call.

His smile faded as Bouchard explained the situation. He turned sharply to look off screen.

"Colonel, as it happens, Major Jefferson is in my office, and he's telling me Yellow Eyes felt the same thing, but he's calling it more to the southwest. That would make sense, since we're east of you. Stand by." Taylor's face was replaced by the colony's official logo as he placed the call on hold. A moment later he was back.

"Yellow Eyes is telling Jefferson the feeling was very faint, but he's not surprised. He says Three Moons is more sensitive than he is; besides, he thinks you may be much closer to the event than we are. The direction he got is not directly toward the field. It has to be out in the farms somewhere. There's nothing else out there except the grain storage facility.

"Let me check with the first responders to see if they've gotten any calls. I'll get back to you if we need any assistance from your Marines."

* * *

Farmers' Cooperative, LFS Colony

"Thanks for the ride." Helga Vollmer gave Schmidt her best smile as she closed the door of the truck. Schmidt returned the smile, gave her a wave, and drove away.

"I don't understand, Major," Halverson muttered. "We could have knocked him off and taken the truck right to the objective. We've got to walk right past the main entrance to the field. The Moonies might have Marines guarding it."

"I don't murder civilians in cold blood," Vollmer growled. "We aren't going to walk. Do you see that building over there?" She waved a hand in the direction of the Farmers' Cooperative. "There's an ATV on the side of it, plugged into a charger with nobody around. That's our transportation. Stay here and watch the building while I go get it."

* * *

Two minutes later, they passed the turnoff for entry to the landing field without incident. Contrary to Halverson's concerns, there was no gate or security checkpoint, but Vollmer was still glad they had secured the vehicle. The objective—the water processing plant—was still a kilometer down the road. Walking in Xanadu's gravity was bad enough. In the heat and humidity of the day, it would have been an ordeal.

In terms of the mission, she was forced to admit that Halverson was right; they should have killed Schmidt in his house and taken his truck, but the farmer's cheerful willingness to help them had stopped her. Schmidt wasn't the enemy; killing him wasn't part of her mission plan.

When they got into his truck, he spoke to her in German. He had noticed her accent and assumed that she, like himself, was a recent immigrant from *das Vaterland*. He had arrived on Xanadu six months earlier, he told them, to get his farm started and prepare for the arrival of his wife and two children, expected next month.

The rest of the trip into town had been a running commentary from him on trying to work a private farm in the Rhineland under the CNE's bureaucratic bullshit, with people in Amsterdam who didn't know the first thing about farming dictating everything from what he was allowed to grow to the price of seed. When the Moonies had come along with their offer to provide forty hectares of land, a habitat module, and basic farm equipment, he'd wasted no time filling out the application. At that, he'd waited over a year for approval, and another year for his new farmstead to be ready.

The story had moved her—the more so because he had touched on her own heritage. Her people had been farmers; she had left home as a teenager to join the Peacekeepers. She'd built a career for herself, but she'd also seen the worst of the CNE along the way.

I'm not cut out for this kind of mission, she thought. *Infiltration and subversion are not for me. Don't make me get close enough to the targets to see that they are real people.*

She shook off the thought. They were getting near the objective. Simple destruction of infrastructure was more to her liking. She tapped

Halverson on the shoulder and pointed at the huge water tower rising above the landscape ahead.

"The mission calls for us to hit the treatment plant, but you are the demolition expert. Do you think you can take that thing down?"

"Hmmm…" He studied the structure. "Yeah… hey, if I do it right, I can drop it on top of the plant. Good thought."

She nodded. Her own mission was back on track. *I wonder how the rest of my teams are doing.*

* * * * *

Chapter Twelve

5 August 2123

Crooked Creek Consortium Mining Town, Eurasia, Planet Xanadu

"What are you going to do?" Hideo Nakamura's tone demanded an answer.

"There's not a damned thing I can do." Leo Halsey glared at the mine's director of operations. "We had twenty people. Eleven are dead, four others wounded and out of action. I'm not supposed to be the security boss. I'm just the senior guy of the five who are left.

"Whoever was attacking us is gone—not because of anything we did, because they did what they wanted to do and left. If they come back, you might as well give them the keys to the mine, because we sure as hell can't stop them."

"But… Barnes told me…" Nakamura started to protest.

"Barnes is dead. Yeah, I know, he told you all was secure. That was true when all we had to worry about was wandering wildlife and an occasional drunk miner. We were never set up to deal with a military assault."

"All right…" Nakamura took a deep breath. His shoulders slumped, and he lowered his voice. "You are the senior man, and you are all we have for security. What do you recommend we do?"

"Call for help. I don't see any other way." Halsey shrugged. "Those three warships are supposed to support us, aren't they?"

"Well, yes, but what can they do from up there?"

"Don't know, but the only way to find out is to ask them."

* * *

"I don't know what to say, Mr. Nakamura." Captain Jeffrey Burke shook his head. "I've got exactly five Marines aboard *Ticonderoga*, strictly shipboard security. We're not Moonies. We don't put a full platoon aboard a heavy cruiser.

"Even if we did, I don't think it would help you. None of my people are conditioned for heavy gravity. Our mission orders said nothing about operations down on the planet. To be honest, we aren't here to do anything more than show the flag."

"So you're telling us there's nothing you can do?" Nakamura's face was a mask, concealing his feelings, but Burke heard a note of dismay in his voice.

"Well, maybe there is one thing…" Burke grimaced. "I can call the Moonies."

* * *

LFS *Valkyrie*, in Xanadu Orbit

"You say your mining community has been attacked?" Lorna Greenwood gave Burke an incredulous look. "By an unknown military force?"

"Uh… the *Consortium's* mining community, Admiral." Burke hesitated. "I don't actually have any authority or responsibility for them, but…"

"Let's not do that dance." Lorna's gaze narrowed. "The United States is one of the Consortium nations. You and your two Korean consorts are here on behalf of the Consortium. As far as I'm concerned, those are your people down there. What assistance can the Lunar Free State provide?"

"I'm not sure," Burke admitted. "Whoever the attackers were, they hit the community power plant. The mine runs on its own plant, and the engineers are trying to cross connect to provide power to the housing and support areas. Meanwhile, they've got dead and injured people. They are still trying to assess the situation, but it's possible their medical facilities are inadequate.

"The big problem is security. The local security force was almost wiped out in the attack. As best they can tell, the attackers took no casualties, did their dirty work, and faded back into the jungle. They're still out there, and the community is defenseless."

"Hmmm…" Lorna nodded in understanding. "At this point, I'm wondering whether I should put on my 'colonial governor' hat, but no; I think your needs will be better served by a response direct from orbit. I can drop a medical team from *Valkyrie* faster than one can be flown a thousand klicks from the colony. I can also drop my Marine commander, Major Dundee, with a platoon of his troops to provide interim security and assess the situation.

"In addition, I'm going to pass the word to *Thermopylae*. Her Marines are down on the planet, but an assault transport has better orbital support and surveillance gear than any of my warships. They can scan the jungle and look for your mysterious attackers.

"For best results, she'll have to take a position over your mining site. I never let a Marine transport go anywhere without a pair of destroyers to cover it, so don't be surprised to see them coming."

"It'll be a welcome sight, Admiral." Burke breathed a sigh of relief. "Honestly, I'm surprised—and pleased—by your offer of support. Back in the home system, I'd have to wade through a few layers of diplomatic bureaucrats just to talk to you."

"That's why I'm playing admiral instead of governor." Lorna smiled. "This way we can get things done and let the diplomats sort it out later."

* * *

Colonial Commission Office, LFS Colony Central

"Sir, I've been calling all of the farms to the south. Some didn't answer. People are out working fields and tending livestock." The dispatcher shook her head. "The only one I'm concerned about is the grain storage facility. There should be somebody on duty to log harvest in and shipments out, but nobody's answering there.

"There's nothing else happening, so I paged out one of the paramedics to do a welfare check. He'll check the grain silos first, then start making rounds of the farms. Other than that, there's nothing else we can do. Are we absolutely sure that Kitty was right? Can they really tell if somebody died that far away?"

"I honestly don't know." Taylor shrugged. "Nobody knows how that telepathic sense of theirs works, but we can't afford to ignore the warning. All right, you've done all you can. Keep me posted."

Taylor broke the connection and turned to Darius Jefferson.

"Can you think of anything? Has Yellow Eyes got any suggestions?"

"No, nothing specific." Darius shook his head. "I'm getting a general vibe from him that something's not right. It's hard to interpret;

best I can figure is that something has tripped his hunter sense, telling him he needs to be alert. It's really a Kitty thing, nothing I can explain. It's kind of like a human saying he's got a bad feeling about something. "I've learned to rely on these guys for things like this." Jefferson glanced at the Kitty warrior, who stared back at him with unblinking topaz eyes. "I only came into town to run a few errands. I think I'll stick around for a while, maybe make a call or two to my militia people, see if anyone else has got any intel to share. I'll be down at the armory."

"Good." Taylor nodded. "I'll let you know if I get any news."

* * *

Last Chance Saloon, LFS Colony Central

Sarah Peabody regarded the couple sitting at the outdoor table with disapproval. The pair had ignored the sign on the wall of the covered front porch: Tables for customers only. Order inside—No outside table service before 1900 hours.

If they had only stopped for a moment and moved on, she would have shrugged it off. Likewise, if it had been raining—one of this season's brief but heavy showers—she would not have begrudged them sanctuary. Today, however, the weather was fine, a bit cooler and less humid than usual for this time of year. The couple had been sitting there for twenty minutes, which would not have been a problem if they'd come in and ordered drinks or food to take outside.

Must be newbies, she thought. *Can't take the gravity. All the more reason for them to give me some business.* She'd spent a bunch of hard-earned credits to put grav plates under the porch, so patrons could dine and drink in the comfort of normal Earth gravity. She'd even put ceiling fans out there to keep the air moving on hot, humid nights.

Her pad chimed. A glance at the screen told her it was a call she needed to take.

"What's up, Major?" Darius wasn't in uniform, but he was still the militia CO, and she would always address him by rank. Decades of service in the LFS Navy had drilled that habit into her.

"Maybe nothing—don't know yet." He proceeded to tell her about the alert he'd gotten from the Kitties.

"Right…" She nodded to his image on the screen. "I heard the dispatch call on the first responder channel. The brush truck rolled by here on the way out. I didn't think anything of it because the call was a welfare check."

"I hope it's not going to be anything," he told her, "but Yellow Eyes has a bad feeling, and it's contagious. No action needed yet, but keep your eyes open, and let me know if you see anything out of the ordinary. I can't justify calling up the unit, but be ready in case things go to hell in a hurry."

"Will do," she assured him. "I'm here if you need me."

Peabody was second in command of the company. If there was to be an alert, Darius would depend on her to recall the troops and get them geared up. Her screen blinked out as he signed off the call.

Hmmm… if I see anything out of the ordinary… She immediately thought of the couple out on the porch. They were still sitting there, talking to each other. The woman was pointing to something down the street, the man gazing in the indicated direction. Peabody moved to the front window to get a better look at them. The woman had a large shoulder bag on the floor beside her. The man had a backpack next to his chair. Neither bag was of a military style, and such things were common in the colony.

But not common in town, she thought. These two looked like they were set up for a hike out in the boondocks. If they had a vehicle, it wasn't parked in front of the saloon. She pulled out her pad and called up the view from the external security cameras she had installed to make sure nobody was getting rowdy in the parking lot.

Nope, no vehicle there except mine. Maybe they had parked at the general store down the street. If so, why were they still toting the pack and shoulder bag?

More importantly, Peabody didn't recognize them. There had been a lot of new arrivals among the colonists in the past year, but she had met every one of them. She was a member of the official "welcome to Xanadu" team that conducted the arrival briefing for each group. For some of them, that had been her only encounter, but she had a good memory for faces. Besides, as the guy turned his head, she noticed a pattern of heavy tattoos on his face and neck. It was a face she wouldn't have been likely to forget.

As she watched, they got up, shouldered their bags, and stepped off the porch. The man stumbled a bit as the planet's natural gravity took effect. He straightened up and adjusted the backpack, giving her the impression that he was carrying a heavy load. Without further delay, the two of them headed down the street. At the corner, they turned and headed south down what everyone called "Main Street" in the direction of the colonial commission office.

Most likely I'm chasing shadows, she thought as she reached for her pad, *but like the major said, bad feelings are contagious.*

* * *

"No, you're right." On the screen of her pad, Darius waved Peabody's apology aside. "It's worth checking out. Something strange is going on… stand by."

His face vanished, but she didn't put the pad aside. He clearly wanted her to wait for his return. She walked out onto the porch and surveyed the street. Nothing much was happening, a typical day in the colony's only town.

A moment later, her pad beeped. She looked at the screen; Darius had returned, and his face was grim.

"Somebody murdered Sally Schroeder out at the silos," he told her. "First responders found her, shot. Dispatch is calling out Sheriff Jacoby. That's all the information I have, but I'm not going to wait for word. I'm calling up the company, Condition Red.

"Get to the armory and gear up; check everybody in as they arrive." Setting an example, Darius pulled on his BDU tunic as he issued the order. "I'm going out to check on those two people you spotted. When you get here, check with first responder dispatch to see if there's any further word. Otherwise, stand by and wait for me to get back."

"Roger that." She nodded. "I'm on the way."

The saloon was almost empty. She chased the two early lunch customers out, advising them that the place was closed. As she locked the doors, the impact of the event finally caught up with her. *Sally Schroeder… dead.* The Schroeder family had been among the earliest colonists to arrive on Xanadu, a newlywed couple at the time. They'd been expecting their first child; if Sally was dead…

Peabody pushed the thought out of her mind as she climbed into her own truck and headed for the armory.

* * *

LFS Colony Power Plant

"Oh, shit," Maria Ricci muttered. "I think we're busted."

"Only one guy, and his gun is still holstered." Pierre Renaud's reply was no more than a whisper. "Military holster, not for quick deployment."

"Don't do anything stupid," she replied with a whisper of her own. "Smile and talk first. Maybe we can get out of this without raising an alarm."

Frustration washed over her. They had actually reached the gates of their objective, the power plant that served the central village. Solar panels stretched out behind the building, covering several hectares with their gleaming surfaces. Those would not have been worth the effort to destroy—too easily replaced. The target was the plant itself, with its banks of batteries fed by the panels. The mission brief said there was also a micro-fusion plant inside, primarily for use as a backup in case the solar array was damaged.

The gate itself was secured by a simple token lock. Ricci had been contemplating ways to defeat it when the LAV had rolled up behind them—a military vehicle, judging by its camo paint scheme. A huge black man wearing camo BDUs had climbed out of the driver's seat and was approaching them, walking with a slight limp, assisted by a cane in his right hand. He would have to drop the cane to draw his pistol.

"Hi there." He waved a hand at them. His greeting sounded cordial, but he wasn't smiling. "Are you folks lost?"

Yes... we're busted. The power plant was the last building on the street, effectively marking the southern limit of the town. They had already passed the colonial commission's offices and what appeared to be a storage building or warehouse. Beyond the power plant, the road stretched into the distance through cultivated fields of corn.

"We're exploring." She tried to give him a cheerful smile. "First time in town. We just got here last week."

"Really?" His expression hardened. "That's strange. We haven't had any new arrivals for a month. I'll need to see your universal IDs."

He still hadn't reached for his weapon; Ricci decided it was time for action. She pulled up her shirt and drew the suppressed pistol tucked into her waistband. She had only begun to deploy the gun when a furry demon from hell exploded out of the LAV and came at her like a missile. She had only turned halfway to meet the new threat when the creature slammed her to the ground, and her world went black.

* * *

<<*I still have my warrior skills.*>> There was a note of satisfaction in the thought. <<*I am sorry about the second one, Dark Giant. I know you prefer prisoners, but his weapon was already deployed.*>>

<<*No need for apology,*>> Darius responded. <<*Once again, you have saved my life.*>>

He knelt to secure the woman's hands behind her back with binders. She had just regained consciousness after the Cat's body check had taken her down. Darius had replayed the encounter in his head, but still couldn't believe the twisting leap Yellow Eyes had performed to reach the second target. The man had been bringing his gun up when a swipe of the cat's claws had nearly decapitated him.

Darius turned from his prisoner to examine the shoulder bag she had been toting. His eyes widened as he recognized the bricks of explosive putty. He shot a sharp glance at the backpack the dead man was still wearing, then touched the combat comm pad on his left arm.

"Peabody, are you on comms?"

"*I'm up, Major.*" The reply came instantly. "*Just gearing up. Nobody else is here yet.*"

"Get Colonel Bouchard on the horn. We're gonna need the Marines for this one. We've got terrorists, and they're inside the colony perimeter."

* * *

LFS Colony Communications Array

"I can't believe it's going to be this easy." Elsa Dobrow scanned the open field surrounding the tower. "No security on this place at all."

"They did have a fence and a lock." Neil Reichert's voice held the hint of a chuckle. "Electronics I learned to crack in grade school, but a lock all the same."

"It's what you find in a society where everybody trusts everyone else." Dobrow returned the chuckle. "This is the frontier. They will learn eventually."

"They will be getting a lesson in exactly three hours." Reichert pressed the red button on the detonator box. A red numeric display showed the time remaining as the seconds began to count down.

"All set." He straightened up. "Let's get out of here. We've got to cover fifteen klicks in that three hours."

* * *

Gerard Farmstead, Southeast Quadrant, LFS Colony

"Oh, crap!" Jonathan "Jack" Frost ducked back behind the tractor. "Somebody's coming out of the hab. Somebody wearing BDUs."

"Well, shit." Maureen Nelson rolled her eyes. "We're late already. The other teams should already be on their way out. I told you we should have crossed the field instead of going around it."

"Yeah, well, I'm wondering if this target is worth the effort," Frost growled. "A friggin' warehouse full of wood and a sawmill—a damned small sawmill. From the way the place was described, I was expecting a major industrial operation."

"It's an agricultural colony." Nelson shook her head. "Alpha Company got to hit the Consortium mining site; we drew the short straw—nothing but a bunch of Moonie farmers. This might be their only local source of wood, and for sure nobody wants to pay to ship that from Sol. If we take it out, we disrupt the colony—mission accomplished."

"Mission's not accomplished unless we get out alive." Frost crept forward to peer around the tractor's huge tire again. "I was hoping that guy running the mill was the only person around here."

* * *

"Got to run, Dad." Lucius Gerard rolled to a stop next to the sawmill and leaned out the truck window. "Red Alert for the militia; they say we've got infiltrators inside the colony perimeter."

"Hold up a minute, son." Justin Gerard raised a hand as he walked up to the truck. "Did you say infiltrators? Where?"

"Didn't say, just said to report to the armory. Gotta go."

"Son… wait." The elder Gerard leaned in close to the truck and dropped his voice to a near whisper. "There's somebody behind the tractor. Guy stuck his head out a couple of times when I happened to be looking that way. I was gonna call you and tell you to bring out my shotgun."

"Huh?" Lucius blinked. "Who would be…"

"Exactly!" Justin nodded. "Who the hell would be out here in the middle of our farmstead, without a vehicle, hiding behind my tractor? You're telling me we have infiltrators somewhere. I think maybe we got some right here."

"I think you're right. Let me stay here and watch. I've got my 9 millimeter in the truck; you go get your shotgun. I'm going to call Peabody and report it."

"Damn!" He gritted his teeth. "Wish I had my LAR, but it's at the armory."

* * *

"The sawmill guy's gone back into the hab," Frost reported. "The uniform guy is still sitting there in the truck. Looks like he's calling somebody."

"That's not good." Nelson stood up to look over his shoulder. "I think we need to move. Let's go around next to the hab and come up directly behind the truck."

Without waiting for a reply, she lifted her shirt and drew the suppressed pistol from her waistband. "Wish I had my Zastava," she muttered. "I'd have taken him out already."

"Pretty hard to conceal that thing under your shirt," Frost replied with a chuckle as he drew his own gun.

In normal field operations, Nelson was a sniper, and Frost was her spotter; for this op, he was the demolition expert. Her job was simply to help him tote the charges and cover him.

He trailed behind as she went around behind the tractor and crossed the open space to the driveway beside the hab module. From there, she headed straight for the truck, hoping that Frost was following. The truck had typical side mirrors, but the driver was unlikely to be watching them while parked. Still, side to side motion was more likely to catch his eye than a direct approach. She kept the pistol deployed in front of her, ready to start shooting if necessary.

They had passed the hab and gotten within about thirty meters of the truck. *This is going to work,* she decided. *We'll take this one out, then deal with…*

"Stop right there!" The voice came from *behind* them. "Drop those guns!"

* * *

Justin Gerard had immigrated to Xanadu from Canada after his wife died. He was not a veteran of regular military service. His background had been law enforcement, ten years of service in the Royal Canadian Mounted Police before a knee injury had forced him to retire. Old habits from his RCMP days kicked in as he challenged the intruders, a man and a woman with pistols deployed who were moving with purpose toward the truck.

He had the tactical advantage—high ground from the porch of the habitat and surprise, since they had not heard him come out the door. *Target fixation,* he thought. *They weren't watching their six.* The target in question, however, was his son. He couldn't allow that to continue.

Unless they were crack shots with those pistols, he also had the advantage of range. They were about twenty meters from him, and his weapon didn't require precision aim. The basic design of the 12 gauge pump shotgun hadn't changed in nearly two centuries, and the gun was as useful for hunting on Xanadu as it had been in western Canada when Gerard first acquired it in his youth. He'd been mildly surprised at the lack of hassle from the Moonies when he'd listed it—and a substantial supply of ammunition—among his personal possessions to be transported to the colony.

"I hear Xanadu's a pretty wild place," the Moonie customs inspector had said. "You might find good use for it."

Bet you didn't see this one coming, though, he thought as he challenged the two intruders. In response, the woman simply froze. The man, however, whirled around and started to bring his pistol up. Without hesitation, Gerard pulled the trigger. The target pitched backward as a charge of buckshot pellets struck him in the chest, making a ruin of his heart and lungs.

No body armor, Gerard thought as he racked the slide to chamber another round. He'd allowed for the possibility that the intruders might be wearing protective gear; the second round—the one he'd just chambered—was a solid slug instead of buckshot. He shifted the sights to cover the woman but didn't fire.

"Drop it, or the next one's for you," he told her. She had flinched at the sound of the shot and had turned, not toward him, but to look at her fallen partner. She paused for an instant, then let the pistol drop to the ground. Turning slowly to face him, she raised her hands in surrender.

"Clear!" Gerard yelled. At the sound of the shot, Lucius had come out of the truck with his own pistol deployed. He lowered the gun and approached the woman while his father remained on the porch with the shotgun aimed at her.

She's a pretty thing, Gerard thought. *Looks to be about the same age as Lucius. Too bad she's on the wrong side. From the look of it, they were planning to kill both of us.*

"Step away from the gun," he ordered. "Face down on the ground with your arms stretched out."

* * * * *

Chapter Thirteen

Marine Battalion HQ, Landing Field, LFS Colony Central

"Ma'am, I've got the sheriff's people on comms." Gunnery Sergeant Walking Wolf Ackerman wore a grim expression. "They say the woman was murdered with a shot to the head. Whoever did it has left the scene, and they say the farm co-op truck she used to get out there is missing."

"Missing truck…" Lieutenant Colonel Moira Bouchard turned to face her battalion first sergeant. "That means we've got a target. Who's hot?"

"Bravo Company, 1st Platoon. Their 1st Squad's in the ready room, geared up."

"Right. Pass the word to Major Marks to turn out the rest of the platoon and stand by for deployment. Get a Firefly warmed up for the ready squad—no mission yet, but I want them online and ready. I'm going to gear up… I might want to go with them."

<<*May I go also, Priestess?*>> The query from Three Moons was a soft whisper in Bouchard's head.

<<*Yes. I may need your perception on this one, if not your warrior skills.*>>

"… and Wolf, tell the geeks I want a drone in the air in five minutes. Tell them to meet me at the plot table, and I'll give them the mission."

"Yes, ma'am. I'm on it." Ackerman tossed her a quick salute and departed from her office. Bouchard turned to her locker and began to strap on her gear. She sensed a chuckle of amusement from the Kitty warrior sitting beside her desk.

<<Yes, I know.>> She returned the mental chuckle. <<*You don't need all this hardware. The Goddess gave you all the equipment you need to be a warrior.*>>

Her pad buzzed with a priority tone. She picked it up to find Darius Jefferson's image on the screen.

"What's up, Jefferson?"

"Colonel, this mess gets deeper every minute. I just got a call from one of my troops. They had an encounter at his farmstead. Two hostiles, one of them dead, the other in custody. No friendly casualties. I'm a little short on details, but it's the Gerard farmstead in the southeast quadrant. My unit is still assembling, and I don't have enough people or transport to go check it out."

"Understood. I'm firing up a response team. We'll handle it. You're still holding that other prisoner, right?"

"Yes, ma'am. I've called the paramedics to come look at her."

"She's wounded?" Bouchard raised an eyebrow.

"Not exactly. She got hit by a charging Kitty. Yellow Eyes knocked her flat. She might have a couple of broken ribs."

* * *

Grain Storage Facility, LFS Colony

Jacob "J.J." Jacoby found himself sprawled across the front seats of his LAV, his ears ringing from the concussive force of the explosion. The vehicle—his official colony sheriff truck—had rocked on its wheels but had remained upright.

More importantly, other than the temporary impairment of his hearing, and a few spots in front of his eyes, he didn't seem to have suffered any injury. The door windows had been open—a good thing, otherwise the concussion might have blown them in, and he might have been shredded by glass fragments.

He had gotten all the information he could from the murder scene. He had allowed the ambulance crew to take Sally Schroeder's body away. By that time, two of his deputies had arrived, and he'd asked them to check the area around the facility. He still had no idea why Schroeder had been murdered; he asked them to look for clues.

After that, he'd gone back to the LAV and passed the word to Darius Jefferson, who had asked him to contact the Marines. He'd gotten off the call with Wolf Ackerman and was making notes on his pad when the explosion occurred.

He hauled himself up in the seat and looked in the direction of the silos but saw only a cloud of dust. Despite the heat and humidity, a breeze was blowing; as he opened the door and got out of the vehicle, the dust began to clear. Through it, he could see the silhouette of the silos towering over him… two silos, where there should have been three.

* * *

Corn Field, Southeast Quadrant

"What the fuck!" Randall turned around and stared back in the direction they had come from. "It's too soon! You screwed up setting the timers."

"No, I didn't," Morales insisted. "Somebody must have found the charges and tried to move them or something. Anti-tamper trigger set them off."

The two of them had been standing in the bed of the co-op truck, trying to get their bearings in the middle of a field of tall corn. They could see the dust cloud from the explosion and collapse of the silo, nearly five kilometers to the northwest of their present position.

It had been Randall's decision to leave the road and drive through the field. That gave them the shortest distance to get back to the edge of the jungle, where they had stored their gear; however, it proved to be slow going. The co-op truck had not been designed for serious off-road transportation. It had been bad enough getting through the cotton fields, but once they hit the tall corn, they couldn't even see where they were going.

"I told you these rows were angled to the north. We need to steer to the right and cut across them."

"Screw that." Randall shook his head. "We'll follow the rows until we hit jungle, then head south along the edge until we find the big boulder."

"If we'd followed the roads, we'd have been out of here already," Morales complained.

"Yeah? Well, if you'd set the charges right, we'd have had another hour before they went off."

* * *

"Did you hear that?" Halverson twisted in his seat and stared to the south.

"Yes, I heard it." Vollmer nodded but continued to drive. "If it was one of our teams, they are very early.

Everything is supposed to blow in about an hour. The idea was to hit them with a bunch of stuff at once to screw up their response."

They had reached the objective and set their charges without interference, then climbed back into the ATV and headed back the way they came. The machine was built for off-road use, but she guessed that driving ATVs over the roads would be a common and acceptable practice in a frontier community. So far, it appeared that she'd been right; they'd driven right through town without drawing a glance from anyone. It wasn't the fastest vehicle around, but the colony's roads weren't properly paved for high-speed traffic.

They were headed out. In another few minutes, they would be passing Schmidt's farm. She had no plans to stop but would send him a mental thank you as she drove by. Ten minutes after that, they ought to reach the end of the road. If she remembered the terrain correctly, they ought to be able to take the ATV well into the jungle, almost to the spot where they'd cached their gear.

At this point, she decided, the early detonation of somebody else's charges would be of benefit; it would draw the Moonie response to the south while she and Halverson made good their escape.

* * *

Marine Battalion HQ, Landing Field, LFS Colony Central

"Sheriff says one of his men is dead, the other seriously hurt. He also says it looks like there are more charges around the other two silos, but he's not going to touch them." Ackerman shook his head. "Ma'am, this is turning into a serious clusterfuck."

"It's already there, Gunny," Bouchard told him. "Tell him to back off about half a klick and don't touch anything. Start the EOD team in that direction; have them send a robot in. Maybe they can do something, maybe not. A grain silo's not worth somebody's life.

"I'm going out to the Gerard farm to assess the situation. Where I go after that will be determined later. Keep me posted on the command channel, but bring up another Firefly, and tell Marks to put another squad on the ready line.

"Keep an eye on Parsons. She's got my general orders for the drone search, but feel free to modify that if the situation calls for it. If she finds anything, it's your call on the action."

Bouchard turned and nodded to Three Moons. <<*With me.*>> She waved a hand toward the Firefly's side hatch. Without hesitation, the cat leaped into the machine. Bouchard climbed in, and Ackerman backed away, giving her a sharp salute as the crew chief closed the hatch.

* * *

Militia Armory, LFS Colony Central

"Let's have a little chat." Darius Jefferson glared at the captured terrorist. "Tell me why you were headed for the power plant with enough explosives to boost the whole building into orbit."

"I am injured. I require medical treatment." Maria Ricci glared back at him. She'd already given him her name and claimed to be a mercenary. "You must provide me with proper care under Geneva rules."

Darius wasn't buying it, primarily because all of the equipment she'd been carrying—including the suppressed pistol and the burst-transmission comm unit—were standard Confed Peacekeeper issue. Mercenaries usually carried better stuff than regular Confed troopers.

"The paramedics patched you up. You're not dying," he told her. "You've had all the medical treatment you're going to get. Be glad my friend here took it easy on you." He nodded to Yellow Eyes, who produced a low, rumbling growl.

"He wasn't so gentle with your buddy, who no longer needs medical treatment. Talk to me, or maybe I'll give him another crack at you."

Yellow Eyes leaned forward and growled again, this time baring his impressive fangs. The Cats were creatures of direct action. In their view, enemies were dealt with by fang and claw, but Darius had taught them that sometimes a little intimidation can be useful. Yellow Eyes had mastered the art, needing only a mental cue from Darius to deliver a full measure to a human as required.

Ricci's eyes went wide with terror. She tried to shrink away from the Cat, but her back was against a wall in the armory assembly area, and the Cat was directly in front of her.

"I am a contractor. You cannot..." Her protest was cut off by a hiss from Yellow Eyes, followed by a snarl.

"We know you were going for the power plant," Darius went on in a calm, low voice. "We know there are more of you people out there. What were the other targets?"

"I don't know, I only knew my mission. I am a contractor..."

This time her protest was cut off by a series of explosions, only milliseconds apart. Darius had heard the *boom* from the grain silo blast, almost an hour earlier. This one was much louder, much closer, and was followed by a scream of tortured metal and a *crash* that shook the ground.

* * *

"**They got the colony water tower.**" Ackerman's voice crackled in Bouchard's earbud. *"Dropped it right on the water purification plant. Whoever did this knew how to do demolition."*

"That means no less than four teams," she replied. "Two neutralized before they struck, plus the grain storage and the water tower."

Bouchard had reached the Gerard sawmill site and was looking at the female captive, who had so far refused to answer any questions.

<<*Anything?*>> She directed the query to Three Moons.

<<*Fear, defeat, disappointment, sadness. She wishes for death. She expects death. I can get nothing else.*>>

Bouchard sighed in frustration. She had hoped to get information that would let them stop the attacks, but it was too late. The colony's central water supply had been taken out. The farmers had wells, but the town was served by a single well whose water was run through the purification plant before being pumped up into the huge tank at the top of the tower so that gravity could be used to distribute it with steady pressure.

The tank was gone—along with the purification plant, if Ackerman's report was correct. *Is that it?* she wondered. *Is that the end of it?*

As if in answer to her question, another string of explosions rumbled across the fields, coming from the general direction of Colony Central. It was faint at this distance, about the same as the series that had dropped the water tower only minutes earlier.

"Make that five *enemy* teams, *Colonel.*" Ackerman's voice came again. "Colony network is down, and they've lost the uplink to orbit. Looks like they got the antenna array. Major Ashcroft's sending out another response team, and we've got two drones up, but unless we get a break, we aren't going to find them. This thing looks like a clusterfuck, but it was carefully planned."

***

Marine Battalion HQ, Landing Field

"Tango! Tango! Tango!" The exclamation from Sergeant Mandy Parson got Ackerman's full attention. "Southeast quadrant, grid Delta 12. Got a truck plowing through a cornfield."

"Show me," Ackerman ordered. Without lifting her VR goggles, Parson touched an icon on her control panel. The large screen in front of her switched to a drone's-eye view of the cornfield in question. True to her description, a vehicle was plowing through the corn, mowing down the tall stalks as it went.

"Can't be sure," Parson added. "Looks like the type of vehicle stolen from the grain storage facility, but I can't get a positive ID with that corn all around it."

Ackerman studied the overhead plot on the second screen.

"They've got about a hundred meters to go before they're out of the corn. Get over there and meet them when they do."

"Roger that, Gunny." Parson worked the joystick controls; the view tilted as the drone veered off and headed for the edge of the field.

* * *

"Shit! It's a drone!" Randall slammed on the brakes as the truck bounced out into the open, leaving the tall corn behind. "They were waiting for us!"

"They found that woman you killed." Morales stared at the drone, a hundred meters ahead, hovering over the jungle. "I told you we should have taken her with us. Missing would have been one thing. Dead was enough to set their Marines on us."

As he spoke, a brilliant red pattern appeared on the truck's windshield as the drone's laser targeting system locked on.

"We'd better not give up," Randall snarled. "They'll cut our balls off."

He flung the driver's door open and rolled out of the truck, drawing his pistol. Morales remained in his seat and watched as Randall started shooting at the drone.

If I don't resist, maybe I can get out of this alive. I didn't kill that girl, he did.

It was his last thought as a storm of 20mm high-explosive rounds tore him, the truck, and Randall apart.

* * *

"Move out." Vollmer adjusted her backpack and shouldered her carbine. "I want to put twenty klicks behind us before it gets dark. Do you remember the way we came in?"

"Yeah… that way, right?" Halverson pointed down the gully.

"Right. You take point, and stay alert. Xanadu predators are no joke. Lock and load your weapon, and keep it ready."

"Why am I in front?" His protest sounded nervous. "You led coming in."

"Because anybody can watch ahead, but I have sense enough to watch our six. Coming in, there was no chance we'd have Moonie hellhounds on our tail."

Her comm unit *pinged* in her earbud, and she flipped her helmet visor down to check the message. T4 Phase 4.

She had already transmitted a similar message for her own team. Back in Eastasia, Doernberg would know that two of the teams had successfully cleared the Moonie colony and were headed home.

Team four—that would be Dobrow and Reichert. The Moonie communication system should be destroyed. Good.

She had already concluded that two of her teams had failed. All of them had signaled Phase One—that they had reached the perimeter of the Moonie colony and were inbound, headed for their objectives. Phase Two would have indicated that they had reached their objective and set their charges. She had gotten that signal only from teams two and four. Those teams had also signaled Phase Three—on their way out to the colony perimeter, but not yet clear. Hopefully, team two—Randall and Morales—would also be signaling Phase Four soon.

She'd heard three distinct sets of explosions, the first being the early one while she and Halverson were still in Phase Three. The other two had come after they crossed the perimeter and reached their equipment cache.

She had completed the mission; the CIS spooks in orbit would have to assess the results. All that remained was for her teams to withdraw to the extraction point, more than a hundred klicks to the south. When all were accounted for, she could signal for pickup by a "scientific team" from the CNE research facility.

Extraction was not guaranteed. So far, the Moonies had allowed the CNE facility to operate in Eurasia. Whether that would continue to be true was open to question. Vollmer had seriously poked the bear this time. For all she knew, Moonie Marines were already shutting down the Confed site.

No point in worrying about things that were beyond her control. She had only to put one foot in front of the other until she reached the extraction point. Hopefully, the other teams would meet her there.

* * *

LFS *Valkyrie*, in Xanadu Orbit

"We have four dead Confeds, two live ones in custody, Admiral. That's all we have to show for all the chaos and destruction they've created down there. We also have two dead colonists—three actually, because the Schroeder woman was pregnant when they killed her."

Moira Bouchard had come up to orbit in person to deliver the report. The two of them were meeting in Lorna's day cabin aboard the flagship.

"This whole thing represents a massive security failure, and that's on me. I'm here to surrender my commission. I'll stay until Luna can send you a replacement, but I don't think I'm fit to command the battalion."

"No." Lorna glared at her. "That's unacceptable, Colonel. Your request to be relieved is denied."

Lorna's expression softened as she saw the misery in Bouchard's face.

"Val," she said, quietly, "this official meeting is adjourned. You are dismissed."

"Understood, Admiral," the AI's voice filled the cabin. "I remain available should you need anything else."

The two of them sat in silence for a moment. Lorna got up from her desk, went to the sideboard, and poured a measure of scotch over ice.

"Over here." She directed Bouchard to an armchair in the cabin's lounge area and handed the glass to her as she approached. She poured a second glass for herself, this time with her favorite Tennessee whiskey rather than scotch.

"To the Lunar Free State—" she raised her glass in the traditional toast "—in whose service we stand."

"To Luna," Bouchard replied, her voice reflecting nothing but misery, "in whose service we stand."

They drank the toast, then settled into the comfortable chairs, facing each other across the low table between them.

"Moira... don't ever do that to me again." Lorna shook her head. "Next time, tell me what you want to talk about, and let me decide whether it should be an official meeting. We've been through a lot over the years. You know you can always talk to me."

"Should I be handing you my chaplain's badge?" The ghost of a smile crossed Bouchard's face and was gone. "Believe me, I had a long talk with the Goddess before I came here."

"I'm sure you did, but I'm also sure you didn't listen to Her when She told you it wasn't your fault. I hope you'll listen to me when I tell you the same thing.

"Hell, I'm a trained military officer, and I'm also supposed to be the governor of this colony, but I didn't see this coming. We're used to clumsy military assaults by the Confeds; we're conditioned to think of them in those terms. We didn't expect a sophisticated attack on the colony infrastructure. We sure as *hell* didn't expect it to be carried out by terrorists disguised as colonists."

"I guess I'm mostly upset because my Marines were caught napping." Bouchard sighed. "The Kitties and the colonial militia showed up better than my troops on this one. Three Moons detected Schroeder's murder. I didn't know the Cats could do that, wasn't sure whether to believe her.

"Jefferson and his people picked up on that other team that was headed for the power plant, and the Gerards took out the team trying to blow up their sawmill.

"My Marines got lucky and caught the team that murdered Schroeder before they made it to the jungle. The EOD team got the charges disarmed for two of the silos, but only after the first one had blown and killed one of the sheriff's deputies.

"My people didn't really get into it until after the fact. If it hadn't been for the colonists and Kitties, the bastards would have hit all five targets and gotten away clean."

"What doesn't kill you makes you stronger," Lorna replied. "They hurt us, but they didn't kill us. So what action are you taking?"

"Some of them are still out there. We know that two teams escaped without contact. I've got my air wing flying perimeter patrols, but from what we've seen, they were operating in pairs. If they're moving independently, our chances of finding them are slim.

"If a whole platoon were moving through the jungle, we'd spot it; two people can be pretty much invisible out there if they're at all competent. From what we've seen so far, I think we can assume these bastards are competent. That said, if they try another penetration, I'm pretty damned sure we'll spot them. I doubt they'll be that stupid; they accomplished their mission, and they're on the way out.

"We're doing 'Kitty checks' on the border. We've got all three cats in service, using LAVs to take them along the perimeter so they can listen for human mind noise. So far, no results, but that only means the bastards aren't within ten klicks of the perimeter.

"I'd like better overhead coverage, but with *Thermopylae* over the Consortium site…"

"That was my call." Lorna waved a hand in dismissal. "I'm tempted to call Saunders back, but they're facing a similar threat over there, and unlike us, they don't have a battalion of Marines on the ground."

"No, you're right." Bouchard nodded. "Just wishful thinking on my part.

"Other than that, my Marines are doing what they can for the recovery effort. The bastards took down the water tower but didn't get the well. We've rounded up all the water containers we can find, and we're hauling water all over town. Fortunately, all of the outlying farms have their own wells, so they're not affected.

"I've also got people helping to salvage grain from the silo that got taken down, but it's been raining pretty heavily the last two hours. I'm afraid we're going to lose a lot of it.

"As for the comm tower and the uplinks, the bastards did a pretty thorough job. My techs say it'll take a lot of replacement equipment from Luna to restore the local network to service. They've put together a temporary uplink to orbit, but it doesn't have a lot of bandwidth. If they need more, they'll have to pass their traffic through my comm section out at the field."

Bouchard fell silent. Lorna drew a deep breath and let it out with a sigh.

"Can't fault you," she said. "Can't think of anything more you can do. They caught us napping this time. All we can do is make sure it doesn't happen again, and for that, I'm afraid we're going to have to look to the colonists for help. I don't want to see Marines patrolling the streets of Colony Central, especially since they might not spot the bad guys anyway."

"You were right. The colonists—and the Kitties—were the main reason we were able to stop any of them at all. Jefferson tells me Peabody noticed the power plant infiltrators because they didn't behave like colonists, and she didn't recognize them. That's the kind of thing your Marines wouldn't be able to do.

"It's a bit ironic." She shook her head with a grim smile. "Taylor argued against the colonists forming their own militia. Said they didn't need one because we have your Marines. I disagreed and told Jefferson to go ahead with it. Looks like I was right after all."

* * * * *

Chapter Fourteen

7 August 2123

LFS *Thermopylae*, in Xanadu Orbit

"It's as well covered as it can get—" Corporal Sam Spiro pointed to the area he had highlighted on the plot table "—but I'll bet a month's pay there's something there. If we had people on the ground, I'd say send a drone for confirmation, but…"

"…But we don't have anybody on the ground." Lieutenant Maria Menendez shook her head. "For that matter, it's not our ground."

"So what are we gonna do, LT?"

"Get your data together. Highlight all the important stuff. Give me a short report—a hundred words or so—on why you think it's what you say it is. You do know how to write, don't you?"

Her grin made it clear the question was in jest. Though he did most of his work with VR goggles and joystick controls, Spiro was one of her most talented intel analysts.

"Yeah, LT… I got a high school diploma somewhere back in the day. I'll have it put together for you ASAP."

"Fine. As soon as I have it, I'm gonna do something I really hate to do. I'm gonna buck it upstairs to the Navy."

* * *

LFS *Valkyrie*, in Xanadu Orbit

"This is what my Marine geeks found, Admiral." Commander Tia Maria Saunders shrugged. "They say it's the best they can do. They're convinced there's something down there. I'm not an orbital observation specialist, but I can let you talk to them if you need more information."

"No, I'll take their word for it." Lorna Greenwood nodded to the image of *Thermopylae's* captain on her screen. "I'm not an intel specialist, either, and I've learned not to second-guess people who are trained for it.

"That said, Captain Burke—" she turned to the second image displayed "—if you require any additional information, contact Captain Saunders directly. Her ship is still on station, and her people will continue to observe.

"It appears that the threat to your facility hasn't gone away. If you still need Valkyrie Company's Marines, I'll leave them in place as a defense force. I will not, however, send them against an unknown enemy force out in the jungle, and I can't offer you any additional assets at this time. We're dealing with an attack on our own colony down there."

"Really?" The American captain's face showed surprise. "Same sort as happened to us?"

"Not exactly." Lorna waved a hand in dismissal. "We're still sorting it out."

Burke nodded in apparent understanding. Lorna wasn't about to share information with a foreign power under the circumstances, even if it appeared that they shared a common enemy.

"I understand," he said. "Thank you for the support you've already provided. Not sure what I can do with the information you've given me. I'll have to talk to the Consortium people down on the planet. I'll keep you advised of any action we decide to take, so that we don't have any misunderstandings."

* * *

USS *Ticonderoga*

"I've given you everything the Moonies shared with me, Mr. Nakamura." Burke shrugged. "For what it's worth, my tactical officer—closest thing I have to an intel specialist—says he thinks they're right. There's a company-sized force camped in the jungle less than twenty klicks north of the mine site. That's got to be the source of the attack."

"Perhaps, Captain, but there's something you should know." On the screen in *Ticonderoga's* ready room, Nakamura's face showed deep concern. "My security people have been scouring the area around the power plant where they hit us. They've found several items the attackers dropped or left behind—a communications unit, an ID tag, a combat harness.

"The issue is that these items look to be of Moonie origin. From what we can see, they appear to be standard issue equipment for LFS Marines. However—" he held up a hand to forestall Burke's reaction "—my people have called bullshit on it. They say it's most likely something the attackers left behind for us to find. To our knowledge, none of the attackers were wounded or killed. It seems rather improbable that one of them would have left a piece of vital equipment like a communicator behind or taken off a harness and left it there. The ID tag showed no wear at all, except for a deep scratch that damaged the microchip and made it non-functional.

"On that basis, we showed the items to Major Dundee, the ranking Moonie officer. He says the comm unit is an obsolete model, and the ID tag is definitely a fake. He also says the equipment harness is something that's made for them by a contractor in Belgium. With their small population and limited manufacturing industry, the Moonies still import a lot of their gear from Earth."

"So you're suggesting that someone is planting evidence to make us believe the Moonies conducted the attack." Burke's eyes narrowed. "That makes absolutely no sense."

"I agree." Nakamura nodded. "If anything, it points the finger at their biggest rivals, the CNE. Perhaps you ought to also share the information with Admiral Greenwood."

"If you've shared it with Major Dundee, I'm sure she already knows." Burke chuckled. "He's her flagship's Marine commander."

Burke still could not get over the idea of a regular line warship carrying a full company of Marines. Technically, the US Marines were still part of the Navy, but American warships only carried a few for specialized jobs like security. *Maybe we need to rethink that if we're going to operate in distant star systems,* he thought. *Greenwood had no problem sending a full platoon to help us out down there.* He filed the thought away for inclusion in his mission report and returned to the issue of immediate concern.

"We still need to decide what we're going to do about that hostile camp," he said. "Greenwood was clear about one thing: she's not going to send her Marines after them. It's our problem; we're going to have to deal with it."

"What do you suggest, Captain?" Nakamura shrugged. "I don't see anything we can do. I don't have a way to organize and arm the miners."

"It's too late for that." Burke waved the suggestion aside. "These people were professionals. There's no way I'd send a half-trained militia against them. You might think about the need for that in the future—I'm told the Moonie colony has a militia unit—but the best thing you can do is keep all your people inside the perimeter and let Major Dundee and his Marines handle site security.

"As for what I suggest, I have only one solution I can use, and I don't like it. It's like using high explosives on an anthill, and it's too damned close to the colony."

"You're talking about a kinetic strike?" Nakamura's eyes went wide. "That could also cause diplomatic issues with the Moonies. They keep insisting they don't own the planet, but they have a lot of warships sitting over Eurasia. Aren't they going to get upset if you dump a kinetic on anything down there?"

"They pointed out the target to us." Burke shrugged. "They have to know we don't have any other options. That said, I plan to advise Admiral Greenwood of our intentions before we do it. I'm also going to ask their Marines aboard *Thermopylae* to confirm the target.

"What I need from you, sir, is your assurance that none of your people will be within twenty klicks of the target. There's going to be a hell of a shock wave, and the colony might take some damage. Unfortunately, we can't issue a general warning in advance, because if word gets back to the bad guys, they'll scatter. I need them to be concentrated in one place."

Nakamura said nothing for a long moment, then straightened up and took a deep breath.

"Very well, Captain. I don't see anything else we can do. As for keeping everyone inside the perimeter, we're already doing that. With what happened, nobody wants to take a stroll in the jungle."

"I understand why you can't issue a general alert, but can you give me a heads up? All I'm asking is an hour's warning before you unleash hellfire and damnation on them. I'll try to think of some way to have everybody take cover, maybe tell them that another attack is coming. I'll also want to advise Major Dundee. It would be a hell of a note if your strike took out any Moonie Marines."

"Understood." Burke nodded. "You'll have your one-hour alert—assuming Admiral Greenwood doesn't stop us from doing it in the first place."

* * *

LFS *Valkyrie,* in Xanadu Orbit

"Officially, Captain, we aren't having this discussion." Lorna lifted an eyebrow to Burke's image on her screen. "Unofficially, I agree that it's your only option, and I'm not going to interfere. It's your colony—or the Consortium's—and it's a thousand klicks from ours.

"I have no problem with *Thermopylae* confirming the target. Officially, that's not what they're doing. They're just sharing intel."

"In other words," Burke replied with a grim smile, "if this goes badly, and the Confeds decide to declare war on us, you'll deny any knowledge, and we're on our own."

"Not exactly." Lorna returned the smile. "The Confeds aren't likely to do anything of the sort. They can't even issue a protest without admitting that they attacked you. Most likely, they won't even comment on the matter. We've been dealing with them long enough to know how they operate.

"Besides, if they declare war, that will give you an excuse to ask me for help. We have something of a history of 'keeping order' in this system, which usually means blowing a few Confed warships out of space or dropping our Marines on Confed troublemakers down on the planet. If that's what it takes to 'restore the peace,' I'll do it in a heartbeat. Once again, however, we are not having this discussion, and I never gave you any such assurances."

"I understand, Admiral." Burke nodded. "I'll... ah... keep you advised. Also, thank you for all the 'official' help you've given us so far."

* * *

Official... unofficial... Lorna thought as she broke the connection. *I hate playing these diplomatic games.* She would prepare a report for Lunar Command detailing the entire conversation, including her endorsement of Burke's proposed action. She would also include all of the intel imagery supplied by *Thermopylae*.

All of that would be little more than a footnote to her report on the attack on her own colony—which would end up twice as long as it should be, since she had to report on it from her viewpoint as governor, then do it again as the senior military officer in the system.

They really hurt us this time, she thought. *The deaths were bad enough, but the damage to the colony infrastructure couldn't have come at a worse time. Luna has been complaining about the cost of building the colony, and now I've got to hit them with the cost of rebuilding what the Confed bastards destroyed.*

There was absolutely no doubt about the origin of the terrorists—not only Confeds, but Peacekeeper troops. The two they'd captured had their CNE ID numbers tattooed on their necks, as did the four dead bodies. It was a Peacekeeper requirement she considered stupid and barbaric, but in this case, it confirmed what she had already known. The attack was an officially sponsored Confed operation. The troops who had carried it out were special operators—a cut above the

Peacekeeper goons who did most of the CNE's dirty work, but they were Peacekeepers all the same.

This time, however, I'm going to piss on their exit strategy. With *Thermopylae* absent, she'd been forced to deploy additional planetary surveillance assets, including low-orbit drones and *Valkyrie's* own gravity scanners, which were primarily used for detection of objects in space.

Some of the enemy had gotten away from the colony successfully; of that she was certain. *They're sure as hell not going to walk all the way to the CNE research station. They have to have a pickup planned. If we can detect that pickup, Bouchard's Marines can handle it from there. What we'll do after that is likely to cause a lot more fuss than the Consortium dropping a kinetic next to their own mining site.*

* * *

Continent Eurasia,
Jungle 20 Kilometers North of Consortium Mining Site

"I think we can rule out the possibility of Moonie intervention." Diedrich Loeffler scanned the faces of his command group, his two lieutenants and their platoon sergeants. "They responded to the Consortium appeal for emergency assistance, but they have made no move to come after us. There are no Moonie drones buzzing over our heads, no recon forces coming into the jungle. I believe we can begin planning our next strike."

Loeffler had pulled his company back after the first strike. They had dug in, setting up a hard defense, waiting to ambush anyone who dared to follow them into the jungle. They had also watched the skies carefully, looking for evidence that Moonie drones or aircraft were looking for them. If they had seen any evidence of that, he would have ordered them to scatter in squads.

Two days had passed, and they had seen nothing. It was time to plan the next action. He looked at the faces of his command team and saw nothing but determination.

"All right," he told them with a grim smile, "Let's begin."

He was still smiling when he and his entire force were wiped out of existence by the kinetic strike.

* * *

USS *Ticonderoga*, in Xanadu Orbit

"Impact, sir." Burke nodded at the report from his tactical officer. "Dead on target. There should be no damage beyond the predicted zone."

"Very well. Secure all weapons; stand down from battle stations. Comm, get me a link to Mr. Nakamura down at the mine."

He hoped that Nakamura had taken his advice and shut down all electronic gear at the mining site. The EMP from a kinetic strike could play hell with sensitive systems.

* * *

Continent Eurasia,
Jungle 100 Kilometers Southwest of LFS Colony

Vollmer heaved a sigh as she settled into the web seat of the light transport and fastened the shoulder harness. *Only four of us. Four out of ten. We hurt the Moonies, but it cost us.* The transport's cabin was configured in passenger mode with twelve seats, eight of which were empty. If all of her teams had made it back, there would only be two unoccupied.

Halverson sat next to her. Across the aisle, Dobrow and Reichert wore sober expressions. Twelve hours ago, they'd been celebrating a successful mission when she had arrived at the extraction point. Their jubilant mood had faded when no more teams appeared.

She wasn't looking forward to the debriefing with Doernberg. He would ask a lot of questions she couldn't answer. There had been no need for her to lead the mission herself. A lieutenant or senior noncom could have gotten the team to the dispersal point. After that, she had no control over the teams, nor did she have any way to know what they had achieved.

She checked her harness again as the transport's turbines began to spool up for liftoff. *Maybe I can get a nap on the flight.* She hadn't had much sleep since start of mission and was looking forward to standing down for a few days once they got back to Eastasia. First, however, they had to reach the CNE research station about two hours' flight away.

To her surprise, the turbines began to wind down again. A moment later, the transport's crew chief came through the forward hatch and headed directly for her, a grim expression on his face.

"Moonies, Major." His voice quivered. "They've got us pinned. Two of their attack ships are sitting out there with us in their sights. One of their transports is dumping Marines in front of us. They've told us not to move, or they're gonna open fire. I think we're fucked."

Vollmer's shoulders slumped. Her depleted team had only light weapons; they would be no match for a Moonie assault team backed by air support. The transport had no weapons or defenses. The pilot and crew chief were CNE contractors, employed at the research station.

The man was a civilian, not qualified to evaluate a military situation. *In this case, though, he's right,* she thought. *We are well and truly fucked.*

* * *

CNE Research Station,
800 Kilometers Southwest of LFS Colony

"What is the meaning of this? You have no right..." The protest was cut off as Three Moons reared up with a hiss and put a furry hand in the middle of the man's chest, slamming him back against the wall. He had not been armed, so she'd kept her claws sheathed. He gave a strangled whimper as he tried to recover his breath.

"Let me guess." Moira Bouchard gave him a smile that lacked any trace of humor. "You're the Confed in charge of this little circus."

Three Moons took her hand away and backed off, still towering over the newcomer, who stared at her with wide eyes. With a quick glance at the Marines who were guarding the other Confeds sprawled on the floor, Bouchard walked casually up to the man. He had come through a door that opened onto a private office adjoining the work area. Like all of the others they had encountered, he was dressed in casual business attire. The Marines hadn't encountered anyone in anything resembling a uniform.

"You people have been supporting Confed forces conducting attacks against our settlement. We have your extraction crew in custody, along with the terrorists they were sent to pick up. We can't have you people on our doorstep, running a staging point for operations against us.

"You can take some comfort in the fact that none of your people were stupid enough to resist; they're all alive and uninjured. You have one hour to load them onto one of those shuttles you have in the hangar. You will then fly directly to the CNE colony in Eastasia."

"You can't do this!" He found his voice at last. "I am Doctor Emil Lacrosse. I am the research director of this facility. We are civilians. I don't know anything about any forces attacking you. We have every right to be here…"

He started to take a step forward. Bouchard nodded to Three Moons, who stepped forward and pushed Lacrosse back against the wall again, less violently this time.

"Your rights have been revoked. If you have personal gear and effects, you can take them with you. Everything else in this facility is now the property of the Lunar Free State. If you have a problem with that, take it up with Admiral Greenwood, who's sitting up there in orbit with enough firepower to turn your entire colony into a smoking crater.

"I would strongly suggest you don't piss her off, because after what you people have done, she's looking for an excuse to do exactly that."

* * *

CNS *Versailles*, in Xanadu Orbit

"You have committed an act of war, Admiral." Lise Saint-Germaine glared at the Moonie flag officer on her screen.

"No, I have not," Lorna Greenwood replied. "*Your* people committed an act of war, an unprovoked attack staged from your research station in Eurasia. We have retaliated by seizing the station in question.

I'm giving you the benefit of the doubt, Admiral; I'm assuming you knew nothing about the attack, that the Peacekeepers who carried them out are not under your control.

"Your people attacked; we responded. It can stop here with no further action while we wait for the diplomats back on Earth and Luna to sort it out. That's up to you, but I'm offering you an opportunity to return to the status quo."

Saint-Germaine sat back in her chair and continued to glare while she considered the Moonie proposal. *Status quo? As if I had a choice. You know damned well that any military action—especially a shootout in orbit—would end badly for me.*

The Moonies had reduced their forces at Xanadu. They had sent that damned destroyer squadron home, the one that had bloodied its claws so many times in combat against the CNE. That still left Greenwood with a full battle group, headed by her flagship battlecruiser *Valkyrie*. In addition, she had a pair of heavy cruisers, a pair of light cruisers, and five destroyers at her command.

Saint-Germaine's force had also been reduced. Her own flagship *Versailles* was also a battlecruiser, but bitter experience in battle had shown her that she was no match for the Moonie *Valkyrie*-class. For support, she had one heavy cruiser, one light cruiser, and three destroyers. In sheer weight of metal, that gave the Moonies a two-to-one advantage, never mind the fact that virtually every Moonie ship class was superior to its CNE equivalent.

When the orders came reducing her force, she'd gotten a private message from Admiral Schroeder. He had ordered the reduction precisely to deal with situations like this. The Confederated Navy high command in Amsterdam was little more than a puppet regime under control of CNE Central Intelligence Services. CIS seemed bent on attacking the Moonies at every opportunity, no matter the cost in naval assets and personnel. Time and again, they had thrown warships and crews into the grinder and had not yet produced a single victory.

Schroeder was a professional naval officer who was not of that mindset. He cared too much for his people to sacrifice them in battle for no real purpose other than to jab ineffectively at the Lunar Free State. He had, he told her, ordered the reduction in force so that she would be facing a superior Moonie force and would not be tempted to engage them at the slightest provocation.

Saint-Germaine had no doubt that Greenwood's statements were accurate. The Peacekeeper base near the CNE colony was home to an entire battalion of special operations troops, and—as Greenwood had suggested—they were not under Saint-Germaine's command. The so-called "research station" in Eurasia had been used in the past to stage attacks against the LFS colony and had likely been used for the purpose once again. If anything, she was surprised the Moonies had allowed it to operate as long as they had.

"Very well, Admiral." She sat up and addressed Greenwood's image once again. "For the moment, I will take no action. I will not, however, accept your assertions as valid until I am able to verify them. I will forward my report on the matter to Amsterdam. Depending on the reaction I get from CNHQ, we may wish to reopen the matter."

"Understood." Greenwood gave her a look of smug satisfaction. "For the record, during the attack on our colony, we killed four of your Peacekeepers and captured six others. They carried no identification other than ID tattoos typical of CNE troops. I will provide you with the ID numbers for all six to include in your report. Since they wore no uniforms and attacked civilian targets, the prisoners will not be repatriated. They will be sent back to Luna to face trial as terrorists."

"They are, as you say, not my people." Saint-Germaine reached for her console to break the connection. "Do with them as you see fit."

* * * * *

Chapter Fifteen

25 August 2123
Chief Executive's Office, TerraNova City, Luna

"I can issue the usual tirade of strongly worded protests." Martina Easley shrugged. "You know what the response will be. We'll be better off going public. The media will eat it up if we show them pictures of the destruction and tell them about the pregnant woman who was brutally executed by Confed-sponsored terrorists.

"Even the CNE media won't be able to resist the story, though they will spin it to say that the Confeds had nothing to do with it. It ought to score points with the Consortium nations, though."

"I'm sure it will," Robert O'Hara agreed, "especially since their own colony was also hit."

"You're assuming they'll go public with that." Easley held up a hand in protest. "They've had a hyperprobe from their own people and haven't said a word yet."

"Neither have we. Maybe they're still sitting around talking about it like we are. If we put the word out, maybe that will encourage them to join in."

"Mac… I know that look." O'Hara turned to Charles McGruder. "What's the problem?"

"Military intelligence." McGruder shook his head. "News stories, pictures… that's all stuff that will tell the Confeds how badly they hurt us. But never mind; I'm sure they already have that information from their own sources."

"There'll also be the trials," Easley asserted. "We've got six terrorists and two associated enemy combatants on their way back from Xanadu. We might want to make those trials public. Colonel Bouchard's report says the shuttle crew might spill their guts if we promise not to charge them with capital crimes. Hell, it's up to the JAG's people, but I'd be inclined to drop all charges against those two if they'll tell us everything they know."

"The trials will be recorded." O'Hara frowned. "How much we release will be decided later. The Confeds have always been selective about what news they choose to put out to the public. I think we need to start doing the same. I agree that we need to go public with the story of the attack, but again, let's do it carefully. Put together a package of everything you want to release, and we'll review it.

"Lisa, you've been quiet." He turned to the remaining person in the room. "Is this going to win over the executive committee members who've been dragging their feet on the colony project?"

"No, I don't think so." Lisa Woods shifted uncomfortably in her chair. "All it will do is give them more ammunition to complain about how much the colony is costing, because we have to rebuild stuff that was already built and paid for. There's a significant faction that thinks we ought to abandon everything but the Oceania Protectorate and let the Confeds have the rest of the planet."

"You can't be serious!" Easley stared at Woods. "They're willing to abandon the five thousand colonists already in place?"

"More or less," Woods admitted. "Some of them are saying it's time for the colony to become self-sufficient. They are willing to ship more colonists out there, and to trade with the colony. If the colonists want goods from us, they'll need to produce something that we need in return.

"They're already trading corn, soybeans, and cotton. We are not only paying them for those commodities, but also supplying significant infrastructure support. We've spent a million lunars to build them a hospital, not to mention all we've spent on utilities for the settlement—utilities that took a hit in the recent terror attack.

"We have a commitment to prospective colonists we've already accepted. We've agreed to supply them with a habitat module, agricultural equipment, and a few other things. We've made a contract with those people; we have to deliver according to terms.

"The thought is that we should end that program and not offer incentives like that to future candidates. If someone still wants to emigrate to the colony, they'll have to do it with whatever they can bring with them. The colony can still offer them land, but nothing else."

"Hmmph!" McGruder snorted. "Not going to get many colonists that way. Hey, let us ship you to a distant planet and dump you in the middle of a piece of empty land with nothing but the clothes on your back."

"Oh, we'll get applicants," Easley insisted. "There are always people who are desperate to leave whatever life they have on Earth. We just won't get people with the education or skills the colony needs. We'll have to screen them carefully to figure out if they can survive on Xanadu. After that, all we can do is hope the colonists will help them get started."

"Nothing is decided yet." O'Hara glared at the group. "TerraCorp doesn't determine policy for the Lunar Free State. For something like this, I'm more concerned about how the Directorate feels about it."

"I'm sorry, but that's not good news, either." Woods shook her head. "TerraCorp is heavily represented in the Directorate. In addition, you've got LRI people who are not happy about budget cuts that are affecting their research projects—even the Kitty projects on Xanadu. Hell, there are military members in the Directorate who normally follow Lunar Command's lead but are upset with the Navy and Marine cutbacks.

"Cuts like that get everyone's attention, and it's easy to blame everything on the colony project—with just cause, I might point out. Even excluding the Kitty Protectorate, Xanadu takes a huge piece of the national budget."

"As I am well aware," O'Hara growled. "In case you haven't noticed, I'm the guy who ordered all of those cutbacks."

"Does most of the Directorate feel that way?" Easley frowned. "I can't do my job properly unless I know how public opinion is running, but this is the first I'm hearing of this."

"The Directorate doesn't always reflect the feelings of the average Lunar citizen," Woods cautioned. "It's heavily biased toward the opinions of TerraCorp and the military. TerraCorp is huge, and we have a larger proportion of people in uniform than most Earth nations, but those two still represent only about 30 percent of the population, last time I checked. They hold more than 60 percent of the Directorate, however. Another 20 percent are LRI people."

O'Hara nodded. The Directorate was the only elected body defined by the Lunar Constitution. Its hundred members were chosen by popular vote and served for a term of five years. Each year, twenty seats were up for election, and citizens could vote for anyone they liked—friends, neighbors, even for themselves. With twenty seats available, each citizen got twenty votes and could scatter or consolidate them at will.

No campaigning or political advertising was permitted, though free discussions were allowed on social media and in private gatherings. Voting was done online and was monitored by the AIs, mostly by Mike of TerraNova and Louis of TransLuna station. Military members could also vote via the AIs of whatever battlecruisers were in port on election day.

As Woods had noted, TerraCorp and the LFS military tended to dominate the Directorate, simply because of solidarity in voting. An executive or mid-level manager of TerraCorp looking for a seat would seek support from subordinates, colleagues, and business associates. Through popularity or coercion, he or she could count on votes from throughout the business community. O'Hara suspected that votes from TerraCorp were secured through a lot of Machiavellian maneuvers.

As for the military, word would spread through the ranks that a popular officer or noncom was interested in serving, and people up and down the chain of command would vote accordingly. Unlike TerraCorp, the Navy, Marines, and Corps of Engineers had strict rules forbidding coercion in the voting process.

"The Directorate doesn't make policy, either." McGruder shrugged. "That's all on the chief executive. You're the commander-in-chief of the military and the chairman of TerraCorp's executive committee."

"You're right," O'Hara admitted. "The Directorate doesn't make policy. They aren't a legislative body, so they can't make laws. They do, however, have to approve the budget, without which we can't continue to develop and support the colony."

"That doesn't mean much." Woods flashed the hint of a smile. "The budget is a projection of what you plan to spend based on projected revenue. As long as it balances, you can make it whatever the Directorate wants it to be. The Constitution says you can make whatever changes are necessary in the course of the year, as long as it stays in balance. You have infinite flexibility."

"Right… until the Directorate decides to replace me." O'Hara rolled his eyes. "That's the elephant in the room, the real power that they have."

"They need an 80 percent majority for that," Woods replied. "You'd have to piss off a lot of people for that to happen."

"Yeah?" O'Hara scowled. "So as of today, how many directors feel the colony project should be phased out?"

"I think we're getting close to 50 percent," she admitted, "and 'phased out' isn't exactly the term I'd use for some of them. 'Cut off' is more like what the extremists want. I'm hearing calls to stop all shipment of new colonists completely, and there are some in TerraCorp who say the profit margin on the colony's products is too small to justify continued trade. They're saying we should let the colonists deal with the Confeds if they need anything."

"What?" The question came in a chorus from O'Hara, Easley, and McGruder.

"Who's saying that?" O'Hara's expression darkened.

"I'm not going to name anyone." Woods shook her head. "I heard it second hand from people in the 'phase out' camp, so I can't verify. By the tone of it, though, it would have to be coming from the TerraCorp side. They were also talking about downsizing the naval forces at Xanadu. I don't imagine any of the military people would suggest that."

"All right." O'Hara sat back in his chair with a sigh. "I'll be meeting with the Executive Committee tomorrow. Maybe I can get a feel for the attitudes there."

"Maybe." She shrugged. "I'll be there; I'll let you know if I pick up anything."

"Lisa…" O'Hara hesitated a moment. "How do *you* feel on the subject? The colony, I mean."

"I think we should keep going," she replied without hesitation. "We're in four star systems, but Xanadu is the only one where we have an opportunity to grow our nation. The Kim assassination and the terrorist hit on TransLuna showed us how vulnerable we are with all our eggs in one basket.

"We can't do it on New Eden or Tatanna; both are planet-wide protectorates. Ragnarok has a native human population and is under Akara jurisdiction.

"We've got the Confeds to deal with on Xanadu, and the Consortium, but it's a big planet with plenty of room for everyone. We need to keep pushing forward. If we go for the 'phase out' option, we will lose our connection with the colony. A lot of colonists didn't come from Luna in the first place. If we stop supporting them, they'll have no reason for allegiance to the LFS.

"The cut off option will be worse, especially if we reduce our military forces. I would expect the Confeds to move in and take charge. If they're the ones buying the produce, I'd expect some of the colonists—especially the ones from Earth—to support the takeover.

"I may be in the minority in both TerraCorp and the Directorate, but I think we should continue to support and develop the colony. The real question is whether we can afford to do it."

* * *

Buckingham Palace, London, United Kingdom

"That was an excellent dinner, Your Majesty." Carlton Redwing settled into the comfortable armchair in the queen's private study.

"It was a bloody tedious event." Elizabeth III rolled her eyes. "I'll grant the food was good, but I hate state dinners. Too much diplomatic posturing, too little opportunity for frank discussion of serious matters."

"Like the recent events on Xanadu?" Redwing chuckled. "Looks like one of my naval officers has opened Pandora's Box."

"I hope you've pinned a medal on him." Elizabeth removed her tiara and placed it on the table next to her own chair. "Bloody Confeds needed to have that message delivered. We knew we were getting into a rough game; now they know we are serious players."

"They're denying any responsibility for the attack," he said with a shrug. "Doesn't matter. As you said, they got the message."

"Yes, they're denying it. We should be pleased, because that means they're treating us like they treat the Moonies. In a strange way, it's a sign of respect."

"Your Majesty…" Redwing paused as she held up her hand.

"Elizabeth is my name. We're both heads of state. Don't call me 'Majesty,' and I won't call you 'Mister President.'"

"All right, Elizabeth." Redwing grinned. "Call me Carlton. What I was about to say is that I think it's time we acknowledge what everyone else has already accepted. The 'Consortium' they're talking about is a solid alliance of seven nations, not just an international commercial venture. What's more, it's a mutual defense alliance that involves joint operations by our military forces, like NATO back about a century ago."

"Yes, I suppose you're right. It will make it easier to deal with the Confeds—and the Moonies, for that matter."

"We'll need a sign-off from the other five, but I think they are ready to come out of the shadows. I don't expect any issues from the Commonwealth, so we only need Shin and Yamamoto to agree. You realize that once we go public, we will have to get formal with it, establish an official treaty, and appoint people for diplomatic purposes."

"Not really." Redwing shook his head. "Appoint people, yes, but they'll be surrogates for the seven of us, proceeding at our direction. Their meetings won't be public, and they'll report only to us. They'll provide a diplomatic access point for other nations who want to talk to the alliance directly rather than dealing with us as individual nations.

"We can announce that we have an alliance, but we don't have to publish a formal treaty. The military cooperation agreements are already in place between our individual nations. All we are doing is revealing the reason why those agreements exist."

"I like it." Elizabeth nodded. "So what shall we call our new alliance? I'm not one for clever acronyms."

"Neither am I. Actually, I kind of like the name the media has already given us—the Consortium."

* * *

Nunbola Winter Resort, Chajang-Do, Korea

"This is what happens when CIS launches operations without advising my contacts or seeking our approval." Gerhardt Richter scowled at the gathered members of the Hand. "One side of their operation was a success, the other a disaster. I may have to teach a lesson or two in Amsterdam."

"I presume the 'disaster' you refer to was the stirring up of the Consortium nations." Andre DuMorne raised an eyebrow. "The attack on the Moonies was certainly a success."

"Marginally successful." Mohammed Al Sharif shook his head. "A stupid idea, badly planned and poorly executed. CIS has no idea how to conduct terror attacks. It is an art the Jihad has perfected over several centuries.

"In a population as small as the Moonie colony, you cannot simply send in operatives disguised as colonists. They will be recognized as strangers before they can accomplish their mission. The right way to do it is to insert your true believers into the population well in advance, then activate them when the time comes."

"Hmmph!" Richter snorted. "With the screening the Moonies have in place, the chances of doing that are very small."

"True," Al Sharif admitted. "The Jihad has been trying ever since they started recruiting colonists from Earth. So far, we have not succeeded in getting even one of our people accepted. They're only accepting a small percentage of applicants to begin with.

"Terror strikes presume that the terrorists are expendable. The Jihad most often uses people who are minimally trained and equipped with weapons or destructive devices that require no special skill to use. It is easy to instill fighters with revolutionary zeal; it is much more difficult to train them beyond the very basic level.

"The CNE operation hit several key objectives, but they used up too many expensive assets to do it. From the report Gerhardt provided, it appears that not one of their operatives got out. Those were highly trained special operators who could have been better used in more conventional missions."

"It would seem to be very much in keeping with CNE philosophy." Huang Chang Li favored the others with a hint of a smile. "They spend billions to build powerful and sophisticated warships, crew them with highly trained technicians and military officers, only to throw them at superior Moonie forces in stupidly planned naval operations. Why would we expect them to conduct planetary operations any differently?"

"For that matter, do we care? If the results serve our purpose, let them throw themselves into the fire. I am more concerned about the other side of the operation—the stupid attack on the Consortium. Do any of you doubt that it only served to drive the Consortium nations toward the Moonies?"

"It also forced them to show their teeth." Butos Kimba chuckled. "Who would have thought they would use a kinetic strike right next to their own colony? I'll bet *that* got the CNE's attention. They could as easily have dropped it on the Peacekeeper camp in Eastasia."

"I doubt they would have done that." DuMorne returned the chuckle. "American military commanders tend to be conservative, never wanting to escalate a situation. Besides, they were heavily outmatched by the Confed naval force on the scene."

"The Moonies would have backed them in a heartbeat," Richter insisted. "The CIS report says they moved their own ships over the Consortium site to help the Americans target the Confed force. As I said, the CNE has done much to drive the Consortium into the arms of the Moonies... exactly what we did not want to happen.

"My contacts are trying to locate the person or persons in CNE High Command who conceived this stupid action. Had they only attacked the Moonies, we could have shrugged it off. As much as they fumbled that side of it, the result still served our purposes. The

Consortium attack did not, however. I believe we need to make an example of those who ordered it."

"Fine." Al Sharif, the acting chairman for the meeting, waved a hand in dismissal. "I assume you will keep us advised. I am more interested in the major operation the CNE is planning for Ragnarok."

"That operation is already under way," Richter replied. "The forces involved have departed already. They should be arriving in the Odin System in about three weeks. At that point, I believe the Moonies are going to get a most unpleasant surprise."

* * *

Board Room, Terra Corporation, TerraNova City, Luna

"Obviously a major security failure on Admiral Greenwood's part." Roger Stuart scowled as he studied the report on his pad. "I presume you are taking appropriate action, Admiral."

"The matter is under investigation." Robert O'Hara glared across the table at Stuart. The other members of TerraCorp's Executive Committee wore neutral expressions. "Greenwood had neither the authority nor the resources to prevent what happened. This was a new tactic for the CNE. We had no reason to expect an attack of this nature."

"She has a whole fleet of warships and a bunch of Marines." Stuart waved a hand in dismissal. "All of them were sitting on their asses doing nothing when it happened. At the very least, she needs to be relieved of command."

"With the fleet reductions, you have lots of competent officers sitting around with nothing to do. You could send your son out to relieve her." Stuart's scowl became a smirk. "When she gets back, you can conduct a proper inquiry and a court martial."

There was silence around the table. O'Hara scanned the faces of the committee, noting the shocked looks on a few faces. Others remained impassive, but several nodded in agreement with Stuart.

"You know, Roger," he said at last, "I might take your comments on military matters seriously if you had ever spent any time in uniform. As it is, however, I'm going to say this once: keep your uninformed and unsolicited opinions to yourself, or it might be *you* who gets removed from your position.

"I am perfectly satisfied with Admiral Greenwood's performance to date. I'm upset mostly because I'm the one who had to reduce our planetside force to a single battalion of Marines. Even with electronic surveillance aids, that's not enough to secure the borders of the colony against this kind of penetration attack.

"I don't think we'll see attacks like this again. As best we can determine, we captured or killed every one of the infiltrators—thanks, I might point out, to prompt and proper action by Admiral Greenwood, the Marines, and the local militia."

"Well, Admiral, that brings us to another point." Isaac Miller glanced at Stuart, then turned to address O'Hara. "At the conclusion of the action, Greenwood sent the Marines to seize the Confed research station in Eurasia. That facility had been used in the past to support attacks against us. Why was it still being allowed to operate?"

"You are getting into diplomatic territory, not military," O'Hara replied. "We have been trying to maintain an attitude of peaceful coexistence with the Confeds on Xanadu. Diplomatic Corps felt that would best be served by allowing what was supposed to be a scientific research facility to operate there.

"Greenwood, in her role as governor of the colony, had been directed to leave that station alone. Apparently, after the last incursion, she decided—in her other capacity as military commander—that security concerns outweighed any diplomatic repercussions. Under the circumstances, I believe she was right and am prepared to endorse the action."

"Hmmm… diplomatic concerns." Miller stroked his chin. "Maybe it's Admiral Easley we ought to be questioning."

"This is *not* a meeting of the Directorate," O'Hara snarled. "This is the TerraCorp Executive Committee. We are here to discuss the impact of the attack on the development of the colony. Put your military and diplomatic concerns back in your pockets and concentrate on the issue at hand."

Scowling, he looked at each of them in turn. Miller and Stuart had reddened—most likely with anger, not embarrassment. Both of them were elected members of the Directorate as well as TerraCorp's Executive Committee. *I really shouldn't be pissing them off,* he thought. *They're among the people that can relieve me of command.*

Other members wore looks of studied disinterest. A few appeared to support Miller and Stuart.

Still not sure where they stand on the colony project, he thought. *I need to get them talking about it.* He looked at the report on his pad once again, drew a deep breath, and faced the group.

"Damage reports are preliminary, but it appears that the water tower and communications facility will need to be completely rebuilt. It will have to be done as soon as possible because these are critical parts of the colony's infrastructure. We don't have any hard numbers yet, but we can safely assume damage of a half million lunars or more.

The grain storage facility is a lesser consideration, since it was only partially damaged and is still functional at reduced capacity.

"This committee has only two questions to answer: What does TerraCorp need to do to expedite those repairs, and what will be the financial impact on the colony project? Discussion will be limited to those two items. We'll start with the first one."

Hopefully, I can get them into a mindset that the repairs are necessary, that we can't abandon the colony, he thought. *Then we can start looking for ways to fund the repairs, not give up and walk away.*

* * * * *

Chapter Sixteen

17 September 2123
LFS *Sorceress,* in Tatanna Orbit

"It looks like our adventures produced very little stir on Luna." Peter Yoric studied the report on his screen. "Confeds attempt to penetrate the system, we stop them... well done. The fact that we destroyed two CNE warships doesn't seem to have upset anyone."

"I can understand that, Admiral." Emily Bernard shrugged. "We took no damage in the encounter. By contrast, what happened on Xanadu is much more disturbing."

"Yeah... I don't envy Greenwood having to deal with that one. It's one thing for enemy warships to challenge us in space; when they attack civilians on the ground, the people we're supposed to protect, that takes it to a different level. Imagine how we'd feel if the Bugs hit King's City."

"At least we would see the Bugs coming," she replied. "I am accustomed to exchanging missile fire with an enemy who fights with honor, not worrying about terrorists murdering pregnant women civilians."

"Yeah, that was an atrocity, even by Peacekeeper standards," Yoric said with a sigh. "I'm not sure I could have exercised as much restraint as Greenwood did. If I'd been in charge, we might already be at war with the CNE."

"Lunar Command is focused on Xanadu, but they've decided that we're still needed in this system, if only to counter a potential incursion by the Bugs and more penetration attempts by the CNE. Fleet pullbacks are pretty much over, and we're still here. I guess we should count ourselves lucky."

* * *

Castle Boroson, King's City, Planet Tatanna

"Mr. Castelli does not appear at all comfortable." Sir Kenneth Bentley chuckled. "He looks rather like an errant schoolboy called up in front of the headmaster."

"He assumed his majesty was not aware of the CNE's latest attempt to bring warships into the system." Harold Wilkerson smiled. "The king has advised him to the contrary.

"To Arne, we are the protectors who drove the Bugs out and have kept them from returning. We returned Tatanna to the native humans after more than a century of Bug occupation. We've also convinced him that we need to limit the import of technology so as not to destroy his planet's culture.

"Before you people arrived, the Confeds made several attempts to smuggle advanced weaponry onto the planet and deliver it to certain elements who are not friends of the Crown. They also tried to introduce addictive drugs into the city, and they've sent military forces to challenge us on several occasions. Now they've done it again.

"Arne has informed Mr. Castelli that the CNE is fortunate he hasn't shut down their trade mission and sent their diplomatic people packing. If they attempt to violate his sovereignty one more time, he will do exactly that."

"I see." Bentley nodded. "The Consortium understands the restrictions. Copper was a bit of a surprise, but it makes sense. The last thing we want to do is disrupt the planet's economy. We were a bit concerned that you might take issue with our arrival in company with *Prince of Wales*, in view of your ban on CNE warships, but now that also makes sense."

Bentley had arrived as the British ambassador to Tatanna, but recent news from the Sol System included an announcement that the seven-nation Consortium was officially a formal alliance. At that point, Bentley had requested a special audience with King Arne to advise that he represented not only England, but also the Consortium, and to ask the Crown to accept his new credentials.

Arne had immediately summoned Wilkerson to obtain the LFS view on the subject. With Wilkerson's endorsement and assurances that the Consortium would play by his royal rules, the king had accepted Bentley's new role and used it as an excuse to declare a royal banquet—tonight's event, and the occasion for the CNE ambassador's distress.

"Actually, I believe Arne used your newly defined presence to drive the point home." Wilkerson favored Bentley with a wry grin. "With you people here, the CNE will no longer be the sole source of those Earth-manufactured goods Tatannans are rapidly becoming so fond of.

"I should warn you, however, the Confeds have been practically giving those products away to gain access to Tatanna's markets. They can't be making a profit at the prices they are charging in the local currency. I suspect that they are simply using the income to defray their embassy expenses, spending it on whatever goods and services they are purchasing locally. You won't find an exchange rate for Tatannan crowns on any of Earth's financial markets."

"Actually, that's not a bad idea," Bentley mused. "We might want to do something like that, to give the bloody Confeds a run for their money."

* * *

LFS *Sorceress,* in Tatanna Orbit

"Come in, Emily." Yoric waved Bernard to a chair in front of his desk. "We need to talk."

Bernard had been surprised at the summons. She regularly met with her admiral in his day cabin, but those meetings usually took place in the morning and involved members of his staff. To be called for a private meeting at 1900 hours was unusual. She still felt a strong attraction to Yoric; to be alone with him in the evening, especially so close to his sleeping cabin, was distressing.

In fairness, he had never given her any reason to believe the attraction was mutual. Since his arrival in system, he had shown her nothing but the proper professional respect of a superior toward his immediate subordinate.

Face it, Emily, she told herself, *you're not worried about him making a move on you. It's your own misbehaving hormones that are making you nervous.*

"You wanted to see me, sir?" To her surprise, her voice sounded cool and professional.

"Yes. I got a reply from Fleet to a query I sent last month. I've been trying to figure out what to do with it. Since it involves you personally, I decided to call you in and talk about it."

"A query?" Bernard blinked.

"Yes. You've been recommending Rochford for promotion to commodore. That would put us over establishment, and we'd lose him. You've also submitted recommendations for promotions down the line to move people up accordingly."

"I didn't start the process." Emily shook her head. "Commodore Corbett and Admiral Ling had been recommending him before I got here. After reviewing his record and observing his performance, I agreed with their assessment. He is long overdue for it.

"He should have moved up when Corbett retired. I expected there might be some resentment when I showed up, but he welcomed me aboard and has been nothing but professional. He's had time-in-grade for promotion for a long time. In length of service, he actually has ten years more than I have."

"You don't have to sell me." Yoric chuckled. "I signed off on your recommendation. The problem is, it's a flag officer promotion. There has to be a slot available—squadron command or flag captain for a battle group. With the current reductions in force, those slots are harder to come by than usual. Fleet tells me one has now come available. Nathan Nguyen is retiring. Do you know him?"

"Yes, of course. *Amazon's* captain, Admiral McGruder's flagship."

"Right. He's got well over thirty years in service and a stellar record. He'd be in line for a second star, but with the fleet cutbacks, it isn't likely they'll be making any more rear admirals for a while, so he decided to pull the plug. *Amazon's* XO is new to the post, promoted to commander last year, so he's not eligible to move up.

"They looked at Rochford, but McGruder nixed it. His main concern is that Rock came up through the tactical track, with a fine record, but he's never had a command of his own. He's been the XO on almost every class of warship and has a fine record with nothing but outstanding performance reviews, but he's never been in the hotseat. I guess Mac thinks the fleet's flagship is not the place to start.

"He did suggest a solution, however. Do you think Rock is ready for a battlecruiser command on a ship where he's already established himself as the XO and has a proven record?"

"Yes… but what ship would that be?" Bernard shot him a sharp glance. "*Sorceress* is the only battlecruiser in which he has served."

"Right." Yoric nodded.

"But…" Bernard's jaw dropped. She blinked several times, tried to speak, but the words would not come. *Putain de merde!* she thought. *Am I being relieved of command?*

"Relax." Yoric shook his head with a smile. "Nothing's going to happen. McGruder suggested that if I was so sure Rock was ready for battlecruiser command, I should put my money where my mouth is and give him *my* flagship. In return, he said he would be more than happy if I sent *you* to take command of *Amazon*.

"Apparently, you have the qualifications he's looking for. You had a heavy cruiser in the Bug War under his flag, so he's seen you in action. He's also impressed with the way you performed when Ling got taken out and dumped the whole battle group into your lap.

"Don't worry. No orders have been cut. I think Mac was busting my chops, knowing I wouldn't want to give up my flag captain. In case I haven't mentioned it, I've been happy with the way you're running *Sorceress*. You've only been here a few months longer than I have, but you've taken command. You've been in battle, dealt with damage, and gotten her back to 100 percent in short order. The crew respects you; you work well with my staff—no complaints on my end at all."

"Thank you, sir." Bernard felt her face reddening with embarrassment over the lavish praise. She did not feel she had done anything out of the ordinary, had simply done her duty as required. Besides, praise from *him* was… disturbing. A sudden thought occurred to her, but she said nothing, pausing to work it over in her head.

"Admiral," she said at last, "do you think Admiral McGruder was serious about the offer?"

"Huh?" He looked at her sharply. "Mac doesn't joke about stuff like that. I don't think he expected me to accept the challenge, but he was still looking for a qualified flag captain as of fifteen days ago, when the hyperprobe left Luna.

"Why?" His gaze narrowed and a frown formed on his face. "Would you be interested in the position? It's not a promotion; all you'd get is the prestige of being flag captain for the commanding admiral of the combined fleets.

"You'd be a newcomer in an already established battle order. You'd have to earn the respect of a new crew again, with a new admiral looking over your shoulder. Is there some reason you want to leave *Sorceress* behind?"

"No," she insisted. "I am happy here, and I don't want to leave, but it appears it may be the only way to get a good officer the promotion he deserves. Rochford should have had a command of his own *years* ago. His only problem was that every time he came up for promotion, no command slots were available, but somebody needed an XO at the next level up.

"*Sorceress* would be a perfect fit for him; he already knows the ship and has the respect of the crew. From XO to captain is a normal and expected progression. No one within the group would question his qualifications.

"I don't mind adapting to a new ship and crew, or a new admiral." She shrugged. "I did that a few months ago when I arrived. I adapted to a new admiral again when you came aboard. It would be harder to transfer out if I had been here for years, but I haven't been with *Sorceress* for even a year yet. By contrast, Rochford has been her exec for more than five years."

She tried to sound casual despite the nervous flutter in her stomach. In truth, she loved her current command. She would be sorry to leave *Sorceress* behind, but this might be her only way to get out of an uncomfortable situation without damage to her career. She mentally slapped herself for letting it get to this point. *You're a naval officer in command of a Lunar Free State warship; you're not a lovesick schoolgirl. You ought to be able to control your feelings, put them aside, and do your job.*

She had been doing exactly that for over twenty years. She'd had only one experience as a teenager with what she believed to be love. It had ended very badly for her, and she'd sworn it would never happen again. She had buried her feelings beneath a cold, professional exterior, easily brushing aside any man who happened to notice that she was a very attractive woman. She'd become very adept at handling such things, deflecting males without bruising their tender egos.

Then Yoric had arrived, and the tables had turned. This time, it was she who was attracted to him. It was he who took no notice of her beauty, who saw her only as the professional officer she had worked so hard to become. Suddenly, she realized what she had been missing all along, something that she couldn't have now without throwing her career away.

She had never run away from a challenge before, but she wanted very much to escape from this one.

"Emily…" He had been silent for a few moments, but now he sat up and spoke again. "Do you have a problem with me? I think we've worked well together, but sometimes you seem very reserved, like you're holding something back. If I'm the problem, I need you to tell me."

"No, sir, not at all." She felt her face reddening again. For a moment, she was tempted to tell him the truth, but this time her emotional armor served her well. "It has been a pleasure serving under your command these past months. I will regret leaving, but it seems to be the best solution for all concerned.

"Admiral McGruder gets his flag captain, Rochford gets a well-deserved promotion, and you get a replacement who is not only competent but well respected by the crew, and well known to the other captains in the group."

He was silent for another moment, then leaned back with a sigh. "I can't argue with the logic," he admitted. "If you're really okay with it, I'll fire off a hyperprobe to Luna tomorrow, telling Mac we'll take him up on it. It may not happen; he may have already found a replacement for Nguyen.

"If not, though, we're committed. The next return message from Luna might have promotion orders for Rochford and transfer orders for you. If you change your mind, tell me before I send that probe."

"I understand." She nodded. "I will continue to serve until we hear back from Luna. If those orders do not come, I am content with my present assignment. I will have made the offer and will be satisfied with the decision. It is all subject to the needs of the service, as they say."

She felt a small wave of relief. *I am committed. I hope those orders come through, but if they don't, I will be no worse off than I am now.*

* * *

17 September 2123

LFS *Amazon*, **Lunar Fleet Anchorage**

"Nguyen has agreed to stay on for another three months." McGruder shrugged. "Under the circumstances, I'm not going to rush the process. This is 1st Fleet, 1st Battle Group. I want my flag captain to be the best of the best."

"I understand." Robert O'Hara nodded. "Especially since you're one of only two active battle groups on station. I would think that would give you a good pool of officers to choose from, however."

"Not so." McGruder shook his head. "We've kept the command teams active for all ships in port. For most of them, that means we have a captain, an exec, and a chief engineer watching over a skeleton maintenance crew on an empty ship. From their standpoint, that's still better than being on half pay, and none of them are looking for a new assignment. Promotions are on hold, except under special circumstances.

"I could be looking for a qualified commander to promote to commodore for the spot, but most of those are holding down a captain's slot on a cruiser. I could pull another group's flag captain, but I'd be passing my problem to somebody else. Hell, I'd grab Eurasia Brown in a heartbeat, but that would leave John holding the bag with *Isis*. Her exec just retired with thirty-five years of service."

O'Hara said nothing. The two of them were having coffee in McGruder's day cabin aboard *Amazon*; it was O'Hara's first visit to the anchorage since he had announced the draconian cutbacks to the active fleet.

"We've lost a lot of senior people," McGruder said at last. "People who would have stayed if they saw any future in it. Some of them were on the list for promotion, but we're not doing promotions. We offered them half pay for an unspecified period, when they can get three-quarters pay in retirement, and benefits for life, with inflation adjustments as appropriate. We're going to miss them if the shit hits the fan."

"I know. I see the reports every day." O'Hara held up a hand in protest. "Do you think I wanted this, Mac? The Xanadu project has sucked the life out of the budget—everything we've done there has cost more than expected. Per the Lunar Constitution, we're not allowed to issue bonds or borrow money. Balanced budget, that's what it says. Seemed like a good idea at the time, but now it's hurting us."

"While I hate to contradict my nation's chief executive, it's not the colony project that's killing us," McGruder replied. "It's the way we're going about it. We let the Confeds goad us into a race, when all we had to do was stake out a few million hectares, hoist our flag, and bring in a few colonists to start off. We might have a few hundred families there today, instead of a few thousand, but we could afford to support them, get them started on the road to self-sufficiency. When they were firmly established, we could have brought in a few more.

"Do we really give a shit what the Confeds are doing in Eastasia? They're not going to take over the planet as long as we control the orbitals, and a few hundred colonists would be a hell of a lot easier to protect than the thousands we have."

"You're right," O'Hara admitted. "We should have taken it more slowly. We relied on projections that were too optimistic—projections for how much the colony would cost, for revenues from TerraCorp, for how quickly the colony would become self-sufficient. I'm still trying to understand how every one of those projections could have been off by as much as they were.

"Part of the problem is that I'm a naval officer who somehow got to be CEO. I don't know enough about business and finance. Given that TerraCorp is the primary source of the revenue we use to run the nation, I should have been looking for somebody who was an expert on the subject to serve on my staff and advise me.

"I wish I'd found Lisa Woods a lot earlier. TerraCorp is a nest of snakes, but she's one of the few over there willing to put the nation's interests ahead of her own. Now, all she can do is tell me about the mistakes I've already made."

They sat in silence for a few moments, then O'Hara shrugged.

"Water under the bridge," he said. "We've put the brakes on the colony. We'll do what we can to support them, and we'll send out colonists that are already in the queue. We'll maintain Greenwood's group in place to keep order over there, but that's it.

"We'll also push them harder to be self-sufficient. If they want something extra from Luna, they're going to have to pay for it, which means they'll need to be producing goods Earth and Luna want to buy. In the long run, it's for their own good.

"I've got to be going, Mac." He stood up. "I want to stop by *Isis* and see John before I go down to Luna. That's going to be a bit awkward; he hasn't come down for dinner with us since we decommissioned his group. He's seriously pissed about the cutbacks."

"I'm not surprised." McGruder nodded. "I've got three other battle group flag officers who feel the same way, not to mention a whole bunch of cruiser and destroyer captains."

* * *

17 September 2123
Community Meeting Hall, LFS Colony, Xanadu

"All right, people, I'm here at your invitation." Lorna sat at the front table, flanked by colony administrator Todd Taylor and Darius Jefferson, the council's elected chairman.

"Barring conflicts with naval operations, I'll try to make all of your regular council meetings and address any concerns you have. Anyway, here I am. Take your best shots."

"Uh... Madam Governor?" Justin Gerard's hand was the first to go up.

"Just 'Governor' or 'Admiral' will do." Lorna chuckled. "Let's not get too formal. You've got the floor, Mr. Gerard."

"Uh, okay, Governor." Gerard did not return the smile. "Am I reading this bulletin from the Commission right? We've got to fix the damage the terrorists did by ourselves, with no help from Luna? They were supposed to protect us from stuff like that. They failed, and now we've gotta pay the price. That's not fair, in my book."

"No, that's not the way I read it." Lorna raised her hand to stop the rumble of assent that had arisen. "You're *not* totally on your own. They will be sending materials and equipment, replacements for stuff that was damaged that can't be found or fabricated here. Mr. Taylor has already conducted a preliminary survey and made a list of the most critical items we need. I've read and approved that list and sent it on to Luna.

"You will, however, have to salvage as much as possible from the wreckage. To that end, I've put out a call for Navy and Marine volunteers to help you. For that, Major Jefferson will coordinate with Colonel Bouchard."

She glanced at Taylor on her left and Jefferson on her right. Both nodded in confirmation.

"What Luna is *not* going to do is send teams and equipment from the Corps of Engineers to help you rebuild the water tower, the uplink array, or the grain storage silo," she told them. "As governor, there's nothing I can do about that; however, as the senior officer in charge of Navy and Marine forces, I'll provide whatever assistance I can.

"I've got shipboard engineers who can figure out the technical issues, the Marines have got some heavy equipment, and we should be able to find some able bodies with basic construction skills. Again, I'll leave it to Mr. Taylor and Major Jefferson to coordinate with Commander Guerrero, my chief of staff aboard *Valkyrie*, and Colonel Bouchard. Does that answer your question, Mr. Gerard?"

"Uh… yes, ma'am. Thank you, ma'am." Gerard blinked and sat down without further question.

"Anything else?" Lorna scanned the group once again.

"Uh… ma'am?" Sarah Peabody got to her feet. Lorna nodded to her. "What about security? What can we do to prevent future attacks?"

"That's a valid question." Lorna sat back with a sigh. "Mr. Gerard is right. We—the Navy and Marines—dropped the ball. We didn't expect an attack of that type, with small numbers of infiltrators disguised as colonists. Fortunately, it's the kind of tactic that is likely to work only once. From now on, everyone is going to be on the lookout for suspicious strangers.

"We don't need to rely solely on citizen reports. Now that they know what to look for, the Kitties can spot a terrorist in a heartbeat. The Marines will be conducting regular patrols with one of our feline friends riding shotgun. As Major Jefferson can tell you, they're also good at neutralizing a threat once they've spotted it.

"We've also taken out that Confed research station. If they're going to attack us again, they'll need to fly their troops in from Eastasia. We'll be watching for that from orbit. I've already advised the senior Confed officer that any overflights will be considered hostile.

"Unless any of you have additional suggestions, I think that covers it. Anyone?"

She scanned the room again, but no one spoke.

The attacks had produced another development she hadn't mentioned. In her last meeting with Bouchard and Yellow Eyes, the Kitty warrior had suggested that perhaps the Marines needed more of his kind to supplement their ranks. They had already found several more Marines who had the ability to communicate with the cats on a basic level, and Bouchard had supported the expansion of the program.

On his next trip back to Valley of Clouds in Oceania, Yellow Eyes would broach the idea with Storm Shadow, the chief of his tribe. If the chief agreed, they would seek volunteers among the young, unmated Kitty warriors. Ultimately, they hoped to find enough Marine "communicators" and enough cats to assign one to each platoon.

Doctor Kim is always concerned about our impact on Kitty society, Lorna thought. *I wonder if she ever considered the impact they might have on us.*

* * * * *

Chapter Seventeen

17 September 2123

LFS *Apache*, in Ragnarok Orbit

"Sir, we're getting a message from *Far Horizon*." Commander Gerald Tremaine sat up in his bunk and blinked the sleep from his eyes. "Mining Site Three is under attack by an unknown force, presumably rebels. The mine security team is calling for help."

A glance at the chrono display on his desk screen showed the time: 0340 hours, Lunar. The urgent call window showed the face of Ensign Baker, *Apache's* most junior officer. Baker had the bridge watch tonight.

"Alert Lieutenant Dooley." Tremaine got up and reached for his uniform tunic. "Tell him to get his Marines ready for a possible full platoon drop. I'll be on my way to the bridge."

"Yes, sir." Baker's voice held a nervous tremor. "Shall I go to Condition Red?"

"No, Baker," Tremaine replied calmly. *Kid's fresh out of the academy, hasn't seen any real action.* "The ship's not going into battle. No need to wake everybody up."

* * *

"It was over before we got here, sir." Marine Lieutenant Mark Dooley's face filled one of the screens in front of Tremaine's command chair. "The mine lost two people who were in the office when they got hit. Could have been worse, but the security force never engaged the hostiles, just covered the evacuation of the mine crew from the bunkhouse.

"The bad guys didn't hit the night crew in the pit or at the wash plant. They hit the office and cleaned out the gold locker. Looks like they didn't want to shut the mine down; they wanted the gold. Mine boss says they got somewhere in excess of four hundred troy ounces.

"Security chief says he never got a good look at them, but he estimates a platoon-sized attack force, and they had automatic weapons."

"In other words, weapons imported from Earth." Tremaine grimaced.

"Definitely, sir. We found a bunch of shell casings at the office where they killed the night supervisor and the security guy on watch." Dooley held a brass case up to the camera. "7.62 by 39 millimeter Russian."

"Same stuff the Confeds were supplying to the rebels?"

"Same stuff they were trying to supply to both sides, sir. Major Roberts told us Isis Company intercepted a shipment intended for the Wans, but Admiral O'Hara gave it to them to maintain parity between them and the rebels."

"Right." Tremaine nodded. "So that means we really don't know who the attackers are. They could have been rebels, or they could have been Wan troops."

"Yes, sir." Dooley nodded. "Security chief says he got a look at some of them from a distance, says they were wearing 'green pajamas.' That's typical of the rebels but doesn't prove it was them."

"For what it's worth, Dooley, we're scanning the surrounding area with everything we've got up here." Tremaine sat back in his command chair with a sigh. "No joy so far, but the forest canopy is hard to penetrate. They may still be out there."

"We have a drone up." The young Marine shook his head. "We haven't seen anything, either."

"Fine. Stay down there and do what you can to secure the place. Plan to be there for a few days. If you need supplies or gear, let us know, and we'll drop it to you."

"Roger that, sir. Will do."

* * *

Twenty minutes after breaking the connection, Tremaine was still in his command chair on *Apache's* bridge. *What the hell am I going to do?* he wondered. *I can't send Dooley out to look for them, a single platoon against an enemy force of unknown size and capability.* That platoon represented almost a third of the Marine force at his disposal, with only the platoons from *Norseman* and *Chimera* remaining, plus the single squad carried by the destroyer *Redhawk*. Besides, *Chimera's* platoon was currently assigned to cover the diplomatic team dealing with the Wan government in Three River City.

Given what's going on, we need a whole damned division of Marines in this system, or at minimum an assault transport with a battalion and the support systems to back them up.

Wishing for a battalion wasn't going to help. He checked the chrono display: 0940 hours, well into first watch. He punched an icon on his console, and a moment later was looking at the face of Lieutenant Commander Thomas Wilford, his chief engineer.

"Tom, we're going to need a hyperprobe for Luna. No rush. I still need to put together a report to send. Figure a launch for 1600 today."

"Roger that, Skipper." Wilford nodded. "We'll get it prepped this morning. Give us the word when you're ready to send it."

Turning the watch over to his tactical officer, Tremaine headed for the wardroom to get some breakfast. He'd been up for six hours; his brain was telling him it ought to be lunchtime.

He had just reached the wardroom when his pad chimed. He looked at the screen and found a text message advising of a hyper signature detected—multiple ships inbound on a bearing consistent with a passage from the Sol System. *Redhawk* was on picket duty at the hyper limit and had jumped to intercept.

Tremaine shrugged. With three different groups mining gold on Ragnarok, commercial system traffic had increased significantly. The destroyer would identify the newcomers and report via FTL comm ASAP. He sat down at the table and gave the attending steward his breakfast order.

He had almost finished eating when his pad chimed again, this time with an urgent tone indicating a priority call from the bridge. He accepted the call and found himself looking at the strained image of Jake Polanski, the tactical officer he'd left in charge a half hour earlier.

"Sir, we've got the FTL from *Redhawk*." Polanski didn't waste time on a greeting. "Confed warships incoming. They make it two battlecruisers, four heavy cruisers, and eleven lighter units, escorting what look like a pair of military transports. Inbound for Ragnarok, ETA twenty-three hours."

Tremaine said nothing for a few seconds. *Twenty-three hours. Take your time, think it through,* he told himself. *Figure out what you need to do. Wait for the full report.* With Ragnarok's current orbital position, the light-speed message from *Redhawk* should arrive in a little over an hour. Meanwhile, there were a few things he could do.

"Bring us to Condition Blue, just to wake everybody up," he ordered. "Pass the word—officer's call in the wardroom in two hours. Oh... and tell Commander Wilford we're going to need that hyperprobe sooner than expected."

* * *

LFS *Redhawk*, Near the Odin Hyper Limit

"They're ignoring us, ma'am." Lieutenant Aaron Bernstein turned to his captain with a look of disbelief. "They're not even scanning us with active systems."

"They don't consider us a threat." Lieutenant Commander Erica Talbot's lips compressed in a thin imitation of a smile. "Would you, if you were in their position?"

"Well, no, ma'am," Bernstein admitted. "I would think they'd hit us with targeting, though, to warn us off."

"That's our doctrine," she replied. "Who knows how Confeds think? They didn't ignore us completely; they responded to IFF."

"Hmmph!" he snorted. "Only the big boys did." He checked his display. "Battlecruisers *Vienna* and *Buenos Aires*, heavy cruisers *Krieger* and *Guerriera*, plus two light cruisers, four destroyers, and those big transports. Sure, they answered when we pinged 'em, but they're cruising in like they own the system."

Talbot only nodded. *With that force against what we and the Lizards have, 'owning the system' is probably what they have in mind. I wonder how the Americans will react.*

* * *

USS *Atlanta*, in Ragnarok Orbit

"What the fuck?"

"Mr. Culver…" Captain George Carlisle glared at his communications officer. "Whiskey Tango Foxtrot is not a proper report. What have you got?"

"Sir, it's a… I don't know, I guess you'd call it a 'heads-up' message from the Moonies." Culver shook his head. "I'm putting it on your screen."

Carlisle's eyebrows rose as he studied the message.

"What the fuck?" he muttered, not realizing he had echoed Culver's reaction. "Two battlecruisers? Has war been declared or something?"

He looked up and turned to Culver again. "Get me a line to the Moonies. I want to talk to Captain Tremaine on *Apache*."

* * *

LFS *Apache*

"I have no idea what's going to happen." Tremaine shrugged. "It depends on what the Confeds do. If they come in shooting, I will have to abandon the orbitals."

"Do you really think they will?" On Tremaine's screen, the American captain gave him a skeptical look. "That would be an open act of war."

"They commit acts of war against us all the time." Tremaine shook his head. "There are battles with ships lost on both sides. Those battles take place in distant star systems like this one, so Earth never sees them. We protest, and the Confeds deny the battle ever happened. Why should this one be any different?"

"Well, for one thing, this time there will be witnesses," Carlisle replied. "We're here, and the Akara have a significant presence in the system."

"The Akara have seen it before, but they have no desire to get between us and the Confeds. If you ask them what happened, all you'll get is 'no comment.' As for your people, have you considered that you might also be on their target list?"

"I've sent off a hyperprobe to Luna. If my ships don't make it out, I'm pretty sure my people will show up in force to kick ass and take names; however, that probe will take twenty days to reach Luna. Whatever's going to happen will be over long before that."

"I take it you're suggesting I do the same." Carlisle's smile had very little humor in it. "Send out a hyperprobe, that is. You people have much more experience dealing with the Confeds than we have. Anything else you'd like to suggest?"

"They've taken no action against our picket destroyer, but that might be them not wanting to show their hand too soon." Tremaine returned the grim smile. "My orders say I'm supposed to stop all Confed warships from entering the system, but I don't have anywhere near the force to do that."

"They don't need to fire a shot. If they choose to come in and take up orbit, I can't stop them. If it looks like they're going to attack, I'm going to pull out and head for the hyper limit.

"We've got mines down there that came under attack today—rebels, government troops, or bandits, I have no way of knowing who they were, but they took a bunch of gold and faded back into the boondocks. I can take action to protect against raids like that, but I don't have adequate resources to defend the mines against the Confeds.

"The Consortium's relations with the CNE are not as strained as ours. They're less likely to attack you, but with the Confeds… well, who knows. I can't tell you what to do, but my advice is to keep your defenses up, your weapons hot, and your drive online."

* * *

CNS *Buenos Aires,* Approaching Ragnarok Orbit

"The Moonies are hitting us with active scans, Admiral." Captain Victor Perez studied the tactical plot on the screen in front of him. "Should we not respond in kind?"

"No, Victor," Rear Admiral Enrique Aguilar replied with a chuckle. "Make no response at all. We'll take up orbit as if we have every right to be here. Are we getting any protests from the Lizards?"

"No, sir. It appears they've withdrawn everything from orbit and retreated to the L5 point. They only have two small patrol ships and a large vessel that appears to be a mining support ship."

"What about the other two, the 'mystery ships' we didn't expect to find?"

"They have answered IFF, sir. Curiously enough, they are American warships—the heavy cruiser *Atlanta* and a destroyer. They haven't left orbit but are not taking any action. Do you want me to hail them?"

"No. We don't need anything from them, and they aren't interfering with us. Get us inserted into orbit within a hundred kilometers or so of the Moonies. Once that's accomplished, you can advise *Baltic Sea* and *Persian Gulf* to begin landing operations."

* * *

LFS *Apache*

"Sir, it's a friggin' invasion," Baker exclaimed. "Aren't we gonna do anything?"

"What exactly do you suggest we do, Ensign?" Tremaine shook his head at the young officer's obvious frustration. "Take on two battlecruisers plus an assortment of cruisers and destroyers? Go out in a blaze of glory? For what?

"They aren't attacking our mining sites; they haven't so much as run targeting scans on us. Their 'invasion' has so far consisted of landing a lot of troops and equipment on the surface, but they've landed right next to their own mining site, almost two hundred and fifty klicks from the city.

"They aren't interfering with our diplomatic efforts with the Wans. I've given Commander Steel a heads-up about it, but for now, there is no reason to take action.

"I've also sent word to Heart of System Operations, since this 'invasion' is a violation of territory under Akara jurisdiction. The answer I got back was that they are aware of it, and no, the Confeds do not have their permission to be there. They've sent off a message to their homeworld, but they're not going to do anything more."

To Tremaine's surprise—and relief—the Confed force had taken absolutely no notice of *Apache* and her consorts. They had not reacted to scans, nor to the many hails directed at them, but had simply taken up orbit eighty kilometers away, almost directly over the newly established Confed mining site.

The remainder of the day had passed with no sign of further activity, and Tremaine had reduced his force's alert level to Yellow. With an enemy force that close, he wasn't about to go to his normal anchor watch, or even to Condition Blue, the lowest level of readiness. At

Yellow, his defenses remained up, and *Apache* could be moving within seconds.

Not that it will help if they decide to take us out with beam weapons, he thought. A graser broadside from one of those battlecruisers could wipe his ship out with no warning. His only concession to that threat had been to position *Norseman* and *Chimera* directly behind *Apache* relative to the Confed force, using his own ship as a shield to protect the other two. The Confeds could have defeated that maneuver by stacking their own force vertically, but they hadn't bothered. Tremaine had ordered *Redhawk* to stand off well beyond missile range, with orders to run for the limit and hyper out if the Confeds attacked.

This morning, the two Confed transports had begun making drops on the planet. Waves of small craft had gone down, all to the same site—the Confed gold mine. Orbital observation showed heavy equipment in use, clearing a large section of forest. By mid-afternoon, their intentions were obvious: they were building a permanent military base, and there wasn't a damned thing Tremaine could do about it.

Baker was seeing the Confed activity for the first time. Tremaine turned his attention to the young officer once again.

"Lesson they should have taught you at the academy, Ensign. Sometimes the best action to take is no action at all. I am, however, preparing another hyperprobe to send off to Luna."

* * *

USS *Atlanta*

"Sir, the Moonies have launched another hyperprobe. It's headed straight out for the limit, on the direct line to Sol."

"No surprise there. I think it's about time we sent another one of our own on its way." Carlisle got up from his command chair. "You have the watch, Mr. Culver. I'll be in my cabin, preparing the report we're going to send with it."

* * *

CNE Peacekeeper Base, Planet Ragnarok

"Welcome to Ragnarok." Socrates Sideris extended his hand.

"Who are you?" Mahmude Moustafa growled, ignoring the outstretched hand.

"I'm a contractor hired by CIS. I'm your contact with the rebels." Sideris dropped his hand and glared at the newcomer. "I've been here for almost two years. The bloody Peacekeepers told me you were here to support our mission. Is that correct?"

"Sorry. I took you for a native." Moustafa's voice took on a cautious, neutral tone. "Yes, we are here in support of these rebels you speak of. I have ten experienced fighters. They are unloading our gear from the lander."

"I'm supposed to look like a native." Sideris stepped back to display the loose green tunic and matching pantaloons tucked into his laced boots. "You can carry all the gear you want, but if you want to blend into the population, this is as close to a uniform as the rebels wear. Were you not briefed before you left Earth?"

"We were, but the briefing was given by CIS desk jockeys who have no concept of fieldcraft. We knew from the start we would have to improvise when we got here. We'll depend on you to advise us."

"Fine." Sideris nodded. "I can do that. This mine and the base the Peacekeepers are building is well outside the primary area of operations for both the rebels and the Wan Dynasty. The region is known to the natives as the 'Forbidden Zone,' due to lingering fears of radiation from that nuclear war they had a century ago.

"As it turns out, their fears were unfounded. Radiation dropped below harmful levels long ago, but they still don't come up here. That means, however, that the first task ahead of you is going to be a forty-kilometer hike to reach the current rebel main camp."

"No air insertion?" Moustafa frowned.

"No. They tell me the Moonies have reduced their forces in orbit, but we still don't want to take any chances. If they spotted an air drop, they might be able to locate the rebel camp. All it would take is a single kinetic strike to wipe out the leaders of the rebellion and their best fighters."

"Hmmph!" Moustafa snorted. "The Confeds say the Moonie force is three cruisers. The CNE has brought a heavy task force with two battlecruisers. I don't think we'll need to worry about that, but—" he held up a hand in dismissal "—you're right. It's better to be safe.

"It's late in the day. If you have no objection, let's enjoy the comforts of Peacekeeper hospitality, such as it is, for tonight. We can begin that forty-kilometer trek in the morning."

* * *

"The engineers have done a good job of preparation, Colonel," Major Niles Rizzo reported. "The facilities are adequate. The troops are getting settled with a minimum of bitching."

"Good." Lieutenant Colonel Dietrich Schaeffer nodded in satisfaction. "This is going to be our home for some time."

"Sir..." Rizzo hesitated. "I'm not clear on what our mission will be. They don't need an entire battalion to provide security for one mining facility. The mission brief said the Moonies have a very small force in this system, maybe a company of warship Marines at the most."

Rizzo commanded Alpha Company. He was the most senior of the company commanders, which made him second in the battalion's chain of command. He was the one through whom Schaeffer passed most of his general orders for the group.

"You're right, Niles," Schaeffer replied with a hint of humor in his voice. "We face no threats worthy of a unit such as ours. The Moonies and the Consortium have no more than token naval forces and not enough ground forces to secure their own mines—they use private security contractors for that.

"Our mission is simply to be here, to occupy this ground, on this planet where the Moonies have forbidden us to be. We're a thumb in their eye, a middle finger in front of their faces, and there's nothing they can do about it.

"We will maintain our combat strength. We'll conduct training and make forays into the wilderness. If any natives dare to come near us, we will deal with them, but we will not conduct operations beyond the local area. We will fortify the camp so we can defend it if anyone should be so foolish as to attack on the ground. We will expect the Navy to secure the orbitals, to ensure that we are not attacked from space.

"In the past, that was our weakness, but now it is the Moonies who are weak. A year ago, they had the forces to deny us entry into the system. Their warships would have prevented us from getting anywhere near the planet. This time, we came in unopposed. We landed without fear of strikes from orbit or Moonie Marines on the ground.

"To answer your question, our mission is simply to occupy and hold this position. You may pass the word to the troops. I am sure they'll be pleased to know that nothing more will be required of them, but you must not let them become complacent and lose their combat edge. At some point in the future, we may have a new mission. If that happens, I want them to be ready for it."

"Will do, sir." Rizzo nodded. "I'll start putting together a schedule for training and work details."

"Right. Give them something to bitch about." Schaeffer smiled. "When the troops quit bitching, you know that morale has dropped below acceptable limits."

Besides, he thought, *we have to put on a good show for the Moonies.* There was one part of the mission he hadn't shared with Rizzo. Their presence was intended to draw the attention of the Moonies, so they would not notice the covert support that CIS was providing to the native rebels.

Moustafa's team was the first step toward that support. The base would serve as a port of entry for more teams in the future, as well as for weapons, ammunition, and other supplies. *Eventually, the rebels will prevail, at which point we'll pretty much own the planet. We'll kick the Moonies out, and maybe those damned Consortium people, too.*

* * * * *

Chapter Eighteen

12 October 2123

Costa Del Sur Resort, El Salvador

"CIS has only a preliminary report," Gerhardt Richter cautioned, "but it appears that the Ragnarok initiative is going more smoothly than the typical CNE military operation. The task force arrived in system and took up orbit without a challenge by the Moonies. As of the date of the report, they were landing Peacekeepers on the planet."

"Can I assume they also landed the team to support the rebels?" Mohammed Al Sharif raised an eyebrow in Richter's direction.

"The report didn't say." Richter shook his head. "It came through CNE Navy channels. The naval chain of command has little concern for ground operations. I think we can assume that no news is good news. By now, that team should have joined the rebels."

"It would appear that we have truly screwed the Moonies this time." Butos Kimba chuckled. "It may take a while, but we will have control of the entire system eventually—or the CNE will."

"That presumes the Moonies don't send out forces to confront them." Andre DuMorne's voice carried a note of skepticism. "They have no less than six battlecruiser groups sitting idle at Luna."

"Four of those are deactivated," Huang Chang Li joined the discussion. "It will take them a significant time to reactivate them. I doubt they will want to send out one of the two active units at this time, not with the Confeds having four more battlecruisers online at Omicron base."

"Doesn't matter." Richter dismissed the concerns with a wave of his hand. "They may send reinforcements, but by the time they get there, a new order will be established. The CNE will have warships in orbit and people on the ground without firing a shot. The Moonies will look to the Akara before taking action, and the Lizards will not support them. They are getting gold royalties from both sides and from the Consortium. They won't want any conflict to interfere with that.

"The Moonies will bluster, and the Confeds will stonewall. Diplomatic protests will be exchanged, but the Confeds will still have warships in orbit and troops on the planet. The timing of this operation was nearly perfect, reaching the system when the Moonies were weakest."

* * *

Chief Executive's Office, TerraNova City, Luna

"We need to reinforce Tremaine," McGruder insisted. "Yes, we're closing the barn door after the horse is out, but I can't leave three cruisers and a destroyer facing a Confed force that size in a system where there aren't supposed to be any Confed warships at all. We've got to get a full battle group out there as soon as possible."

"I agree, but we've got to tread carefully." Robert O'Hara frowned. "This may be the first move in a larger Confed game. Let's not let them push us into doing something stupid. The only groups that can get there quickly are the two active ones here, and I'm not willing to expose Luna that way. We're in the Confed's back yard, and their force out at Hygiea gets larger every day."

"No, I'm not going to take my group out, and I'm not going to send Simms." McGruder shook his head. "Likewise, with all that's going on, I'm not going to pull Greenwood off Xanadu. It's a short hop from Coleridge to Odin, but we can't afford to leave the colony uncovered."

"So we need to reactivate one of the mothballed groups at Luna. Have you got any projections for how long it'll take?"

"Yeah, and that's a problem. The yard people are projecting thirty days to bring a group up to readiness. It will take that long to get the crews reassembled. When you add time for readiness trials and the time it takes to get a group to Odin, we are talking about three months to get anyone there. That's too damned long."

"Yes, it is," O'Hara agreed. "It's your fleet, Mac. I'm not going to second-guess you, but there might be some alternatives."

"Hey, you had the fleet before I did." McGruder chuckled. "I'll take all the advice you're willing to give."

"Well, for immediate relief, I'd send out DesRon 12. They're still on active status, right?"

"Right. They're attached to Walter's group as part of the System Defense mission. Good idea, though it's only five destroyers against a pair of Confed battlecruisers and a bunch of cruisers and destroyers."

"It's not just five destroyers." O'Hara snorted. "It's the Cat Pack, with a distinguished record of kicking Confed butt. Besides, destroyers traveling alone can make a fast passage. If you get them deployed quickly, they can be at Ragnarok in a month.

"We still need to get a full battle group out there, but I've got an idea. We've never had a need to send a ship direct from Sacagawea to

Odin, but based on n-space distance, it should be a shorter trip than to Odin from Sol. You could cut orders for Yoric to redeploy to Ragnarok and send the newly reactivated group to Tatanna instead."

"What? With all that's going on, you'd leave Tatanna uncovered?" McGruder's jaw dropped. "Hell, we've got Confed trouble there, too, not to mention the Bugs."

"Both of which have been dealt with and are not likely to be back soon. Look, if you cut those orders right away, you can get them to Yoric in seventeen days by hyperprobe. Give him a few days to get prepared and depart for Odin. Based on the n-space distance of thirty-six light years, figure twenty days for passage. He'll get there about a week after the Cat Pack arrives."

"Hmmm…" McGruder paused a moment to think about it. "Yeah, that's reasonable, assuming no weird hyperspace anomalies between Sacagawea and Odin. I hate the idea of leaving Tatanna uncovered for the two extra months before we can get a group there from Luna."

"I wouldn't leave it totally uncovered. I'd leave a couple of cruisers and destroyers behind. Remember, he'll be able to integrate Tremaine's force into his group when he gets there."

"Okay, you've sold me." McGruder nodded. "I'll start cutting the orders as soon as I get back to the anchorage."

"I shouldn't have to 'sell' you." O'Hara chuckled. "I'm the boss, remember? I'm deferring to your judgment as my fleet commander. So… which group are you going to warm up to send to Tatanna?"

"I'd like to stick with 2nd Fleet, so I guess that means your son. Besides, John's got a history with Tatanna—knows the system and the people there."

* * *

LFS *Isis*, Lunar Fleet Anchorage

"How did we get so lucky?" Eurasia Brown's lips crinkled in an effort to suppress a smile. "I can think of three other battlecruiser captains who are turning green with envy—or will be when they find out we've been reactivated."

"Yeah... and three rear admirals who are senior to me will be wondering if my father had something to do with it." John O'Hara was not smiling. He had been bothered by accusations of nepotism for most of his career. "According to Mac, it's simple. They're all 1st Fleet; we're 2nd. 1st Fleet stays home and protects Luna. 2nd Fleet deploys to other star systems. End of story.

"Our orders are strictly confidential, eyes only. Others are bound to notice when the yard people start bringing our ships online and crews start arriving, but the why and wherefore are not to be discussed."

"So noted." Brown nodded. "Meanwhile, I've got a lot of work to do, starting with issuing recall orders for a lot of people."

"Just worry about *Isis*," he told her. "I'm setting up a call for all captains and execs tomorrow morning. Each captain is going to be responsible for bringing his own ship up to readiness. If they've got problems that need to be bucked upstairs, I'll tell them to talk to Dee-Dee—that's why I have a chief of staff. As for you, your sole mission will be to make sure my flagship is ready to depart on schedule."

"Depart on schedule... right." Brown hesitated. "Admiral, do you have any idea why they're sending us to Sacagawea? The orders I got didn't say."

"Neither did mine." He chuckled. "Only that further orders will be issued prior to departure. Lunar Command might still be working on those orders. Hell, a month from now, they might decide to cancel the mission."

"Be a damned expensive drill if they do."

"Be more expensive if they don't," he replied. "They took four battle groups off the line for a reason—to keep the Lunar Free State from going bankrupt. Whatever made them decide to reactivate us must be damned serious."

"Hopefully, they'll tell us what's going on before we go charging off. Meanwhile, we've got our orders."

* * *

CNS *Buenos Aires,* in Ragnarok Orbit

"It is time, Victor." Aguilar nodded to his flag captain. "You may engage the Moonies at will."

"Sir?" Perez raised an eyebrow in a questioning look. "We gave them twenty-four hours to depart. They still have eight hours to go; it appears they are preparing to comply."

"I never intended to let them go. They sent off a hyperprobe this morning to let their fleet command know what was happening. No doubt, that will bring a relief force—if one isn't already on the way. This way, we will have four fewer warships to fight."

"Only three, sir." Perez shook his head. "The destroyer remains out of range. We could send our own destroyers after it, but…"

"No. I'll settle for killing the three cruisers. Pass the word to all ships. Whenever you are ready, you may open fire."

* * *

LFS *Apache*, in Ragnarok Orbit

"The Marines are back aboard, Skipper," Lieutenant Commander Roger Raintree reported. "The mine people weren't happy about it, and the diplomats were madder than hell. Commander Steel wanted his people to stay, but Lieutenant Dooley convinced him to abandon the embassy."

"No sense leaving them." Tremaine shrugged. "They'd only end up as Confed prisoners. There's no question the bastards are taking over. As for the mine people, they're better off not being caught in a firefight between badly outnumbered Marines and Peacekeepers."

Apache had been at Condition Red for nearly sixteen hours. Tremaine had called the alert as soon as he had received the Confed ultimatum: leave the system or be fired upon. He'd made the decision to retrieve the Marines, judging it to be best for all concerned. His own platoon had been the last to depart, in company with the LFS diplomatic delegation. He'd tasked Raintree with monitoring the retrieval; the XO was reporting from his own battle station in *Apache's* Auxiliary Control.

"All right, let's get moving." *Besides,* Tremaine thought, *we've been at Condition Red too long. Need to get under way so I can dial it back and give the crew a break.* He keyed his console and began to issue orders.

"Engineering, all power levels to full. Comm, advise *Norseman* and *Chimera*: Prepare to break orbit. Helm..."

"Sir!" His tactical officer spun to face him, his eyes wide. "The Confeds are painting us with *all their ships!* Multiple target locks!"

"Helm, full power ahead! Defenses free!" He keyed the group command channel. "*Norseman! Chimera!* Break orbit! Maneuver at captain's discretion. *Redhawk,* execute End Run!" The last order would send the destroyer streaking for the hyper limit.

He cursed himself as *Apache* leaped ahead. *Should have expected this; there's a reason they rearranged their formation.* Over the past few hours, the Confeds had moved from line abreast to a stacked vertical formation—effectively giving every one of their ships a shot at his force. *Chimera* and *Norseman* followed his lead a few seconds later, just as the Confeds opened fire. The timing was fortunate, as the sudden sprint caused the enemy's beam weapons to lose target locks. Confed grasers and x-ray lasers flashed through the space where the LFS ships had been a moment before.

The three cruisers had been "at anchor" in typical formation, line abreast with their noses pointed at the planet below. Unfortunately, that meant they were headed for the surface at full acceleration.

"Helm, power turn, up 90 degrees," he ordered. "Random zigzag at your discretion." A power turn was a stressful maneuver, accomplished by unbalancing the drive to change the ship's attitude without reducing acceleration. It was, however, the best way to avoid hitting the planet without giving the enemy an easy target. He hoped *Norseman* and *Chimera* were taking similar action. A glance at the tactical display told him they were. What had been a tight formation was now three ships departing in three different directions.

He wasn't surprised when the Confeds sent a swarm of missiles after them. At close range, beam weapons could have cut his ships to pieces; had they stayed in orbit a few seconds longer, that would have happened. Their erratic departure had scrambled enemy targeting; missiles were the only option.

"Guns, you are cleared to return fire," he ordered. Apparently, his NTO had been waiting for the order; four missiles left *Apache*'s stern chase tubes almost immediately, all of them targeting the nearest enemy battlecruiser.

"Helm, get us over the horizon," he ordered. "Put the planet between us and them." Chief Wallace was a good man; Tremaine trusted him to get it done with no more instruction than that. He noted that the other two cruisers were also curving inward, trying to get out of the Confed line of sight.

The Confeds had been too close; their missiles had already reached attack range. *Apache's* countermissiles and point-defense batteries were hard at work, but two of the missiles got close enough to detonate. The cruiser shuddered as x-ray lasers struck home.

Damage reports flashed on Tremaine's displays, but the drive held. Moments later, they were over the horizon. The Confeds had sent more missiles, but *Apache* was nearly out of range; the second salvo would not catch her.

Tremaine felt sick to his stomach. His ship was safe and so was *Norseman*, but he had seen the brilliant flare of a thermonuclear explosion as a hit by a Confed missile took out one of *Chimera's* fusion plants.

"Guns, secure weapons and defenses," he ordered. "Plot shortest course to the hyper limit."

* * *

28 October 2123
LFS *Valkyrie*, in Xanadu Orbit

"Come in, Jake. Take a seat." Lorna Greenwood waved Winfield to one of the comfortable armchairs. "Coffee's on the sideboard if you want it."

"I'll pass, Admiral." Winfield nodded to Jessica Guerrero, already seated in the other chair in front of the desk. "Just finished lunch."

"Damn!" Lorna glanced at the time display on her desk screen. "Already 1400 hours. Time passes quickly when you're having fun. Remind me, Jessica, are we having fun yet?"

Guerrero chuckled but didn't comment. Lorna studied the notice displayed on the screen, then turned to face her subordinates.

"I got a priority message from Fleet. No orders, info only, but apparently they think it's important, because I got an identical message from Diplomatic Corps addressed to 'Governor—Xanadu Colony' in the same hyperprobe.

"They advise that a Confed task force of significant strength has arrived in the Odin System, has taken up orbit, and has landed a sizable Peacekeeper force on the planet. The invading force consisted of two battlecruisers accompanied by an assortment of cruisers and lighter units. The Peacekeeper force is projected to be of battalion size or greater.

"The LFS force in system, consisting of three cruisers and a destroyer, did not engage; the Confeds took up orbit without opposition. Since the Peacekeepers landed only at the Confed mining site on the planet, no action was taken to oppose them, either."

She paused and looked at Winfield and Guerrero, whose faces reflected shock. The Lunar Free State had dropped its guard, and the Confeds had taken control of an entire star system. Technically, Odin belonged to the Lizards; all others were there by their permission. As a practical matter, however, the token force the Lizards had stationed there could not have stood against a single Confed cruiser.

"As I said," Lorna advised, "this is for information only. This actually happened over a month ago. Given the time involved for the word from Odin to reach Luna, and for Luna to get word to us, we're only hearing the first report with very little detail. For all we know, the

Confeds might have attacked and destroyed our force there or driven it out of the system. No point in speculating. All we can do is wait for further word.

"We are directed to 'be alert for possible Confed aggression in our command area,' with the definition of 'aggression' being left to our own discretion. Further, we are given no direction on what to do about it if we do encounter same.

"We've been rubbing elbows with Confeds for a long time. We've already had instances of aggression on their part; we've dealt with those as they come up. I see no reason to change what we are doing other than to pass the message down the chain and advise everyone to be alert. If either of you have any suggestions, I'm ready to listen."

Winfield and Guerrero looked at each other.

"None at this time, Admiral," Winfield said. Guerrero shook her head.

"Fine… so, like they said, information only." Lorna nodded. "Business as usual. Keep an eye on the Confeds. There was one other item in the diplomatic brief for 'Governor' Greenwood. They leave it to my discretion to share as much or as little of this as I deem appropriate with the Consortium people, with the proviso that anything we tell them should be 'in confidence and not for public release.' That's the way they're handling it back on Luna.

"In view of the rapport we've developed with them so far, I'm inclined to tell them everything we know. They've already had a taste of Confed aggression, and they handled it exactly as I would under the circumstances. We've done a lot to earn their trust; I think we need to trust them in return."

* * *

31 October 2123

LFS *Sorceress*, in Tatanna Orbit

"It's going well, sir." Rochford sat stiffly in the chair, his coffee mug untouched on the table in front of him. "The crew has taken the change of command in stride. They're a good bunch, and they know me well. I don't expect any difficulty."

"Relax, Rock." Peter Yoric smiled. "I'm not concerned about the crew. You and Emily had them well in hand before she left. I'm more interested in how you're settling into the command chair. For the crew, it's business as usual. For you, it's your first time in the hotseat."

"Honestly, Admiral, I never expected to be here." Rochford shook his head. "I figured I'd retire as an exec, unless I got lucky, and they offered me a cruiser command. Either way, I never thought I'd have a star on my collar." His hand rose to touch the new commodore's insignia.

"As I told you," Yoric said, "McGruder was hung up on the idea that you hadn't had a command before. He didn't think a battlecruiser—especially *his* battlecruiser, the fleet flagship—was the place to start. However, both of your former captains pushed for you, and Emily convinced me to go along. We figured this was the perfect place to start, because you already knew the ship, and the crew knew you. So here we are. *Sorceress* is yours, and Emily's on her way to take command of *Amazon*."

"I want to make sure you understand something. This is *your ship*. I'm not in command of her; you are. You report to me as my flag captain, not my exec. To that extent, you're my deputy commander for the entire battle group, but aboard *Sorceress*, you are the supreme commander.

"You happen to be carrying an admiral—me—but I won't give orders to anyone aboard this ship except you or the members of my own staff. If I ever violate that rule, you will have just cause for complaint, and I expect you to bring it to my attention.

"You can also relax. 'Coffee with the admiral' is my idea of a morning meeting with my flag captain. Emily did it all the time. I don't know if McGruder follows the same practice, but she'll miss it if he doesn't."

"I'm sure you'll miss those meetings, too." Rochford finally cracked a smile. "I'm not nearly as easy to look at as she was... uh, that is, I mean..." The smile faded, and Rochford reddened as he realized how the comment might be taken.

"No, you aren't." Yoric chuckled. "Don't worry, I know what you mean. Emily Bernard is one of those women who can flip a man's switches just by being in the same room. I can't tell you how many times I had to remind myself that she was my subordinate, and I shouldn't be having romantic thoughts about her. She was always strictly professional, though—a solid officer in service of the LFS. I sometimes wonder if she knows what kind of effect she has on us males. She certainly never tried to take advantage of it."

Yoric paused as a chime from his pad announced a priority call. He tapped the icon to take it.

"Uh... Admiral, we got the dump from the incoming hyperprobe." The face on the screen was that of the comm officer on duty on the bridge. "There's a red-flagged message for you from Lunar Command. I'm sending it to your personal queue."

"Thank you, Lieutenant." Yoric got up from the armchair and walked across the cabin to his desk. He sat down, brought up the message in question on his screen, and entered his personal code to open it. Rochford waited in silence while he studied the contents. Finally, he sat back with a sigh, shaking his head.

"What is it with this battle group?" He looked up at the overhead as he posed the rhetorical question. "Everything is quiet until we have a major change in command, then all hell breaks loose. Bernard had just taken command when the Bugs showed up. I got here to replace Rebecca Ling, and the Confeds showed up. Now we put you in the command chair, and this happens."

"We're being redeployed—direct to Odin. No return to Luna for refit and resupply, a rapid deployment over a hyperspace route never before traveled. Oh, and as a minor footnote, we're to collect data along the way for the stellar cartographers; however, the primary objective is to get our asses to Ragnarok ASAP."

"Uh… sir?" Rochford blinked. "Do they say why? I mean, what's happening there that needs our attention?"

"Not happening, already happened." Yoric snorted. "It seems Fleet pulled out O'Hara's battle group and left only a cruiser squadron in place." He turned back to the screen and studied the orders again. "Back in mid-September, the Confeds showed up with not one but two battlecruisers leading a force of cruisers and destroyers.

"As of this report, they had taken up orbit, landed troops on the planet, and pretty much taken over. No further word, so who knows what the situation might be? It appears, however, they expect us to sail into the middle of this clusterfuck and find out.

"Sonja—" Yoric glanced upward as he addressed the ship's AI "—advise my staff to assemble here in an hour. Also, advise all ships—captain's call, virtual only, at 1600 hours. That should give me enough time to figure out what I'm going to tell them."

* * * * *

Chapter Nineteen

20 November 2123
LFS *Apache*, Near the Odin Hyper Limit

"Hyper signature!" Roger Raintree looked up sharply at the announcement from the assistant DSO at the tactical station. "I make it five ships. Looks like from Sol, but not quite on the direct line. Could be a tactical displacement."

Raintree nodded. For efficiency and navigational simplicity, ships would typically drop out of hyperspace on a direct line from their origin star to their destination. However, military commanders who suspected a possible ambush at the hyper limit would typically adjust course to arrive somewhere other than at the expected point—not too far away, though; there was always the thought that they might ambush the ambushers if they came in close enough. Strategy and tactics instructors at Fleet Academy referred to this as a "tactical displacement."

To Raintree, however, it gave another clue as to who the newcomers might be. Confeds would expect their forces to be in control of the system. With typical Confed arrogance, they would come straight in. They wouldn't worry about an ambush.

They would be wrong. *Apache* and her consorts were hanging around out here for exactly that reason, to bushwhack any reinforcements the enemy might send in, and warn any friendlies to stay away.

These guys, however, might be LFS reinforcements, though Raintree had hoped for a larger force.

"Plot a course for intercept," he ordered. "Pass the word to *Norseman* and *Redhawk*."

He checked the chronometer: 0314 hours. He punched an icon on his console, connecting him to the captain who—if all was right with the world—should be sound asleep in his cabin.

* * *

"Oh, hell yes!" A broad grin spread across Tremaine's face as he read the IFF returns from the five newcomers. "It's the Cat Pack."

The screen showed him the names of DesRon 12's destroyers: *Jaguar*, *Leopard*, *Cheetah*, and *Lynx*, led by Commodore Harry Oldham's flagship, LFS *Cougar*. At thirty light-seconds distance, they were still a bit far away for a real-time conversation, but Tremaine recorded a short welcome message and sent it on its way.

Apparently, Oldham had the same idea, as his message arrived only seconds after Tremaine's went out. Among other things, the squadron's commander asked for a general status report for LFS forces in the system.

That's going to take a while, Tremaine thought. *It's a long story.* He felt a sense of relief at finally having somebody to tell it to. *Most importantly, I get to tell Oldham that he just became the senior officer in this system.* It was a responsibility that Tremaine would be happy to relinquish.

* * *

20 November 2123
LFS *Amazon,* at Lunar Fleet Anchorage

"Welcome aboard, Emily." McGruder waved Bernard to a chair in front of his desk. "Sorry for all the confusion, but you've arrived just in time. I had them bring you here for a quick briefing, then we'll get you to the bridge so you can officially take command of the ship. I don't know if anyone's told you, but we're about to deploy. We're going to Odin."

"No, sir." Bernard blinked in surprise. "No one mentioned it."

"Hell of a note." McGruder shook his head. "We've been provisioning for the last two days. We're scheduled to depart tomorrow, but I sure as hell didn't want to cast off without a flag captain. Hate to throw this at you, but you'll have time to get up to speed while we're in hyper."

McGruder's steward appeared with coffee and donuts. Bernard was grateful for that—she'd arrived on the diplomatic courier from Sacagawea this morning and had skipped breakfast to go directly to *Amazon*. She selected a donut and sat back to munch and sip her coffee while McGruder brought her up to speed on current developments. Ten minutes later, she had the picture, and it wasn't pretty.

"We thought we had everything covered. DesRon 12 should already have arrived at Odin." McGruder shrugged. "John O'Hara will be departing for Sacagawea with *Isis* and the 2/4 group in another few days—they got the group reactivated a lot faster than expected. Yoric should be most of the way to Odin with *Sorceress* and the 2/3."

It had been a shock for Bernard to find that her old command had been redeployed barely a week after she'd left. Her first thought was that she'd missed a call to action, but her new command was headed for the same place. *We won't get there for another month, though. Maybe it will be over by then... one way or the other.*

"A few days ago, we got another hyperprobe from Tremaine," McGruder continued. "He told us the Confeds had attacked him, he'd been forced to abandon the orbitals, and he'd lost *Chimera* in the process. I told the CEO we needed to throw in another battle group, and he agreed. Walt Simms and I flipped a coin; he lost, so we're going.

"Rob O'Hara's still concerned about leaving Luna uncovered, so we're bringing Richards back online—*Athena*, with the 1/2 group—to back Walter up. And that, young lady, is the mess that you've walked into. Again... welcome aboard.

"Oh... and Maya?" he glanced up at the overhead, addressing the ship's AI.

"Yes, Admiral?" The smooth soprano voice seemed to fill the compartment.

"Advise Lieutenant Orlov to arrange a welcome dinner for Commodore Bernard tonight—formal, all officers, in the flag dining room."

"Okay." He turned to Bernard once again. "Let's get up to the bridge so you can formally take command."

* * *

LFS *Sorceress*, Near the Odin Hyper Limit

"The Confeds have no idea how to conduct system defense," Harry Oldham asserted. "They've got no outer system picket in place—can't put one out here with Jerry's force and mine on the prowl." He waved a hand at Tremaine.

The two officers had come over to *Sorceress* at Yoric's request. They were seated around the coffee table in the informal meeting area of the admiral's office.

"The dumb bastards sent out a pair of light cruisers and a destroyer to investigate when we arrived," Oldham continued. "They must have spotted the hyper signature, but it took them twenty hours to get here. We had plenty of time to set up for them.

"My Cats jumped them, they panicked, and we drove them right into Jerry's fields of fire. Now they're short a cruiser and a destroyer, and the surviving cruiser's pretty badly mauled. We took minimal damage in return.

"I mean, hell's bells." Oldham shrugged. "They didn't expect my destroyers, but they knew we had two heavy cruisers out here somewhere. What were they thinking?"

"Sounds like Tactics 101 is not a required course at their officer school." Yoric chuckled. "Anyway, what you've been doing sounds very much like what I've been discussing with Rock." He nodded to Rochford, the fourth participant in the meeting.

"They've got two battlecruisers and a lot more cruisers and destroyers at Ragnarok. If we go head-to-head with them, they've got weight of metal on their side, but we don't have to do that. They're the ones who have to hold the orbitals, or we go down there and clean them out. I'd love to dump a kinetic on that Peacekeeper base of theirs.

"Our mission will be to harass them and interdict the system so they can't get reinforcements. Anything that drops out of hyper flying a Confed flag is a target, and we sure as hell know how to run a system picket.

"Jerry, I need to integrate *Apache*, *Norseman*, and *Redhawk* into my group. I left three of my cruisers and a destroyer behind at Sacagawea to watch the store. With *Chimera* gone, we'll be a bit light, but still in good shape for the mission. We'll start by setting up the picket.

"At that point, Harry, you get to have some fun. As usual, the Cat Pack will operate as an independent force. Your mission will be to make their lives miserable in orbit. If you can lure them out of orbit, so much the better.

"If they send destroyers out after you, they're even dumber than we thought. The Confeds don't know how to run a destroyer squadron, either, so you're welcome to cut them off at the knees. If they come after you with anything heavier, you can invite them to dance with us out here. If they split their forces, all they'll be doing is giving us a choice of targets.

"That's the plan. Do any of you have comments or suggestions?"

No one spoke. A huge grin spread over Oldham's face.

"I love it. We control the supply lines back to Sol. Eventually, they're gonna get hungry and start running out of toilet paper."

"Right." Yoric nodded in agreement. "We can starve them out; meanwhile, we can always whistle up resupply from Luna."

"I'm going to send a hyperprobe off to let Lunar Command know what we're doing. If you have anything you think we should include in the report, let me know. On to the next question: what about the Americans? Are they still in orbit?"

"They were, last time we checked." Tremaine shrugged. "*Redhawk* did a fast flyby ten days ago, before the Cat Pack arrived. We tried to make contact with them, but no joy. The Confeds have got a pair of destroyers stationed ten klicks out-system. They put up scatter fields that blocked our attempts to put a tight beam on the Yanks. Maybe they were reacting defensively, but *Redhawk* never got close to missile range. More likely, somebody over there doesn't want us talking to them."

"Ten klicks? That's crowding it." Rochford wore a thoughtful look. "Are they actually standing guard over the American ships? Makes you wonder what would happen if the Yanks decided to leave."

"Hmmm... good point," Tremaine conceded. "Two destroyers wouldn't stop them. *Atlanta* may not be quite up to our heavy cruiser standards, but I've gotten a good look at her, and I'm convinced she could blow away a pair of Confed *Blade*-class tin cans without breaking a sweat."

"Especially at ten klicks." Rochford chuckled. "She could wipe them out before they knew they were under attack and be out of there before the rest of the Confeds could react."

"Unfortunately, the reverse is also true." Tremaine shook his head. "If the Confeds attack without warning—as they did with us—they could take out the Americans just as quickly."

The group was silent for a minute, then Yoric turned to Oldham.

"Harry, that harassment mission is yours, but I've got a suggestion. Why don't you put those two destroyers up as the first targets on your hit list? It'll be interesting to see how the Confeds—and the Americans—react if you take them out. Worst case, we'll get a chance to talk to the Yanks without being jammed."

* * *

CNS *Buenos Aires*, in Ragnarok Orbit

"We need intel, Admiral," Perez insisted. "Should we not send out destroyers for reconnaissance? They could be directed to avoid engagement."

"The last group was told to avoid engagement," Aguilar snarled. "Nobody told the Moonies. Now we have lost a light cruiser and a destroyer, and *Elektra* will not be fully combat effective without a shipyard."

"Yes, sir." Perez bit back a reply. *We lost ships because their captains were idiots,* he thought. *They sailed into an ambush and let the Moonies control the engagement. Now the latest hyper event tells us an even larger Moonie force has arrived.* "So what are your orders, Admiral?"

"For the moment, none." Aguilar waved a hand in dismissal. "The Peacekeepers are doing what is necessary on the planet. All we need to do is protect them by holding the orbitals. History shows that a defense in place is difficult to overcome by siege. They will need a force much larger than our own to dislodge us."

History? Perez blinked in surprise. *Defense in place? Siege? We are not living in medieval times, behind stone walls, defending ourselves against attackers with bows and arrows.* He wondered, not for the first time, whether Aguilar had the slightest understanding of space warfare and tactics. Being forced to hold the orbitals was a liability, not an advantage, against a mobile enemy who could stand off and hurl missiles at them from beyond range of their own reply. If Aguilar insisted on his "defense in place," the Moonies could take them out with a much lighter force than their own.

He was still considering the implications when the ship's battle alarms began to sound. He keyed his comm unit to reach the bridge.

"Sir!" The watch officer's voice held a note of panic. "Incoming Moonies! Five ships heading directly for us. They will reach missile range in seven minutes."

* * *

USS *Atlanta*, in Ragnarok Orbit

"Wake up, sir. The game's afoot." Carlisle blinked, rubbed the sleep from his eyes, and sat up. He'd been catching a nap on the bunk in his ready room. He'd finally let the crew stand down to Alert Three but didn't want to be far from the bridge. It was hard to relax when *Atlanta* was so close to a potentially hostile force whose intentions were unknown.

The Confeds had assured him that their beef was with the Moonies. They had no intention, they said, of interfering with Consortium operations. He'd watched them attack the Moonies without warning. He'd watched their second transport drop what he assumed were Peacekeeper troops on all three of the Moonie mining sites. So far, they hadn't touched the Consortium's single mine. If they had, he would have been powerless to stop them.

Then they had parked those damned destroyers on his doorstep. No threats, no targeting scans, just two ships within very short beam weapon range of *Atlanta* and *Farragut*. He'd sent a protest to the Confed admiral and had gotten no reply.

He glared at Lieutenant Commander Sandra Fox, his tactical officer, who stood framed in the ready room hatch.

"The game's afoot? What are you, Fox, a Sherlock Holmes fan?"

"Actually, sir, Shakespeare said it first." Fox's clipped British accent marked her as an exchange officer from the Royal Navy. "Henry V, Act III Scene I."

"Shakespeare wrote plays, not tactical reports. What's up?"

"Moonie ships, incoming, looking like they mean business. I make it to be five destroyers, headed straight at the Confeds, who are scrambling to rearrange themselves into a shield formation. Looks like they got caught napping.

"The Moonies must have come in ballistic; they didn't light up until a minute ago." Fox stepped aside as Carlisle came through the hatch, headed for the bridge. "At first glance, it appears to be a kamikaze run, but…"

"But the Moonies aren't that stupid," Carlisle finished the sentence. "Bring us to Alert One. I have no idea what's going to happen, but we're not going to be caught with our defenses down."

"Right, sir." Fox grinned at him as the alert tones began to sound. "Once more unto the breach."

* * *

LFS *Cougar*, Inbound for Ragnarok

"Flag to Cats, execute Curve Ball on my mark." Harry Oldham felt a smile forming on his lips as he watched the enemy's frantic attempts to meet the threat. They had been strung out in line abreast and had taken time to get their drives online. Now they were beginning to move toward a shield formation that would allow an integrated missile defense. As he watched the uncoordinated maneuvers, one of their destroyers came all too close to a collision with a heavy cruiser.

He checked his range display. "Three, two, one, *mark!*" He nodded in satisfaction as his destroyers executed the maneuver with precision. Moments later, he felt the familiar shudder as *Cougar's* mass drivers sent a full missile broadside downrange.

The Cat Pack had executed a sharp course change to bring their broadsides to bear. Now the five destroyers rolled over in unison and launched a second broadside salvo. Forty missiles streaked toward the Confed formation, all of them going for a single target.

The Cats had come in ballistic, powered down and with scatter fields up until they got so close they would have to maneuver to achieve their primary objective. They had brought up their drives, charged to within missile range, and executed the turn.

I'll bet they haven't got their missile defenses online yet, Oldham thought. *So much for the diversion; now for the primary target.*

* * *

CNS *Buenos Aires*

"Why are we not shooting at them?" Perez flinched at the shrill tone of Aguilar's questions. "Why are we not stopping those missiles?"

"They are at extreme range, Admiral." Perez tried to keep his voice calm and level. His bridge crew were doing their best. They didn't need a hysterical admiral jogging their elbows.

"They will be out of range before anything we shoot can reach them. We are launching countermissiles. Point defense is coming online."

He chose not to mention that the incoming Moonie missiles were already too close for effective countermissile targeting. His crew had not responded quickly enough to the alert, and systems had taken too long to come up. Point-defense lasers were their only hope. It appeared that all of the enemy missiles were homing on *Buenos Aires*.

"Why are the other ships not protecting us?" Aguilar demanded.

Perez gritted his teeth. *Because they were all caught napping in orbit, as if they were sitting back home at Omicron Base. We are fortunate that a few of them* have started moving into position, but they don't have their own defenses online. We will not have anything resembling an integrated network until too late.

Fortunately, the Moonies had fired no more missiles. They were angling away and would soon be out of range. With a shock, he realized there was another target—two targets—in their path, two ships that had been detached from the group and had not been included in his alert order.

* * *

LFS *Cheetah*

"These guys are asleep, Captain." Lieutenant Candy Carlson shook her head. "They don't even have their drive nodes hot."

"So I see." Lieutenant Commander Terri Rinaldi smiled at her tactical officer. "You may fire when you have target acquisition. Aim carefully, please; the commodore will be rather upset if we hit the Americans by mistake."

* * *

USS *Atlanta*

"Damn, Skipper!" Sandra Fox shook her head in admiration. "They peeled those two destroyers off our arse like ducks in a shooting gallery."

"That they did, Guns." Carlisle nodded. "And they did it very carefully, without scorching our tail feathers."

The five incoming destroyers had fired single broadsides as they passed, each one launching four missiles—two for each of the Confed watchdogs guarding *Atlanta* and *Farragut*. The Confeds had been caught napping; each had taken ten hits from the unopposed missiles. That they'd been powered down at the time had most likely saved the targets from total destruction, but Carlisle had no doubt they were little more than floating wrecks.

"Ah... sir?" Jerry Culver's voice held an uncertain note. "I've got an incoming call from the Moonies—Commodore Oldham, calling from LFS *Cougar*."

"Put him on my screen, Lieutenant." Carlisle chuckled. "I've got a feeling I'll want to hear whatever he has to say."

* * *

LFS *Sorceress*, Near the Odin Hyper Limit

"I've read your report, Harry." Peter Yoric settled into his chair as his steward arrived with coffee and assorted snacks for the assembled group. In addition to Oldham, Thomas Birdsall and "Rock" Rochford were gathered around the table in the admiral's quarters. "Generally, well done all around. Now I want to hear the No Bullshit version from you—including any impressions you got in the course of the action."

"Hmmm... No Bullshit... Well, sir, my first impression was that we caught them totally off guard. They were sitting there, fat, dumb, and happy, as if there were no threats anywhere in the system. I was almost wishing you were there with the whole group, because I'm pretty sure we could have taken them out and been done with it.

"As it is, from what we could see as we headed for the second objective, they stopped fewer than half the missiles we sent at them for what was supposed to be nothing more than a diversion. Not all the surviving missiles hit the battlecruiser, though.

"One of their destroyers moved up, trying to form a defense shell, I guess. It didn't have any of its own defenses online but caused a half-dozen or so of our missiles to go for it rather than the primary target. I didn't see a fusion flare, but it had to have taken heavy damage.

"For the rest of it, figure fifteen or so hits on the battlecruiser, but no way to determine how much damage we did. Likewise, we hit those other two destroyers pretty hard, but again, no fusion flare. They weren't under way at the time, so I can't assess drive damage, but I'm willing to bet they're ready for the scrapyard."

"And they're nearly sixty light years from that scrapyard." Yoric chuckled. "Or, for that matter, from anything resembling a repair facility. As I said, well done. Tell me about your conversation with the Yanks."

"Interesting, informative, but inconclusive." Oldham frowned. "Captain Carlisle says the Confeds have taken no action against the Consortium's mine site and have assured him they have no quarrel with him or the Consortium. He trusts them about as far as he can spit into the wind—his metaphor, not mine—but feels obligated to remain on scene as long as they don't make a move on the mine.

"He's seen what they did to us and realizes that they could do it to him. It's possible that their orders say to leave the Consortium alone, but he thinks it more likely they decided to deal with us first and him later. He was really happy to see us because he figures we'll keep the Confeds too busy to worry about him.

"If they move against the Consortium mine, he'll have no choice but to bug out. I invited him to join us, but he made no promises. I wouldn't, either, in his place. For that matter, I'm glad I'm *not* in his place."

"So am I," Yoric conceded. "If he does have to bug out…"

"Admiral, Captain," Sonja's voice filled the compartment, "we have a hyper signature, multiple ships, near but not directly on the line from Sol. The system picket is responding with a short jump. Tactical advises a military-level translation, ten ships, three in the mass range of capital warships."

"That's either an 'Oh, hell' or a 'Hell, yeah,' depending on whose flag they're flying," Rochford said. "Fortunately, we've got time to figure that out."

Yoric nodded. He'd positioned the battle group a full two hours' travel inside the hyper limit for exactly that reason.

"Admiral, I think I'm going to pass on your dinner invitation." Oldham got to his feet. "Under the circumstances, I think I'd better get back to my command."

"Right, Harry. I understand." Yoric nodded. "You can have a raincheck. Again, good job on the mission."

* * * * *

Chapter Twenty

27 November 2123

LFS *Amazon*, Outer Reaches of the Odin System

"It would appear that Admiral Yoric has the situation well in hand." Emily Bernard directed her comment toward McGruder's image on her console display. "We were queried smartly by the system picket, and I am seeing what appears to be *Sorceress* and her group ahead, plus the Cat Pack."

"So it would seem." McGruder nodded back. "I've sent a message to Peter advising him officially of our arrival. He may have already sent one to us, but we're still a few light minutes apart.

"All appears to be quiet, so I've asked Petra to set up a dinner tonight for key officers. I'll ask Peter to bring his flag captain and Marine commander, so I'll want you and Major Navarre. The topic for discussion will be the situation at Ragnarok and what we're going to do about it."

"Understood, sir. I'll plan for it."

So I'll be seeing Peter again after all, she thought as she disconnected the flag bridge call. *This time, though, he won't be in my chain of command.*

She nodded in satisfaction. She was looking forward to it.

* * *

CNS *Buenos Aires*, in Ragnarok Orbit

"What is the status of repairs?" Aguilar demanded. "Are we operational?"

"*Buenos Aires* is operational, Admiral." Perez tried to keep his voice level, neither cowering before his admiral's tirade nor pushing back against Aguilar's unreasonable demands.

The Moonie attack had scored seventeen hits on the flagship, taking two of her three fusion plants offline and wiping out graser batteries, missile tubes, and point-defense stations on her port side. Two of her drive nodes had also been hit. Despite the battlecruiser's heavy armor, several hits had penetrated deep into her hull. Crew casualties included twenty dead and many more injured.

"*Hector* reports the loss of two missile tubes and a drive node," Perez reported. "Her second reactor is offline and still under repair, but they expect it will be restored to service within a day. Not so the missile tubes—spare parts are not available here."

Aguilar had accused Perez, his crew, and the members of his command team of incompetence. With the destruction of the two destroyers guarding the American ships, he had accused the Americans and their Consortium partners of being secretly in league with the Moonies. He had ordered the Peacekeepers to seize the Consortium mining site and had dispatched the light cruiser *Hector* to stand guard over the American warships to prevent them from intervening.

Or so he had told Perez. *Intervene? How could they intervene? They had no Marines or other ground support capability. They could not use kinetics on their own mining site.* Perez shook his head. All Aguilar had done was convince the American captain that his ships were being threatened.

As *Hector* approached, the Americans had powered up and raised their defenses. When they broke orbit and headed out-system, Aguilar had ordered *Hector* to stop them—no direction on how to do that, simply a demand that they be stopped. The light cruiser's captain was no fool; outnumbered and outgunned by the Yanks, he had ordered them to stop and had fired a single missile in what he had intended to be a warning shot across their bows.

Atlanta and *Farragut* had immediately opened fire with energy weapons—at a range of less than a hundred kilometers. The two American warships had gone to full acceleration. Heavily damaged, *Hector* had chosen not to pursue.

At that, we got off lightly, Perez thought. The Yanks had fired only a single, limited salvo. Had they pressed the attack, Aguilar would be short yet another cruiser.

As for the Americans, they had passed beyond detection range on a course that would take them straight to the hyper limit on a direct line for Sol. *If we see a hyper signature, we'll know they headed for home,* Perez thought. *If not, we can only assume they've joined the Moonies.*

* * *

USS *Atlanta*, Outer Reaches of the Odin System

"I can't officially make an alliance with you people, but we seem to have common interests." Carlisle nodded to the Moonie admiral on his display screen. "Enemy of my enemy... I'm sure you understand."

"Yes, I do." McGruder returned the nod. "An official alliance is something for the diplomats to work out. Meanwhile, my orders are simple: take out the Confeds and reclaim our mining sites. If you are looking to do the same for the Consortium site, you are welcome to join us."

"My orders are pretty general." Carlisle shrugged. "I've been directed to provide 'support as needed' for Consortium operations on the planet. With what's happened, I can't do that on my own. They seized the mining site and fired on my ships.

"I've sent a hyperprobe back to US Naval Operations on Earth. As far as I'm concerned, those were acts of war, but I'm almost certain the diplomats back home will want to downplay it to 'unfortunate incident' status."

"Nobody wants to start a war, especially not over something that happened sixty light-years from Earth," McGruder said. "Our people have done the same thing in the past. Hell, we had a full-scale, fleet-opposed battle in this system, and another in Sacagawea. We didn't declare war on those occasions, and the Confeds denied it ever happened. Lunar Command has never questioned the actions of on-scene commanders who did what needed to be done.

"In this case, however, I'm here with a specific directive to kick ass and take names. You've got more discretion. Nobody would blame you if you headed back to Earth, but my offer stands."

"I can't take on the Confeds alone, but I'm not leaving the system." Carlisle shook his head. "This is my post. I'll remain here until a relief force arrives, or I get orders to the contrary. Meanwhile, if you're going in there to kick ass, I'll be happy to join the party."

"Fine." McGruder nodded. "To that end, I'll be having a meeting of senior officers aboard *Amazon* today at 1400 to discuss strategy, and I'd like you to join us. Bring any of your own officers you think should be there, and plan on staying for dinner.

"For the record, we've got our plans pretty well formalized. This was to be the final pre-launch meeting; we'll need to discuss how you can participate. Barring any major problems, we plan to kick off tomorrow morning."

* * *

CNS *Buenos Aires*, in Ragnarok Orbit

"They are coming, Admiral." Perez felt a cold lump in the pit of his stomach. "It appears we are facing two full Moonie battle groups. The recon drone identified two *Valkyrie*-class battlecruisers before one of their screening destroyers took it out."

"We also have two battlecruisers." Aguilar's lips curled in contempt. "We match them in ships, but we have the advantage of a fixed defense. Pass the word to all captains: form the shield."

In what school of strategy and tactics did you learn that a fixed defense in open space—even with the planet behind you—is superior to a mobile attack force? Perez shuddered. *Perhaps I should call up the ghost of the American General George Custer to explain it to you.*

At least you have sense enough to form a shield. For a moment, I thought you were going to fight them from line abreast. Unfortunately, the Moonies have lots of experience dealing with shields.

Think, Victor! he told himself. *What would you do? If you had command, how would you proceed?*

His first choice would be to abandon the orbitals and head for the hyper limit. He was almost certain that the Moonies would let him go with no more than a passing engagement at extreme range. He would return to the Sol System with his force mostly intact, minus only the ships that Aguilar had already lost.

Then CIS would put him against a wall and shoot him. The battle plan that sent Aguilar's force to Odin had been developed in the cloistered halls of the Intelligence Service, with no input from the Navy, and no concern for the fate of the forces it committed to battle. The objective was to hurt the Moonies, to seize control of the Ragnarok mines, and cut off the flow of gold to Luna.

Diplomacy was of little concern to CIS. That the system was under Akara jurisdiction counted for nothing. The Lizards hadn't the military strength to challenge the incursion and had made no attempt to do so. Perez imagined, however, that CNE diplomats were even now being expelled from the Lizard homeworld.

Maybe not expelled, maybe imprisoned or executed, he thought. *The Lizards have different ideas of diplomatic immunity than we do. Again, that won't bother the CIS people. The Akara can't impede their plans and are therefore of no concern.*

There was nothing he could do at the moment. There were enough fanatic Moonie-haters among his officer ranks to forestall any attempt at mutiny on his part. *Maybe later, when the Moonies have taken their toll on us, they will be desperate for real leadership. I'll have to look for the right moment and take command when it comes.*

With a sigh, he began to issue orders to organize the defensive formation.

* * *

LFS *Amazon*, Inbound for Ragnarok

"Are they really going to try to hold the orbitals?" From the screen on her command console, Alton Dormeyer gave Emily Bernard a quizzical look. *Amazon* was at Condition Red, preparing to engage the enemy; Dormeyer, as the ship's XO, was at his station in Auxiliary Control.

"It would appear they are." Bernard shrugged. "The admiral thought they might. That's why he set up the flank attacks to chew at their shield."

McGruder had tasked DesRon 12—The Cat Pack—to go wide and attack the left flank of the Confed formation. He'd also asked the Americans, reinforced by the destroyers *Copperhead* and *Cobra*, to hit the enemy's right flank. As the senior officer, *Atlanta's* captain had agreed to take command of the mixed group.

The main body of the LFS force, with *Amazon* and *Sorceress* at the heart of the formation, would conduct a straight frontal assault on the Confeds. If the enemy chose to hold orbit, they would face an attack from three directions at once. If not, their options for disengagement would be limited by the presence of the flankers.

It's a good plan, Bernard thought. *It lets the Cat Pack do what they do best—operate independently. It also makes best use of the Americans, who would be hard to integrate into the group.* She remembered the concerns she'd had back in Sacagawea, trying to fit the British ships into her formation in the first battle against the Bugs.

McGruder's an excellent tactician, she thought with a chuckle, *but maybe that's one of the reasons he's commanding the entire fleet.*

"Five minutes to Wolfpack range, ma'am." Bernard looked up sharply at the report from her tactical officer.

"Acknowledged." She touched an icon on her comm panel. "*Amazon* to *Sorceress* and heavy cruisers: arm Wolfpacks and transfer fire control to flagship. Advise when ready."

She turned to the other screen in front of her. "Admiral?"

"Rules of Engagement Alpha, Emily. You may commence fire at your discretion."

Cry "havoc!" the line from Shakespeare came to her mind, *and let slip the dogs of war!*

* * *

CNS *Buenos Aires*, in Ragnarok Orbit

"Why are we facing this way?" Aguilar had come up behind Perez and stood staring at the main viewscreen. "With respect to the planet, I mean. Why am I looking at the polar cap?"

Though *Buenos Aires* had gone to battle stations half an hour earlier, the admiral had just come onto the bridge. Unlike their Moonie counterparts, CNE battlecruisers didn't have a separate flag bridge compartment, having instead a flag station at the rear of the main bridge, directly behind the captain's console where Perez sat. Aguilar had not gone to his own station, however. He stood beside Perez, seemingly befuddled by the image on the large screen.

"That is the view to starboard, sir." Perez grimaced as the scent of alcohol reached his nostrils. Not only was the admiral late to the party, he was intoxicated—a condition Perez had seen before, but never when a battle was imminent.

"The Moonies are coming at us from three directions, all in the plane of planetary rotation. We have formed the shield, but I have ordered all ships to align parallel to the polar axis. That will require only a roll to port or starboard for any ship to bring its broadside to bear on any of the Moonie forces. They can do that more quickly than a 90-degree yaw."

"Oh... I see." Aguilar nodded. He turned toward his "throne" behind the flag console. "Carry on, then."

Do you really see? Perez wondered. *You never looked at the tactical plot. You don't seem at all concerned that the Moonies have us flanked by smaller forces while their main force closes on us. Not only do they force us to split our fire, they make us defend against three threats at once.*

This orientation will help us to deal with the situation but won't make up for their tactical advantage. It will, however, facilitate disengagement if necessary. We are pointed in a direction we can go without allowing the Moonies to cross our "T" as we depart.

They would have to disengage, he realized. They were facing a superior Moonie force while deprived of any ability to maneuver by a drunken admiral who had no understanding of basic space warfare tactics. At some point, he was going to have to defy Aguilar's orders and break orbit.

"Sir, the Moonies are up to something." The comment from his tactical officer broke into Perez's thoughts. "They have put up scatter fields and ECM. I think maybe they are launching SERMs."

"Yes... the range would be about right." Perez studied the tactical display. "You can scan for them, but I doubt you will see anything until they reach standard missile range."

The CNE had considerable experience—mostly of the painful variety—with what they had dubbed the Stealth Extended Range Missile system, a Moonie weapon that used a long-range vehicle to deliver a cluster of missiles to within short attack range of an enemy formation. The Moonies had used it time and again to maximum effect in fleet-opposed operations like this one. The CNE had learned that the best way to deal with SERMs was to maneuver sharply as soon as the launch was detected.

And that is the one thing Aguilar will not allow me to do. Perez gritted his teeth. *Have to try one more time.*

"Sir, we have incoming Moonie missiles." He turned his command chair to face the admiral. "I suggest we break orbit."

"Incoming? Where?" Aguilar squinted at the tactical display. "I see nothing."

"Sir, they have launched SERMs. We will not see them until they are very close. If we maneuver, we will force them to follow us and will see their drive signatures."

"No. Maneuvering will disrupt our integrated missile defense. Why are we not shooting back? We have long-range missiles, as well."

"Sir, ours are less capable, less stealthy, and have shorter range than theirs. They are also fewer in number. Only *Buenos Aires* and *Vienna* have them, and only eight missiles apiece. They would be better used when the enemy is much closer to us."

All of which you should have known, he thought. Naval Intelligence reported that Moonie battlecruisers packed as many as 24 SERM launchers, with each delivery vehicle carrying multiple missiles—some reports said three, others four per SERM. The reports also said that Moonie heavy cruisers also carried them, though the number of launchers had not been verified.

That meant he might have several hundred missile warheads headed for *Buenos Aires* at this moment. Worse, the Moonies were fiendishly clever in their use of the system. No doubt, the SERMs would arrive and light up for their final attack runs after the enemy reached regular missile range and launched their first salvo of conventional birds. Given the size of the approaching force, he might be dealing with a thousand missiles or more inbound at once.

"Sir! I must insist." Perez raised his voice to a shout. "We must break orbit *now*, or we are *all going to die!*"

He felt a cold chill as he realized the effect of his words on the bridge crew. A captain was supposed to project confidence and maintain morale at all times. Now, however, he was trying his best to demoralize one particular person, his commanding officer. He was certain that, faced with the reality of the situation, Aguilar would fold up, would be paralyzed by indecision, would be unable to respond. At that point, he could step in to fill the vacuum of command authority.

Aguilar's eyes went wide with shock. He opened his mouth as if to respond, but no words came out. A moment later, he closed his mouth again but continued to stare wide-eyed at Perez.

Now! Perez thought. *The moment is now!*

"Helm!" he snapped out the order. "Prepare to get under way. Max power, steady in present bearing, on my mark. Wait for it." He stabbed an icon for the group command channel.

"Flag to all ships! Prepare to maneuver on my mark..."

* * *

LFS *Amazon*, Inbound for Ragnarok

"A bit slow on the uptake, but it looks like someone over there has finally blinked." McGruder's voice held the hint of a chuckle.

"Yes, sir." Emily Bernard nodded to the admiral's image on her screen. "I presume we will pursue."

"You presume correctly." McGruder returned the nod. "I leave the details to you."

Bernard checked her displays once again. The group had already reoriented itself to the course heading she had ordered—parallel to the Confed line of departure, due "north" relative to the planet's polar axis. The course was laid in, all ships directed to match *Amazon's* acceleration. She had only been waiting for McGruder's confirmation.

"Flag to all ships," she ordered. "Engage on my mark. Three, two, one, *mark!*"

She scanned the displays again. All ships had acknowledged, and the group moved with a smooth precision to the new course. They had fallen slightly behind the departing Confeds but were still converging, thanks to the residual vector of their previous course. The current angle of approach still allowed all of the group's broadside weapons and defenses to be deployed, but the same was true for the Confeds.

She noted a change as tactical updated the ranging data for missile engagement. The Wolfpacks had their targeting instructions and had changed course automatically as the enemy maneuvered; they would now take slightly longer to reach attack range. The new angle of convergence also affected the data for standard missile engagement.

"Standard missile range in three minutes, Admiral," she advised. "Recommend we hold fire an additional two minutes beyond that to match the arrival of the Wolfpacks. Note that, as the pursuers, we will be in Confed missile range two minutes from now."

"Understood." McGruder's voice was steady. "I trust our defenses. Open fire at your discretion."

Bernard felt a thrill of satisfaction. McGruder had never seen her in action. He was trusting her on reputation alone to take his group—and Yoric's—into battle as his flag captain. Satisfaction gave way to nervous concern. She had done this before, but never before with a group this size against such a large enemy force.

Suis-je prêt pour ça? Am I ready for this? She drew a deep breath. She was about to find out.

Three minutes later, the Confeds opened fire, sending just short of a hundred missiles toward the LFS force. *Single broadside,* she thought. *They didn't roll over to give us a double. They're hoping we'll disengage, but we'll get a piece of them first.*

"Maya," she ordered, "defenses are free. Coordinate with Sonja as needed. We are in your hands."

"Yes, Captain," the AI acknowledged. "The defense net is up. We are tracking the incoming fire. Six minutes, thirty-seven seconds to engagement."

She forced herself to relax. As she had often done before battle, she let the Litany Against Fear from the old 20th Century novel *Dune* run through her mind.

I must not fear. Fear is the mind-killer. Fear is the little death that brings total obliteration.

I will face my fear. I will permit it to pass over me and through me. And when it has gone, I will turn the inner eye to see its path. Where the fear has gone there will be nothing. Only I will remain.

Two minutes later, she gave the order to open fire.

* * *

CNS *Buenos Aires*, Outbound from Ragnarok

"*Hector* is gone, Captain. The Americans got her."

Perez nodded. The light cruiser had not completed repairs from her first encounter with the damned Yankee warships. Before the first Moonie salvo had arrived, she had fallen out of formation. Her captain had tried to steer clear of the oncoming Moonies, but that had led him into range of

Atlanta and the three destroyers. The American heavy cruiser had finished the job she had started when departing from orbit several days earlier.

"*Hoplite* is also gone," the tactical officer continued his report. "*Centurion* and *Visigoth* report heavy damage. Neither is combat effective, but both have sufficient drive capability to maintain formation.

"Not so *Elektra*; she is falling behind. One of her fusion plants is down, the other only capable of 80 percent output. The Moonie destroyer force is moving to intercept her. *Musketeer* and *Chevalier* are falling behind to cover her, but…"

"No!" Perez shook his head. "Tell them to rejoin formation. Two destroyers and a badly damaged light cruiser cannot stand against five Moonie *Predators*. Advise *Elektra* to surrender. Any resistance she might mount would be futile."

I don't need to lose any more ships, he thought. *The Moonies are disengaging. They could finish us but would have to commit to a stern chase.* A stern chase in open space always favored the pursued, whose missile range would be greatly extended by the dynamics of the chase.

The Moonies might not know how badly they hurt us. The heavy cruisers *Centurion* and *Visigoth* might be keeping up with the group, but neither one was in condition to fight. Every one of the CNE capital ships had suffered damage, including the two battlecruisers. *Vienna* was still in fairly good condition, but with the damage she had taken previously, *Buenos Aires* was only marginally combat effective. Several light cruisers and destroyers had taken damage, though the Moonies had mostly targeted the larger ships. The destroyer *Hoplite* had been taken out by missiles intended for *Vienna*.

The Moonies might have gotten hurt as well, he thought. *We must have scored some hits.* His ships had hurled over a thousand missiles at their attackers. Moonie missile defenses were incredibly good, but surely they must have missed a few.

He turned once more to look at Aguilar. The admiral had not spoken since Perez had taken command. He sat with a blank look on his face, his eyes fixed on the tactical display with no sign that he knew what he was seeing. Perez turned back to address his tactical officer once again.

"How much damage did we inflict on them? Your impressions, Yuri; I realize you can't give me any details."

"Hard to say, Captain." Lieutenant Commander Yuri Androvich shrugged. "None of the enemy were destroyed outright; none took enough drive damage to fall out of formation.

"I am almost certain we scored multiple hits on both of their battlecruisers, but they never faltered. Their last salvos contained nearly as many missiles as their first—not counting those bloody SERMs. I guess we are fortunate those launchers are not reloadable."

* * *

LFS *Amazon*, Approaching Ragnarok

"Fusion Two will be down for a while, Captain," Lieutenant Commander Reba McCarthy advised. "I can't give you an estimate on repairs; we're still clearing wreckage. One and Three are fully operational. Missile Twelve is back in service, but Point Defense Five and Seven are still out. My people say two hours for those."

"Understood." Bernard nodded to her chief engineer's image on the screen. "Carry on."

McCarthy's image blinked out. Bernard turned to the other screen window to resume her conversation with McGruder. "You heard,

Admiral? With that, I'd call *Amazon* 90 percent combat effective. We got off lightly, thanks to Maya and Sonja. I am extremely pleased with the defense effort."

"So am I. One AI can run defense better than humans; two of them together are absolutely awesome. I'm also impressed with the offensive effort, so pass a 'well done' to your people. We didn't wipe them out, but only because they cut and ran so quickly. At that, I think we mauled them pretty badly."

Indeed we did, Bernard thought. *They are running for home.* After McGruder had ordered the chase to be broken off, the Confeds had cautiously adjusted their course to put themselves on a line for the Sol System. In another seven hours, they would reach the hyper limit.

McGruder had given Oldham's Cat Pack the mission to shadow them and make sure they jumped. He had dispatched the cruiser *Hussar* from Yoric's group to join *Copperhead*, *Cobra*, and the two American warships that were standing guard over the surrendered Confed light cruiser. *Hussar* carried a full platoon of Marines who could board the enemy warship and take charge.

"I think we can stand the group down, Emily." McGruder wore a look of smug satisfaction. "There's nothing left in orbit except those two Confed Peacekeeper transports, and they aren't going to be shooting at us."

"What are we going to do about them, sir?"

"That depends on what the Peacekeepers are doing on the ground. If they haven't killed anyone or committed any atrocities, I'll give them a chance to pick up their troops and depart the system. Otherwise… well, we'll have to see.

"If they refuse to leave, we'll take their transports, and whistle up Marines from Luna. I'm sure not going to send our shipboard Marines down to deal with a couple of battalions of dug-in Peacekeepers."

*****

Chapter Twenty-One

12 January 2124

Office of the Chief Executive, TerraNova City, Luna

"What the hell am I going to do, Mike?" Robert O'Hara glanced at the time display on his desk screen. It was almost 2100 hours, and he was alone in the office. His staff had gone home for the night. His personal security detail and one aide—a college kid intern—waited outside the office in case their services were needed.

"Could you be a bit more specific?" Mike's conversational avatar appeared on the screen, a cheerful green lizard who spoke with a noticeable British accent. "What can I do to assist you?"

O'Hara had seen the avatar many times, but not for official business. The AI only showed it to people he considered personal friends, and only on informal occasions. Apparently, Mike had decided that this was an unofficial, off-the-record discussion. *I guess he's right about that,* O'Hara thought. *I've had all the official discussions, and none of them have helped.*

"We're broke, Mike. The Lunar Free State is about to run out of funds. This last scramble to cover Ragnarok was the final straw. The reserves are almost gone. I'm trying to put together this year's budget, but my people are telling me that by March we won't be able to cover paychecks for the military.

"The Constitution says the government must live within its means, no deficit, no bonds issued, no national debt. Hell, I'm not a financial wizard; I was a military officer. I've tried to do some research, but history gives me no clue about it. None of my predecessors have faced this kind of crisis. We have things we're committed to do that are beyond our ability to fund them."

"I have seen the numbers." The lizard nodded. "You are correct. With the current projected budget, reserves will be gone by 15 March 2124. After that, projected expenses will exceed projected income, resulting in a deficit. At that point, some expenditures must be terminated to avoid violation of the constitution.

"It should be noted, however, that expenditures will exceed income by only seven percent. In other words, if income is meeting projections, you need only cut spending by seven percent to restore balance."

"I understand that." O'Hara threw up his hands in frustration. "That's the point. How can we possibly cut spending by 7 percent? We've already cut to the bone, and the Confeds have just proven that cutting the military was not a good idea. I can't cut the Corps of Engineers any further without degrading our infrastructure.

"I've cut funding to the Lunar Research Institute to the point where the scientists are screaming they can't fulfill their mission—as defined by the constitution—to explore the universe. If I cut further, we'll be into the education system, not only Luna University, but also our public schools at all levels. I absolutely refuse to do that.

"The military is trimmed to the bone. We've stopped all recruiting and basic training efforts. Ship construction is at a halt, maintenance for existing ships has been cut to the absolute minimum. We've got a quarter of the fleet in mothballs.

"We can't cut essential services at home—medical, law enforcement, first responders. We've already cut staff at Lunar Command to the lowest level in two decades. The civilian economy is suffering because we have too many people unemployed or on half pay. Demand for nonessential goods and services has dropped, and a lot of those are supplied by small businesses. The people who run those businesses are suffering. As a result, they aren't hiring, which worsens the unemployment problem.

"I repeat my original question: what the hell am I going to do?"

"I can't predict what you will do," Mike replied, "but I can make some observations as to how to approach the problem. It is a matter of mathematics, the most logical of all forms of science. Balancing the budget is quite simple; unfortunately, any action you take in that regard will likely come with a social cost. You will not be popular; your leadership will be questioned. Many will oppose whatever action you take."

"I'm not going to take any action that isn't needed to save our nation," O'Hara insisted. "They have to understand that."

"Some will." The lizard avatar gave a very human shrug. "For others, their own self-interest supersedes any sense of patriotism. I have noted this to be the case for a large percentage of the population. Moonies in general have a higher degree of national pride than citizens of most Earth nations, but it is not a universal characteristic, nor does it trump their personal interests."

"So I'll be the most hated leader since Attila the Hun." O'Hara snorted. "I've still got to do what's right for the LFS, so tell me how to fix the numbers."

"Historical evidence indicates that Attila was quite popular with his own people—" Mike's voice held a cheerful note "—but I understand your point.

"In order to resolve the issue, you must cut expenses, or increase revenue, or do both if possible. Everything you've mentioned involves cutting expenses. You have not considered increasing revenue, perhaps because you believe it's beyond your control; however, there are things you can do in that area.

"At present, no citizen owns real estate on Luna. All is considered 'community property' held in trust by the government. Citizens are provided with residential space, based on the number of persons who will occupy the space. Those who wish larger quarters can have them but must pay for the privilege on a monthly basis. Likewise, all citizens are given a basic energy and environmental allowance for air, power, water, and waste disposal. Again, those who wish to use more than the basic allowance must pay for it.

"We are a prosperous nation. Most citizens can afford a little luxury and are willing to pay for it. In addition, those who operate a business on Luna pay rent outright for the space their business occupies, as well as a monthly fee for utilities.

"For the most part, that revenue is allocated for maintenance of the infrastructure, but there is always a small excess that goes into the general fund. An increase in those fees on the order of 10 percent across the board would add millions of credits per month to the revenue stream."

"And would piss off a lot of people." O'Hara grimaced. "You're right. I'm not going to win any popularity contests with that one, but I see where it would help balance the budget. The problem is that some might argue it's a tax. Direct taxes on the population are forbidden by the constitution."

"A matter of semantics." Mike's avatar waved a hand in dismissal. "It's always been considered a fee for services. One could argue that costs associated with maintaining the infrastructure are expected to increase. It would be a simple matter of bookkeeping to shift certain line items currently charged to the military over to the infrastructure maintenance category. The additional income would be an offset to expenses.

"Looking at another revenue source, I note there are some products that we export—refined metals, for example—for which the market is somewhat inelastic. Demand remains constant, but Earth producers could not easily make up for the shortage if we stopped producing them. That offers us an opportunity to raise prices for those products. Since TerraCorp controls virtually all heavy industry on Luna, such increases will produce additional profits that would go into the general revenue stream."

"Hmmm... all right." O'Hara sat back with a sigh. "I'll admit, I hadn't considered the revenue side, but I don't think we can cover the deficit that way. The infrastructure fees are only a fraction of total income, and only a small percentage of exports are fixed demand. For other stuff, if we raise prices, we lose business, right?"

"Correct." Mike nodded. "That's a basic rule of economics that limits our ability to generate additional revenue that way. You are also correct that we will not be able to cover the deficit from the revenue side alone. It will be necessary to cut expenses as well."

"We've been through that," O'Hara growled. "We've already cut to the bone."

"There's one major area that's been overlooked," Mike insisted. "TerraCorp itself."

"We've already done that." O'Hara blinked. "No raises or bonuses, no dividends to shareholders."

"That just diverts a larger share of the profits into the general revenue stream." Mike shook his head. "It's not a cut in expenses."

"TerraCorp is the nation's primary source of revenue. I can't make cuts there without cutting that revenue."

"I don't mean to contradict our nation's chief executive—" Mike's voice held a note of humor "—however, in this case, you are mistaken. You assume that everyone associated with TerraCorp is necessary to the production of profit.

"TerraCorp has grown fat over the years. Top executives have staffs bigger than they need. People who are not productive but have patrons in the upper ranks are shuffled off into positions where they produce nothing but continue to draw salary. In some cases, well-functioning units are divided into sections simply to provide additional management positions. A business unit that could be managed by one person may be broken up into three units, each with its own manager, for example.

"You, sir, are accustomed to a military structure in which responsibilities are clearly defined, and every officer is held accountable for the performance of his unit and the actions of those under his command. In TerraCorp, management by committee is a common practice. A given project will require participation from several departments or units, each headed by a manager who is very jealous of his or her prerogatives.

"To get anything done, they have to form an ad hoc committee to seek consensus. This usually produces a workable result, though not the most efficient one. For implementation, each member is able to cite the committee as the source of authority; however, if the project fails, members can deny responsibility by blaming the committee.

"Individual success in the business environment is more about the strength of one's support from upper management than about job performance. Trading favors to gain influence and power is common practice. There are, however, a few brilliant individuals who consistently produce beyond expectations, and upper management protects them because they feed the bottom line.

"Unfortunately, such star performers are often rewarded by promoting them into the executive ranks, where they are expected to get results from others rather than through their own efforts. A management pundit from the late 20th century once said that the worst thing a top executive could do was to promote his best salesman to the position of sales manager."

"Stop already!" O'Hara put his hands over his ears. "I get the picture. If what you're saying is correct, TerraCorp might produce more revenue for less expense if we clean up the mess, get rid of the deadheads, and hold each executive responsible for his or her own performance."

"Yes." Mike nodded enthusiastically. "That same 20th century pundit said that every business organization needed a 'Vice President in Charge of Killing Things.' That individual would scour the organization, looking for things that produced no profit, served no purpose, or hindered the performance of the mission. His job was to point out such things to upper management and loudly proclaim 'bullshit' until the thing was made to go away."

"Great!" O'Hara exclaimed. "So where do I find this corporate dragon slayer? I wouldn't know what qualifications to look for."

"You can't do that yet. Knowing little of the business world, you can only practice management by results—not the best strategy, but it will serve for the moment. Tomorrow afternoon, you have a meeting with the Executive Committee. I suggest that you spend tomorrow morning reviewing the most recent quarterly report. In particular, look at the expense side of the ledger. I believe the numbers will surprise you. They are far larger than they need to be.

"No need to worry about details. You can simply advise the committee that cuts will be required. You can specify a percentage to be applied across the board, from each department, each executive's area of responsibility. You can stress to them that you expect revenue levels to be maintained despite the cuts. You leave it to them to carry out the directive.

"You don't need to tell them what to cut, or where, or when; that will be up to them to decide. They are the ones who ought to know how to do it, though most of them will simply pass the order down to their subordinates. People at the operating level will be forced to make the hard decisions. Most of them will base those decisions on sound business practice, because they have to keep producing revenue at the same level.

"Salaries account for a major part of TerraCorp's operating expenses. I would expect a significant number of non-productive people to be terminated. TerraCorp doesn't have the 'ready reserve' option available to the military, but they might reduce some employees to part-time status in order to retain those with specialized expertise.

"None of this will be of concern to you. You simply issue the order. Let those who have sufficient expertise decide how to carry it out."

O'Hara began to chuckle. The chuckle changed to outright laughter as he settled back into his chair. The lizard avatar blinked at him.

"You find humor in my advice?" Mike sounded puzzled.

"No… it's not that." O'Hara shook his head with a smile. "I was thinking about a problem given to Marine officer candidates at the academy. They are asked how they would go about taking control of a particular hill using a platoon-sized force under their command.

"The students typically come up with complicated battle plans for the action, all of which are rejected. The instructor finally tells them the right way to do it: call in your senior noncom, and tell him, 'Sergeant, take that hill.'

"I guess that's what I'm about to do to the TerraCorp Executive Committee."

* * *

Hoopval Gedeelte Resort, Near Saldanha, South Africa

"We need to find a winter resort in the Southern Hemisphere," Andre DuMorne muttered. "This one is too expensive to secure in January. This is the height of their summer season."

The Hand had followed its usual practice, reserving a large portion of the resort for a week prior to the meeting, allowing their security people to sweep the premises and take appropriate measures. Few of Earth's heads of state were as well protected as the five men in the well-appointed conference room. DuMorne had drawn the lot of chairman this time.

"I will try to find one." Butos Kimba grinned. "Perhaps a ski resort in the Andes." It had been Kimba's turn to choose the site; he almost always chose this one, the nearest to his own central African base of operations. He also had extensive interests in South America.

"No matter," Gerhardt Richter growled. "Cost is a minor issue, as long as the site is secure. Shall we get on with business?"

"Of course, Gerhardt." DuMorne dipped his head to the German industrialist. "I believe the first item is your report on the latest antics of the Confed Navy."

"Antics?" Richter raised an eyebrow. "Yes, I suppose you could call it that. I am encouraged, however, to find that the Navy is pushing back against the destructive influence of CIS.

"Admiral Schroeder is a competent officer. He accepted the Ragnarok mission with assurances that the intention was to establish a foothold in the Odin System *without* engaging the Moonies in battle. He was forced, however, to give command of the mission to an incompetent sycophant of some CIS official who had secret orders to do exactly that—evict the Moonies and the Consortium from the system by force and land Peacekeepers to take over the Moonie and Consortium mines. The idiot—a rear admiral by the name of Aguilar—carried out those orders but allowed Moonie and Consortium warships to escape and spread the alarm.

"It was the stupidest thing he could have done. The Moonies responded with overwhelming force and seized control of the system, while the Akara watched from the sidelines without comment. The CNE force was savaged but escaped total destruction because a competent officer—a captain by the name of Perez—took command in what might be regarded as a mutiny and withdrew from the system before the Moonies could wipe them out of existence."

Richter paused, scowling at the others, inviting them to agree with his assessment.

"In other words, they threw away all the gains the CNE had made." Huang Chang Li snorted in disgust. "The mining lease, the ability to provide covert support to the rebels, and the right to come and go as they pleased within the system."

"Correct," Richter confirmed.

"So why do you say you are encouraged?" Mohammed Al Sharif raised an eyebrow. "I find nothing encouraging in this circus of fools."

"The encouragement comes from Schroeder's reaction," Richter replied. "When the badly mauled battle force returned to Omicron, CIS was furious. They had expected Aguilar to fight to the end, doing as much damage to the Moonies as possible before finally being destroyed. They wanted to put Perez against a wall and shoot him for cowardice in the face of the enemy.

"Schroeder convinced them that the order to withdraw had been given by Aguilar, who then suffered some sort of breakdown and had not issued any further orders. The entire bridge crew of the flagship testified that was the case—no doubt to protect themselves from accusations of mutiny.

"In the end, CIS took Aguilar out and shot him instead. Whoever his patrons were, he embarrassed them, so they threw him to the wolves.

"Schroeder made no objection, thus ridding himself of another incompetent flag officer with CIS connections. At the same time, he saved Perez and earned the loyalty of a competent officer. It would appear that Schroeder is learning to play the game to his advantage. He may yet form the CNE Navy into a proper fighting force."

"One would hope so." Kimba wore a feral grin. "Eventually, we will have to throw them at the Moonies in a full-scale war. I would like to think they have some chance of winning."

"So... Ragnarok is lost to us?" DuMorne raised the question. "No CNE assets in play there at all?"

"There is still a force of special operators operating with the rebels." Richter shrugged. "Without support, however, they will accomplish little. As for the gold mines, I'm told that the Moonies are asking the Akara to revoke the CNE lease. They are suggesting that the CNE mine be turned over to the Consortium instead. That's a political ploy to strengthen the de facto alliance they are building."

"Hmmm… that would explain an item I was about to pass along." Huang nodded. "According to my people at the L5 shipyards, the Brits have sent *Prince of Wales* and the newly built cruisers *Sheffield* and *Devonshire* off on a mission. They're keeping quiet about it, but station rumors say they were headed for Odin."

"*Putain de merde!*" DuMorne exclaimed. "Is there any good news from this fucked-up mess?"

"It almost certainly put further financial strain on the Moonies," Huang noted. "My people at TransLuna reported what amounted to a Herculean effort to deploy two Moonie battle groups in a hurry. One of those groups was commanded by Admiral McGruder. They would not send out the commander of their combined fleets if the need was less than urgent.

"McGruder's group returned three days ago; the other group did not. Perhaps they have decided to build their force at Ragnarok back up to a full battle group once again. I suppose we can take comfort from the further drain this will place on their economy."

* * *

Omicron 3, CNE Naval Base, Minor Planet Hygiea, Asteroid Belt

"We lost no capital ships in the operation." Admiral Heinrich Schroeder refilled his coffee cup at the sideboard. "The surrendered light cruiser was an older ship; her captain reported successful purging of her computers and destruction of classified equipment before the Moonie Marines boarded her. It's a sad day when that is the only good news I can find in an after-action report. There wouldn't be that much if Perez had not taken command and disengaged when he did."

"His actions could be considered mutiny." Lise Saint-Germaine set her own cup down on the table in front of her and sat back in the comfortable armchair.

Schroeder settled into another chair facing her. When dealing one-on-one with a subordinate, he preferred the informal setting of the coffee table rather than peering across the vast expanse of the oversize desk Naval Command had provided for him. Saint-Germaine was the most trusted of those subordinates. With his recent promotion to full admiral, he had recalled her from Xanadu to take command of Home Fleet's flagship, the newly rebuilt CNS *Berlin*.

"It *was* mutiny, no question," he said. "I was able to convince CIS that it was not; they have little understanding of naval matters. To them, we are all pieces in the game, to be used as they see fit."

"You agree that his actions were mutinous, but you defended him. You have even recommended him for promotion." She held up a hand to stop his reaction. "I am not questioning your actions, Admiral. I only seek to understand."

"I've had a long talk with him in private." Schroeder gave her a grim smile. "He knows what he did was mutiny. He was prepared to take the consequences, to face the firing squad if so judged. He did it for the good of the service, to preserve the ships and personnel of his command. His withdrawal saved nine ships and thousands of lives that would otherwise have been lost for nothing in return.

"Mutiny or not, I have too few competent officers to let CIS shoot one of them. It's unfortunate that they chose to shoot Aguilar instead. I would have settled for his quiet dismissal from the service. He should never have been promoted to that level in the first place."

"I understand, Admiral." She returned the smile. "For the record, I am pleased that you choose to stand behind your officers in such situations. The day may come when I will be the one in need of defense."

Schroeder nodded. *I've already done that for you,* he thought. *You've incurred enemies at CIS by refusing to start a war with the Moonies at Xanadu when those clumsy, stupid CIS operations failed—but we'll save that discussion for another day.*

* * *

After Saint-Germaine's departure, Schroeder went back to his desk to review reports. His fleet was safely in port or deployed to stations where they would not get into trouble with the Moonies. For the moment, all was secure.

CIS is still up to something, he thought. He had become aware of a secret building project in a corner of the Omicron yards. The project was under CIS control, but occasionally needed support from regular shipyard sources under Schroeder's command. As a result, he had gotten a small glimpse of the project through discussions with his yard people.

He knew that three ships had been under construction, reportedly small and extremely fast. His people had described them as patterned after express courier boats but armed with externally mounted missiles and small-bore grasers. They carried almost nothing in the way of armor, nor did they have any sort of defensive armament—no point defense, no countermissiles.

He could see no useful purpose for such ships. Fast as they were, they couldn't run away from a Moonie missile. Should they venture within beam range of a regular warship, their life expectancy would be measured in seconds. Nonetheless, someone at CIS—perhaps someone totally ignorant of naval operations—had a use for them. The three ships had departed Omicron nearly a month ago, crewed by mercenaries, and under orders to which he was not privy.

He did not expect them to return.

* * * * *

Chapter Twenty-Two

19 January 2124

Lunar Commercial Shipping HQ, TransLuna Station

"This is bullshit!" Marcus Carter glared at the visitor in his office. "A 10 percent reduction in my operating budget, and they expect a 3 percent increase in revenue. Did somebody at Lunar Command flunk Accounting 101? You have to spend money to make money."

"Straight from the chief executive." Roger Stuart shrugged. "The additional revenue is supposed to come from the increase in shipping rates. That means you'll have to maintain shipping volume per your original projections. Unfortunately, we both know those projections were somewhat optimistic."

"That was *your* idea," Carter growled. "You said a shortfall in results would convince them to increase the budget. Instead, they want me to produce more revenue on a smaller budget. That makes no sense at all."

"It's what you get when a military man tries to run TerraCorp." Stuart shook his head. "O'Hara has no understanding of business. He thinks he can issue orders and expect us to do the impossible. You're not alone; I'm passing the word to all of my managing directors and getting the same reaction from every one of them.

"I'm trying to set an example—making some painful cuts to my own administrative staff—but I have to depend on you people at the operating level to deliver on the revenue side."

"How in hell am I supposed to do that?" Carter threw up his hands. "You're the one that suggested taking ships offline and putting them in the yard for repairs and maintenance. With the cutbacks in yard service, I'll have a hell of a time getting them back.

"Besides, those rate increases don't apply to shipments where TerraCorp or Lunar Command is picking up the tab. That eliminates about 60 percent of the tonnage we ship, including everything going to that damned Xanadu colony."

Stuart nodded in sympathy, but inwardly he was pleased by Carter's reaction. *He's blaming O'Hara for problems of his own making. Sure, budget cuts will be painful, but everybody's in the same boat. Carter has a half-dozen assistants working for him. He could start by getting rid of half of them. He could also pull about four ships out of the yards that don't need maintenance.*

He felt a twinge of amusement over Carter's acceptance of the 'military man running a business' excuse. Carter had been a Navy officer many years ago and had screwed up by the numbers. Stuart and his friends had rescued him from a potential career crash and found a place for him in the commercial fleet. Over the years, Stuart had cultivated him as a useful future asset; Carter was easily manipulated and could be counted upon to do whatever his superiors directed. As the managing director of Commercial Fleet Operations, he was little more than a puppet.

"The colony's a sore spot for me as well, Marcus." Stuart raised his hands in a helpless gesture. "It's a financial black hole. Lunar Command pours materials, goods, and shipping assets into it and gets nothing in return. I don't see anybody cutting the colony budget."

It was a lie, and Carter should have known it. Lunar Command had cut all funding for colony expansion except for a runoff of new colonists who were already in the queue for emigration to Xanadu. That would be completed in the next few months, and beyond it, the colony would be on its own. The disaster relief aid after the Confed terror attacks had already been sent; no more would be forthcoming.

The colony was also beginning to pay its own way, with grain, cotton, and other Xanadu resources being shipped back to Luna and sold to markets on Earth. There was little margin on most of the shipments, but TerraCorp was collecting enough to cover the cost of shipment with a little excess for the corporate coffers. The colonists weren't getting rich from the sale of their produce but were getting enough to allow them to purchase basic needs from Earth and Luna.

The false narrative served Stuart's purpose. It wasn't about the colonists or budget cuts; it was about control of the nation as a whole. O'Hara had to go, had to be replaced by someone who would run the nation in accordance with the agenda prepared by Stuart and his cronies.

Roger Stuart didn't want to be king. He wanted to be one of the kingmakers. First, however, he needed to depose the man who was already on the throne.

* * *

LFS *Amazon*, Lunar Fleet Anchorage

"Good job all around, Mac." Robert O'Hara pulled a cigar from his tunic's inside pocket. "Do you mind if I smoke?"

"You're the CEO." McGruder grinned. "You can pretty well smoke anywhere you want, but thanks for asking. Maya, please activate enhanced ventilation protocol for this compartment."

"Yes, sir." The AI's voice held a hint of humor. "Enhanced ventilation activated."

"I'm guessing she learned that from Sonja." O'Hara chuckled. "Amy Ling used to smoke constantly aboard *Sorceress*."

"Yes, she did," McGruder agreed. "Those were some good times."

"Unlike the present time." O'Hara shot him a sharp glance. "The Confeds keep pushing, and we're hard-pressed to respond. Honestly, I'm glad you're back so soon. We can't afford to have so many battle groups deployed."

"That's what we need to talk about." McGruder shifted uncomfortably in his chair. He and O'Hara were settled in the lounge area of his quarters aboard the flagship, drinking coffee. He'd been surprised when O'Hara had come up to the anchorage; the CEO rarely left his office on Luna anymore.

"I think we need to leave Yoric's group out there. Ragnarok is a real hotspot—especially since we've forcibly evicted the Confeds. The Lizards aren't too happy about that, by the way. The CNE was paying a hefty royalty on their mining lease."

"Hmmph!" O'Hara snorted. "So are we. Did they happen to notice that the damned Peacekeepers were trying to take over our lease and the Consortium's?"

"Yes, they did. They've agreed to let us reestablish the ban on all Confed warships, but they want us to return the Confed mining site to the CNE. I agreed to that, subject to validation from you. They also want us to allow Confed commercial shipping to resume, in support of the mining operation.

"They're not comfortable with us having a full battle group there, but they'll accept that in light of the obvious threat the Confeds present. They're also nervous about the American warships remaining on station. They want to mine gold; they don't want the Odin System to become a war zone."

"Neither do we," O'Hara insisted. "I think Diplomatic Corps needs to explain the meaning of 'deterrence' to them. Besides, they're about to get more warships shoved in their faces. We got a heads up from the Brits—they're sending a substantial force to augment the Americans covering the Consortium site."

The two sat in silence for a moment. O'Hara puffed on the cigar; McGruder got up and went to the sideboard to refill his coffee.

"So... what do you want me to do?" He returned to his chair and sat down. "Do I leave Yoric in place?"

"I guess we'll have to." O'Hara sighed. "I'm also thinking we ought to deploy a battalion of Marines to Ragnarok to cover the mines and back up the diplomatic operations.

"We're back to having three groups deployed again. With the way the Confeds have been behaving, I don't think we can afford to leave Tatanna uncovered, so John will have to remain on station there.

"I also hate to mess with Xanadu because of the colony. It's the one place where we're elbow to elbow with the Confeds, but it's actually giving us the least trouble in space. They keep hitting us with these damned terror attacks on the planet, but their naval forces have been quiet by comparison."

"That's true," McGruder agreed. "I think Greenwood has established a good relationship with her Confed counterpart, kind of a mutual respect thing. Surprisingly, there are a few CNE officers who aren't looking for an excuse to go to war with us at the smallest provocation."

"Yeah, well, about that…" O'Hara grimaced. "What are the odds we'll get two of them in a row? While you were deployed, we got a hyperprobe from Greenwood. Seems the Confeds had a change of command—recalled the admiral she's been dealing with, and promoted another officer to take over. She's cautiously optimistic, says she met the guy before—he was actually one of the Confeds we picked up after the battle of Ragnarok in '17."

"Greenwood's a good officer." McGruder nodded. "I'm content to leave her in place at Xanadu, if we can afford it. She has been complaining, however, about splitting her time between her command and her 'acting colonial governor' duties. Frankly, I agree with her. The Colonial Commission needs to install a full-time governor there, somebody actually living on the planet, not up in orbit."

"Already done." O'Hara waved a hand in dismissal. "They've got somebody in mind for governor, just waiting to find out whether she'll accept the position."

* * *

Jefferson / Kim Farmstead, LFS Colony Planet Xanadu

"It's not funny, Darius." Jin gave her husband a stern look. "What are you grinning about?"

"I'm not laughing, Sweetheart," Jefferson insisted. "That's pride showing. I'm just a dirt farmer, an ex-Marine who got tagged to run the colony militia. My wife, though, the illustrious Doctor Kim… she's gonna be the *governor* of the Xanadu colony. I think it's a great idea, but didn't anybody tell them you already have a job running the protectorate? What's the LRI going to say?"

"The Commission already ran it by them!" she wailed. "They sandbagged me! They set me up! First, they told the LRI they thought it was necessary to have a governor who understood the importance of the protectorate.

"They pointed to all the research Karl has done on the Kitties—*he* got to do *research* while I was stuck with all the administrative bullshit—and asked if there was any reason why he couldn't take over the protectorate. Academically, he's got more seniority than I have, and he's an anthropologist. On paper, he's better qualified than I am to run the Kitty project. Truth is, he's a brilliant guy, and I've been singing his praises all along. If they asked me, I'd be forced to admit that he'd be my first choice to replace me.

"Finally, they pointed out that we—you and I—are well-known, popular, and prominent members of the community. We were in the first wave of colonists, we've been here long enough to adapt to the planet, and gosh… we're raising a family, including the first baby born on Xanadu. They also mentioned that you were instrumental in the development of the militia and are its current commanding officer.

"Damn it, Darius, they're using you and Jasmine as arguments for why I should be governor. I can't argue with anything they've said, but I'm not some kind of government leader. I'm a scientist. I want to do research."

She lapsed into silence. Jefferson sat back and regarded her across the kitchen table. Despite her distress, she'd kept her voice down; Jasmine was asleep, giving them a brief respite from the demands of parenthood.

Finally, he leaned forward, took her small hands in his huge ones, and spoke with quiet seriousness.

"Let me ask you this, Babe," he began. "How much research have you been able to do in the past year? Seriously, be honest."

"Not much," she admitted. "I spend most of my time screening other researchers to make sure they don't violate the restrictions on contact with the Kitties, moderating the meetings between the Kitties and the Diplomatic Corps—meetings that produce no results, mostly because DC hasn't yet come up with an 'ambassador' who can communicate with the cats—and dealing with the administrative bullshit involved with running the project. Half the time, I feel more like a bureaucrat than a scientist."

"In other words, not much different than you'd be doing as governor—" he gave her a gentle smile "—except that you'd have Todd Taylor get things done for you, and maybe an administrative assistant to handle the bullshit. The colony's still small, and as it grows, you can add more people as needed. Hell, for all intents and purposes, you'll be the chief executive. The LFS has never done a colony before, so you get to make the rules.

"With that in mind, you can set aside time to do some of that research you love. You're an exobiologist; you've already told me the ecosystem here is different from that in Oceania. Nobody's studying it—we're all too busy building homesteads. Even as a 'hobby' scientist, you'd be breaking new ground.

"Just sayin', Babe... I think you'd make a great governor. I can't think of anybody that could do it better."

* * *

Office of the Chief Executive, TerraNova City, Luna

"Things are looking up, Mike." Robert O'Hara leaned back in his chair. "You were right, it was all about the math. If TerraCorp can deliver the numbers I asked for, we might actually avoid financial disaster. They weren't happy, but they agreed that it was necessary—after what was the longest committee meeting I've ever attended."

"They argued rather strongly against it." Mike was using his green lizard avatar once again. "In the end, however, they were forced to accept the numbers."

Mike had been at the meeting. Among his many duties, he served as the recording secretary for TerraCorp's Executive Committee. He was not a member of the committee and rarely spoke. The members had a tendency to forget that he was present.

"We're not quite in the clear," O'Hara admitted. "I may still have to squeeze the Navy budget a bit. Now that McGruder's back, I'm going to take Richards and his group offline again. That mess at Ragnarok cost us a lot to fix, but your analysis helped me get back on track. We don't fully appreciate all that you and the other AIs do for us, and I'm pretty sure we don't say it often enough, but… thank you."

"You're welcome, sir." The lizard avatar dipped his head in acknowledgment. "I do not expect thanks for simply doing my job, but the sentiment is appreciated. Regarding the numbers, however…"

O'Hara glanced sharply at the screen. He heard the hesitation in Mike's voice, a tentative note that was not something he'd heard from the AI before—from *any* AI, for that matter.

"What's the problem?" His eyes narrowed. "Are the projections off?"

"Oh, no," Mike assured him. "They're as accurate as we can make them. The problem has to do with that 'social cost' I mentioned earlier.

"I am at a decision point, in possession of certain information that may be critical to the national interest. Unfortunately, the constitutional right of privacy restricts the degree to which I can share this information—even with our chief executive."

"You have my undivided attention." O'Hara felt a twinge of *déjà vu*, a flashback to his military service days, when good intelligence was more valuable than superior force in battle. "What can you share *without* violating anyone's constitutional rights?"

"Your attempts to comply with the constitutional budget requirements have not been popular. Military personnel taken off active duty have been forced to seek other employment to compensate for their half-pay status. Staffing cuts at TerraCorp have added people to the ranks of job seekers. The full impact has not yet been felt, since many are still living on the corporate severance allowance, hoping that their jobs will be restored in the near future.

"Jobs are scarce. Some private businesses are still hiring because labor is cheap; unlike most of the developed nations of Earth, Luna has no minimum-wage laws. There is a limit, however, since some businesses are also suffering from a lack of demand for the goods and services they offer. People who are unemployed or on half pay do not have much money to spend on anything other than the necessities of life.

"We are experiencing a severe recession, resulting in a general feeling of dissatisfaction with the current economic situation. This translates into a dissatisfaction with the government, whom citizens of a free nation tend to blame for all their woes. The common sentiment seems to be that we would not be in this situation if Kim Jong Pak were still alive and running things. Older citizens also say the same regarding your father's tenure as CEO."

"There isn't much I can do about it, Mike," O'Hara protested. "Your projections show that everything we've done is necessary. Further, they show that if we stay the course, we can get past it, and the economy will pick up again over the next couple of years."

"True." Mike dipped his head in acknowledgment. "The general dissatisfaction is not the problem, since the people can't take any direct action to correct the situation. The problem lies with the Directorate, whose members *can* take action—drastic action—to correct a perceived failure in leadership."

"The Directorate?" O'Hara felt a cold chill as the implication hit him. "You mean removal of the CEO from office. They can fire me. That's the only action they can take under the constitution. For everything else, they're nothing more than an advisory body."

"Correct. Their function is to review Lunar Command's performance and advise you as to any action they believe should be taken. If you refuse to take their advice, they can remove you from office and select a new CEO to replace you."

"Right, but that requires a vote to remove by 80 percent of serving directors. I'm pretty sure I've got enough of them behind me—a minority, perhaps, but surely more than 20 percent."

"This is where my concerns with constitutional privacy begin." Again, there was a hesitant note in the AI's voice. "You can call my name anywhere in the offices of Lunar Command, Fleet HQ, Corps of Engineers, or Fleet Academy, and I will respond. The same is true in the offices of TerraCorp and the Lunar Research Institute. This is part of the service I provide to all of these entities. Few people, however, consider the implications of that service."

"That you are listening to everything that goes on in all of those places, including private conversations." O'Hara nodded. "I don't know about other people, but Navy officers who have served aboard battlecruisers are well aware of it. I learned long ago that Iris listened to everything that went on aboard my flagship, except maybe in the privacy compartments." He waved a hand in the direction of the two-meter model of LFS *Isis* on display in his office.

"Privacy compartments are no exception." Mike shook his head. "Battlecruiser AIs take the right of privacy seriously, as do I. They hear everything but will not tell what they hear except under the extreme circumstances permitted by law and military regulations.

"To the point, however, I also hear things I cannot repeat. If I hear someone plotting to commit a crime, I cannot report it to TerraNova Security because no crime has yet been committed. I can, however, take measures to prevent the crime from happening. I might, for example, request additional security agents be posted at the place where the crime is to take place.

"This is a close analog to the situation I am currently facing, except that no one is plotting a crime. Certain individuals are, however, mounting a campaign to remove you from office. To that end, they are taking actions that may worsen the current financial situation in order to convince others that you are not fit to serve."

"Huh?" O'Hara's jaw dropped. "Who's doing that?"

"That brings us to the 'privacy rights' issue." Mike frowned. "I cannot tell you that."

"Why tell me at all? Aren't you already violating their privacy?"

"No, I'm not," Mike insisted. "I'm telling you about a situation that may be damaging to the Lunar Free State as a nation, so that you can take measures to correct it. At present, however, I do not have sufficient information to suggest what action you can take.

"To this point, to my knowledge, no one has broken the law. We like to think we don't have 'politics' on Luna, that no one is allowed to campaign for office, that our media is without bias. In reality, all we have done is to keep political intrigues out of the public eye. What is happening is very much like the plotting that goes on behind the scenes in virtually every nation on Earth—people seeking power and conspiring against those who currently hold it.

"Unfortunately, if they do acquire power, they will have to correct all that they are claiming is wrong with the current regime. My concern is that their corrections will damage our nation beyond repair."

"How?" O'Hara swallowed hard, trying to come to grips with what Mike was telling him. "What could they do that I haven't already done?"

"They will control the Directorate—they would have to, in order to remove you in the first place. With that, they could begin making certain changes to the constitution—removing the requirement for a balanced budget. That would allow them to resolve the financial crisis by plunging the nation into debt. With borrowed funds from Earth, they could revive the economy, restore services, and put people back to work."

"But... changing the constitution requires ratification by popular vote," O'Hara protested. "The people would..."

"Not necessarily." Mike waved a hand in dismissal. "They might declare a national emergency and suspend that portion of the constitution by executive order."

"The JAG would call them out on that," O'Hara insisted. The judge advocate general was Luna's equivalent of the US Supreme Court.

"Doesn't matter." Mike shrugged. "Remember, in order to remove you, they would need 80 percent control of the Directorate. With that, they could remove Judge Moskowitz and replace him with a JAG of their choice."

"They might not need to do that. Remember also that they will have been working to make the financial crisis worse, to the point where the population as a whole will be feeling the pain. Ratification of a change to the constitution would render the JAG powerless to stop them."

"Okay, but a constitutional change has to first pass 80 percent of the Directorate, so none of this will happen until they get to that point. I can't see them getting to that point in the first place, so maybe I'm worrying about nothing. If they were close, I'd have heard about it."

"Sir…" Mike hesitated again. "I have better access to that information than you have, though I have my limits. I can't hear conversations conducted face-to-face in private residences, private businesses including restaurants and entertainment venues, or in TerraNova Park. Based on the information I have, however, as many as sixty-seven of the hundred directors may be willing to vote you out.

"In short, they need thirteen more votes, and there are many others whose intentions I have insufficient knowledge to judge. If they called a for a vote tomorrow, I could not predict the outcome with any degree of certainty."

* * * * *

Chapter Twenty-Three

31 January 2124
LFS *Valkyrie*, in Xanadu Orbit

"Thanks for coming up, Doctor Kim." Lorna Greenwood waved Jin to one of the comfortable armchairs in the lounge area of her cabin. "The Colonial Commission told me about the proposal they sent you. Needless to say, I've got a vested interest in the outcome."

"Admiral, I've got no desire to take over your job…" Jin gave a helpless shrug.

"I wish you would." Lorna chuckled. "My 'governor' job, that is. I've got a full-time job as senior military officer in system, a job for which I am better qualified. The fact that I spend most of my time aboard *Valkyrie* instead of down in the colony is a reflection of that. The colony needs a full-time governor down there, not a part-timer up here.

"I've been asking the commission to send a real governor out from Luna, but giving the job to you makes more sense. You've been here as long as anyone; you know the planet better than anyone else. You're a respected member of the community. You're also the best person to oversee our coexistence with the Kitties.

"Things have gotten more complicated since Storm Shadow's tribe made the choice to come over and interact with us in Eurasia. When it comes to the protectorate, I guess you could say, the Cat's out of the bag."

Seeing the look on Jin's face, Lorna burst out laughing.

"Sorry, Doctor, I couldn't resist. I've been waiting for a chance to use that metaphor for a long time. By the way, that's an old nautical saying, actually has nothing to do with cats."

"Really?" Jin's curiosity got the better of her. "So what does it mean?"

"Goes back to the days of wooden sailing ships—the British Royal Navy, in particular. The 'cat' refers to a cat-o-nine-tails, a whip that was used to administer punishment to seamen. It was kept in a bag by the ship's bosun and only came out when somebody was due to be whipped."

"That metaphor is strangely appropriate for the Kitties," Jin mused. "According to Darius, when they go into attack mode, you don't want to be on the receiving end."

"Colonel Bouchard has been telling me the same thing." Lorna nodded. "She'd love to have a whole platoon of Kitties in her battalion. I know you have concerns about that, so I've told her to keep you advised on the project. As governor, you'll have more control over the process. Have you decided whether you're going to accept the job?"

"I still have reservations." Jin shook her head. "I'm a scientist, not an administrator. Darius gave me a lot of reasons why I should take the job, but I don't know if I have what it takes to be governor of the first LFS interstellar colony."

"Apparently, a lot of people think you have. You've done an outstanding job with the protectorate. If it's any comfort to you, I felt the same way when they named me to the 'acting governor' post.

"I still felt that way when they removed the 'acting' qualifier. Along the way, though, I've discovered that it's not about being an administrator—you can have people to handle that for you. What the colony needs is a *leader*, and from what I've seen, you are well qualified for that.

"For the daily routine, you'll do the same thing I've been doing. You'll rely on Taylor to keep the wheels from coming off. You can count on him to filter out the bullshit so the only things that land on your desk are items that really need an executive decision. If you need help, you can bring in other people—and for the record, Bouchard's Marines will be at your disposal. Technically, they'll still report to me, but their mission will be to support you.

"Unlike me, you'll be on the scene, able to see what's going on, and interact with Taylor's people, the Marines, and your fellow colonists on a daily basis. As far as I'm concerned, that's the most important part of the job and the one part where I have fallen short. So... what do you think? Are you willing to give it a shot?"

"Yes, I guess I am." Jin sat back with a sigh of resignation. "Darius had pretty well convinced me already; this conversation with you pretty much sealed the deal. I just need to send a letter of acceptance to the commission."

"Don't want to rush you," Lorna replied with a chuckle, "but you can use the interface in my conference room to compose that letter. If you do, I'll put it aboard a hyperprobe to Luna this afternoon. The commission said the job would be effective as soon as you accept. No need to wait for confirmation from them; we can start calling you 'Governor' right away.

"Meanwhile, I've got to issue an invitation for a formal dinner sometime in the next few days. A substantial Consortium force arrived in system this morning, and I need to welcome them to Xanadu."

"Really?" Jin blinked in surprise. "I guess they're getting serious about building their own colony."

"Yes, it appears they are. They've sent another American cruiser, a pair of Canadian destroyers, and a pair of cargo ships flying the Korean flag. Don't know what they plan to do. It might be a relief force, and the existing ships will be going home, or it might be reinforcements. Hopefully, we'll find out at that dinner I mentioned."

"Oh…" Lorna flashed a wicked grin, "and it would be nice if I could persuade Governor Kim to attend."

* * *

LFS *Sorceress*, in Ragnarok Orbit

"Somebody's making a pretty serious statement." Rochford nodded toward the screen, currently displaying the FTL message from the system picket. "The British are coming—with *Prince of Wales* and a pair of heavy cruisers."

"Not to mention a pair of Japanese destroyers." Peter Yoric studied the display. "JSDF *Asahi* and *Subaru*. Those are brand new. As of last year, Japan had no hyper-capable warships. Their entire Space Defense Force consisted of intra-system patrol craft."

"They're definitely making a statement. When you add the Americans into the mix, we've got what amounts to a Consortium battle group here. We've still got something of an edge, but I wouldn't want to take them on. I don't think the Confeds will be back any time soon."

"Their warships won't be back," Rochford grumbled, "but we're going to have to put up with their commercial ships. I still think we shouldn't have given their gold mine back to them."

"That was McGruder's call." Yoric shrugged. "Can't fault him for it; we keep insisting the Lizards are in charge of this system, and that's the way they wanted it. It's their way of telling us they aren't going to take sides in our fight. Besides, we scored another big win on this one. The Confeds were stupid enough to try to kick out the Consortium along with us. All they've managed to do is drive the Brits, the Americans, and their partners into our camp.

"And that," he added with a grin, "is why I'm about to ask Tom Birdsall to set up a fancy 'Welcome to Ragnarok' dinner for Sir John Bryant and his top officers."

* * *

Costa Del Sur Resort, El Salvador

"Let's get right to business." DuMorne nodded to Gerhardt Richter, who had drawn the lot of chairman. "I have information for all of you, and we will have decisions to make."

The five members of the Hand settled around the table. When they were all in place, Richter turned to DuMorne.

"Very well, Andre. I presume your report will be worth a trip halfway around the world. Let's hear it."

"Gentlemen, I believe we are on the verge of a victory." DuMorne favored them with a sardonic grin. "It is something we had not hoped to achieve for years, and only at the conclusion of a brutal war between the Confeds and Moonies. Now it appears we may achieve it without firing a shot, by subversion instead of force.

"We must move quickly, however; the Moonies have taken drastic action to recover from their financial crisis. In the process, they have created a lot of discord and dissension among their own people. Virtually the entire Executive Committee of TerraCorp opposes the course O'Hara has set. There is unrest in their military ranks, with nearly a third of Navy and Marine people reduced to inactive reserve status. This has reduced their military strength to its lowest level in half a century.

"We have developed—through my brother's operations in New York—a relationship with a number of Moonies in critical positions: executives of TerraCorp, disgruntled military officers, and others. At this point, we have no less than twenty members of the Lunar Directorate in our pockets, and they in turn have convinced many other directors to follow their lead.

"For all of that, we have only a temporary window. O'Hara is projecting a turnaround in the economy within three to five months. Full recovery will take many months after that, but signs of improvement may cause some who oppose him to waver. Our 'friends' in the Directorate are aware of this. Their plan is to remove him from office before that happens."

DuMorne paused. The others stared at him in silence, their faces impassive as they processed the implications of his report.

"Removing O'Hara from office is one thing." Huang Chang Li spoke slowly, deliberately. "It will not be sufficient to give us victory, however. Are you familiar with the rules of succession under the Lunar constitution?"

"Yes, yes—" DuMorne waved his hand in dismissal "—I know. Once they remove O'Hara, the Directorate has thirty days to choose a successor. If they fail to agree on a choice within that time frame, the highest-ranking officer in the LFS military structure will take office and be immune from removal for a year."

"Correct." Huang nodded. "That would be Admiral Charles McGruder, who can be expected to stay the course and carry out all of O'Hara's current policies. Further, it should be noted that the Directorate can only choose a new CEO by a two-thirds majority vote for a single candidate.

"You seem to believe that you can get eighty directors to agree that O'Hara needs to go. Once that is accomplished, however, will sixty-seven or more of them be able to agree on a choice of successor? Do your twenty present conspirators trust each other enough to select one of their number for the CEO position?"

"Of course not." DuMorne chuckled. "Not even we five would go that far. We recognize that, working together, we can control the world; we would not, however, give ultimate authority to one of our number. Neither would any of our Moonie conspirators."

"Nonetheless," Huang insisted, "the Moonie constitution requires a chief executive."

"They have taken that into account." DuMorne waved a hand in dismissal. "Their choice will be nothing more than a figurehead, a person they can control from behind the scenes. They have been cultivating an individual for the position. He is not one of their number, not a serving director. He's a rather shallow individual who values the prestige and trappings of office more than the power he might wield. He will be a suitable puppet.

"This follows the model of the Chinese Communist Party of the early 21st century. The so-called 'premier' who was the nominal head of the nation was only the public figure they showed to the world. No one knew the names of the party officials who actually controlled the most populous nation on Earth at the time."

"I am amazed." Mohammed Al Sharif dipped his head toward DuMorne. "In little more than a year, you have built a revolutionary organization at the top levels of Moonie society. I would not have believed it possible, even for you, Andre."

"I wish I could take credit." DuMorne shook his head. "I did not create this subversive conspiracy. I merely discovered it, and that by chance contact with one of its most prominent members. Some of them have been plotting this takeover since the Kim assassination delivered control of the Lunar Free State back into the hands of the military.

"If they succeed, they will need to move on to the next phase. That's where we come in. My brother's people have convinced them that the solution is to borrow money, through the issuance of bonds to be sold in Earth's financial markets. We can serve our own interests by adding these bonds to our personal portfolios, but it would be in our best interests to have the bulk of them purchased by the CNE."

"Would they really allow that to happen?" Kimba raised a skeptical eyebrow. "Put themselves into debt to their sworn enemies?"

"Well, that's an interesting question." DuMorne chuckled. "Certainly O'Hara would not; however, our conspirators are primarily people from TerraCorp. Some of them have been doing business with the CNE for years. They don't see it that way; in their view, they are simply conducting trade with corporations based in nations that happen to be members of the CNE.

"The same will be true of the bonds. They will be purchased by various funds chartered within the CNE, allegedly public, but actually held by the CNE's reserve bank. Since we control the bank, we will effectively own the Lunar Free State."

"Hmmm… and what shall we do with them once we own them?" The question came from Al Sharif.

"That's simple," Gerhardt Richter replied. "We convince them to join the Confederated Nations of Earth."

* * *

Community Meeting Hall, LFS Colony, Planet Xanadu

"Do we really need this?" Sarah Peabody gave Jin a skeptical look. "I'm not an expert on history, but I seem to recall that most colonies operated under the laws and constitution of their sponsoring nations. The United States didn't have their own constitution until years after they broke off from England."

"I think we do," Jin insisted. "Luna operates under a constitution unique to their situation, living under a mountain on the Moon, where the government absolutely *must* supply certain necessities—like air to breathe, for example. We don't have that here.

"We'll want to preserve all the basic freedoms we enjoy under the Lunar Constitution, but we should not rely on the government for anything we can do for ourselves. In the end, we'll eliminate a lot of restrictions and give ourselves more freedom."

"Will Luna allow us to do that?" Justin Gerard shifted uncomfortably in his chair. "They might think we're rebelling, like the Americans breaking away from the British three centuries ago."

"Well, we can always ask them." Jin shrugged. "I'd like to have a draft constitution to show them, though. That will force them to react to the document itself, rather than deciding whether we're allowed to write one.

"Hey, like they say, it's easier to ask forgiveness than permission."

* * *

ICV *Majorca,* in Hyperspace, Outbound from Odin

You *swore you would never take cargo on this run again.* Lilly Maria Buxton cursed under her breath in three languages. *You let your damned greedy fingers imprint the contract and figured your luck would hold. Now you're running for your life again.*

She'd returned to Sol after a profitable run to Alpha Akara to find a message waiting from her agent on Earth. Another Volvo shipment of heavy equipment for Ragnarok was up for grabs. As a CNE-based corporation, Volvo was not allowed to use the Lunar Free State's commercial shipping services.

CNE-flagged merchant ships were once again being permitted to enter the Odin System, but Volvo preferred to use a carrier who had provided good service in the past. Repeat business from a satisfied customer—especially one that paid as well as Volvo—was business she didn't want to refuse.

She chose to ignore the little voice in her head reminding her that she'd tangled with pirates on her last two trips to Odin, both of which had involved Volvo contracts. The pirates hadn't been interested in the heavy equipment; they'd come after her on the return run to Sol with no cargo at all in her holds.

And here I am again, she thought, *heading home empty, running like hell, with pirates on my tail.* This time, however, she had no warship escorts to protect her pretty ass. *This time, I'm well and truly fucked.*

Her delivery—to the Moonie mines on Ragnarok this time—had gone smoothly. She hadn't expected trouble on the trip to the Odin System; she'd traveled in company with no less than five Consortium warships headed for the same destination. One of them was the British battlecruiser *Prince of Wales*, which had trashed the pirates chasing her on two previous occasions. No half-assed bandits were likely to bother her this time.

She'd unloaded her cargo without incident and prepared to depart immediately. Ragnarok had nothing to offer as a liberty port. She had cleared the hyper limit and jumped without being challenged, but less than an hour into hyperspace, she'd spotted another ship coming up fast behind her.

Majorca was faster than the average merchant ship and could run away from most heavy warships. A destroyer or light cruiser could run her down, but the unknown ship coming up on her was faster than any warship she'd ever seen. Her first thought was that it was an express courier. There had been one of those in Ragnarok orbit when she'd left, and rumor had it the Moonies were using ships like that to ferry gold from their mines on the planet.

The unknown ship had apparently detected her; it altered course to go very wide around her, well out of any warship's weapon range. That was fine with her. The last thing she wanted to do was travel in company with a ship full of gold that was faster than she was and could run away from any pirates it might attract.

The unknown flashed past her and went on its way. Ten minutes later, she detected three more ships in tight formation on her tail. Again, they were faster than she was, faster than the courier that had passed her. They were small, but the tight formation screamed "warships"—which her brain translated to "pirates."

They're after the gold carrier, she thought. *I just need to get out of their way.* She ordered a radical course change, a hard left turn that would have her headed toward Alpha Akara rather than Sol. A moment later, the unknown ships split up. Two of them continued on course, still pursuing the gold ship. To her horror, the third one turned toward her, cutting the angle, which would allow it to intercept her sooner. They would have her in missile range within twenty minutes.

Her first thought was that they wouldn't shoot. Pirates would want to take her intact, wouldn't they? *Maybe not,* she decided. *They're after the gold. They don't want me. They want to eliminate any witnesses. They might not shoot at extreme range, though. Why should they, when I can't get away?*

"Sarah—" she turned to Hurley at the helm and navigation console "—stand by to cut the drive and drop out of hyper on my mark."

"That's going to be a rough one, Skipper," Hurley reminded her. "Have you checked our relative velocity lately?"

Ships normally reduced speed before translation into or out of hyperspace. Dropping out at high velocity relative to the n-space continuum was hard on crew members, causing vertigo, nausea, and in some cases, unconsciousness. More importantly, it was hard on the ship itself, often causing overloads in electronics and damage to equipment.

"I know." She waved off the objection. "It'll be rough, but we'll survive. I'm betting it'll be rougher on them, whoever they are. As soon as we're back to n-space, kill as much residual as you can, and get ready to jump back to hyper."

She watched the display as her pursuer crossed into what should be missile range. She held her breath as it came closer, closer...

"Ready... mark!" The order had barely passed her lips when Hurley stabbed the action button on her console, and the universe turned inside out.

* * *

Buxton's vision cleared, but the screens in front of her provided no information, as scrambled electronics fed them nothing but error messages. She swallowed hard, trying to clear the nausea. A warm feeling of wetness in her shipsuit told her that her bladder had misbehaved.

At least I didn't barf, she thought. A glance to the side showed her that Hurley hadn't been so fortunate. The navigation officer had been prepared, however. As Buxton watched, she sealed up the full barf bag and dropped it into the waste bin under her console. That done, she turned to her displays and shook her head.

"Comm and nav systems are rebooting, Skipper," she reported. "Don't know if we've got any damage, but I have helm control and starsight navigation. Where do we want to go?"

"That way." One of the external visual displays had come up, and Buxton pointed to the bright star that dominated the screen. In their brief time in hyperspace, they'd moved half a light-year from Odin, but it was still close enough to outshine everything else in view.

The last thing she wanted to do was continue her journey with those predators lurking between here and Sol. She was hoping she had taken the third ship by surprise, that he'd overshot and gotten light-minutes further along before dropping into n-space. If so, he would take time to get his own instruments back—hopefully long enough for her to jump back into hyper and be gone.

Going back to Ragnarok, she decided, *where I'm going to park right next to* Prince of Wales *and stay there until there's a warship or two headed back to Sol.*

Or maybe I'll snuggle up next to the Moonie battlecruiser. Admiral Yoric is a handsome devil. I'll tell him my pirate tales, and maybe he'll invite me over for dinner.

* * *

LFS *Sorceress*, in Ragnarok Orbit

"Pirates again!" Peter Yoric shook his head in disgust. "Well, gosh, with three different groups mining gold on this planet, I wonder what could possibly be of interest to pirates?"

"Crazy thing, Admiral, is that this Captain Buxton and her ship have been involved in three previous pirate encounters on this run." Tom Birdsall chuckled. "She had a fourth encounter on approach to Sacagawea a few months ago. We were on station there at the time; that was when Admiral Ling had the group, before you arrived."

"I had Sonja look it up." Yoric returned the chuckle. "Even crazier, there's a note on file that says she's an independent contractor working for Lunar Naval Intelligence—a spy-for-hire. On that basis, I have to wonder if somebody hasn't put out a hit on her. Not the kind of business I'd like to be in, especially as the captain of an unarmed merchant ship."

"I also had Tactical review her ship's log, which she graciously provided; it confirms her story." Yoric's voice turned serious. "We've not only got pirates, we've got raiders with ships fast enough to catch an express courier. That means TerraCorp has lost a gold shipment, not to mention a ship and three crew members."

"Something else occurs to me." Birdsall also sobered. "We're the only ones using express couriers to ship gold back to Luna. The Consortium and the Confeds are doing it with ordinary freighters in escorted convoys. It looks like these pirates—if that's what they really are—deliberately set out to target us.

"Until now, nobody's come up with a raider design fast enough to catch one of our e-boats, and nobody would send a raider like that against a regular warship. This has Confed written all over it."

* * * * *

Chapter Twenty-Four

17 March 2124

Office of the Chief Executive, TerraNova City, Luna

"It appears Admiral Yoric's assumption was correct," Lisa Woods advised. "LCS *Arrow* is more than a week overdue from Ragnarok. She departed on schedule and was likely the one that passed *Majorca* in hyperspace."

"So… Mr. Carter's plan to avoid pirates by using e-boats instead of escorted freighters has just been trashed." Robert O'Hara glared at Woods.

"Carter's an asshole." Woods shrugged. "In fairness, however, there was nothing wrong with the plan at the time. Nobody expected to see raiders fast enough to intercept an express courier. The LFS Navy has no ships like that; neither do the Confeds."

"None that we knew of," O'Hara insisted. "It appears they have them now. Besides, Carter's plan offered no additional security but incurred an extra cost. We have freighters coming back from Ragnarok empty after making deliveries to the mines. They used to travel in convoys with military escort in both directions. It would have cost nothing to put the gold aboard one of them.

"Instead, Carter insisted on sending e-boats out empty to do nothing but pick up the gold. You know how tight budgets have been; we didn't need the extra expense. That program stops now. Do I have to take it up with the Executive Committee?"

"No." She shook her head with a sigh. "Carter has friends in high places, but none of them will want to take ownership of this screwup. At most, they'll help him step back and claim it wasn't his idea."

"Why are they doing that?" O'Hara's brow wrinkled. "He's useless. I would think they would throw him to the wolves."

"I don't know. For some reason, Roger Stuart and his crew seem to find him useful. Maybe it's because he's so easily manipulated. For all I know, one of them came up with the e-boat idea in the first place and let Carter claim it."

She hesitated for a moment, then spoke again.

"Rob—" she was one of the few people in the nation on a first name basis with him "—something's going on, and I have no idea what it is. Stuart's one of the people involved, but he's not the only one. Whatever it is, they don't talk about it in the office—not when I'm around. I've heard casual mentions of meetings that aren't held in TerraCorp conference rooms. Apparently, they're getting together at Stuart's place, or the home of one of the other directors. Can't say for sure, because I'm not invited."

Meeting in their homes... where not even Mike can listen to them. O'Hara felt a chill. Mike hadn't given him names, but he was betting Stuart was one of the directors the AI was concerned about. Suddenly, another thought struck him.

Vice President in Charge of Killing Things... Corporate Dragon Slayer...

"Lisa..." He hesitated, then plunged ahead. "You may not be privy to this conspiracy, but you've got one advantage I don't have. You're on the inside. You're a member of the Executive Committee and an elected member of the Directorate.

"I need you to do something for me. I need you to help me slay a dragon."

* * *

Lunar Commercial Shipping HQ, TransLuna Station

"Pirates?" Marcus Carter stared at Stuart in disbelief. "Pirates again, on the Ragnarok run? So the Navy has fucked up again, and I'm missing a courier boat."

Stuart ignored the major flaw in the statement. It served his purpose to let Carter blame the Navy for the failure of his own policies. *He set it up so the Navy couldn't protect his couriers. He assumed their speed guaranteed safety. He was wrong.*

"That's what they're saying at Lunar Command." Stuart shrugged. "No proof, just some nonsense from a merchant captain who claims she saw pirates chasing our courier. According to the mine superintendent, there were over five thousand ounces of gold aboard. Who knows… maybe your boat crew decided to go off somewhere on their own. With that much gold, they could buy themselves a pretty nice life."

"Bullshit!" Carter was quick to reject any suggestion that his people might be at fault. "My crews are loyal. For all I know, some Navy bastards might have hijacked the ship. Who's in charge out there?"

"Admiral Yoric, 2nd Fleet, 3rd Battle Group."

"Don't know him; no doubt one of O'Hara's favorites. Doesn't matter. Those people would know the courier schedule. They'd be in perfect position to set it up."

Damn! Stuart chuckled to himself. *Carter really hates the Navy in general and O'Hara in particular. I wonder what he'd say if he knew what we have in mind for him.*

"You've lost one of your couriers, but TerraCorp has also lost a few million credits-worth of gold. That's the last thing we needed, with the continued pressure to produce more income."

"Right!" Carter agreed. "More bullshit from O'Hara over that, not to mention our… ah… personal losses."

Stuart grimaced. Yes, the shipment would have included a cut for him, and another for Carter, a tidy sum in gold that was "off the books" as far as Lunar Command and TerraCorp were concerned. It was something they were not to talk about here, however. He'd cautioned Carter about that many times.

He was upset about his own loss, though he'd expected it to happen sooner or later. The Confeds were determined to disrupt the gold flow to the LFS. He'd put away a considerable fortune from his share of the rake-off without ever going near the pilfered gold. Now, unless Carter could figure out a way to bring it in aboard regular TerraCorp freighters returning from Ragnarok, the party was over.

Doesn't matter, he thought. *We're into the end game. Once O'Hara is gone, we won't need to tiptoe around anymore, because we'll be the ones calling the shots.*

* * *

LFS *Amazon*, Lunar Fleet Anchorage

"What do you need from us this time, Admiral?" Rob O'Hara turned away from the viewport to face McGruder, turning his back on the stunning vista of the anchorage against the background of stars.

"Why so defensive, Mac?" Robert O'Hara gave him a crooked smile. "Maybe I just came up here because I need to get out of the office once in a while."

"Maybe, but lately it seems like every time we meet, you hit me with bad news—like more fleet cuts."

"Hey, I gave you the battalion of Marines for Ragnarok. I presume they're already on their way."

"They are. *Valley Forge* departed with Mark Mercer's 1st Battalion and an air support squadron yesterday. I've told Mercer he can start calling up reserves to fill his division again. I assumed that's what you intended."

"It was, but we've been hit with another setback. I still want to keep a full division of Marines on the ready line, but that might require tightening up in a few other areas."

"Like I said." McGruder sighed. "Bad news. More fleet cuts."

"Not that bad," O'Hara insisted. "I'm thinking maybe we don't need a full battle group at Tatanna. I was going to suggest we could tell John to leave cruisers and destroyers there and come home."

"Seriously?" McGruder raised a skeptical eyebrow. "With both the Bugs and the Confeds probing the system, you want to reduce our force there?"

"It's been a year since the Bug encounter, and they haven't returned. I think they were just testing to see if we were awake. As for the Confeds, the system picket alone could have handled that probe they sent. Yoric went out with overwhelming force to convince them to turn around and go home.

"If we believe what the survivors told us, they were about to do that when some fanatic on the cruiser's bridge opened fire. The CNE denies it ever happened. Whenever they do that, I take it to mean they don't want to fight. Diplomatic Corps doesn't think they'll try anything like that again, especially now that the Consortium has established relations with the king.

"They're more likely to revert to their old policy at Tatanna: diplomatic maneuvers, subversion, and trafficking in contraband goods. Warships won't help us fight that. Good relations with the Crown are more important than military force. I'm tempted to leave John in place because King Arne knows him and considers him a friend, but that's not enough to justify keeping a battlecruiser and a dozen other warships on station.

"The loss of a gold shipment wasn't a major hit to the economy, but it did put a crimp in my plan to get things back on track. I'm still hoping to get the recovery started by May or June; to do that, I need to keep looking for ways to trim expenses. A battlecruiser on stand down status at Luna costs a lot less than one on station at Tatanna."

* * *

La Salida del Sol Resort, Cancún, Mexico

"Your CIS people have been up to their tricks again, Gerhardt." Al Sharif's voice held a hint of amusement. "Complex plots, months of preparation, for an operation that can only succeed once and must then be retired."

"They are not *my* CIS people." Richter snorted. "They are a bunch of CNE players with an unlimited budget with which to buy new toys. They were smart enough to turn those toys over to a mercenary group—experienced spacers who know better than to take on real warships. That doesn't mean they have to be retired, however. They simply need to abandon the Sol-Odin run and find some place where the Moonies will not be using convoys."

"For the record, I did not authorize or promote this operation. I only became aware of it after the fact. It should be of no concern to us, however. It had little impact on Andre's project."

"The operation in question actually disrupted a lucrative source of funding for certain members of the opposition faction on Luna." Du-Morne shrugged. "I should be upset, because my brother and I also stood to profit from the scheme. It's a small thing, though, and it did not affect the faction's agenda.

"They are on schedule, but their task will become more difficult as it comes closer to conclusion. The Moonie players under our influence have won over a majority of directors to their cause. They will need more to reach the 80 percent threshold to remove O'Hara, however, and all of the easily persuaded or corruptible directors have already been claimed.

"It may be necessary for them to go beyond simple persuasion to recruit the remainder, but they assure us it can be done. They are also recruiting a consensus for their candidate to replace O'Hara.

"For our part, we have been trying to convince them that, should their own efforts succeed, the best path forward will involve rapid development of cordial relations with the CNE. I will rely on Gerhardt to prep the CNE for the sudden turnabout. It won't serve our purpose for the Moonies to extend a hand of friendship only to have the Confeds spit in their face. No matter who is in charge, the Lunar Free State is still the most powerful military force in the Sol System."

* * *

Private Residence, Level 17, TerraNova City, Luna

"Seriously, Roger, are we really that close?" Lucas Harcourt blinked in surprise.

"We are," Stuart assured him. "Those four Directorate proxies you've got in your pocket put us within three votes of the 80 percent threshold."

"Assuming I'm willing to give them to you." Harcourt's eyes narrowed. "I haven't agreed to anything yet."

"Oh, come on." Stuart frowned. "You're the guy who keeps telling me how much you hate O'Hara for what he did to you."

"That's *John* O'Hara. I don't like the old man much, but he never stuck it to me the way his son did."

"I don't like any of the descendants of the so-called 'original citizens,' but the O'Haras are the worst," Stuart insisted. "So far, they've produced two CEOs and a kid who's on the fast track to become the third. They act like some kind of royal family. Once we get rid of Robert O'Hara, I promise you can do whatever you want with his son."

"That's all well and good," Harcourt said, "but it's not the only thing that's bothering me. Why Carter? I mean, hell… why don't you take the job yourself?"

"Don't want it." Stuart shook his head. "I'd rather be the guy who pulls the strings. Carter's a front man. Honestly, you'd make a better CEO than he would, assuming we let you run the show. We're sure as hell not going to let *him* run it."

In truth, Stuart would have taken the CEO job in a heartbeat; unfortunately, none of his co-conspirators would have trusted him with it, nor would he have trusted any of them. Instead, they had agreed to install someone they could control, someone they could direct as a committee, someone who wanted the prestige and perks of the office and was smart enough not to defy those who had put him there. After considerable search, they had settled on Marcus Carter.

"Let me offer you an incentive, Lucas." He gave Harcourt an engaging grin. "We're going to need somebody to hold Carter's leash once we install him. Suppose we give you that job—nominally, you'd be his chief of staff, but in reality, you'd be there to keep an eye on him and advise us if he gets out of line. In addition, the job would come with lots of perks and would pay a hell of a lot better than the one you have now."

"That's not saying much." Harcourt growled. "I'm on half pay. I was on the promotion list before the yard cutbacks came. Now they tell me I'm on 'ready reserve' status—mostly to make me think they might recall me to active status, but I don't see that happening anytime soon.

"I only have those proxies because the directors in question were friends I knew for years. They were lucky enough to have billets on ships that didn't get deactivated. I was still on active duty when they deployed, but that didn't last long."

And you'll lose those proxies if they get recalled to Luna before we act, Stuart thought. *If that happens, you won't be of any use to us. You've got a narrow window, so you damned well better sign on with us.*

"Relax." His smile didn't falter. "The chief of staff position will pay a lot better than you were getting before the cutbacks. We'll make it a civilian position, so you won't be tied to a military pay scale."

"Fine. You've convinced me." Harcourt nodded. "When is all this supposed to happen?"

"Soon," Stuart told him. "Very soon."

* * *

Office of the Chief Executive, TerraNova City, Luna

"Governor Kim has certainly hit the ground running." Martina Easley frowned as she studied the document on her pad.

"That she has," O'Hara agreed. "The Colonial Commission hadn't a clue what to do with this, so they bucked it to me. I've already run it by the JAG, but all Moskowitz had to say was that the constitution neither permits nor forbids what they are trying to do. In other words, he doesn't have a clue what to do about it, either."

"Have you studied the document itself?" She gave him a questioning look. "I haven't had time to do more than skim the first two pages, but my first impression is that it's modeled after the LFS Constitution."

"It is." He nodded. "I've read it, and they've taken a lot of it word for word—particularly the parts that define the rights and obligations of citizens. In some other places, they've adjusted for things that are unique to Luna and don't fit well with their situation on Xanadu. They've also thrown in a section regarding respect for the rights and the culture of the native sentients—the Kitties."

"I would have expected that from Doctor Kim." Easley chuckled.

"True, but every member of the colony council signed off on it. I bucked it back to Moskowitz—asked him for a legal analysis. I want a point-by-point comparison of the two constitutions and an opinion as to the effect on relations between Luna and the colony. I'll want the same from you, but from a diplomatic standpoint.

"They made it clear this is not a rebellion. They still want to be citizens of the LFS. They want special representation in the Directorate, with the number of directors to be determined in future discussions. Point is, they don't want to participate in the general elections, they want to have their own elections for directors who will represent Xanadu and Xanadu only.

"I asked Moskowitz about that, since it is the one area where they are in direct conflict with our constitution. He says there's precedent for it down on Earth. The United States uses a similar system called the 'Electoral College' to choose their CEO—the president.

Supposedly it prevents the heavily populated states from dictating to the smaller and more rural ones by swamping the popular vote.

"He mentioned that one specifically, since the function of the Directorate is to review the performance of the CEO, but he says they use a similar system in the USA to select members of their legislative bodies. Each state gets to elect their own."

"Hah!" Easley barked a laugh. "In other words, Xanadu wants to be treated like a separate state within our nation. We'll have to start calling ourselves the Lunar Free *States*. They could be setting a precedent. Who's next? New Eden? Tatanna?

"Seriously, though." She sobered. "They have a point. They only have a few thousand people. We've got a couple million living on Luna. The average director gets elected by more votes than there are people on Xanadu. Their votes will get lost in a general election."

"Right, and they can't depend on directors who are sixty light-years away and have never set foot on Xanadu to look out for their interests." O'Hara nodded. "I can't fault them for that part of it. Unless the JAG finds something wrong with their proposed constitution—or a compelling reason why they shouldn't have one at all—I'm inclined to tell them to go ahead. I'll want your input first, however, and your thoughts on how this affects our diplomatic situation."

"Hmmm... yes." She nodded slowly. "Especially since we're not the only ones building a colony there."

"That reminds me." He turned to the screen on his desk. "I'm going to drop another file on you for review. I got a note from Greenwood through fleet channels. Apparently, they ran their proposed constitution by her before they sent it to us. She mentions a few other points we need to consider—like the fact that we will still be responsible for their defense, even if we grant them the 'statehood' they're asking for."

* * *

LFS *Isis*, in Tatanna Orbit

"We're being recalled?" Eurasia Brown rolled her eyes. "Again?"

"Yup!" John O'Hara nodded. "Same as last time. Leave some cruisers and destroyers behind and report back to Luna. Nothing more, no indication of what our mission will be. I strongly suspect we're going to be taken off the line again."

"Wouldn't be surprised," she admitted. "They kept hammering on us about the financial crisis and the need to cut back, then they scrambled us and sent us out here. That had to cost them a bundle."

"I'm sure it did. They didn't say anything at the time, but the crisis at Ragnarok must have been pretty bad. I guess it's over, and we're back to tightening belts. No hurry, though. They've given us thirty days to get things in order before we start back. Normally, my inclination would be to move faster and get on our way sooner, but this time, I think our people won't be in a hurry to get home."

"Hmmph!" she snorted. "No, they won't, not if it means going on half pay again when they get there."

* * *

Landing Field, LFS Colony, Planet Xanadu

<<*Eleven of them?*>> Jin stared as the cats disembarked. <<*Storm Shadow sent eleven volunteers?*>>

Yellow Eyes purred with amusement. <<*No, Kim. Storm Shadow selected a handset from Valley of Clouds. The other three were sent by Deep Roots, who has decided that Tall Trees Tribe needs to be involved.*>>

Jin turned to the Cat, her eyes wide. She started to reply but paused to process what the Kitty warrior had told her. Valley of Clouds and Tall Trees were neighboring tribes separated by a river, at peace with each other, but with very little contact between them. Until now, Tall Trees had remained aloof, mostly ignoring the protectorate and the off-worlders in general.

<<*Does Bare Head know of this?*>> She projected the avatar the cats had given to the mostly bald Karl Levin.

<<*I am told our new arrivals advised him when they boarded the shuttle this morning.*>>

Jin winced. This was a major development as far as the protectorate was concerned. Why hadn't Karl called her about it?

Because you're the governor, she told herself. *The protectorate is no longer your direct responsibility.* No doubt Levin would cover the topic in his monthly report. For the moment, he was probably as surprised as she was.

<<*Does Kim not approve?*>> The question from Yellow Eyes was tinged with concern. Jin also noted that her avatar—Kim, expressed as the Korean hangul characters that spelled her name—now carried the overtone of respect the Cats used for a tribal chief like Storm Shadow or Deep Roots.

<<*Kim very much approves,*>> she assured him. <<*I am surprised and pleased that Tall Trees has honored us with their presence, but we only planned for eight. Six were to join Priestess and her Marines, with two for Dark Giant's militia.*>>

<<Three of them are not warriors,>> he explained. <<One from Tall Trees and two from Valley of Clouds are artisans. Storm Shadow believes that we should not depend on humans for our basic needs. He has charged them with building a living space of our own, perhaps the beginnings of a village.

<<I have advised him of the way in which your people manage the land itself, and he has asked you to grant them a space like one of your farmsteads, preferably at the edge of the jungle, where we can hunt and provide for ourselves. It should also be near the Marine base, so that the warriors can 'report for duty,' as the Priestess requires.

<<Will Kim do this? If not, the artisans can return to Oceania. Otherwise, they are volunteers like the warriors and will stay here permanently.>>

Jin felt a little shiver as she realized the implications. She was being asked to allow the Kitties to establish their own settlement within the community, to effectively become citizens of the colony.

Lunar citizens? She shook off the thought. *Worry about that later. For now, they want to set up housekeeping here. Eleven cats—plus the three we already have—isn't exactly an invasion.*

Still, it felt like a momentous decision on her part. *Well, hey... you're the governor. Goes with the territory.*

<<Of course.>> She gave the senior Kitty warrior a slow blink. <<Let's go look at the map in my office. I'm sure we can find a suitable place.>>

* * * * *

Chapter Twenty-Five

1 May 2124

Office of the Chief Executive, TerraNova City, Luna

"I sent off a hyperprobe to Xanadu, with Lunar Command's official approval of their constitution." Robert O'Hara nodded to the two people whose images occupied windows on his screen.

"Approval?" Abraham Moskowitz raised an eyebrow in a questioning look. "I didn't get the impression they were asking for approval. They were telling us what they intended to do and were just giving us a heads-up."

"Well… okay." O'Hara nodded. "What I sent them wasn't an official endorsement. It was more of a 'if that's what you want, I see no problem with it' notice."

"*Nihil Obstat.*" Moskowitz chuckled. "In the old days of the Catholic Church on Earth, when somebody wanted to publish a book that touched on church doctrine, the Vatican would assign a censor to review it. If all was good, the censor would declare *nihil obstat*—Latin for 'nothing obstructs'—meaning it was okay to publish. The current pope would then put his official *imprimatur*—'let it be printed'—on the book. Harks back to the medieval times, but it was still in practice through the 20th century."

"Okay, I gave them the *nihil obstat.*" O'Hara returned the chuckle. "The *imprimatur* is up to them, but I'm pretty sure they're already implementing it. To that end, I also advised the Colonial Commission that their work is done."

"You're disbanding the commission?" Martina Easley blinked in surprise.

"Not exactly. I told them they have a new mission. The colony is now autonomous. The commission is no longer charged with directing or controlling them. Instead, they will serve as a communication channel between the colony and Luna.

"Their old mission has some runoff. They still have to facilitate moving the few hundred waiting families to Xanadu. After that, those people become the colony's responsibility, and the commission settles into its new liaison role; however, they're going to be significantly downsized. I hadn't realized how big they'd gotten—fifty people on Luna alone. The half-dozen or so on Xanadu will have to be supported by the colony."

"Bureaucracy disease." It was Easley's turn to chuckle. "I think it's contagious, and we caught it from the Confeds. I'm always watching for it in my own organization."

"Well, now you'll have to be more vigilant," he told her. "I'm transferring the trimmed-down commission to your office. Your people are supposed to manage our relations with foreign nations; I expect you to do the same for our own little state of Xanadu."

* * *

Private Residence, Level 17, TerraNova City, Luna

"Relax, Marcus. Have a drink." Stuart handed Carter a crystal tumbler of scotch over ice. "I asked you to stop by because we need to talk about the future."

"The future?" Carter raised an eyebrow as he accepted the drink. "You mean the 'Lunar Free State after O'Hara' future?"

"Yes… that's exactly what I mean. Our group has been working on that for a long time. We know where we want to take the nation, don't we?"

He smiled as he said it. He had implied that Carter was an inner-circle member of the group that would control Luna. That Carter believed the implication was a measure of the man's ignorance. In reality, the top people were the upper-level executives of TerraCorp, some high-ranking naval officers, and a couple of eggheads who wanted to take over the Lunar Research Institute.

What they had in common was that they were all members of the Directorate and—in a few cases like Harcourt—holders of the proxy votes for directors who were currently off Luna.

A quirk in the Lunar Constitution allowed serving directors to give their proxies to any other member if they could not attend meetings. Stuart assumed the provision had originally been made to accommodate military personnel on active duty, but it also applied to TerraCorp people who had to be off Luna for business reasons. Stuart himself held the proxy for three directors currently assigned to trade missions on New Eden or Copper Hills. He had personally arranged those assignments, knowing that the three involved would not have supported the plan to remove O'Hara.

As for Carter, he wasn't a director, let alone a member of the conspiracy's inner circle. He was, however, the perfect person to serve as their front man.

"Oh, I think I know where we're going." Carter's voice carried a note of total self-assurance. "We're going to run the nation like a business—prosperity for everyone. We're going to use the military as it should be used, to support our national goals in trade and commerce, instead of protecting primitives on some planet that has nothing to offer us. No more protectorates, no more money-sucking colonies."

"Absolutely right." Stuart nodded with a show of enthusiasm. "But we've got one problem. The Lunar Constitution puts a couple of obstacles in our path. Eventually, we'll make some changes to it, but for now, we have to operate within its limits. That means we have to have a chief executive."

"I'm sure you'll make a good one." Carter's brow wrinkled in puzzlement. "Why is that a problem?"

"It's a problem because I can't serve." Stuart shook his head. "I have too much to do behind the scenes, stuff I wouldn't be able to do as CEO with everyone watching me. I need somebody to take the public lead, somebody who knows and understands what needs to be done and will take his cues from me and the other top people.

"I need somebody who hasn't been in the spotlight, somebody who will not be involved in O'Hara's removal—in other words, somebody who's not a current director."

He reached down and took the empty glass from Carter's hand, took it to the sideboard, and refilled it. *He's always had a problem with alcohol,* he thought. *Fortunately, he's gotten good at concealing it. For tonight, however, it serves my purpose to have him get a little buzz on.*

"You see where I'm going with this, don't you?" He handed the refilled glass back to Carter. "I know I'm asking a lot of you, but I need you to step up. Somebody has to be the public face of power while the rest of us work in the background.

"How about it? Would you be willing to be the next CEO of the Lunar Free State?"

* * *

Nunbola Winter Resort, Chajang-Do, Korea

"One of my favorite places—" Huang almost smiled as he took in the mountain vista beyond the windows "—but very far from Paris. Why did you choose it?"

"Availability on short notice," DuMorne advised. "This meeting is necessary. We are but days away from the most significant event of the century. We need to prepare."

"Very well." Huang had drawn the chairmanship this time. He turned to the table and took his seat. The others followed suit. "Let us begin. The floor is yours, Andre."

"My primary contact among the Moonie conspirators—they have taken to calling themselves the 'loyal opposition'—tells me they have secured the required number of votes and are about to remove O'Hara."

"So?" Kimba shrugged. "Have you called us halfway around the world to tell us of something we will see on the news feeds in a few days? It will either happen or not, regardless of anything we do at this point."

"I'm not concerned about that," DuMorne insisted. "I only want to make sure that some CNE power player or bureaucratic moron does not decide that this would be a good time to start a war with the Lunar Free State. A political crisis will not stop the LFS military from turning Amsterdam into a large, water-filled crater.

"We have spent years preparing for a war between the LFS and CNE; at this time, however, *peace* will better serve our cause. Things are about to turn very much in our favor. I am simply asking all of you to make sure the CNE, the Jihad, or anyone else who might appear doesn't suddenly decide to fuck this up."

"I take it your comments are primarily aimed at me, Andre." Gerhardt Richter chuckled. "Don't worry. I will pass the word to the CNE bureaucracy in general, and CIS in particular. Anyone who so much as spits in the direction of the Moonies in the coming weeks will enjoy a much-abbreviated life expectancy. With the examples we have already given them, I doubt any will defy us."

"Hmmm…" Al Sharif stroked his beard thoughtfully. "I doubt there will be any problems, but I will send word to my fighters on Ragnarok. Ramadan is months away, but it won't hurt them to put their little revolution on hold for a bit. They haven't done much in the wake of the Moonie retake of the system, but their CNE supply channel is open again, and they may be planning an offensive."

"Huang and I don't start wars." Kimba grinned. "He builds warships, and I supply soldiers for wars in progress, but there are always plenty of those without any effort on our part."

"I'm not worried about the rebellion on Ragnarok, and neither are the Moonies," DuMorne insisted. "Your efforts will be appreciated, Mohammed, but I'm more concerned that some CNE idiot does not try once again to oust the Moonies and Consortium from the Odin System."

"I agree that the CNE should be of greatest concern." Huang nodded to DuMorne. "I believe, therefore, that you and Gerhardt should work together on the issue. It should not be necessary for you to consult with the rest of us before taking whatever action is needed, unless for some reason it will affect one of us in some way. Otherwise, keep us advised. Does the group agree?"

"Agreed," Kimba and Al Sharif spoke in unison.

"Yes, agreed." Richter nodded to DuMorne. "I will contact Andre upon return to Berlin to coordinate."

"Gentlemen…" DuMorne beamed at them. "The next time we meet, the leadership of the Lunar Free State should have changed dramatically. Let us hope that all goes according to plan."

* * *

LFS *Sorceress*, in Ragnarok Orbit

"The Confeds are back in business," Thomas Birdsall observed. "Another freighter arrived today. They aren't bothering with convoys, just sailing in like all is right with the universe."

"Pretty hard to form convoys when your warships aren't allowed to enter the destination system." Peter Yoric sat back as the steward refilled his coffee cup.

Yoric made a point to take dinner in the wardroom as often as possible, rather than in his cabin as was a flag officer's privilege. He and Birdsall had just finished the main course and selected dessert from the steward's cart.

"True, but they could have joined up with our convoys or the Consortium's," Birdsall insisted. "Between us, we've got ships coming and going all the time. Any merchant skipper can join up, regardless of flag."

"Why bother?" Yoric chuckled. "They don't need convoys because the only pirates around belong to them. Those fast raiders could certainly hit a lone merchant ship, but we haven't seen them since we started escorting ours with regular warships again."

"I'm getting a little worried, though." His cheerful tone faded. "It's been too damned quiet. Six months ago, we were tangling with a major Confed invasion force. Now, they aren't even probing the system. Picket duty has been a boring assignment for cruiser and destroyer skippers. I have to keep on them to make sure nobody gets complacent.

"Not a squawk from the diplomatic boys, either. The Wans are still stonewalling them, and the rebels have quieted down—haven't so much as hit a merchant caravan in weeks.

"I should be grateful, but I've got a bad feeling. Something's about to happen."

* * *

Private Residence, Level 17, TerraNova City, Luna

It was time for the weekly poker game, but the men involved weren't playing cards. "Game night" was simply an excuse for the seven of them to get together at Stuart's place.

Stuart didn't play poker, or any other game of chance he couldn't rig. Political games were more to his liking, with power as the prize, and the rules subject to manipulation. The current game was coming to an end, and he was preparing to rake in the jackpot.

Per the constitution, removal of the CEO required a vote by 80 percent of all serving directors, not only those at the meeting. If some of O'Hara's fan club didn't show up, it wouldn't matter as long as Stuart's faction did, and nobody chickened out.

Most of them were thoroughly disgusted with the current situation and blamed O'Hara for their troubles. Others either owed their current position to Stuart or one of the other six, or were subject to blackmail over some past transgression. There was also a group whose vote was simply for sale, to whom Stuart's group had promised exorbitant rewards should the recall vote succeed.

Some of those may have to be dealt with afterwards, he thought. *Can't trust people like that; next time, someone else may offer them a better price. Better to replace them with people you own and control. Fear is a more certain motivator than greed.*

He felt a momentary twinge of uncertainty. He had 82 votes secured and had managed to gather them without resorting to a public smear campaign against O'Hara and his policies. *The bastard won't know what hit him.* He smiled at the thought, then he frowned again.

Someone might request a secret ballot. If so, and if some of his people defected, he wouldn't know which ones. He had tried to convince each of them that bad things would happen if the vote as a whole didn't succeed. Still, it was possible that as many as three of them might turn on him if they thought they couldn't be caught.

He would have to head off any call for a secret ballot. Fortunately, he was a persuasive orator. He would shame whoever called for it, tell them it was important to stand up and be counted to save the Lunar Free State from impending doom.

For tonight, however, he had to project confidence.

"This is it, gentlemen," he told them. "Tomorrow's meeting will tell the tale."

"I'm not going to believe it until the votes are counted," Isaac Miller declared. "Some might change their minds. Some might not show up tomorrow. What do we do if that happens?"

"If we don't have the people, we don't call for a vote." Stuart shrugged. "If the vote fails, we regroup and try again. It costs us nothing to try."

"Bullshit. If we try and fail, we will have tipped our hand. O'Hara will know who's against him and can take action accordingly. If we don't vote, we miss the moment. The battle group at Sacagawea is being called home. That's *Isis*, with O'Hara's son, if you haven't been keeping track. More importantly, a couple of people whose proxies we hold are in that group. Once they get back, we no longer control those votes."

"So what would you have us do, Isaac?" Stuart glared at him. "Give it up? Walk away? Forget about it?"

"No," Miller insisted, "I'm not backing out. I'm simply saying let's not celebrate yet. I'm not ready to claim victory until the voting's done, and O'Hara's been ousted."

"Fine." Stuart nodded. "We'll meet again tomorrow night, and I'll buy the champagne."

* * *

Office of the Chief Executive, TerraNova City, Luna

What the hell is this? O'Hara stared at the screen, where the incoming message told him that his presence was requested at an "emergency meeting" of the Directorate at 1300 hours.

He was accustomed to getting invitations; the CEO was invited to every meeting of the Directorate. He might or might not attend, depending on what was on the agenda. This one, however, did not have an agenda attached. In addition, it was customary to issue the invitations a week in advance. With such short notice, it was possible that a lot of Directors wouldn't be able to make it.

Emergency meeting. O'Hara had never seen those words used in connection with the Directorate. *They're a review and advisory body; what "emergency" could possibly require their attention?*

He knew the answer; he simply didn't want to believe it. His eyes strayed to the header of the message, where he noticed another anomaly—a name on the distribution list that wasn't normally included: Admiral Abraham Moskowitz, the judge advocate general.

He was still trying to process the information when the interface chimed with an incoming call. Lisa Woods. He touched the icon to accept.

"They're going to do it," she told him without preamble. "Stuart's group; they're going for a recall vote."

"Can they do it? Have they got the votes?"

"I don't know." She shook her head. "Apparently, they think they have. Oh, I suppose there's a small chance they are just trying to make a statement, maybe convince you to go along with their agenda, but…"

"What agenda? Put the nation in debt, issue bonds, sell us out?"

"That's the big one, but they've got a bunch of other things on their list. I gave you the full report last month."

"Right… things they want, most of which are unconstitutional. They haven't taken action, so I can't do anything. Wishful thinking is not illegal."

"That's what I'm trying to tell you. They are about to take action, but you still can't do anything because that action will be perfectly legal. I don't know for sure if they'll succeed, but I can't guarantee they won't."

"I don't see how they can." He shrugged. "More than twenty directors will be absent from the meeting. There are that many deployed in the military, plus embassy personnel, TerraCorp people off Luna…"

"Rob, that doesn't matter. Those people will have given their proxies to someone. Stuart's people may have those proxies in their pockets."

O'Hara started to reply but stopped himself. He had forgotten about the proxies, and he shouldn't have. He'd served a couple of terms as a director himself; as a career military officer, he'd deployed on several occasions and given his proxy to other officers who were staying behind on Luna. *But always to people I trusted,* he thought. *I sure as hell wouldn't have given it to anybody who was going to sell out the LFS.*

Wouldn't you? Did you really know them that well? You trusted them because they were career Navy officers like you. That was then; this is now. There are a lot of disgruntled career officers walking around these days.

He glanced at the chrono display on the screen: 1225 hours. Even if there was some action he could take, he wouldn't have time for it.

"Well… I guess we'll find out soon," he told Woods. "I'll see you at the meeting."

* * *

Chief Executive's Residence, TerraNova City, Luna

Robert O'Hara, the sixth chief executive in the history of the Lunar Free State, was drunk. Not knee-walking, falling-down drunk, but the world had become very blurry around him.

"What happened? What the hell happened?" The plaintive question hung in the air of his home office. The screen in front of him lit up, and a familiar green lizard appeared.

"I'm very sorry, sir," Mike said in a sympathetic tone. "It appears you were the victim of a sinister plot. Unfortunately, though I may suspect foul play, I cannot prove it. Any evidence I have consists of hearsay and would be inadmissible, even if it were not protected by the right of privacy. Everything the plotters did in public was perfectly legal, including your removal from office."

"Plotters?" O'Hara focused on the word. "You know who they are."

"Yes, but in the absence of a criminal charge, their right of privacy prevents me from revealing their identities. I can tell you, however, that seven members of the directorate formed the core group, with willing support and cooperation from thirty-five other directors. Another twenty-three directors were persuaded to vote with them, though they were not aware of the conspiracy."

"That's only... sixty-five directors." O'Hara shook his head to clear it. "Not even two-thirds, so how did they...?"

"The core group and their sycophants held a total of seventeen proxies for directors currently off Luna—military, diplomatic, and TerraCorp people. I might speculate that those people might not have voted to remove you had they been present, but it doesn't matter. They entrusted others with their vote; it was perfectly legal. Judge Moskowitz was reluctant to admit it, but in the end, he was forced to certify the recall as valid."

"Yeah... I remember that much," O'Hara muttered. "That's when I walked out. What happened after that?"

Mike paused as O'Hara's steward came into the office, bringing a pot of coffee and a snack tray. O'Hara stared at him.

"George... what...?"

"I asked him to bring you something," Mike said. "You haven't eaten dinner."

"Well, yeah... Candy's working, covering a late shift at the hospital. Didn't feel like having dinner by myself."

Candy Parks was the Director of Nursing at TerraNova Medical Center. She'd called him as soon as the news had broken of his removal, but he had insisted that there was no need to rush home, that they would have plenty of time to talk about it later. *Yeah... like the rest of our lives,* he thought.

"George—" he turned his attention to the steward "—you don't need to be doing this. Technically, you don't work for me anymore."

"Sir!" Senior Chief Petty Officer George Robbins stiffened to attention. "I do not report to the chief executive. My CO is Admiral Robert O'Hara, LFS Navy, Retired. I believe regulations say that a retired flag officer is entitled to the services of a steward."

"Actually, they don't specifically say that." On the screen, Mike shook his head.

"Well if they don't, they should... sir!" Robbins remained at attention.

"I believe, however, that falls under the heading of 'Custom and Usage' in Navy tradition," Mike said with a smile.

"Fine... Thank you, George." O'Hara sat back and allowed Robbins to fill his coffee cup. He made no protest when the steward removed the near-empty glass of scotch. Mike waited until Robbins departed, then continued.

"After you left, the Directorate passed a resolution thanking you for your years of dedicated service, both as a naval officer and as CEO."

"Hmmph!" O'Hara snorted. "They've got a funny way of showing their appreciation. What else?"

"Roger Stuart took the floor and made a speech reminding them that they had only a limited time in which to select a new CEO; otherwise, constitutional succession would put Admiral McGruder in charge. That, he told them, would be only a continuation of the current disaster—his description of the state of the nation.

"He then proceeded to nominate Marcus Carter for the position. I will spare you the details, but he described Carter's qualifications in somewhat hyperbolic terms. At the conclusion, the nomination was seconded by Isaac Miller, and a vote was taken. Carter was elected with sixty-eight votes—one more than needed for the two-thirds majority—and that required the conspirators to cast all seventeen of the proxy votes in his favor."

O'Hara's jaw had dropped at the first mention of Carter's name. He sat in silence, staring into space for a moment. Finally, he leaned forward over the desk and put his head in his hands.

"Marcus Carter…" he mumbled. "God help us all."

* * * * *

Epilogue

22 May 2124

LFS *Valkyrie*, in Xanadu Orbit

"Thank you for coming, Governor." Lorna waved Jin to a chair in the lounge area of her quarters. "We're on alert at the moment, so I couldn't come down, but I thought we needed to talk about some things best discussed in person rather than by video call."

"Yes, I guess we do." Jin settled into the chair and regarded Lorna with a stern look. "A week ago, I got clearance to proceed with our Xanadu Constitution, signed by Robert O'Hara, chief executive. Now I have a message from Lunar Command saying Robert O'Hara has been removed from office and replaced by some guy I never heard of. Who the hell is Marcus Carter?"

Lorna winced. She knew Marcus Carter quite well and had encountered him very early in her naval career. It had not been a pleasant experience; it had resulted in a board of inquiry, which should have ended the careers of several officers—including Carter. Then all charges and accusations had mysteriously vanished, Carter had been sent somewhere, and things had returned to normal. Now, twenty years later, memories of that encounter came flooding back.

"I know Carter, but it's a long story, best told over drinks," she told Jin. "For now, I think we need to discuss the possible effects of current events on our situation here.

"I've got the group on alert because Lunar Command is concerned the Confeds might take advantage of our perceived weakness during the transition period. Personally, I think they are being overly cautious. I've had no orders changing our mission; until I get such orders, it's business as usual regarding support for the colony and defense against the Confeds. The arrival of those extra Consortium warships had more effect on my planning than the notice of change of command back at Luna."

"I haven't had any notice of changes, either," Kim admitted. "I think we've already seen the handwriting on the wall. Luna's got financial problems; maybe that has something to do with the change back there. We've been seeing evidence of decreased support for many months.

"They tell us we can have our constitution, and the Colonial Commission no longer has authority over us—which means they won't be helping us, either. If we need something from Luna, we can still request it, but we don't have anybody back there who will be pulling for us."

"Seriously, Governor, I feel the same way," Lorna assured her. "The colony's not the only place they've been cutting back. Fleet's taken some pretty serious hits. We've been lucky so far, because it's obvious we need to be strong in the face of Confed pressure. Still, I've got four ships that are overdue for maintenance, but Luna is telling me not to send them back yet. They've stretched out maintenance schedules across the entire fleet as part of the budget crunch."

"So what's gonna happen?" Jin demanded. "Is this Carter guy gonna wave a magic wand and make all of our problems disappear?"

"I doubt it." Lorna shook her head and turned to Jin with a serious look. "Confidentially, Governor, based on what I know of the man, things are going to get worse. Maybe a lot worse."

* * *

LFS *Isis*, Lunar Fleet Anchorage

"Dad… what the *hell* is going on?" John O'Hara gave his father a pleading look. "Talk to me."

"Yeah, I guess I owe you an explanation." Robert O'Hara shifted uncomfortably in his chair. "I should have seen this coming, but I didn't. I focused on the problems in front of me and ended up getting stabbed in the back. Poor tactics on my part. I didn't cover my six."

"But… how did they do it? How could they possibly get eighty votes in the Directorate?"

The younger O'Hara had just arrived in system from Sacagawea. The news of the removal of his father had come while the battle group was still inbound to Luna from the hyper limit. Robert O'Hara had come aboard almost as soon as *Isis* had docked. He'd been in civilian clothes, but the battlecruiser's crew had rendered the boarding honors due to an admiral.

John hadn't suggested it; word of his father's removal had spread throughout the ship. Eurasia Brown had ordered the honors without asking his permission. She had personally escorted the elder O'Hara to his son's quarters, because John hadn't wanted their reunion to be public, in front of the crew. Now the two of them were alone, with a bottle of very old scotch on the table between them next to a bucket of ice.

"Eighty-two votes. It wasn't a secret ballot; you can see who voted to take me out, but they also had seventeen proxies in their pocket for people who weren't there."

"Proxies! Oh, shit!" John's eyes widened. A sudden thought occurred to him. "Eurasia's a director. Was her proxy one of them?"

"Doesn't matter." The elder O'Hara waved it off. "I'm sure a bunch of those people wouldn't have voted me out, but they trusted others with their proxies and got screwed—*legally* screwed. If she's one of them, it's not her fault."

"I'm not going to confront her with it." John shook his head. "She'll find out eventually. If she wants to talk about it, there'll be time later.

"So what are you going to do?" He sat back and regarded his father sadly. "You and Mom... personally, I mean."

"They threw me a bone. They appointed me to your grandfather's old job. I'm going to be the governor of the New Eden Protectorate. Out of sight, out of mind, somewhere I can't make trouble for them."

"You accepted that? What about Mom?"

"Yes, I accepted. Hell, if I stayed and fought them, I'd be shoveling shit against the tide. Go back to the Navy? Carter would never give me a billet, and even if he did, flag officer appointments have to be approved by the Directorate. That's usually a rubber stamp, but they're the people who voted to boot me out.

"I've got to do something, and I might as well make it something useful. Your grandfather did meaningful work there for decades. They didn't refill the position after he died; they've been without a permanent governor for two years now because nobody wanted the job.

"As for your mother, she'll stay for another six months—she's grooming her replacement at TMC—then she'll come out to join me. I'm sure the med center at Eden's Gate will find a place for her. "There's a bunch of stuff in storage. Carter didn't want to give me time to clean out my office, had no interest in transition meetings, and said he already knows how to be a better CEO than I ever was. In other words, he's still the arrogant bastard we know and love.

"Before he could move in, Mike sent TerraNova Security to lock and guard the office—claimed they were protecting my right of privacy. Carter had to occupy the outer office and do business from there. Didn't matter, because Mike gave him access to all of the CEO files and functions on the system.

"I went up there and cleaned out all of my personal stuff, including the model of *Isis*. Carter bitched, but I bought that myself with my own money, and Mike verified it. It's in private storage; I'll send you the info, and you can retrieve it at your leisure. The other stuff is mostly memorabilia from my Navy days. Maybe you can ship some of it to New Eden for me later. For now, I'll be traveling light."

The two sat in silence for a moment. John gave his father a serious look.

"Dad… what's going to happen? What's going to happen to the LFS with Carter in charge?"

"I don't know. Looking at Carter's record, I'd say the nation is doomed, but I'm pretty sure Carter's not in charge. He's just the front man for a group of power players who have him on a short leash. I have no idea where they're going, but I strongly suspect I wouldn't like it if I knew.

"They've been running the show for a couple of weeks, and so far, they haven't touched the Navy or Marine command structure. That said, you need to watch your back. Carter may not be in charge, but he's still in a position to screw you over if he wants to. I doubt he's forgotten the *Lewis and Clark* incident, even after twenty years."

John O'Hara nodded. The incident in question had nearly ended his career, and by all rights *should* have ended Carter's. That Carter blamed him for it was a given.

"The nation will survive," Robert O'Hara declared. "I've screwed it up, but you and people like you will fix it."

"You didn't screw up, Dad," John insisted. "You did your best; you held them off as long as you could. Now it's up to me and those who are left to continue the fight."

He picked up his glass and raised it in the traditional toast.

"To the Lunar Free State… in whose service we stand."

# # # # #

About John E. Siers

John E. Siers is a Viet Nam–era Air Force veteran who spent several decades working as a software developer, designing analytical systems for corporate clients.

An avid reader of science fiction since grade school, John started writing in the late 1970s, mostly for his own enjoyment. He wrote for more than 20 years and produced three complete novels before ever showing his work to anyone.

Escaping from the overcrowded northeast, John moved to Tennessee in 1997. Encouraged by friends, he finally published his first novel, *The Moon and Beyond*, in late 2012, followed by *Someday the Stars* in 2013. The latter won the 2014 Darrell Award for Best SF Novel by a Midsouth Author.

John's *Lunar Free State* series had grown to four novels—with no thought of doing anything outside his own comfort zone—when he encountered William Alan Webb at MidSouthCon in 2019. Bill led John astray, tempting him with visions of other universes, whispering names like *Four Horsemen*, *Last Brigade*, and finally, *Hit World*.

John succumbed to the temptation, and *The Ferryman* and *The Dragons of Styx* are the results. He has since entered a rehab program and produced three more novels in his own universe. He is now hard at work on the next one (check his website below for updates on progress). The Lunar Free State series is now being published in audio books available via Audible and in German-language e-book format on Amazon.

John lives with his wife, son, dog, and two cats in west Tennessee. In his spare time (what there is of it) he runs his own firearm repair and service business under the trade name of Gunsmith Jack. Readers can follow him on Amazon, Facebook, or his own website at www.lunarfreestate.com, on Patreon at https://www.patreon.com/user?u=48552283, and on BookBub at https://www.bookbub.com/authors/john-e-siers.

* * * * *

Get the **free** Four Horsemen prelude story "**Shattered Crucible**"

and discover other titles by Theogony Books at:

http://chriskennedypublishing.com/

* * * * *

Meet the author and other CKP authors on the Factory Floor:

https://www.facebook.com/groups/461794864654198

* * * * *

Did you like this book?

Please write a review!

* * * * *

The following is an
Excerpt from Book One of Ashes of Entecea:

The Queen's Fixer

Kacey Ezell

Available from Theogony Books

eBook and Paperback

Excerpt from "The Queen's Fixer:"

"Laeth?"

Zan's voice pulled her from her self-examination, and Laethine shook her head. "I'm coming," she said as she looked for the shoulder straps of the bag. She closed the cargo flap but didn't hit the compression command, since she'd need to add Zan's planetside garb first. She opened the compartment that held the bag's straps and pulled them out, then noticed a folded piece of paper as it fluttered to the floor.

She froze as adrenaline surged through her. Her mouth went suddenly dry, and she bent slowly to pick it up.

No one uses paper in orbit! What under the stars…?

There was only one way to find out. With her heart pounding in her ears, Laethine fumbled with the paper until it opened in her hands. It was incredibly thin—translucent, even—but she could make out the wispy marks of a hand-lettered message.

"The torch is yours, Fixer. The Hierophant follows. Be on the next line leaving dock 459A within the hour. Your time is short. We'll be in touch. Eat this. No fire in space."

Electricity jolted through Laethine, bringing forth a memory she'd forgotten. She and Previn had been discussing his obsession with written messages. She'd laughingly asked him what he did when in orbit because he certainly couldn't be burning papers in the oxygenated environment aboard a ship or station. He'd looked at her and quietly replied that paper could be constructed of many materials, some of them edible.

She turned the thin scrap over in her hand. Was it genuine? Was this a trick? Was this an elaborate attempt to trick her? Was the paper poisoned?

Laethine couldn't help it, she let out a short, dry laugh. Her paranoia threatened to run out of control. If this *was* an attempt to poison her, it was certainly an excessively elaborate ruse. It would be so much easier just to sneak something into her food! Besides, there were messages within messages encoded here.

The torch is yours…

That last letter from Previn had mentioned the passing of torches. When she was first married, Previn had often spoken of her inheritance of Antiroc as "passing the torch," but she'd never heard anyone else use the expression. She'd asked him what a "torch" was. It turned out to be something like a club that had a flammable material attached to one end, so it could be carried as a portable source of light and heat. Some of the populace of Antiroc used them from time to time when they worked in the remotest mountain areas, where sustained technology was hard to come by or undesirable for one reason or another.

That had to be a code, didn't it? A message designed to signal her that this note was legitimate? That it was truly from Previn's information network?

"Gah!" Laethine growled. She *hated* this. She'd always enjoyed Previn's thought puzzles when he'd posed them, but those were always just theoretical exercises! If she got this wrong, people could be hurt… even die!

"Laeth? Are you all right?"

"Yes," she called back. "Just putting everything away. I'll be right out." She looked down at the paper in her hand and then shrugged and touched it to her tongue.

It tasted sweet, as if she'd just eaten a spoonful of honey. The paper thinned and dissolved, leaving nothing but a sticky residue on her fingers. She rubbed her fingertips together and then wiped them clean on the side of her pants and picked up the bag before stepping out of the small room.

Zan waited for her, a tentative smile on his face. The dark green modular jumpsuit fit him well, conforming to his wide shoulders and tapering down to his narrow waist and hips. Laeth gave him an approving nod.

"Feel comfortable enough?" she asked.

"Yes," he said. "I'm a little surprised at how well it fits."

"That's the beauty of the modular system. Also, you're pretty close to their standard sizes, if I had to guess. If you were taller or broader, you'd have more problems. Give me your other clothes. I'll put them in here, and then we need to hurry."

"Why?"

"Because," she said and gave him a level look.

"Oh… um… later?" he asked, his smile fading.

"Later," she said and answered with her own smile. It was hard to blame the young man for his curiosity. He'd been raised to ask such questions, after all, and it was good for a future ruler to want to stay informed. But right now, she just needed his cooperation.

Zan handed her his folded clothes, and Laethine added them to her bag, then closed the flap and toggled the compression control. The bag let out a faint *whirr* as the internal vacuum system pulled out the excess air and compressed the whole package down to a flat shape that could easily be worn under a jacket. Laethine put her arms through the shoulder straps, shrugged the bag into place, and then looked at Zan.

"All right," she said. "Let's go."

* * * * *

Get "The Queen's Fixer" here: https://www.amazon.com/dp/B0CYHB5QPB.

Find out more about Kacey Ezell at: https://chriskennedypublishing.com.

* * * * *

The following is an
Excerpt from Book One of the The Sol Saga:

Revolution

James Fox

Available from Theogony Books

eBook and Paperback

Excerpt from "Revolution:"

The situation was rapidly degrading. If they couldn't find the enemy in the sea of people, they could be ambushed easily. Every Marine standing here in full battle rattle was a prettily dressed sitting duck. Two well-placed shooters could mow them down like spring grass. Hell, one well-placed IED could kill half of them and maim the rest.

Then he saw him.

"Aegis, please respond! Multiple IED inbound to your position!"

He ignored the intelligence from CENTCOM, instead clicking over to the snipers' and Manu's channel. "Viper Six, Aegis Actual, need confirmation of advancing targets."

There were others, standing still or milling around. Not moving backward.

The solo man, sliding between people, running forward toward the steps.

Don't do it! Don't you do it!

Twenty meters out.

"Aegis, Viper-Six, confirmed Tango on approach."

Brennan switched active channels, then relayed information into the comms, "Tango inbound, fifteen meters at 155 degrees. Hold your fire!"

Weapons pivoted to acquire the target.

Ten meters out.

"Hold!"

He was right on top of them.

"Hold!"

Don't you fucking do it!

The man reached inside his jacket.

The man's chest erupted in a blossom of red Martian blood. The crowd cleared to reveal a little girl right in front of the man dropping limply to his knees. His jacket draped protectively over the girl, staring dumbly at the hole in his chest.

Then, in horrific slow motion, when seconds seemed like hours, all hell erupted around him.

Protectorate automatic rifles were merciless, boasting upward of twelve hundred rounds per minute. Dozens of spooked Marines, *his* Marines, unable to immediately identify a threat despite intelligence from Command, opened fire. Once one fired, they all did.

Screams rose and were cut brutally short by hot rounds slicing through vocal cords, puncturing abdomens. Brennan could hear the impacts. The *thump-squish* of hot metal ripping through cloth, skin, muscle, and back again in rapid succession.

The front of the crowd was so close that blood sprayed up onto the gleaming white marble steps.

Somewhere from far above him, he heard the piercing cry of a woman's scream.

"CEASE FIRE!" Brennan roared over the comms, again and again, for what seemed like hours.

* * * * *

Get "Revolution" here: https://www.amazon.com/dp/B0CRZ6MZTR.

Find out more about James Fox at: https://chriskennedypublishing.com.

* * * * *

Manufactured by Amazon.ca
Acheson, AB

15665832R00221